LIZZETTE GRAYSON CARTER

# THE *Across* COLOR LINE

C L Press

C L Press
P. O. Box 1
Hallieford, VA 23068

**PUBLISHER'S NOTE**
This book is a work of fiction. Names, characters, places and incidents either are the product of the author's imagination or are used fictitiously, and any resemblance to actual persons, living or dead, business establishments, events, or locales is entirely coincidental.

ISBN-13: 978-0-9816073-0-6
ISBN-10: 0-9816073-0-6

Library of Congress Control Number: 2008926875

Printed in United States of America

Cover Designed by Shelia Reneé Smith

Interior Designed by The Writer's Assistant
www.thewritersassistant.com

# Dedication

*For my beloved family members who've passed:*

*Aunt Christine, Uncle Charlie, Uncle David, Gail, Aunt Mary, Aunt Bertha, Uncle Shack, Sue, Derrick, and Great Grandmother Ethel.*

# *Acknowledgments*

My Heavenly Father, my Lord and Savior Jesus Christ, I thank You for everything that you've done in my life and allowing this ambitious and momentous project to come into fruition. For with You, Lord, nothing shall be impossible. Thank you for keeping me humble.

Thank you...

To my husband, Michael. I praise God for your love and devotion.

To my beautiful daughter, Brienna. You are truly Heaven Sent and I love you.

To my grandmother, Marie Golden, for your love and strength in holding the family together.

To my mom, Emaline Creamer, and step dad, Gregory Creamer, for your belief and care.

To my dad, James Grayson, for your comforting 'daddy' voice.

To my 'second parents,' Herbert and Doris Carter, for your strong words of wisdom.

To my siblings: Bryant Grayson, Rodney Grayson, Gregory Creamer, Georgette Creamer, and 'brother' Charlie Banks.

To my aunts and uncles: Martha Ann Paden, Faye Shackelford, Julia Leonard, Jane Hayward, Lucille Blakey, Shirley Golden-Carter, Virginia Golden, George Blakey, George Carter, Roger Golden, Golden family, Carter family, Grayson family, and the Johnson-Barton Switzer family. Thank you for your continual encouragement and love.

To Reverend and Mrs. Eric D. Robinson and the Ebenezer Baptist Church Family for grounding me in the Word, and for a blessed church to call 'home.' Thank you for your fellowship, loving support, guidance and generosity to Antioch, Emmaus, First, Wayland and Zion Baptist churches.

To the Mathews County residents and public school teachers, faculty, staff and students; Mathews County Library; Gloucester County residents; Gloucester County Library.

To Tawanda Ferguson; Lettice Mayfield; Vanessa Boyd Knight; Lisa Shields Robinson; Franklin Jarvis; Mr. and Mrs. Raymond Willis; Ray Willis; Yvette Willis; Ceandra Scott; Staci Spencer; my 'guinea pigs,' Crystal Coleman and Christie Henderson and The Henderson Family; Mark and Delphia Ferguson; Tonya Speed; Dyretta Bates; Diane and David Ashberry; Dwayne and Vivian Blake; Janine Burns; Virginia Kelly; and Marlon and Eileen Davis.

To my editor, Jessica Tilles; my graphic artist, Shelia Reneé Smith; Nikki Turner; Katrina Boswell; Mandy Malone with *The Daily Press*; Frank at Office/Copy Max; Black Expressions Book Club; The Sista Book Club; The Sweet Soul Sisters Book Club; Waiting 2 Exhale Book Club; and World Victory Book Club.

To Miss Grace Bihr; Randy and Lisa Hollomon; Terry and Debbie McKinney; Karen Hudgins; Nona Pritt; Richard Harfst; Evelyn Thompson; W. Lee Chaney III; Brian Leonard; Sheila Rucker; Becky Norwood; Darlene Patterson; the UPS freight family; Rusty at Ozark; Frank at ExactBind; and many, many more.

My first time out as an author with my novel, *The Color Line*, was a dream come true and it has blossomed into a glorious experience, because of all who are mentioned above.

Again, I say, thank you.

Blessings,
Lizzette Grayson Carter
April 11, 2008
Mathews County, Virginia

Leon:
You are such an incredibly, incredibly endearing human. Thanks for ... busta out ... be the great force ...

"heading ... Century out ... that you'll ... for our support!
Thanks for your support ...
God Bless you!

Lynette Thurman Carter

THE COLOR LINE

# Chapter 1

# Lacie

Who'd have thought I'd fall in love with a white man?

Me? A sista, with a white dude? Huh, never in a million years, I thought.

That is, until I met Tony.

I glanced over at him sleeping peacefully and smiled. It was nine o'clock in the morning, the first day of the New Year and also our first official day as a couple. It already felt as if it was going to be a good year.

An idea suddenly came to mind and I got out of bed quietly. I grabbed his shirt from off the bedside chair and smiled, remembering the last time I'd worn it.

After freshening up in the bathroom, I went into the kitchen and looked in the refrigerator. It was well stocked with all of the ingredients I needed. I took the ingredients out and went to work while I pondered the events that had transpired in the last twenty-four hours, as well as the past four months.

So many positive things had changed in my life. After years of dissention and strife between us, Mama and I had finally made peace with each other. We were communicating better and there no longer seemed to be a wall separating us. The anger in me was gone and I felt her every effort to change and become a better mother.

My little sister, Reneé, was now engaged to Danny and the happiest I'd ever seen her. She was steadfastly attaining a remarkable sense of maturity and confidence, which in me, had been absent at her age. Despite being a pregnant teenager, she was all the more determined to continue her education, be a good mother and marry her man.

Then, of course, there was Tony.

The moment we met, it was electric.

The problem? He was my boss and white. Those two reasons alone were taboo. Yet, the attraction and the chemistry we shared was too magnetic and I enjoyed being around him.

I shook my head, recalling my futile attempts at denying my feelings for him. I had all of these preconceived notions and ideas running around in my head, constantly telling me the consequences of even imagining being with him. Still, I couldn't shake my feelings for him. The issue became more problematic when we shared our first intense kiss in Washington, DC. That's when I knew I was in trouble and had to put a stop to whatever was going on between us.

So I started dating his friend, Joe—that had to be stupidest thing I'd ever done in my life.

Black, rich and devastatingly handsome, Joe was, in essence, every black woman's idea of the perfect black man. I knew Joe was the one for me, but my attraction for Tony kept pulling me into his direction. It should have been clear when I slept with Tony.

But my penchant to make it work with Joe was resolute. So still confused and torn, with an odd sense of obligation, I continued my relationship with Joe and even accepted his proposal. It didn't suppress my feelings for Tony, however. In fact, they intensified, especially when Simone came into the equation.

Simone was a very beautiful model and Tony's ex-fiancée. She was also a thorn in my side. Jealous knots would develop in the pit of my stomach whenever she was around, which was ironically and equally met with her jealousy. I mean, the girl had issues.

Simone immediately let me know that she didn't like me. She also had no problem telling me that she'd come back into Tony's life, and was ready to get him back, at any cost. Hey, I was fine with that, I thought. I was with Joe and I was engaged to him. It wasn't going to have any effect on me.

I couldn't have been more wrong.

It was a Saturday night, during a Christmas party, when the tension between Simone and I finally came to a head. It was also the beginning of an agonizing affirmation for me. Heavily intoxicated,

Simone had followed me into the ladies room after an argument at the table, spewing out accusations. Then, she had the nerve to call me the n-word. Oh, how I had wanted to kick her butt! Fortunately, on her behalf, my good friend, Robert, interrupted me from giving her a beat down and took me home.

Tony came over my house a while after, seeking an explanation of what had happened between us. He had picked the wrong time. The nerve of him to question me instead of blasting her out! I was already disturbed and emotional from the argument with Simone, and jealous from seeing him dance so intimately with her at the party.

My defense mode came on immediately and that started an argument. Essentially, it was merely a lover's spat because we were both frustrated and jealous of both of our significant others. We were in love and it took that spat, along with both of our emotional and strong confessions of love toward each other, for me to realize the truth. That's basically what did it.

I had been in love with Tony all along but had been foolish and afraid. It was a pivotal, but bittersweet, moment to acknowledge our feelings for each other because other people were involved and were bound to get hurt. Undoubtedly, there was going to be drama.

It came, too.

My decision to break up with Joe was agonizing, but I had already wasted enough time for both of us and didn't want to prolong my engagement with him any further. I had to tell him and when I did, Joe took it hard. When I told him I was in love with Tony, he took it even harder.

Life at home wasn't so great, either.

Mama was incensed and strongly voiced her disapproval, which complicated my relationship with her even more. She was angry because I had screwed up a perfectly good relationship with Joe—a successful black man—for Tony, a white man. In response, I, full of years of anger and resentment, lashed back and ridiculed her for her irresponsibility toward me when I was growing up.

That scare of Reneé being rushed to the hospital was the only thing that finally knocked us into our senses. We realized that we had to reconcile and forget about the past and work on our future as mother and daughter. Once that happened, it got a little better between us.

Everything and everyone around us seemed to fall into place. Danny had popped the question to Reneé; Joe forgave me; and eventually, and somewhat reluctantly, Mama gave her blessing for me to be with Tony.

I smiled and started to hum, *You and I* by Stevie Wonder, while I flipped the omelet over and thought about how happy I was, to finally be with Tony. I'd done the right thing.

Tony was handsome, respectful, easygoing, confident, ambitious, and had a way of crooning out *You and I* by Stevie Wonder that I'd never heard a white man do before. He was the coolest white man I'd ever known and he had a great spirit. That could have been why I'd fallen for him so easily, but it wasn't. It was much more.

Much more.

# Chapter 2

# Tony

I'd never seen a woman look so sexy in my life.

Smiling and standing back quietly, I watched Lacie at the stove with one of my shirts on, and nothing else, humming as she lightly tapped the spatula on the frying pan in deep thought.

Man, was I in love with her!

Her lovely brown skin, full lips and nice curves were all for me.

I continued to observe her silently, not wanting to mess up the view that I was getting, as she bent over, and recalled the first moment we'd met.

Three months fresh from my break up with Simone, I'd left my old job and had taken a lucrative position at Ryan & Company. It had been my first day and I'd had the mindset of all work, no play and *definitely* no women. The door of the elevator I was in was about to close when I heard this woman yell for me to hold the door, as she dived for the elevator. She fell, spilling everything out of her briefcase.

One look at her beautiful face and sexy legs, and she had me. No other woman had ever affected me in such a way and, although I'd promised myself no more women for a while, I felt a strong urge to get to know her. I was quite elated after that initial meeting when she unknowingly informed me that we worked for the same company and that I was going to be her boss.

However, our second meeting didn't go off so well. Lacie had been embarrassed and angry once she found out that I was her new boss and she let me know it. Thankfully, her demeanor changed after I'd given her a smooth apology and suggested that we start anew. After that, our working relationship got better and stronger.

So did my feelings for her.

I found Lacie to be extremely captivating; I had come close to asking her out several times, but was constantly reminded of the fact that I was her boss and I really didn't know if her feelings were reciprocal. I thought I'd had an inkling of an idea of her feelings the night we shared a kiss in the hotel elevator in DC, but after we agreed not to let it happen again, I figured that was it.

Yet, I still wanted her.

Then Joe came into the picture.

It was ironic and unfortunate for me to find out that my friend, Joe, who we were trying to attain as a client, had met Lacie at a club prior to him doing business with us. To my chagrin, they hit it off instantly and Lacie started seeing him. I had started to wonder if there was a chance for me.

I thought I'd gotten it when Lacie and I shared a night together after celebrating the business deal with Joe's company, but was sorely mistaken. The next morning, we'd gotten into a heated argument where she claimed she didn't want me and wanted to pursue things with Joe.

I was bewildered and disappointed because I was confident that she loved me, but was simply afraid. Her rejection was hard for me to accept but because I loved her and wanted her to be happy, I relented and gave her my best wishes. I promised her that I wouldn't pursue her anymore.

But that was a fallacy. I wanted Lacie, and deep down, I knew she wanted me too. Giving up on her was not an option.

I'd finally gotten my chance to spill out all of my feelings to her after she'd had a heated row with Simone. Her apparent jealousy over seeing me with Simone had given me the green light and I took it eagerly. I was filled with so much joy and relief when she verified that I hadn't been wrong about her feelings. Lacie really did love me after all, but when she said the words, it became that much more real.

And now she's my girl. She's finally mine and without a shadow of a doubt, I want her to be my wife.

Yeah, we'd been through a lot to get together, and while chasing her had been one of the hardest pursuits in my life, it had been worth it.

I smiled, still watching her cook.

Man, if she didn't look as if she belonged there! It was surreal seeing her there in my clothes and in my kitchen.

I couldn't resist the temptation any longer. I tiptoed up to her quietly, bent down and slowly ran my hands up her legs. She gasped instantly but relaxed once I stood up and kissed her neck softly.

"Umm," she managed to murmur. "Tony, don't you know it's dangerous to touch a woman that way when she's got a hot frying pan in her reach?"

"Mmm," I replied, enjoying the taste of her skin on my lips. "I didn't notice. All I saw was you in my shirt. Anyway, you should know that it's dangerous to walk around in a man's shirt with nothing underneath. A man can get ideas…" I whispered, moving my hands to her legs again.

"Stop, Tony," she gasped again with a little giggle. "Look, this food is almost ready and if you don't want a burnt omelet, I suggest you stop."

"All right," I chuckled, starting to rub her hips instead. "But you just look too good in my shirt." I peered over her at the stove. "Is this your infamous Spanish omelet you never got to fix for me?"

She turned around to face me. "Yes, it is, Mr. Douglas. Now will you stop touching me and sit down," she replied, laughing.

"Okay, okay," I chuckled, walking over to the table. I looked back at her. "Wow. The kitchen table's all set and everything is nicely laid out. I'm getting the star treatment today," I bantered.

"Maybe not the star treatment, but you are getting a good breakfast," she quipped in return, placing both of our plates down and taking a seat across from me.

"Mmm…this is very good," I murmured after a few minutes.

"Did you even doubt?" She winked and took a bite from her fork. "I told you that I'm a good cook."

Amused, I countered, "No, but I do know one thing you're better at." She blushed immediately. "C'mon, Lacie. I know you're not going to get all modest on me."

"What is wrong with you this morning?" She shook her head and gibed, "I tell you a white man gets a little brown sugar and now he doesn't know how to act."

"That was good," I pointed and grinned, taking a sip of my orange juice. I put the glass down and looked at her intently. "Listen, all jokes aside, Lacie. I can't tell you enough how glad I am that we're finally together."

"You know what? So am I," she beamed. "It's something about this whole thing between us that seems so right."

"Yeah, but honestly, at one time, I didn't know if you were ever going to own up to your feelings for me." Shaking my head, I added, before taking a bite from my fork, "Woman, you really put me through it."

She looked at me tenderly. "Tony, you know why I did."

I stopped chewing enough to add with a nod, "Yeah, 'cause you were scared."

She nodded her head several times. "Yes, very, very scared."

I swallowed and eyed her seriously. "Are you still scared?"

Her eyes showed the answer before she spoke. "A little, yes," she admitted. "I'm new at this kind of thing. But I told you last night that I'm willing to give this a try."

I reached over to take her hand and said, "Thank you for giving me—*us*—a try." I stood up to lean over the table and kissed her earnestly for a brief second then sat back down.

"Mmm," she uttered with a smile.

We ate for a few minutes and when my plate was almost clear, I glanced at her fleetingly and said, "I gotta tell you, though, Lacie. I don't think you had a choice in the matter." She looked up with a curious frown. "With giving us a try, I mean," I explained.

She put her fork down and said, "Excuse me?"

I gathered some food onto my fork and avoided looking at her because I was going to crack up any second. I repeated, "You didn't have a choice."

Peripherally, I saw her place her hand on her hip. "Oh, I *had* a choice."

"Woman, please, after me? C'mon, now."

"What about Joe?" I felt her eyes bearing into me but still didn't look at her.

I had expected her to say that and shook my head. "He was still after me." I took a bite from my fork.

"No, he wasn't. I met him first."

"Right, but who got the panties first?" After a brief pause, I finally looked up to see Lacie's fierce eyes on me and winked with a smirk. "Come on, woman. You know you wanted this." Her mouth dropped and then I burst out laughing.

"You know, I really must have given you too much last night for you to be acting like this," she said, shaking her head with a chuckle.

Suddenly, the doorbell rang.

"Just in time," I said, checking my watch and rising out of the chair to go to the door. "I'll be back."

The roses the delivery guy handed me were perfect. I reached into my robe pocket and handed him a fifty-dollar-bill, and said, "Thanks, man."

Lacie was staring out the window when I returned.

"Penny for your thoughts," I whispered in her ear, handing her the bouquet.

"Tony?" she questioned. "Why? When?"

"I called the florist earlier," I explained.

Tears welled up in Lacie's eyes as she stared at the bouquet in awe. "These are so beautiful. This was so thoughtful of you."

"Well, you know," I said, blowing on my fist and then rubbing it on my shoulder. "What can I say?"

She looked at me oddly for a moment and then we started laughing.

"Come here," I said, taking her hand and helping her out of the chair to hug her.

Having her in my arms was beyond words. It felt like home. I cupped my hands around her face and said, "I love you so much."

Lacie brushed her lips with mine and whispered, "I love you, too."

Hearing those words come out of her mouth again made me kiss her that much more passionately. I lifted my head after a moment and said softly, "Why don't we go out and spend the day together? This being our first day out as a couple and all."

"What do you have in mind?"

I had already decided but didn't want to tell her yet. I shook my head. "It's a surprise."

She leaned back and looked at me with a small frown. "Tony, I didn't bring any extra clothes with me."

I looked her over. "Just wear one of my shirts and blue jeans and tuck the jeans in your boots and that'll be fine. I've got a warmer coat and hat that I want you to wear also because it's going to be very cold outside."

"Tony, are you out of your mind? I'll look crazy with your clothes on. I can't go out looking like that."

"Lacie, you'll be fine. I'll be wearing jeans also. Don't worry. We're not going anywhere fancy."

A scowl came on her face suddenly. "Nowhere fancy, huh? What? I'm not good enough for that?"

She couldn't be serious. "No, I'm just saying that you…" Her scowl slowly turned into a grin and I shook my finger at her. "Bad, very bad."

"I know. I couldn't help it," she giggled with a nod. "Okay, Mister Surprise. You've convinced me. I'm yours for the day but after that I've got to get home."

"Fair enough." I whispered in her ear, "I've got another idea. Why don't we go in the bathroom and take a shower together?"

"Umm," she murmured. "Sounds nice, but you know what'll happen if I go in there with you."

I grinned, pulling her closer. "That is the idea."

"Uh, uh," she uttered, easing out of my arms. "That ain't happening. You've already kept me out all night, Tony, so let's not work on all day too. Mama's reluctantly agreed to this union between us and I don't want to tick that woman off."

"All right," I chuckled, walking out the kitchen. "You can always change your mind, though. Matter of fact, I'll even leave a crack in the door."

*Chapter 3*

# Lacie

I smiled and shook my head as I watched him retreat from the kitchen. His suggestion was tempting, but I'd never get home if I took his invitation. With a contented sigh, I started gathering the dishes from the table and loaded them into the dishwasher.

Though I was excited and curious about where he was going to take me, I couldn't help but be a little apprehensive. This was going to be our first adventure out together and it was literally going to be a test for me. I'd never dated a white man before and the anticipation of the looks and stares that I was certain we were bound to get from some, was indeed a bit scary. But was I going to shy away from going out in public places with him? No. I loved him too much for that. Furthermore, we deserved better.

The telephone rang suddenly. Tony was still in the shower, so I decided to answer it and picked up the portable phone hanging on the wall by the refrigerator.

"Hello?"

There was a brief pause before the female on the other end replied, "Hello? Is this Anthony Douglas' residence?" Her voice sounded older.

"Yes, it is," I confirmed.

There was another brief pause. "This is his mother. Is he there?"

"Uh…yes he is, but he's in the shower right now. May I take a message?"

"No, don't bother." A third pause and then, "I'm sorry. With whom am I speaking?"

"Uh…Lacie," I answered, feeling a nervous knot in my stomach.

"Oh, you must be the housekeeper! Anthony told me he was thinking about ordering a housekeeping service and I'm so glad he did. He stays so busy." She sighed. "Oh well. Tell him I'll try to reach him later on tonight. Good-bye."

Flabbergasted and confidence somewhat shaken, I stood there holding the phone after his mother hung up for a good second before I hung it up. She'd thought I was the housekeeper and I hadn't corrected her.

Fresh out of the shower, with a towel wrapped around his waist, Tony reentered the kitchen.

"What's wrong?" he asked, coming up to me with concern.

I gave him a small smile. "Nothing."

"You sure?" I nodded in reply. He studied my face for a moment, and then said, "Okay." He kissed my forehead. "Babe, it's almost eleven. Go ahead and take your shower and get ready. Don't worry about the kitchen. I'll finish cleaning up," he offered.

I walked slowly toward the bedroom, anesthetized by the initial taste of reality. I'd had my first conversation with Tony's mother and had been too afraid to introduce myself.

It was a shame that it was too early to have a drink. I sure felt like I needed one.

�����

Tony's surprise was a carriage ride through Central Park.

Romantic as the ride was, I brooded over the short conversation I'd had with his mother throughout its entirety. I was mad with myself for not telling her who I was and a little offended when she thought I was the maid. Then again, how could I have introduced myself to her? I doubted that Tony had told her about me 'cause we'd recently gotten together.

Tony squeezed my shoulder gently when the carriage came to a halt. "Enjoy the ride?" I nodded with a small smile. "Good," he said, looking at his watch. "It's a little after one. You want to get a bite to eat before I take you home?"

"Okay, that's fine," I replied, as he helped me out of the carriage.

Once we entered the restaurant, I realized that one, I'd never been to this one before and two, it was very elegant and very expensive. There we stood, Tony and me, wearing matching black bombers and black knitted hats and I was not comfortable. We were way too underdressed.

"You'll be fine. We're not going anywhere fancy," I mimicked Tony softly, while the host looked at the reservation list.

"Shh," Tony whispered, squeezing my hand reassuringly. "You're fine. Don't worry about it."

He held my hand while we were led to a table in front of a huge window with a breathtaking view of Central Park. With snow on the ground, the park looked amazing.

Tony whispered in my ear once the host left, "Nice view. Isn't it?" as he gently pushed my chair close to the table.

"Very nice," I replied, glancing around the restaurant as Tony sat down.

Nope. I couldn't see any of my people. I shook my head and he caught it.

"What's wrong?" he asked.

"Nothing," I replied quickly.

"Uh, uh. Something's wrong. Tell me."

"It's nothing. Forget it," I dismissed, shaking my head.

"Lacie…" Tony began, but I ignored him when my peripheral vision caught sight of the host pointing to our table as he talked to a blonde woman.

After a curt nod, the blonde woman strolled slowly to our table.

"Good afternoon," she said in a frosty tone, only looking at Tony. "My name is Iris and I'll be your server today." She handed him two menus and he passed one to me. "What would you like to drink?"

Iris continued to watch Tony while he viewed the menu. Not once did her eyes veer my way.

Tony glanced up and asked, "What choice of wine would you recommend for special occasions?" After Iris ran down the list, keeping eye contact only with him, he nodded determinedly. "Okay, the last one sounded good. Give us that one." He looked at me. "Are you fine with that, babe?"

Finally, Iris eyed me out the corner of her eye. Making sure that my stance was well conveyed to her, I put my hand over his with a wide grin and replied in a syrupy tone, "Yes, baby. Anything you say."

Tony nodded. "Okay, we'll take that one," he finalized, giving the waitress a smile.

Iris pursed her lips. "Fine, sir. I'll be back with your wine. I'll give you time with your order," she stated and walked off briskly.

Satisfied that my point was made, I opened my menu and asked Tony in the same syrupy tone, "What are you going to order, baby?"

🙰

We arrived at my apartment a little before three. Given the unexpected telephone call from Tony's mother and the waitress' attitude at the restaurant, I was beginning to wonder how Mama was going to act toward Tony.

I hesitated to put the key in the lock to unlock my apartment door and looked at Tony warily. "Are you ready?"

"For what?" he asked.

"The wrath of Josephine," I whispered.

He stared at me blankly. "Lacie, wasn't she part of that whole ruse along with Robert and Carrie to get us back together last night?"

"Yes, but…"

"But?"

I sighed. "Look, all I'm saying is just prepare for something outrageous to come out of Mama's mouth because she is not at all tactful. She might be okay with us being together, but she's still not crazy about white people."

He shook his head. "Lacie, just open the door."

I inhaled and turned the key and once I opened the door, the aroma of some good cooking immediately smacked us in the face. No one was in the living room, but I heard rattling in the kitchen.

"Sounds like someone's busy in the kitchen," I murmured to Tony while he took our coats and hung them up. "Mama! Reneé! I'm home," I yelled.

Mama came out of the kitchen with one of my aprons on, wiping her hands on a dishtowel and exclaimed, "Well…look who finally decided to come home!" She stopped short, put her hands on her hips and looked me over. "Lacie, what in the world are you wearing?"

Slightly embarrassed, I gave her a tight smile. "Mama…don't start, please."

"Umm, hmm. That's what you get for staying out all night," she teased, walking over to give me a hug. "Happy New Year, Lacie." She let go of me and looked at Tony with a kind smile. "Happy New Year, Tony."

"Happy New Year, Mrs. Taylor," he replied, returning a smile.

"Ah," Mama scolded lightly with an index finger. "I prefer that you call me Josephine. Even though I'm going to be a grandmother soon, I'm still in denial. I don't want to feel any older. That's one thing you need to know about me. Although, I'm sure Lacie's told you a lot about me already."

"Okay, Josephine," Tony chuckled.

"Good." Mama nodded.

I sniffed the air. "Mama, what's that you're cook…" Then recognizing the smell, I asked, "Shrimp gumbo, Mama?"

She nodded and replied as she started for the kitchen, "Yes and if you two don't mind, I would like some company, not to mention some help. Reneé and Danny went baby shopping with his parents and left me here alone. You two come on in here and put some aprons on and help me with this food."

Tony and I glanced at each other with a shrug and then followed her into the kitchen.

I grabbed an apron from underneath the sink and put it on. "I can't believe you're fixing shrimp gumbo. You know how much I love that." I caught sight of piles of dough rolled into the shape of rolls on a sheet of aluminum foil. "And your homemade rolls, too? Aw man! What did I do to deserve this?" I exclaimed softly, going over to the other sink to wash my hands.

"Child, please. It's got nothing to do with deserving. This is New Year's Day. Plus, I didn't know when you were coming home, so I thought I'd fix dinner so you wouldn't have to cook when you got here," she explained. "Lacie, you can start cutting the potatoes and make big chunks too. Not them small ones that I don't like, either." She glanced over at Tony who was sitting on a stool at the counter watching us. "Do you know how to cook, Tony?"

"Yeah, I can cook a little," he replied.

"Well, good. Come over here and cut up these green peppers," she commanded lightly.

"Mama, maybe he doesn't want to help," I spoke up for him and grabbed a paper towel.

"No, that's okay, Lacie. I don't mind," he said easily, coming around with me to wash his hands.

"You see, Lacie? He wants to help," Mama declared with a triumphant smile.

I only shook my head.

Tony did more than cut up the peppers. He did everything he could to help Mama. I watched and listened while he and Mama cooked and carried on simple conversation about food.

After a while, Mama turned to me. "Lacie, would you mind going to the store to get a few items for me?" She handed me a small list out of her apron pocket.

"If you want, I'll go for you," Tony offered.

"No, that's okay. Lacie will do it," Mama insisted lightly. "Won't you, darling?" I peered at Mama, but couldn't make out her expression. She sensed my unwillingness. "It's okay, Lacie," she mouthed to me silently.

"Okay, I'll go," I relented. "Tony, walk me to the door." As we walked out of the kitchen, I turned back around and mouthed, 'behave yourself' to Mama. She hunched up her shoulders innocently and waved me off.

"You know what she's going to do, don't you? She's going to ambush you while I'm away," I whispered anxiously while Tony helped me with my coat.

"Probably so, but it's going to be all right."

I looked at him incredulously. "You're not the least bit concerned."

"No." He shook his head and gently guided me toward the door. "Now don't worry. Just go to the store and don't take too long before I have to come looking for you." He gave me a peck on the cheek and headed toward the kitchen.

I stood there with uncertainty, before I realized that the longer I waited, the longer he'd be alone with Mama.

I rushed out the door.

# Chapter 4

# Tony

"Okay, Tony. Enough pleasantries. What do you want with my daughter? Besides the obvious, of course," Josephine said when I returned to the kitchen.

Eyeing me sternly with her arms folded, she leaned against the counter and waited for my answer.

Lacie was right. She didn't mince words. Instinctively, I knew she wasn't going for any bull and would smell it a mile away if I even bothered to give her a charming smile. There was no time for charm. This woman was serious.

She raised her eyebrow when I swallowed and cleared my throat. I held up a hand and expressed with honest sincerity, "I just want to love her, that's all."

There was an uncomfortable stillness while she continued to stare at me. And I mean, she stared me down. I heard every sound in the kitchen while I waited for a response—something—anything from her to get the imaginary sweat to stop running down my face. Hours seemed to fly by before she finally responded.

"But why a *black* woman?" she emphasized, not backing down on her stare.

"I don't care about her color, Mrs… I mean, Josephine." I cleared my throat.

"Why not? Everyone else does, the world does," she stated straight-forwardly.

Man, she sounded exactly like Lacie. "Uh, Josephine, I don't mean to be rude, but I've had this conversation with Lacie a while ago…"

She quirked one eyebrow and held up an index finger, silencing me. "Tony, I don't care if you've talked this over with Lacie a million times. You're talking to her mother now and I need to hear every word out of your mouth and see your face while you utter them. I've been around for a long time, Tony, and I'll know your hand before it's even played."

She was sharp and she wasn't giving me a way out. I nodded in compliance. "Okay. What do you want to know?"

"Are you really in love with Lacie or are you just a wigga?" she queried without batting an eye.

"A wigga." It wasn't a question, rather a statement.

"Yes…a wigga," she repeated with a sparkle in her eye. "C'mon, you know what I'm talking about. White men trying to be black, liking our music, and even having a little rhythm. A white man wanting to be a…"

"C'mon now…" I stopped her, feeling immediate discomfort with the stereotyping and suggestion.

"No, you c'mon," she contended, raking me over. "Black women are some of the most beautiful creatures on this earth, Tony, and white men have continually lusted after us." She held out her hand. "Our various complexions tell the story." She refolded her arms. "Whether it was rape, consensual or love, the attraction has always been there and still is. But when it was love, we were left with broken hearts because white men couldn't deal with the discrimination."

"Have you experienced this?"

"I just know the tale all too well, is all." She inhaled, sizing me up. "Tony, Lacie is a very strong woman, but like most women she turns to mush when she's in love. She's quite vulnerable and even more so now, given this type of relationship. I want to know if you're prepared to go that extra mile when things get tough. Are you with her for the duration or are you just going through some phase or something? 'Cause if you are…"

I had to stop her right there. "Hey, I'm in *love* with Lacie. *Really* in love with her." I held out my hands. "This isn't a phase and I'm not using her. This is real to me," I expressed earnestly. "There's no other way to explain it. She's got me."

We stared at each other for a long time, but I was determined not to break this one.

"But you still didn't answer my question; are you prepared to go that extra mile?" she repeated.

"Yes, I'll do anything for her...for us."

"I have your word on this, then?"

"Yes, ma'am."

"Okay," she stated, nodding decisively and backing off her stare. "I'm sure Lacie's told you this also, but you're hearing this from me now; I have a problem trusting white people, Tony. Especially white men. Lacie is whole-heartedly in love with you and while I love her and recognize that this is her life, this thing between you and her is very difficult for me. It opens a lot of wounds for me as a black woman. You're very vocal about your feelings for her and now you have to own up to them. *So I'm warning you...*if you hurt my daughter in anyway or even think about calling her the n-word, then her business becomes mine. I will hunt you down and skin you alive. Is that understood?"

This woman was on point and I couldn't help but admire her. I cleared my throat. "Yes, ma'am."

She grimaced and held up her hand. "Tony, if you and I are ever going to be on one accord, don't ever call me ma'am again." Then she smirked. "But that's all right. At least it shows you've got some manners." She took a deep breath. "C'mon, let's finish this food and act like we've been cooking all this time."

She started to turn toward the oven but I placed my hand on her shoulder, stopping her. "Can I give you a hug?" I asked.

She looked surprised for a second but smiled warmly and opened her arms wide. "Oh, come on here, boy," she exclaimed softly, laughing. "I'll still be watching you, you know."

I chuckled. "I wouldn't have it any other way... Josephine," I said, giving her a warm embrace.

Josephine. What could I say about her, except she was a mother protecting her child? She was blunt—amazingly blunt—but I respected her for it. She needed to tell me where she was coming from and needed to know where I stood.

Point blank.

Thirty minutes later, Josephine and I were still cooking and talking when I heard keys in the door. It had to be Lacie, so I went to the door. Taking the bags out of her arms, I gave her a kiss on the cheek and smiled at her.

"What did you do? Buy up the whole store?" I teased, closing the door behind her.

"How did it go while I was gone?" she asked at once, ignoring my question and hanging up her coat.

"It was interesting. We had a nice talk," I replied, walking to the kitchen.

"Umm, hmm, what did she say to you?" she asked, following me. "Mama, what did you say to him?" she asked Josephine when we entered the kitchen.

"What he and I talked about is between us. What are you so worried about?" Josephine replied calmly and sweetly.

"Mama, I know you said…"

"Lacie," I said calmly. "Really, it's fine."

"And quit bothering the man and put up the groceries," Josephine stressed. "We got too much to do and you're busy worrying about what I said to him."

I chuckled while Lacie looked from Josephine to me. She narrowed her eyes at me and started taking out the groceries, but not before whispering to me, "That wasn't cute, Tony. Not at all."

*Chapter 5*

# Robert

It was six o'clock on New Year's morning when the call came. I picked up the phone.

"Robbie," my mother's voice on the other end cried, "your father's in the hospital. He had a massive stroke last night."

I sat up immediately and asked, "What? How did this happen?"

I heard my mother let out a deep sigh and automatically knew the news couldn't be good. "Well, you know your father. He's so stubborn and I told him not to bring that wood in because it was too heavy. He'd just been feeling so ill lately…" her voice trailed off and she started crying.

"Okay, Ma," I said softly, trying to calm her down. She didn't hear me. "Ma?"

"Yes, Robbie," she answered, sniffling.

"I'm going to see about getting a flight out as soon as I can. It shouldn't be that difficult now that the holidays are over. Are you at the hospital now?"

"Yes," she sniffled again.

I scrambled to find a pen and scrap paper and said, "Give me the number and I'll call you back when I get some details."

Once I got off the phone with her, I started making plans.

*Chapter 6*

# Dawn

What the *hell* was I doing?

I stood in the lobby of the classy restaurant debating whether I should go in.

It was last night when I saw him....

*I felt a light tap on my shoulder and turned around. He was all smiles and looking fine. "Dawn? I thought that was you. What are you doing here?"*

*Equally surprised to see him there, I stammered, "Uh...a few of my friends that I work with invited me to this party. And you?"*

*"Same here. I know the guy that's giving it. He and I go way back."*

*A few seconds of silence, then, "Mind if I sit down?" he asked, indicating the bar stool with his hand.*

*"Uh...no. Go ahead," I replied.*

*We sat at the bar wordlessly watching everyone mingle. Practically everyone had drinks in their hands, ready for the New Year to arrive.*

*"So why are you here? I mean, I know why you're here at this party, but what are you doing in Miami?" he asked.*

*"I got a bit part in a low budget film and my agent recently hooked me up with some fashion shows here," I explained with pride.*

*"Congratulations, Dawn! How long will you be in town?"*

*"Oh, I've moved here. I packed up my things after my agent informed me of the gigs and said goodbye to the Big Apple." I shook my head. "There were so many bad memories, you know? I just needed a fresh start."*

*He nodded. "Yep, I know a few things about bad memories, too."*

*Knowing what he meant, I said nothing because I was uncertain of what to say. A crowd of people gathered in front of the television set. The countdown was beginning in Times Square and the ball was slowly coming down.*

*"Five...Four...Three...Two...One! Happy New Year!" the crowd yelled.*

*Everyone exchanged hugs and couples kissed. We looked at each other and smiled uneasily. Without warning, he got off his bar stool, took my hand, helped me off mine, and embraced me.*

*"Happy New Year," he said softly in my ear.*

*"Happy New Year," I returned.*

*"Hey, come over here, man!" A tall black man was waving at him from across the room.*

*"I'm being summoned," he said with an apologetic smile.*

*Nodding in response, I said, "Sure, go ahead. I see my friends waving me over there also."*

*He started walking off slowly. "You take care, all right?"*

*I smiled. "Yeah, you too."*

*He continued walking away, then stopped and turned around. Despite all the commotion in the room, I heard him say, "You want to meet me for lunch tomorrow?"*

*For whatever reason, I replied, "Sure."*

*He strode toward me, told me the place after we agreed on a time, and then walked over to the tall black man, who was now waving frantically for him.*

So here I was, pacing back and forth nervously, with little steps on the soft carpet, in the lobby of the restaurant. I could feel people watching me as they walked past my pacing figure to enter the restaurant.

*There's nothing wrong with what I'm about to do. This is perfectly innocent and only a simple lunch between acquaintances.*

Both hands on the twelve on my watch, indicated that it was time for me to go in.

Straightening up, I walked toward the host and told him my name. He checked his list and told me to follow him.

I admired the décor of the restaurant as we glided past tables filled with people in earnest conversation. This was a classy restaurant, indeed.

The host suddenly stopped short and then I saw him standing at the table. Smiling, Joe was immaculate from head to toe in an expensive suit.

This man had it going on and I was in trouble. Crap!

Lacie was going to beat the hell out of me.

# Chapter 7

# Joe

I was headed for danger, I thought, watching Dawn walk through the restaurant with grace and purpose. Tall and astoundingly beautiful, I hadn't noticed her—not until last night.

*"I've gotta tell you, man. We can do some serious business together,"* Trevor was saying as a familiar looking female in an awesome red dress passed by me.

*"Hold on, man,"* I said to Trevor as my eyes followed her to the bar. *"Look man, I gotta check something out, okay? I'll be right back,"* I said, stepping away from him.

*Was that Dawn, Lacie's friend? I caught a side view of her. Yep, it was. What was she doing here?*

*I moved a little closer but stood at a distance, checking her out. Hair swept up elegantly, long legs and perfectly manicured hands loosely holding a champagne glass, she was looking righteous.*

*Was I going to simply stand there like an idiot and not say anything to her?*

*Boldly, I walked up to her, tapped her on the shoulder lightly, put on my best smile and said, "Dawn? I thought that was you. What are you doing here?"*

*Her gorgeous, dark brown, doe eyes blew me away when she turned around and then widened with surprised from seeing me there. She seemed different, more confident even. Why hadn't I noticed her before?*

*We made casual conversation, both explaining why the other was there and drifted off while we watched everyone yell the countdown. But I was watching her every move.*

*"She's Lacie's friend! She's Lacie's friend!" the white imaginative figure on my right shoulder cautioned repeatedly. But the red imaginative figure*

>ACROSS THE COLOR LINE

on my left cheered me on saying, "Man, you'd better go for that. She is hot!"

The New Year came and everyone was exchanging hugs and kisses. I didn't know what to do and figured she didn't either. Impulsively, I went for it.

I got off my bar stool, simultaneously helped her off hers, embraced her gently and said, "Happy New Year." She felt good in my arms and for some reason I didn't want to let her go.

I heard Trevor's beck and call, apologized to her and started walking away. Then I stopped and realized that whether it was to reminiscence about New York or not, I wanted to see Dawn again. I walked back to her after asking her out for lunch and told her to meet me here at twelve o'clock.

And here she was heading my way.

Standing, I watched the other men in the restaurant follow her figure as she walked behind the host. Dawn didn't appear to notice and actually looked a little dazed upon reaching the table.

"Hi," she said softly.

"Hi," I replied.

The host told us our server would be with us shortly.

I smiled and watched Dawn as I helped push her chair under the table. She seemed nervous. She didn't know it, but I'd seen her when she arrived five minutes earlier and noticed her pacing back and forth.

"So how are you feeling?" I asked politely, rubbing my hands together under the table once I sat in my chair.

"I'm fine and you?" she returned.

"A little groggy from last night, but I'll make it."

"Too much to drink?"

"Yeah. Way too much," I admitted. "I've been doing that a lot recently."

"Oh," was all she said.

"I must admit," I said, leaning over the table a bit. "I didn't know if you were going to come."

She gave a little smile in reply. "The thought did come to mind. It was a difficult decision."

"I can understand that." I nodded. "I'm glad you came, though."
She peered at me. "Really?"

"Yes, 'cause I'm starving!" I said and we both chuckled. That seemed to break the tension. "C'mon," I said, opening the menu. "Let's decide on what we want to order, okay?"

"Okay," she said, opening hers as well.

Hearing the imaginative white figure on my shoulder saying, "You dummy!" I brushed him off my shoulder.

*Chapter 8*

# Lacie

Mama had said something mean to him. I just knew it.

Figuring that neither of them would speak about it unless I was alone with one of them, I put the subject on hold while we continued helping her in the kitchen.

It wasn't long after that Reneé and Danny arrived, after being dropped off by his parents. They came in carrying a load of baby stuff, looking like the most adorable couple.

Reneé grinned at me and put her arms around my shoulder as Tony helped Danny take the packages upstairs. "So the plan worked, huh?"

I grinned sheepishly. "Yes, it did."

Reneé nodded her head toward the kitchen where Mama was and asked, "Is she behaving herself?"

"I don't think so. She sent me on an errand for some groceries, while Tony helped her cook. I was gone for a good half-hour."

"A half-hour?" Reneé's eyes widened. "You left him alone with Mama for a half-hour?"

I nodded. "I know, Reneé. I know. And Mama knew what she was doing, too. I mean, who ever heard of black people having Tacos and Tortillas on New Year's Day?"

Reneé burst out laughing as Tony and Danny came back downstairs, and Mama came out of the kitchen.

"Okay people, the food's ready. Reneé, Lacie, you two set the table. Tony and Danny come in here and help me with the food," Mama announced.

Within five minutes, the table was set with Mama's shrimp gumbo, black-eyed peas and rice, corn bread and cabbage.

"Where are the Tacos and Tortillas, Mama?" I mocked Mama when all of us sat at the table after prayer.

"You know, it's the funniest thing," Mama said innocently, spooning some rice on her plate. "I decided not to use them after all." She looked at Tony. "Tony, it's our family tradition to have black-eyed peas and rice on New Year's Day. It's supposed to bring good luck throughout the year. You know anything about that?"

"Yes," Tony replied, passing her the black-eyed peas. "It's a tradition in my family also."

"Umm, interesting," Mama uttered. "Are you looking forward to the New Year?"

"Very much so," he answered, looking at me. "I see a lot of good things happening this year."

"Oh? With Lacie?"

"Mama," I warned her lightly.

"Lacie, I'm just asking the man some questions. How am I supposed to get to know him better if I don't ask questions?"

"We've only been together for twenty-four hours, Mama. Not to mention that you've already given him the third degree while I was out. Give the man a break…"

"Well, I have some news!" Reneé interrupted loudly. All eyes turned toward her. Beaming she said, "Danny and I have decided that we want to get married the weekend before Valentine's Day."

"What!" Mama shrieked.

Here we go. Arguments always seem to get started at the dinner table.

Not affected by Mama's outburst, Reneé smiled. She took Danny's hand in hers. "We don't want anything elaborate—just small and intimate—enough to make it official," she said easily, looking from me to Mama. "We want you two to give us your blessing."

Mama spoke before me.

"But this is so soon and you're both so young…" Mama objected. "Have you two thought about what you're going to do?"

Danny explained. His parents had offered to help them out. They owned another house and offered it to them. After graduation, Danny would work so Reneé could stay home with the baby and go to school part-time.

"I guess you two have thought it through then," Mama mumbled.

"What do you say, Mama?" Reneé asked her softly.

No one spoke while we waited for Mama to speak. She took a deep breath and looked at me. "Lacie?"

I shrugged. "Mama, if this is what Reneé and Danny really want..."

Understanding, Mama nodded and took another deep breath. "I must be getting really old," she murmured as she stood and went over to Danny. She embraced him tightly after he stood and said tearfully, "Congratulations and welcome to the family."

Reneé yelled with joy and Tony and I clapped.

At that moment, I couldn't have been more proud of Mama.

❧

I walked Tony to the door when he was getting ready to leave. Danny had left and Mama and Reneé were upstairs.

"Today was good, don't you think? Your mother agreeing to Reneé and Danny getting married so soon," Tony suggested, putting on his coat.

"Very," I replied, looking at him pensively. "Tony, are you going to tell me what you and Mama talked about while I was at the store?"

He sighed. "Why are you so concerned about what we talked about?"

"Because I know how Mama is and you're not telling me anything," I shot back, squinting at him.

He shook his head. "Let it go, Lacie. It wasn't as bad as you think." He planted a kiss on my lips. "Listen, I'll call you tomorrow and I'll see you at work on Monday, okay?"

"Okay, but..." I started.

Silencing me with a longer kiss this time, he ended it with, "I'll see you Monday. I love you." He closed the door behind him.

"I love you, too," I murmured to the closed door. "Mama!" I shouted, turning around and walking to the bottom of the stairs.

℅℃

I was right.

Sitting in the living room with Mama, I shook my head as she reiterated the conversation she had with Tony.

"You asked him if he was a wigga, Mama? A wigga?" I groaned.

She dismissed me with a little wave. "Girl, hush. I just said that to startle him a little bit. You know, catch him off guard."

Standing up in a daze, I began walking toward the kitchen, muttering, "I don't believe you said that to him. I just don't believe you said that to him."

"I had to do it, Lacie," Mama defended, joining me in the kitchen, while I started filling the dishwasher with dirty dishes. "I had to find out. I had to find out if he was genuine."

"By telling him you'd skin him alive if he ever called me the n-word?" I asked her, stopping for a second to look at her. She hunched up her shoulders before I continued with the dishes, shaking my head. "Mama, when we go to church tomorrow, I'm going to ask for a special prayer at altar call for you."

"Lacie, you ought to know how I am by now," she defended. "In the back of my mind there's always going to be this idea that he may say that to you, when he's upset or something. And white or not, people usually blurt out their true feelings when they're angry or during a heated argument. So I decided to shake him up, be upfront and let him know where I was coming from."

I straightened up after I'd finished filling the dishwasher and looked at her with the past two incidences coming into mind. "Mama ..." I said exasperatedly, holding out my hand. "You know, I really...you know what? Just forget it!"

"Forget what?"

Unsure if I should tell her, I shook my head.

Her motherly instinct came on instantly and she came closer and leaned against the counter with me. "Lacie, did something happen today?" I shook my head again. "Lacie, c'mon, we said we'd work on our communication, now," she reminded.

Her reminder was enough incentive to tell her. I was not, however, expecting the reaction she gave me after I'd told her.

"Ow!" I said after she had pinched me on the arm. "What'd you do that for?"

"Lacie, why in the hell did you let that woman call you a maid?" Mama asked crossly.

"I didn't. She just assumed that I was," I replied, rubbing my arm. "That really hurt, you know."

"It was supposed to," Mama said. "Regardless of her assumption, you've come too far to let someone refer to you as a maid. Lacie, didn't you learn anything from that girl, Simone?"

"Mama, that's different. This is his mother."

"So? Does that mean that she's supposed to assume you're the maid because she hears your black voice?"

"Mama, how was she going to know that I'm black?"

"You sure don't sound white, Lacie," Mom wisecracked. "You know very well that black people speak differently than white folk. I bet she wouldn't have thought that if she heard a white woman on the phone!"

"Mama, I couldn't tell her that I was his girlfriend. It was too soon and how else was I going to explain my reason for answering his phone and being in his apartment in the morning?"

Mama didn't answer but shook her head, still incensed. "I can't wait to see that woman so I can break her off some kind of proper!"

"Mama, it wasn't her fault."

"The hell it wasn't! Lacie, why are you defending that woman and you haven't even met her?" Mama exclaimed. "Girl, you've got to get a thick skin about the type of relationship that you're in. You're across the color line now and you already know that society shuns interracial relationships. Family can be even worse, so you've got to be prepared. How are you and Tony going to work if you can't deal with his mother?" I put a hand to my head wearily. "Did you tell Tony about the waitress?" I shook my head. "Lacie!"

"Mama, I handled it," I defended. "I just simply rubbed our relationship in her face, that's all."

"What you should have done was tell the manager about her nasty attitude."

I held up a hand. "Mama, I handled it. Okay?" I strained out, trying to hold on.

Mama noticed it and sighed. "Oh, come here, Lacie," she said immediately hugging me. "I'm sorry, Lacie. I didn't mean to get so riled up."

"Yes, you did," I said between a sniffle and laugh.

"Yeah, you're right. I did," Mama chuckled, pulling away to look at me.

"Mama, I really need your support here."

"You've got it. You know you do. All I'm saying is that if you truly want this with Tony then realize that you might be in for the fight of your life. This is only the beginning. Do not let anyone break your spirit and what you and Tony have down. Not even me. You understand?"

"Yes, Mama," I said with a nod. Then I tilted my head to the side. "So, Mama, what do you think about Tony?"

She leaned back against the counter again, crossed her arms lightly and tilted her head to the side thoughtfully. "You know, he's quite smooth and very charming. I can see why you were attracted to him."

"Does this mean that you like him?"

She nodded her head slowly and narrowed her eyes. "You know what? I really do. He's just a cool cat."

I snickered. "A cool cat, Mama?"

She swiveled her head to look at me. "Yeah…he's quite all right. And because I know you're going to ask him about our little conversation, you can tell him that he passed my little inquisition, so far." She raised her arms over her head and stretched. "I'm going upstairs to see about Reneé and then go to bed." She started out of the kitchen and before she got out of eyesight, she turned to look at me. "You know, if it wasn't for Tony's obvious lack of color and my apparent prejudice, I'd swear he had a little black in him."

I stood there with my mouth agape as Mama walked out. Then I burst out laughing.

# Chapter 9

# Dawn

The woman that landed Joe was going to be very lucky indeed.

It was three hours later and I was standing in the lobby of the restaurant, observing Joe making light conversation with the manager.

Joe was the first man I'd been out with since my move to Miami. Offers had come, but truthfully after all of that mess with Ronnie, I'd promised myself to take my time with romance. So it was quite ironic that the first man that I'd decide to go out with would happen to be my best friend's ex-man; and a fine one, too.

I sighed deeply and recalled how apprehensive I'd been to meet him only three hours earlier. Lunch had been a shaky start for me, but after Joe broke the ice with a light joke, the date—if I were to call it that—got better. It had to be the best lunch date I'd ever been on with any male. We clicked instantly and talked about everything under the sun, from ourselves to our goals. But we never talked about Lacie. And that was the problem. Lacie was my best friend and it was only a month or so ago that they'd been engaged.

Joe was strolling over to me with a warm smile. He was debonair, confident and terribly handsome, but I knew that I couldn't see him anymore. He was the hot chocolate syrup on my ice cream that I wanted, but couldn't have. Although lunch with him seemed innocent enough, there was no question of its secrecy. Had it been any other guy, who was as handsome as Joe and had asked me out to lunch, I'd have called Lacie immediately.

"Okay, where would you like to go now?" Joe asked me easily, giving my arm a light squeeze.

"You know... actually, I have a lot to do. So I'm going to go home and practice some of my lines for the movie," I answered, looking directly at him.

He locked eyes with me and I didn't look away. I wanted him to listen to the unspoken words. He nodded and grinned slightly. "Okay," he said in compliance. "But did you enjoy lunch?"

"Yes, I did, very much. And the conversation as well."

He nodded again. "Me too." Clearing his throat, he looked toward the exit door then back at me. "You gonna be okay? Do you need a ride or anything?"

"No, I'm fine. I drove so..."

After a brief moment of silence, he took a deep breath and said, "Well, Dawn, you take care of yourself and thanks for having lunch with me."

I chuckled softly. "You're welcome. It was my pleasure," I said and extended my hand.

He shook his head. "You know better than that," he scolded softly, moving closer to give me a hug.

After we ended our embrace, I said, "Take care also, Joe."

I walked swiftly toward the exit door without looking back, still heated from our embrace.

*Why did he have to hug me?*

*Chapter 10*

# Joe

I shouldn't have hugged her.

I really shouldn't have hugged her because now the urge to see her again, and get to know her, was there even more.

Now she was leaving.

Impulse told me to go after her, but I figured that I'd play myself if I did. Not to mention, I know she didn't want me to and I understood why. She'd probably felt that I'd compromised and challenged her friendship with Lacie by even inviting her to lunch.

Who could blame me, though?

I'd never been the kind of guy to shy away from a beautiful looking woman and something about seeing her last night prompted me to invite her to lunch. I was glad I did, too, because I'd enjoyed lunch with her and our conversation was like breathing fresh air.

Ambitious with her modeling and acting, Dawn seemed to have a lot going for her. That made her even more appealing because I was as equally ambitious. Even better was how autonomous and more assured she was. She wasn't looking for a man to support her while she stayed at home.

I'd been on a few casual dates since my return to Miami, and had been turned off by them. It was annoying to go out with sistas who only saw dollar signs and wanted to retire once they found out my profession. Dawn appeared to be different.

But she was Lacie's best friend.

I strolled slowly back into the restaurant and went to the bar and ordered a light drink. I sat there taking little sips, examining the dilemma I was in and wrestled with my emotions. Reasoning and a little bit of conscience told me to leave Dawn alone because there was too much of a conflict there. While impulse, again, told me to take my chances and go for her.

I slammed my empty glass down. "Oh, hell," I grumbled, irritated with my decision. I took out a twenty-dollar-bill, placed it on the bar and walked out swiftly.

My impulse was going to get me in trouble one day.

# *Chapter 11*

# Tony

It was back to work as usual and the insistent ringing of the telephone welcomed and reminded me of it, when I strolled into my office early Monday morning.

Stifling a yawn, I put my briefcase on the desk, sat down and answered, "Ryan & Company. Tony Douglas speaking."

"Anthony, Happy New Year!"

I smiled. Everyone I knew called me 'Tony', but my mother still insisted on calling me by my given name.

"Happy New Year, Mom. How are you and Dad and how did the party go?" I asked.

"Oh, it went along nicely. Everyone was asking about you," she hinted.

"Yeah, I had another party to go to here in New York. It was very important."

"Still, you should have come, Anthony. The Sanders brought their daughter, Rachel, and I wanted you two to spend time together."

I sighed, knowing where the conversation was headed. "Mom, do you think you can try to stop fixing me up?"

"Anthony, don't get perturbed. Your father and I just want you to settle down, that's all. You are our youngest son and both of your brothers are already married with children. I think Rachel is a fine girl. Speaking of her, I'm calling to remind you that her sister, Lauren, is marrying Harold Foster in March. You're supposed to perform at their wedding, remember?"

"That's right, I forgot," I grumbled.

"Also, your twin nieces, Amber and Alicia's birthday party is the next day at our house, so we're expecting you there."

"Okay, Mom. I'll put it in my planner."

"Anthony, dear, being that this is a wedding, maybe you need to start thinking about settling down since you know that Rachel is going to be there. That would be a perfect time for you two to catch up on things," she suggested.

She was starting again. "Okay, Mom. I'll think about it and call you later. I've got a load of stuff to do today, okay?"

"Okay, Anthony. I won't push, but please be sure to return my calls. I called you at home, and on your cell phone Saturday morning and yesterday. I even left a message with your maid for you to call me because Rachel wasn't due to leave town until this morning. You've been very hard to catch up with." Mom sighed. "But I forgive you. I love you and I'll talk with you soon, dear."

"My maid?" I stated softly, perplexed and still holding the receiver after Mom hung up.

Pensive, I turned around to the window overlooking the Manhattan skyline. No wonder Lacie had been so aloof during the ride in Central Park. Why didn't she tell me? She didn't even mention it to me when I talked with her on the phone yesterday.

I was tempted to call Mom back and correct her, but changed my mind once I thought about Lacie. I knew Lacie was in love with me, but this was her first go at this type of relationship and we hadn't really had time to discuss my family. Plus, she was still quite fragile. No. I had to smooth things over with her first, before even tackling my mom.

My phone rang again. I turned around and looked at the flashing light, indicating that it was an in-house call.

"Tony, speaking," I answered.

"Happy New Year, Tony. This is Richard."

"Happy New Year, Richard. How's everything?"

"Going very well. Has Lacie arrived at work, yet?"

"No, not–" I replied, but stopped when I glanced outside my office door and saw Lacie hurrying my way through the department. "Wait a minute. I see her now."

"Good. I would like for you and Lacie to come to my office once you get settled in. I have some news that I have to discuss with you two about the William Carr account."

"Okay, we'll be there," I replied, looking up to see Lacie's amazing figure standing in my doorway.

Lacie waited before I put the receiver down before she said, with a contrite expression, "Tony, I am so sorry for what my mother said to you Saturday."

I strolled over to her casually and closed the door behind her. "Boy, you really know how to start a morning off right, don't you? What ever happened to 'good morning'?"

She turned around to look at me. "I'm serious, Tony. Mama told me what she said to you and I'm—"

I shook my head. "There's no need for apologies, Lacie. I didn't take offense to anything she said. If anything, I should be apologizing for what my mother said to you."

"Huh?" she asked, stunned. "When did you find out?"

"A few minutes ago." I sighed. "She shouldn't have assumed you were my maid. So, I'm sorry. Why didn't you tell me?"

She hunched up her shoulders. "I guess I was trying to figure out how to deal with what she said myself. I mean, I was shocked and then she hung up before I could say anything."

"Yeah. She did that to me, too. Come here," I said, holding out my arms. She walked into them and I cupped my hands around her face. "Listen, I don't ever want you to feel as if you can't talk to me about anything. There's nothing we shouldn't be able to say to each other. I love you and I'm not ashamed of you. Don't ever feel any less than the remarkable and beautiful woman you are."

"I don't."

"Are you sure?"

"Yes."

"Despite how the waitress treated you in the restaurant?"

"You noticed that?"

I nodded. "Yep. That's why she didn't get a tip. I also made a complaint to the manager about her." More shock came over her face.

"Maybe next time the only color she'll be concerned about is green."

Shaking her head with an amused little laugh, she said, "Once again you've surprised me, Tony."

"Hey, I went to hell and back with your mother defending my love for you. Do you think I want to risk seeing Josephine's wrath?" I joked.

"No, I know you don't," she chuckled. "So you're really okay? You're not at all offended by what Mama said to you?"

"I'm not going to lie. Your Mom really laid it out. She is definitely not to be played with," I admitted with a light chuckle. "She readily admitted how leery she is about my intentions and everything, but I respect her because she was so straightforward. Not to mention, you did give me plenty of warning beforehand, so I can't be mad about that. Does that make you feel better?"

She smiled. "A little, yes." Then she frowned. "You know, we haven't even discussed how your parents are going to feel about us."

I shook my head. "They're not going to have a problem."

Leaning her head back to peer at me, she asked, "How can you be so sure?"

"Lacie, we've just begun this relationship. Let's just try to concentrate on each other and deal with one issue at a time."

"You're right," she said.

"I know I am." I laughed at the little scowl she gave me as she put one hand on her hip.

"Ha, ha, ha, Tony," she mimicked. "But again, you are right," she admitted, taking a deep breath. "All right, I'm going to walk over to my office and get settled in. I'll see you later, okay?"

"No, it's not okay. I need my morning kiss first." I grinned and kissed her. "Mmm...sweet lips." I lifted my head after a moment. "Thank you."

"My pleasure," she said, smiling. "Now, let go of me, so I can get to my office," she scolded. She removed my hands off of her hips and started toward the door.

I chuckled. "Just so you know. Richard just called and he wants us in his office shortly. So you need to remember to behave yourself."

**51**

Lacie turned around after opening the door, gave me a sexy wink and pointed to the front of my pants. "Oh, I think *you* need to remember that," she punned.

I watched her switch sexily out the door, then looked down and chuckled softly. No wonder

*Chapter 12*

# Lacie

Still walking with a sexy stride, I smiled and giggled softly, knowing that Tony was watching me. I'd only dared to do that because no one else in the department had arrived yet.

Ease and relief overwhelmed me when I unlocked my office door, walked toward my desk and sat down. I'd come to work fully prepared to give Tony a huge apology for what Mama said to him on Saturday, and instead he'd apologized to me about his mother.

His genuine concern for my feelings seemed to be equally or even more important than how he felt. How he'd handled the whole waitress matter at the restaurant was a prime example. No other man had ever defended me in that way before.

Fifteen minutes later, Carrie knocked on my door before she walked in. "So… how did it go after you left the party with Tony? Are you guys back together or…"

I raised an eyebrow at her. "Aren't you nosy?" I teased.

Carrie put one hand on her hip. "Look, we went through a lot of trouble getting that party arranged at the last minute. I had to call in a whole lot of favors in order to get that piano in my house, the food, and the wine. David and I spent all day yesterday cleaning up. You wouldn't even believe how many vomit stains were on my carpet. Now you better tell me something or we are going to have words!" she stressed lightly.

I beamed in answer and that said it all.

Carrie rolled her eyes upward in relief. "Thank God!" she exclaimed and I laughed. "I told myself that if you two didn't get together after that, then *I* was going to give up."

"Well, your plan worked, albeit a little underhandedly, I might add. But it worked," I scolded lightheartedly, wagging my finger at her.

"Thank you very much," she said with a bow, then sat down in the chair across from me.

"Carrie, I gotta tell you, having the piano there was brilliant. How did you even know that Tony played and sung?"

"Girl, you already know the answer to that question."

"Yeah, you're right. Nothing gets past you," I laughed.

"You know that's right," she said, chuckling as she stood up. "Look, I'm going to get some coffee. Do you want some?"

"Yeah, and I only want…"

Carrie stopped me with a hand. "I know. I know. I'll be back."

"Carrie," I stopped her with my voice and she turned around. "Yes?"

"Thank you," I said warmly. "For everything."

"Girl, it was my pleasure," she said humbly, waving it off. Then as she walked out, I heard her say, "Hey, partner. Happy New Year! You can go on in, Lacie's in there."

Robert walked in the door.

"Hey!" I walked over to him swiftly to hug him. He hugged me tightly in return but I got an unsettling feeling when he did. I let go and searched his face. "What's wrong, Robert?"

"My dad had a massive stroke and he's in the hospital," he said sullenly.

"Oh, Robert! I'm so sorry." I hugged him again. "What do you need me to do?"

He released me gently and placed a set of keys in the palm of my hand. "Watch over my apartment for me. I've got to go home to Georgia and I don't know how long I'll be there. All of the numbers to contact me are in the kitchen on the refrigerator. You've still got my cell phone number, right?"

"Yeah, yeah, I've got it," I assured softly, rubbing his arm. "Are you going to be okay going by yourself? You need me to go with you?"

"No. I'll be fine. You've got a lot of good things going for you, with Tony and everything. I don't want to steal your moment."

"You won't be…"

Tony entered my office then. "Hey, Robert. How are you, man?" He extended his hand.

My heart went out to Robert as I watched him put on his best face and shake Tony's hand. "Things could be better. My dad's in the hospital, so…"

"Man, I'm sorry to hear that. Is there anything, I can do?" Tony asked.

Robert shook his head. "No. Lacie's agreed to watch my apartment while I'm gone, so that's all I really need. Just make sure she doesn't get into trouble," he said with a grim smile, then cleared his throat. "Listen, I'm going to go. My taxi's waiting downstairs and I've got a plane to catch." He leaned over and kissed my cheek. "Lacie, I love you and behave while I'm gone. Be good to Tony as well. I'll give you a call and let you know what's up." With a last quick glance at me and Tony, he said, "It's wonderful to see you two together," and walked out.

Tony looked at me. "You think he's going to be okay?"

I frowned, watching Robert step into the elevator. "I don't know. Even though it's warranted, he's really shaken up. I'll feel better once he calls me with word on his father." I glanced at my watch. "Is it time to see Richard?"

"Yep," Tony replied.

"Okay." I sighed. "Let's go."

&#9822;&#10086;&#9822;

Richard Ryan greeted us with a broad smile when we entered his office. "How are things going between you two?" he asked directly after we sat down. Tony and I looked at each other in surprise. He shrugged. "Hey, things don't stay a secret around here for long."

Tony answered. "Things couldn't be any better between us."

"Great. I'm glad. Secretly, I was hoping you two would work it out because you work very well together." Richard nodded. "Listen, the reason I wanted to see you two is because I've got good news."

Richard began by telling us that word was spreading rapidly about the huge deal we made with Joseph Mitchell and the upcoming deal with William Carr. Richard was getting flooded with calls from prospective clients wanting the company's business and they were specifically asking for us.

"I anticipate a busy and prosperous year for this company and here's what we're going to do to prepare for it," he said.

Richard continued by explaining that he felt that Tony and I were going to need assistance with the anticipated workload and wanted us to create an understudy team. This team would do a great deal of the necessary footwork and research for each company wanting our services. Richard wanted Tony and I to focus our attention on friendly and relaxing rendezvous with potential clients to alleviate some of the superficial aspects of the business. This would mean a considerable amount of travel, in which Richard announced our first trip of the year.

"In a month, you two are going to Miami to meet with William and his lawyers. But before that, you'll meet with them here in New York. I must caution you though, about William's main lawyer, Trevor Weeks. William recently acquired him to help with his legalities just because of his reputation alone. So be aware. He's notorious for his ruthlessness. "

"How long do we have to be there?" I asked.

"Only for a couple of days. William's interested in a few business ventures and he's asking for your input. So you two get ready for some sunshine. I'd love to go with you but I have to hold up fort here." Richard took a deep breath and clapped his hands. "Okay. We've got a lot ahead of us and the year's already starting off on a good note. Let's keep it going."

Tony and I left Richard's office a little overwhelmed but excited at the opportunities ahead. Richard had named a few clients we knew of already and Tony and I were conferring about some ideas on our way back to our department.

"You know, I'm surprised that Richard was okay with us being together," I said to Tony when the elevator landed on our floor.

"I don't see why. He's always said that we make a great team," Tony replied, holding the door to the department open for me.

"Yeah, but sometimes relationships like ours can backfire."

As Tony looked like he was about to comment, I noticed Carrie signaling to me that I had a phone call.

"Tony, let me get back with you. Carrie's summoning me," I joked, before walking toward my office.

"I thought you'd want to take this call personally," Carrie remarked when I came up to her. "It's on line one."

Concerned, I walked into my office hoping everything was okay with Reneé or Mama.

"Hello?" I breathed anxiously into the phone.

"Hey, baby girl!" My father's voice greeted on the other end.

"Daddy!"

*Chapter 13*

# Dawn

I looked up and there he was. Joe.

He was watching me intensely as Adrian, the photographer, continued instructing me with every pose.

It had been three days since I'd seen him, and there he stood—with no warning—he'd appeared.

"Okay, just a little to the left, Dawn. That's it. Great. Okay, now, just move your head over. Great. That's good," Adrian coaxed.

I tried to concentrate while Joe continued to observe, but couldn't help feeling nervous by his lingering gaze.

Adrian went on with, "Okay, Dawn, I want a small smile, now. No, don't stretch it. Just a small smile. Relax and concentrate. C'mon, a little more to the left. No, that's too much. No, Dawn, you're.... what is wrong, woman?" Adrian looked up from his camera with exasperation and threw up his hands. "Okay, that's it. Everybody, let's take five. I think Dawn needs it."

Although Adrian had called for a break, everyone's eyes watched as Joe made his way toward me. Still stunned, I remained standing in front of the backdrop as he approached and eyed every inch of me.

He nodded. "You make a beautiful bride, Dawn."

"This *is* a photo shoot, Joe," I whispered fretfully in return, aware that some of the people in the studio were listening to us, pretending to be on their break. "What are you doing here? How did you find me?"

"I wanted to see you," he said with an amused smile. "I'm very resourceful, you know."

"Oh, I don't believe this," I fumed in a low tone and started to walk past him. His cavalier attitude was not impressive.

"Okay, okay, I'm sorry," he said in a soothing voice that halted my footsteps. "But I just wanted to see you and I figured that you'd hang up on me if I'd tried to call you."

I turned around to look at him. "Why didn't you?"

A smile came on his face. "You wanted me to call you, then?"

Darn! The words had come out before I could stop them. Honestly, I had wanted him to call me, but I didn't want to admit it to him. I'd been thinking about him ever since we'd had lunch and felt like a complete heel the whole time. Afraid my thoughts would come out verbally; I merely shook my head and started walking away again.

He stopped me again by placing his hand on my waist proprietarily. "Okay, look, it doesn't matter." He took a deep breath. "You're almost finished with the shoot, right?" I nodded. "Good. Can I take you out to lunch again?" In answer to the disapproving look I gave him, he held up a hand. "Hey, I just want to have a friendly lunch with you. If you're still uncomfortable and don't want to ever see me again, all you'd have to do is say the word and I'll leave you alone. No pressure, honestly."

Giving in, I replied, "Okay. But just coffee."

It turned out to be more than *just* coffee.

Joe and I sat in the coffee house for hours, talking and laughing. Our conversation never became anything serious and felt like casual talk between friends. He was so easy to talk to. That was what was so unnervingly appealing about him.

"Dawn, do you have any plans this weekend?" Joe asked me offhandedly.

"No. Why?"

"This buddy of mine is hosting a party this Saturday at his house for charity. Everyone invited must bring at least one other person. Would you like to come with me?"

Guardedly, I answered, "Why me? I'm sure you don't have any problems getting dates, Joe."

"No, I don't," he replied. "But all the girls that I've been out with have some sort of motive behind them and you don't. I know you and I feel comfortable with you."

I hesitated.

"I've already told him I'm coming," he pressed.

I took a deep breath. "And this is not a date, right?"

"Right."

I was inclined to reject his invitation, but answered "yes" instead. I had to be out of my mind.

෫෬

Saturday was here.

I stood in my bedroom in front of the floor length mirror feeling nervous and anxious. I must have changed dresses fifty times before finally making a decision on a provocatively fitting white sundress and white three-inch heeled sandals.

Over the past few days, Joe and I had talked a couple of times on the phone, getting everything confirmed before today. He'd seemed relaxed the last time we'd spoken, so there was no need to be nervous. But I was.

The doorbell rang. Fretfully, I checked my dress; made sure my hair was tight and grabbed my purse.

He gave me a smile when I opened the door. I looked at his arms.

*What? No roses, Joe? You did it for Lacie on your first date with her.*

*Shut up, Dawn. This is not a date.*

"Are you ready?" he asked.

"Don't I look ready to you?" I wanted to say. Instead, I replied and nodded with a tight smile, "Let's go."

Outside, Joe led me to a sleek, black, convertible BMW and opened the passenger door.

*Where's the limo? Dawn, this isn't a date. Remember?*

"Thank you," I said.

"You're welcome," he replied, before closing the door.

Thirty minutes later, a massive beach house came into view. Contemporary and completely white with sharp angles and large windows, it was striking. A valet came to the car immediately and took the car keys when Joe opened the door on my side.

"It's amazing," I remarked to Joe as we walked toward the entrance.

"Yeah, Trevor is quite known for his extravagancies," Joe explained before a tall black man opened the door.

"Joe!" The familiar looking tall black man bellowed, immediately giving Joe a grip. "I'm glad you made it, man." Then he glanced at me. "Who's this fine lady with you?"

"This is my friend, Dawn. The instructions were to bring a guest along, so I asked her to come along."

He made it sound so obligatory. I was beginning to get offended. I offered my hand to the tall black man.

"It's nice to meet you. You have a beautiful house," I complimented.

"My name is Trevor," he replied, planting a gentlemanly kiss on my hand. "And thank you for the compliment." He turned back to Joe. "Come on in. Everyone's out back."

The house was as equally impressive on the inside. Trevor led us through a massive great room with high ceilings, supported by thick white columns. Tall glass windows gave an immediate view of the patio in the back of the house, where people were gathered poolside, and in the distance was the ocean.

After we walked through the large French doors to the back, Trevor said, "Dawn, I have to pull Joe away from you for a second to talk to him. There's a huge buffet of catered food over there. Help yourself." he said, motioning with his hand before he pulled Joe to a corner.

That was the most I saw of Joe throughout the rest of the night. He spent the majority of the night mingling with Trevor, and other invited guests, while I struggled not to be annoyed at being left alone and maintain some dignity by engaging in casual conversation with others. Though I'd been approached by a few nice looking men asking for dances, I'd turned them down. I don't know why I did, because Joe had practically left me to fend for myself.

My fury grew more with Joe as the night went on. Why had he even invited me if he was going to ignore me the whole night? What ever happened to the nice gentlemanly personality he'd given Lacie? Where in the world was the Joe that I'd had that amazing lunch with the other day? And why did I care?

Boiling, I was ready to leave when Joe finally came over to me at the end of the night.

By then, I didn't care if I ever saw Joe Mitchell again.

# Chapter 14

# Joe

She was mad.

Dawn didn't utter a word in the elevator as she stood frowning with arms folded. Still, she was gorgeous. Taking a sideways glance at her in the thin cotton white sundress, I shook my head.

She had every right to be upset. I'd basically left her alone at the party, and it was done on purpose.

When Dawn opened her door, when I picked her up earlier, I knew I was being put to the test. I literally had to restrain myself from touching her and respect her wishes, and I decided that it was better to distance myself from her. So, when Trevor pulled me away from her, I took advantage of it and stayed with him throughout the entire party, and mingled with other guests. But my eyes followed Dawn as she strolled around the pool. I even felt a tinge of jealousy when men kept coming up to her. That's when I knew that I couldn't be *just* a friend with her. I wanted more.

The elevator door opened and I followed her purposeful stride down the hallway toward her apartment door. She took out her keys and started to put it in the lock, but I gently took them from her.

"Here, let me do this for you," I offered.

She shot me with fiery doe eyes. "I've got it. Just go." She held out her hand for me to give them back.

I couldn't leave her thinking I was that much of a jackass. Ignoring her hand, I put the key in the lock, turned it and opened the door.

"Can I come in so we can talk?"

A frown came on her forehead, then relaxed as she gave me a small smirk. "Joe, just go home." She pointed down the hall. "Walk down this hallway to the elevator and press the button to go down." She stepped over the threshold to close the door.

"Listen, I just want to explain about tonight," I said in a hurry.

Halting from closing the door, she hunched up her shoulders and said, "Joe, do you really think I want to hear what you have to say after the way you treated me tonight?"

"The door's still open, isn't it?" I contended confidently.

Dawn gasped exasperatedly, held up a hand and began blurting out what seemed to be years of pent up frustration. "You know, it's cocky comments like that that are so infuriating! I am so *sick* of men playing games and treating women as if we don't matter. As if we don't have feelings—real feelings. You men all are exactly alike. Women *do* have brains and common sense and more importantly, we know bull–"

I walked up to her and started kissing her. Dawn's body slumped weakly against the door, entangling her tongue with mine, with equal passion. While she moaned and rubbed my head and we continued kissing, I managed to move us in the apartment hallway and close the door. With her leaning against the apartment door, at long last I was able to caress her torso with my hands. She pressed her body against mine, and in response; I lifted up her white dress and began enjoying the warm offering of her body.

After making a swift-eyed sweep of her apartment, and noticing the sofa in her living room, I picked her up and laid her on it. Once Dawn started licking and sucking my ear—a sensitive spot—that did it. I was ready for her then.

Her phone rang suddenly.

Damn! I was about ready to get really busy.

Somewhat dazed, Dawn sat up. I moved to the side of the sofa simultaneously offering her my hand to help her stand. She walked to the living room side of the bar and picked up the portable phone. Her back was facing me as she spoke.

"Hello? Oh, hey," Dawn said into the phone. "Mmm, hmm. Yeah, I can be there. Okay, what time?" She started scribbling something on a note pad by the phone. "All right, thank you." Her face was a little flushed when she turned around after placing the phone in its receiver. "My agent," she explained shyly.

"Oh," I replied, watching her every expression. "Another job?"

Nodding, she replied, "Yeah, it sounds pretty good, too."

"Great," I said softly, standing up.

Dawn gazed at me intently and uttered quickly, "I'm not going to be your second hand prize, Joe."

"Is that what you think you are?" I took a few small steps toward her.

Solidly staying her ground, she shrugged and nodded once. "I'm just letting you know where I stand."

"Okay. Then let me explain something to you. That was the original agenda, you know—to explain, I mean." I smiled and moved closer to her as I pointed to the front door. "That party that we went to was not for couples only and it wasn't for charity either. It was an impromptu house party I had Trevor do."

"Why?" Dawn asked.

"Because I *wanted* to see you again, despite your objections," I explained, reaching her. "I'm sorry for leaving you alone tonight. It was just so hard to be around you because you've been tempting me with this dress all night and all I wanted–" I cupped both of my hands on her face and kissed her longingly. "...was to do this," I said after ending the kiss. I smiled and brushed her cheek with the tip of my index finger.

"What now?" Dawn asked.

"It depends on you. The ball's in your court." I shrugged. "Do you want to see me again?"

She nodded, then uttered, "But..."

I stopped her before she headed there. "Listen, let's just go out a few times and go from there. No obligations or anything. Just the two of us having fun and enjoying each other's company. All right?"

She heaved a huge sigh and said, "All right."

I leaned in to kiss her again and then the phone rang again.

"What now!" I exasperated.

Dawn stifled a laugh. She turned around and picked up the phone on its third ring.

"Hello?" Her eyes were wide when she turned to look at me. "Happy New Year to you too, Lacie. Hu, hu...how are you, girl?"

# Chapter 15

# Lacie

"Hey, girl! Where have you been?" I chuckled, hearing Dawn's voice on the other line. "I've been calling and leaving messages and everything! You got a man there with you now, don't you?" I teased.

I thought I heard her cough. "Girl...what makes you think that?" Dawn returned. "I've been working!"

Laughing, I said, "Well, you better be. It was hard to see you leave New York, so you'd better be doing your thing."

"You know I am. So what's up?" Dawn asked a little too abruptly. "I mean, how's everybody and how are you and Tony doing?"

"We're fine," I answered, but I sensed that something wasn't right. "Dawn, are you okay?"

A split second pause and then, "Girl, yeah, I'm fine. I've just got this new job that my agent called me about and I'm kind of nervous."

"You sure?"

"Yeah. I'm fine."

"Hmm. Okay, then," I said. Still wanting to push the issue, I decided instead to give her an update on everything. I told her about Robert's dad being in the hospital, Reneé and Danny's wedding date and also Mama and Tony's talk. Dawn got a kick out of that.

"Well, that doesn't surprise me. You know Miss Josephine doesn't hold back on her words," Dawn said, laughing.

"Yeah, I know. But guess what, girl?" I didn't give her a chance to respond. "Tony and I are coming to Miami!"

A small pause. "You are?"

"Yeah, girl. We'll be down there next month. So you know we've got to get together," I stressed excitedly.

"Yeah...sure," Dawn said.

I paused before I said anything else. There was something odd in the way she was responding to me, but I'd already asked her what was wrong.

"All right, girl," I said. "I'll give you a call once we get all the details. I can't wait to see you. Love you."

"I love you, too, Lacie," Dawn replied almost soundlessly.

I hung up my cell phone and frowned in contemplation.

"Lacie, do you want extra butter on your popcorn?" Tony interrupted my thoughts as he came over to me from the concession stand.

We were in a movie theater in the heart of Manhattan.

"No, too fattening," I replied.

"Okay. I'll be right back with our popcorn and drinks," he said. He gave me a kiss and walked back to the concession stand.

As I watched him go back, I suddenly felt someone's eyes on me. I looked to my right and there was a brotha giving me a disapproving look and shaking his head as he stood in line at the concession stand. I gave him a look back and then he turned his head around.

Within a minute, Tony returned carrying a huge tub of popcorn, two sodas and a pack of Twizzlers. "You ready, babe?"

I saw the brotha out of the corner of my eye, watching us again. I took Tony's arm, nodded my head and kissed him sweetly. "Yep," I answered. "Let's go."

This color line thing was getting too old and I was enjoying myself with Tony too much to let someone's ignorant stare get to me. Not to mention, I had so many other things to be concerned about.

Unexpectedly, Daddy had called and informed me that he was coming for a visit next month. He didn't explain his reason when I'd talked with him on the phone, other than he wanted to see me. I was overwhelmed and excited because, except for a few calls here and there, I hadn't seen him in over two years. And I'd no idea how to tell Mama. I hadn't even told her I'd talked to him and that was for a good reason. They hadn't spoken to each other in a very long time and Mama still had a lot of resentment toward him. Thankfully, I had a month to get up the courage to tell her.

On a good note, Mama, Reneé and I had decided to have a small ceremony at our church, followed by an intimate reception held at my house. Mama wasn't too keen on everything being so small, but agreed even so. We started making plans immediately, knowing that our time was limited. I volunteered to do the catering as a gift to Reneé and Danny. Mama would pay for the flower arrangements and Reneé's wedding dress, and any of the other expenses. I offered to go in half with her, but Mama insisted on doing it herself. She argued that I had enough responsibilities, along with my job and the catering, and that it would be senseless for me to add on any extra work.

She was right.

Between time on the phone selecting and ordering food and arrangements for the reception, the meetings at work, and of course my relationship with Tony, I was extremely busy. All the same, I was enjoying it.

Tony and I spent long hours working and meeting with many prospective clients and were overwhelmed by the amount coming our way. We soon hurried to get our understudy team together. I immediately chose Carrie; between the two of us, Tony and I had four people working with us and three were interns.

By now, everyone at work was aware of my relationship with Tony and there seemed to be a considerable amount of acceptance about it. I did, however, get some raised eyebrows from a few other black women in the office, but Carrie told me that she knew that some of them were jealous because of some of the comments that she had happened to overhear in the cafeteria. But that didn't bother me.

My relationship with Tony was going too marvelously for me to care and I was falling deeper and deeper in love with him as the days passed. Despite the long hours at work, sometimes not leaving until the late evening, we still managed to go out. Tony would take me to plays, concerts, comedy shows and museums. He was simply amazing and gave me the utmost respect, love and attention. He treated me as his own, never once acknowledging or caring about the negative whispers or speculative stares we'd get. Though sometimes, I would.

The time I spent with Tony seemed to bother Mama very little. She was apparently developing some sort of nesting period with Reneé and was too busy concentrating on Reneé's wedding and reception. Interestingly enough, I didn't see Danny with Reneé much, but every time I'd ask her how things were going with the two of them, she would reply with a positive answer.

I hadn't heard a thing from Robert except a message on my answering machine saying that he'd arrived in Georgia safely. Other than that, he'd been quiet. I'd used all of the numbers he'd given me and called him several times, but kept getting his answering machine. I was beginning to get concerned.

Dawn was also a concern. I'd attempted to contact her also, but like Robert, kept getting the answering machine. What was up with that? Dawn and I were so close and she'd never had a problem returning my calls. This piqued my curiosity. There was something going on and I had an idea that it involved a man. I wondered who the flavor of the month was for Dawn this time. Maybe she'd finally met her match. If she did, she deserved it and I couldn't wait to meet him.

The beginning of February was finally here and Tony and I were now a month into the relationship. I knew this for sure because I'd been counting each day of our relationship and so had he. Though it was a weekday and we knew we were going to have an important meeting with Mr. Carr and his lawyers in the morning, Tony had made special plans for our one-month anniversary.

He took me to a popular Broadway play that I'd been anxious to see, but had had difficulty in getting tickets. We dined at a nice restaurant after, where he'd arranged for us to eat at the chef's table.

Next, we ventured to his apartment building, and as the elevator went from floor to floor, I slipped my arm through Tony's and nestled my head against his shoulder. It had been a special day for us. I was happy and delighted by how much time and effort he'd devoted into making our first month anniversary so pleasant and meaningful. I glanced up at him, really comprehending how madly in love I was with him. It seemed alien that I'd ever fought against my feelings for him.

Tony smiled at me and asked, "You okay?"

I smiled. "Mmm, couldn't be better," I said.

"We made a month," he stated softly, stroking my arm.

"Yes, we did," I replied.

"You ready to throw in the towel yet?" he teased.

"Not a chance," I replied.

"That's what I like to hear," he said, leaning down to give me a tender kiss.

"Mmm, that was nice," I uttered.

"Very. Hold that thought," he said and moved to the elevator buttons and pressed the 'Hold' button.

"Tony?" I questioned.

He shook his head. "It's fine. I know the owner of the building. Now where were we?"

He moved over to me slowly with a devious little grin and I giggled, half-excited and half-nervous. What was he thinking about doing in the elevator? That thought left my mind once he touched me.

He gently pressed me up against the elevator wall while his right hand caressed my waist. The other hand held my head as his mouth moved from my ear lobe, to my neck and then to my lips. I returned his kisses with the same amount of passion as he was giving. My temperature started to rise and our passion began to mount as I simultaneously felt his excitement.

Suddenly, his right hand moved down to my legs and I knew where it was headed next. It was going to be easy access for him because, for some reason, I'd chosen to wear a casual dress. He had me as soon as his hands started to caress my inner thigh. I had to stop because we were both getting too hot.

What *was* it with us and elevators?

"Tony…baby, we've gotta stop," I said breathlessly. "As kinky as this is and as excited as I am, we can't do this in here."

I felt him nod his head as he breathed heavily into my neck. "You're right, you're right. I'm sorry." He managed to push the 'Hold' button while he still held my waist. "Lacie, I can't wait to get you in my apartment," he uttered as the elevator started moving again.

"I know. I can't wait either," I smiled.

Once the elevator stopped and let us off on his floor, Tony hurriedly opened the door to his apartment and then it was on! We were frantically touching and kissing each other, and stripping off each other's clothes as we made our way to his bedroom.

We slowed down a bit and started to kiss each other languorously, enjoying the dance our tongues made. Then he carefully picked me up, laid me on the bed and began planting kisses down my body. My body arched in satisfaction, responding to the skillful way he used his hands and mouth for my pleasure for what seemed to be an eternity.

At last, in answer to my excitement, Tony entered me gently, taking my breath away. Kissing tenderly but feverishly, we locked hands over my head and moved in complete and endless harmony. We blocked everything out around us as we continued to explosive ecstasy and held onto each other before we finally fell asleep.

80C8

I felt Tony gently nibbling on my ear.

"Hey, you," he whispered. "It's time to get up. We've got an important meeting ahead of us."

With a yawn, I opened my eyes and saw Tony holding a mug of cappuccino in front of me. "Thank you," I smiled gratefully, sitting up and taking the cup. I took a sip and a quick glance at the clock on the nightstand before a thought occurred to me. "Tony, it's nine o'clock! Why didn't you wake me sooner?" I said with alarm, automatically getting ready to get out of the bed.

He put a hand on my shoulder and gently pushed me back. "Relax. I already called Richard and told him we'd be in late. He knew about yesterday so he was pretty cool about it. The meeting with Mr. Carr and his people isn't until eleven, so we've got some time."

"You sure?"

"Yeah, it's cool." He smiled and watched me drink my coffee.

"What?" I asked.

"This was your first night staying over here during the week. I liked that you stayed over."

"You do?"

He nodded. "Yeah. It felt like you belong here."

I gushed. "I kind of feel that way, too."

"Uh, listen, I was thinking…"

The doorbell interrupted him and he looked at his watch. "That must be breakfast. I ordered out. I'll be right back," he said as he got up and walked out the bedroom.

I sat up in the bed for a while, looking out the window, enjoying the coffee and enjoying being in his apartment. Tony was right. *It did* feel like I belonged here.

I took another quick glance at the clock. Tony sure was taking his time coming back. Curiously and quite hungry, I decided to find out what was taking so long. With habit, I grabbed his shirt; put it on and with mug in hand, walked toward the living room.

"Tony, what did you get me…?" I asked, entering the living room, but halted in my tracks when I noticed the attractive older looking couple standing in the front hallway of the apartment.

The woman turned at the sound of my voice, and,with the same tone I'd heard during our short conversation on the phone a month earlier, said, "Excuse me?"

Oh, no! This was not good.

# Chapter 16

# Tony

Lacie stood there like a petrified statue.

My parents looked at her and then at me with surprised and inquisitive expressions.

Mom raised her brow and asked, "Anthony, what is going on?"

I immediately walked over to Lacie and put a comforting arm around her shoulders. I felt her limp against me slightly and pulled her up.

"I told you, Mom...I'm getting ready to go to work," I said evenly, and then looked at Lacie. "Uh...actually, *we're* getting ready to go to work," I clarified with a chuckle. I looked back at my parents and saw that they were not laughing. "A-hem. We're just running a bit late, that's all. Uh...this is Lacie. Lacie Adams. Lacie, these are my parents, Johnathan and Abigail Douglas."

Uncomforting silence filled the room as Lacie and my parents stood, staring at each another. The silence was broken by a knock on my open front door by a deliveryman bringing the breakfast I ordered.

"Uh...I have a delivery for Douglas," the deliveryman said awkwardly.

"Uh, sure," I said, leaving Lacie's side to pay the deliveryman. "How much do I owe you?"

The silence continued as the deliveryman and I handled our transaction.

"Okay, thanks, man," I said after the transaction was done.

"Okay, then," Mom said, taking a deep breath and walking over to me. "Anthony, we're going to leave so that you can go on to work." She gave me a kiss on the cheek. "We'll talk later, dear," she said and walked out to the elevator.

Dad followed, but stopped at the threshold and whispered to me. "I'll talk with you later, son," he said with a wink, then joined Mom as the elevator opened.

"Okay, see you later," I called out to them before the elevator closed and went down.

By the time I'd closed the door and turned around, Lacie had already retreated to the bedroom.

ഔങ്ങ

I glanced at Lacie fleetingly as I pulled into the underground parking lot of the office building. She'd been mum ever since my parents left and had remained that way even after she'd dressed and ate the cream cheese bagel I'd ordered for her.

I put the car in park and turned it off, and looked at her. "I didn't know they were coming, Lacie," I asserted. "I told you they were here visiting the Sanders last night and decided to drop by to see me."

"I know."

"Then why the silent treatment?"

Lacie turned and looked at me dubiously. "Tony, did you stop to think that maybe I'm just a little embarrassed by how I met your parents?"

"Listen, there's nothing to be embarrassed about. It's my apartment."

"Tony, that was not the way I wanted to meet them. They saw me in your apartment with just your shirt on. That's not what I call making a good first impression." She ran a hand through her hair and looked back out the window. "And despite the obvious, they must think I'm very cheap."

"I'm sure they don't think that," I said, getting out of the car to go to her side. "And what do you mean, despite the obvious?" I asked, opening the door for her.

She shook her head. "Tony, I don't even know if you're ready for what I have to say," she murmured, getting out with our briefcases.

I took them from her gingerly and closed the door. "Hey, I'm listening," I offered easily as we started walking toward the underground elevator.

She pushed the 'Up' button on the elevator and looked at me pointedly. "Your parents were very shocked to see me, Tony."

"Of course they were. They weren't expecting to see a woman there—"

"No," she interrupted. The elevator door opened and we got on. "It wasn't that I was just a woman, Tony. It was that I was a *black* woman that shocked them and they didn't seem to like me either." She pushed the number twenty button to our floor.

"You can't be serious," I scoffed. "How are my parents going to have an opinion of you so quickly when they weren't even in the house for ten minutes?"

"Sometimes it's not the amount of time that determines whether someone likes you," she hinted. She blew out a deep breath and added, "Listen, Tony, you told me a while ago that you were very close with your parents."

"And I didn't lie."

"But did your parents ever know that you liked sistas? I mean, how could your parents be so shocked about me if your relationship is so close? How could they not know that you have an affinity for sistas?"

The elevator stopped and a few people got on.

I moved closer to her and whispered, "Because my personal life, and who I date, is none of their concern."

"But yet you brought Simone home," she whispered pointedly.

"Lacie, I didn't bring..." I grumbled and stopped. A couple of the other passengers kept looking back at us, evidently listening to our conversation. "Listen to me," I said much softer. "I know what you're trying to suggest. Do not turn this into something that it's not. You don't know either of them and you're judging them without getting to know them first."

The people got off of the elevator and we were alone again.

She huffed and nodded. "They don't know me either—in particular, your mom. Yet she couldn't help but stare at the *black* girl that was in her *white* son's apartment! Tony, don't patronize me. That woman did not like me being there," she whispered heatedly. "She was all in my face."

"You're not being reasonable," I seethed.

"And you're insulting my intelligence!" she shot back, turning to look at me with a glare. "I have been through this enough and seen this too many times to not notice the signs, Tony. Reasoning has nothing to do with the way your mom looked at me, and her expression was not by any means friendly."

"Lacie…"

The elevator door opened on our floor and she snatched her briefcase from me and hurried out.

"Lacie…" I called after her, but she was already through the double doors, hurrying to her office.

The front receptionist eyed me uncomfortably.

"Good morning," I said with a curt nod and walked through the double doors.

As soon as I reached my office, my cell phone started ringing.

"Who is it?" I barked, flipping it open.

"Whoa! You all right, man?" Joe asked on the other line.

"Naw, man. I'm not."

"You and Lacie haven't had a fight already, have you? I told you about messing with black women. They ain't white. They'll cut you," Joe joked.

Not missing a beat, I shot back, "Hey, man, at least I *got* a woman." I suddenly realized what I'd said. "Joe, man…"

"Yo, Tony, don't sweat it. You and I already made peace about Lacie. Remember? Plus, I do have a woman. Or at least I'm working on it anyway."

I put my briefcase on the desk and sat down. "Oh yeah? Who are you working your game on this time?"

"Naw, man. It's not a game. I'm really feeling this girl."

"Joe, besides Lacie, how many times have you said this and then wind up ditching the girl over something stupid like the color of her toenails?" I bantered.

"Whatever, man. But look I didn't call you to talk about my love life," Joe said.

"Okay. What's up?"

"Last month, I went to a party an old high school buddy was giving. His name is Trevor Weeks. He told me that he's working with William Carr now. You heard anything about that?"

"Yeah. Good timing. Lacie and I are supposed to meet with them today as a matter of fact. Why? What's up?"

"I'm gonna tell you now. Watch out for him. This dude plays no shorts."

"Yeah. Richard told us that he's quite ruthless."

"He's also very hard on women. So watch out for Lacie."

"Thanks, man," I said. "Look, Lacie and I are coming down this weekend. We gotta get together or something."

"Yeah, I heard…" Joe stopped.

I picked up on it. "What do you mean, you heard? How did you…?"

"Yeah, yeah, yeah, we gotta get together," he said quickly. Then, "What the…?" he exclaimed. "Look man, I gotta go. These people are driving crazy out here. They're going to get me killed. Holla' at me when you guys get in town."

"All right, man."

"Gone."

I was about to hang up when the call waiting beeped.

"Hello?"

"Hey, dear," Mom's voice on the other end sang.

"Hey, Mom."

"Anthony, darling, your father and I will be in town for two extra days and we wanted to invite you and your friend to have dinner with us on Friday."

"O…kay," I uttered, surprised by the invitation. "I thought you two were leaving today."

"Oh, a few things just came up," Mom replied offhandedly. "Shall I make the reservations?"

I couldn't make a decision until I talked this over with Lacie first.

Their initial meeting had not gone well and I was unsure of whether she'd want to see them again so soon.

"Uh, Mom, let me get back with you later and I'll give you an answer then," I replied.

"Good," Mom said. "We'll be waiting for your call."

I glanced at my watch after I hung up the phone. It was a few minutes until the meeting with Mr. Carr and his lawyers would begin, and hearing Joe's warning about Trevor Weeks concerned me. He never warned me about something without reason.

I took a deep breath, leaned back in my chair and thought back to the brief meeting between my parents and Lacie. Lacie was obviously ill at ease over the awkwardness of the situation. Our quarrel only a few moments ago made that clear. She hadn't been prepared to meet them so soon and was understandably defensive. Now that my parents wanted to meet her formally, I wondered how she was going to handle it. In a way, I was glad that my parents were initiating the second meeting. At the same time, I didn't want Lacie feeling anymore uneasy than she already was.

"Hey."

A sight for sore eyes, Lacie stood in the doorway of my office. I stood automatically and walked over to her.

"I'm sorry, Tony," she said when I put my arms around her.

"Don't be," I reassured, caressing her back with one hand.

"I didn't mean to go off on you like that. I was just so angry with how everything went down. I wasn't prepared..."

"I know. I know," I said softly. Knowing that I needed to get it over with, I held her back gently to look at her and uttered apprehensively, "But uh...you might want to get prepared right away because my parents just invited us out for dinner."

She stiffened at once with panic in her eyes. "What?"

"Okay, listen. Don't get worried," I soothed calmly, trying to reassure her. "This is only dinner."

Unconvinced, she shook her head. "Things are moving way too fast, Tony. I...I'm not equipped for this. I'm barely able to get over the embarrassment of this morning."

"Lacie, this was bound to happen. I was going to have to meet your parents and you were going to have to meet mine—regardless of how." I smiled tenderly. "Hey, I had to go through the wrath of Josephine. The least you can do is have dinner with my parents."

She smiled slightly, shaking her head.

I took her hand in mine and looked at her earnestly. "Do you love me?"

She frowned. "Of course, I do."

I squeezed her hand tightly. "Do you trust me?"

Lacie held her head down for a moment before she pulled it back and replied softly, "Yes, I trust you."

Relieved, I put my forehead against hers, reached behind her head and looked into her eyes tenderly. "Listen, I know it was awkward meeting my parents the way you did, but understand that you're not in this alone," I said. "We should at least give this a try." I kissed her forehead in an attempt at some comfort, but she still looked wary. "Look, just think about it. Okay?"

She blew out a deep breath and nodded. "Okay."

I squeezed her hand again. "All right. We are in this together. Know that, believe it and remember it."

It was then that I noticed a group of suits walk past my office door. The entourage began with Mr. Carr and ended with one tall black man, who in particular, stopped for a split second, looked at me with a frown, and then followed the rest toward the conference room.

"Listen, we'd better get moving. Our guests are here," I said.

⊱⊰

I got a bad vibe from the tall black man as soon as Lacie and I entered the conference room. Dude's gaze followed us when we went to sit in our chairs at the other side of the table.

Lisa, one of our interns, closed the door once everyone was seated.

"Okay," Mr. Ryan began. "Let's get started, shall we? Let's open our book—"

"Wait a minute, Richard," the tall black man interrupted curtly. "I'd appreciate knowing everyone's names before we start."

With respect, Richard said, "Of course. Excuse me." Richard introduced everyone around the table in order. When he got to Lacie and me, he said, "And these two are Anthony Douglas and Lacie Adams. They are the head of the team and will join you and William in Florida."

Dude cocked his head to the side and smirked at me. "Anthony Douglas. You were involved with William's daughter, Simone, right?"

William let out an uncomfortable cough.

Concealing my annoyance at the direct question, I answered, "Yes, but that's in the past, now."

Dude raised his eyebrow and nodded toward Lacie. "Oh, I see. Moving on to bigger and more *colorful* things, is that it?"

"Yep," I declared with a meaningful nod.

Richard cleared his throat and said, "Uh, Mr. Weeks, let's proceed with the meeting. We do have a lot of ground to cover."

I shook my head. I should have known he was the same fool Joe warned me about as soon as he opened his mouth. In those few statements he made, I knew where Trevor was coming from. He didn't like me and definitely didn't like that I was with Lacie.

That didn't bother me one bit, as long as he didn't over step his boundaries.

# Chapter 17

# Lacie

Richard interrupting Tony and Mr. Weeks couldn't have come sooner.

I glanced at Tony uneasily while he and everyone else continued looking at the booklets in front of them. I'd never seen him react in such a defensive way.

Suddenly, I turned and locked eyes with Mr. Weeks who'd obviously been observing me for a few seconds. Uncomfortable with the cocky grin he was giving me, I immediately looked away and turned my attention to the booklet in front of me. I felt him looking my way a couple of times during the meeting and was glad to be out from under his gaze twenty minutes later when Richard adjourned the meeting.

Everyone started leaving the conference room, except for Tony, who Richard had held back to speak with privately.

"Lacie, I thought that meeting would never end!" Carrie exclaimed when we returned to my office. "But girl, did it get exciting at the beginning! Lacie, what is up with all of the attitude between Mr. Weeks and Tony? Did they know each other before this or something?"

I shook my head and sat down. "Nope. Neither one of us have met him before. All we know is that Mr. Carr just recently acquired him because of his ruthless reputation."

Carrie nodded, sitting down. "That's obvious. He was so arrogant with his demands and just kept interrupting Mr. Ryan." She shook her head contemplatively. "I don't know, Lacie. I've got a bad feeling about him, so you better watch yourself around him."

"Yeah, I will. Don't worry." I took a deep breath and leaned my head back and looked up. "But I've got more important things to be worried about now, Carrie."

"What? Are you pregnant?" she asked.

My head immediately came up and I shook it at her smiling face. "No," I replied firmly. "I met Tony's parents this morning." Then I proceeded to tell her the details.

Carrie let out a low whistle after I finished. "Wow! Talk about an introduction! How did his parents react?"

"Oh, his mom couldn't take her eyes off of me. Carrie, I've never had someone stare at me the way she did. I'd never been scrutinized like that before and I... I couldn't move." I ran a hand through my hair. "But that's not my only problem. Now they want to meet me formally and invited us out for dinner."

"Umm, how do you feel about it?"

"Nervous as hell," I stressed, shaking my head.

"Are you going?"

"That's what I'm contemplating, but," I replied, then sighed. "Carrie, I just don't know. I'm sure they've got a bad impression about me already."

Carrie shook her head. "Are you that insecure about yourself, Lacie?" she asked softly.

"Insecurity is not the issue here. Sometimes we only have one chance to make a good impression and I think I blew that with his parents."

Carrie exasperated, "Okay, so they got to see you in Tony's shirt and now know that he's not a virgin. So what? Are you going to let that stop you? If anything, that should be more of a reason for you to go and show them what a great person you really are. Lacie, every now and then life offers us opportunities to get out of the little safe boxes that we put around ourselves because we're afraid and we have to take those chances. You should know, because you wouldn't be with Tony if you didn't," she contended.

"Still, Carrie, Tony and I've only made a month. I wanted us to be more settled before this happened. I don't feel ready for this."

"So *when* are you going to be ready, Lacie?" Carrie asked. "Listen, all I can tell you is that the best way to conquer fear is to face it head on. If you don't, you'll never know what you're made of." She sighed and stood up. "You know, I need to start charging you a fee for all of the advice I'm giving you. Let me get out of here. I've got a ton of research ahead of me because of this Mr. Weeks so, I'd better get with the rest of the team."

I sat silently, reflecting over what Carrie had said and realized that she made sense. Then again, she usually did.

My phone rang.

"Hey, Lacie," Robert said after I'd picked it up.

"Robert, I am so glad to hear from you! I've been calling your cell phone and all the numbers you had on your refrigerator and leaving messages. How is your dad?"

His voice sounded a little strangled when he replied. "He's looking pretty bad, Lacie, and the doctors are really starting to get concerned."

"How's your mom handling it?"

"As best as she can." He sighed. "Lacie, I'm sorry for not calling you sooner. Things are so messed up here and Ma is by herself. I don't know when I'll be back."

"Hey, don't worry about anything. This time, it's my turn to look after your apartment and pick up your mail."

"Thank you, Lacie. I appreciate that."

"Is there anything else I can do?"

"Just pray." He was silent for a second. "Listen, I promise I'll call you soon and give you an update."

"Okay. And listen, if you need me to come down there, just say the word, okay?"

"Okay. I'll be in touch soon."

I hung up the phone realizing how minor my problems were compared to Robert's. Robert might very well lose his father and I was worried about having dinner with Tony's parents.

I made my decision.

Tony was elated when I told him the news. Mama wasn't. "They want to have dinner with you? Why?" Mama asked. We were in the kitchen and she was slicing some onions for the stew she was making.

I shrugged. "They just want to meet me formally. It surprised me also."

She turned away from the stove. "It's a load of bull, is what it is. They just want to size up this new black girl their white son is dating and all." She nodded. "Yeah, I know that game all too well."

"Mama, even if it's a game, I feel I owe it to myself and Tony to go. I just can't hide away in a corner. And Mama, Tony had to go through the Spanish Inquisition with you. I don't see why I shouldn't have to go through it for him."

"Lacie, black people have been through enough, what with four hundred years of slavery, those stupid Jim Crow Laws and the civil rights movement. And we're still not wanted among some white folk. I don't like it. White people are always trying to be in control and have us under their thumb. No. I think that you should invite them over here and have them in your own environment. That way if they start to act up then I can kick them out."

"Mama?" I laughed, shaking my head in disbelief.

"What?"

"Must this always be about black and white?"

"Yes, because that's what you and Tony are—black and white," she asserted with a nod. "Huh, just wait. You'll find that out at dinner."

"What dinner?" Reneé asked, strolling into the kitchen. I motioned for her to sit down.

"Your sister and Tony are going out to dinner with his parents this Friday," Mama informed her, before turning back around to stir up the stew.

"Wow," Reneé said, giving me a fleeting look. "Are you ready for that?"

"Oh, she's already met them," Mama answered for me. "They caught her in Tony's britches when she stayed over last night."

"Mama!" I protested and Reneé giggled.

"What?" Mama turned around innocently with a chuckle. "That's what happened, isn't it?"

"No, I was in his shirt," I maintained.

"Same difference," Mama said.

"Anyway," I expressed with a huff and turned to look at Reneé. "I haven't talked with you in a while. How's everything going with you and Danny?"

Reneé looked down at her protruding stomach and rubbed it. "It's going okay."

"Just okay?" I asked.

"Mmm, hmm," she replied again, avoiding my gaze.

"Reneé, are you not telling me something?"

"Lacie, she's fine," Mama answered for her. "Danny just has the jitters and she's making a mountain out of a molehill. All boys get nervous right before their wedding," she assured, going to the refrigerator.

"Speaking of that," I said, still eyeing Reneé, "Mama and I are just about finished with the arrangements for the reception. There are a few minor details that I have to check out, but I'll make sure they're done before I leave for Miami on Saturday." I took out my planner. "Now, the bridal shop is expecting us early Friday afternoon. I've made arrangements to leave work early and I think…"

I heard sniffling and looked up to see tears running down Reneé's face. Hearing it also, Mama turned around from the refrigerator, with the container of milk in her hand, and looked at Reneé with a concerned frown.

"Reneé, what's wrong?" Mama asked.

That seemed to make it worse and Reneé suddenly burst into tears and ran up the stairs. I looked at Mama and she shrugged.

"I'll go after her," I offered.

"Come in," Reneé answered to my soft knock on her door.

She was sitting on the bed and blowing her nose when I entered. I took a seat beside her. "You want to tell me what's going on?" She shook her head, but I wasn't letting her off the hook. "Reneé, if something is wrong you should tell me or at least tell Mama." She rolled her eyes at that suggestion. "Okay, tell me, then. I won't leave until you do."

She blew her nose again and took a deep breath. "I don't think Danny wants to get married."

"What? Why do you think that?"

She shrugged. "I don't know. He's been acting weird lately and even though we go out, he doesn't give me the same attention he used to. It's as if he doesn't want to be seen with me." Her lips quivered when she added, "And I'm always catching him looking at other girls."

"Have you tried talking with him about it?"

She nodded. "Yes, but he claims that there's nothing wrong and that I'm being silly."

I blew hard and spoke. "Okay, let me tell you one thing about boys, well... guys. Ninety-nine percent of the time they are going to look at other females." I hunched my shoulders. "That's just the reality of the situation. But that doesn't mean that Danny doesn't love you any less. Reneé, Danny is still young and his eyes might wander from time to time, but what matters is who he comes back to. Whom he has in his heart. And Mama might be right. Maybe he is a little nervous about getting married, but that doesn't mean he doesn't want to marry you." I took her hand and squeezed it. "You want me to talk to him?"

"Naw," Reneé shook her head and sighed. "I might be blowing this up and making something into nothing. Or it could be my hormones. I don't know."

"You might be right about the hormones part." I nodded with a chuckle. "You feel better?"

"A little," she admitted.

I heard the sound of pots and pans clanging and said, "I guess that's my cue. I'd better go downstairs and make sure Mama's okay in the kitchen." I stood up. "Why don't you give Danny a call and try to talk things out?" I suggested. More clanging came from the kitchen. "All right, give him a call. I gotta go."

∞

It was Friday.

Mama and I were in the bridal shop waiting for Reneé to come out of the dressing room in her gown. I had a couple of hours before Tony would pick me up at my house and then we'd head over to meet his parents at the restaurant.

"You heard from Robert?" Mama asked.

I shook my head. "Not since the last time I talked to him."

"How's his father?"

"Not well."

Mama nodded. "I'll make sure he and his mother are added to the prayer list at church." She looked at me. "Lacie, will you stop biting your fingernails," Mama scolded softly. "Look, I know you're nervous, but honey, c'mon. Tony's parents are just people. I'm sure they wipe their tails just like we do."

"Mama, that's disgusting." I laughed.

"But it's true," Mama said. "Listen, notwithstanding all the white and black comments I made the other day, I just want you to know that all you have to do is be yourself, Lacie. You don't have to go the extra mile to impress them or be extra kind to them because they're his parents. They're going to think and believe what ever they want to and that's just a fact. But no one can disrespect you for being yourself and no one can take that away from you."

I smiled at her. "Thanks, Mama."

"I admire you, Lacie," she said out of the blue, startling me. "I know I tease you about being with Tony and all, but I gotta tell you... you're very brave. Times may have changed some but we still have a long way to go. People still have issues with race and color. There's just too much history of hate and dissention and distrust. But you know, love…" she shook her head, choking up. "…is such a powerful thing. That's what I see in you and Tony. I see it when he looks at you and in the way he treats you. Mmm, now that's saying something."

"You really loved Daddy, didn't you?" I asked her suddenly.

She looked at me in surprise. "Now why did you bring him up?"

I shrugged, sizing up the right time to tell her. "You were getting so sentimental and everything and I was wondering if you were thinking about him."

She smiled wistfully. "I loved your dad, Lacie, but sometimes love is not enough."

"But you just said…"

"I know what I said. But you and Tony don't have the kind of problems your father and I did…." Mama said pensively.

We sat in silence for a moment when I suddenly decided that now was a better time than any to tell her about Dad's upcoming visit. I took a nervous breath and was about to speak when Reneé came in with the bridal shop assistant holding her train.

Reneé's gown was cream colored and detailed with lace and exquisite pearls. Her belly barely showed through the full gown as she looked at herself in the mirror and smiled broadly.

"So… how does it look?" Reneé asked, looking at us through the mirror while the bridal assistant straightened her train out on the carpet.

With tears in our eyes, Mama and I could only smile. Our baby had grown up.

ഇൗൖ

"*Remember, they wipe their tails just like we do. They're no different,*" I kept hearing Mama's voice say to me when Tony and I walked into the restaurant.

Tony squeezed my hand softly and gave me a comforting smile. "How are you feeling?" he asked, while we waited for the host to finish with another couple.

"Umm...I'm a bit nervous," I answered honestly with a deep breath.

He brought my hand up to his lips and kissed it softly. "Remember. We're in this together, okay?" I nodded. "By the way, you look amazing tonight. I'm sure my parents will like you."

That's what I'd hoped at least.

Tony's parents were already seated when the host led us to the table.

Johnathan Douglas, resembling what Tony would probably look like in twenty or so years,, stood once we reached the table. "Ah, good evening, son," he said, embracing Tony.

Lips slightly pursed, Abigail Douglas remained seated while Tony kissed her cheek after his embrace with Johnathan. I stood there feeling awkward while the two heads of the Douglas family exchanged greetings with their youngest son and made small talk. Elation came over me when Johnathan looked at me with a kind smile and offered a hand, which I gladly shook.

"Hello, Lacie. I'm glad you two could join us for dinner," he said.

I smiled and returned, "Thank you, so am I."

Abigail, sans greeting me, gave me a fleeting look instead and spoke briskly. "Let's sit down and order."

Our waitress couldn't have appeared a moment too soon. She introduced herself, handed us the menus and took our drink orders.

Tony whispered to me, "See, I told you they'd like you."

I gave him a tight smile in answer. He hadn't noticed the hard looks his mother had started giving me before we'd even approached the table.

After the waitress returned with our drinks, and took our dinner orders, Tony and his parents made small talk about family stuff. I sat back idly, absorbing their conversation. All the while, I felt Abigail's eyes on me.

"So...Jennifer is finishing her courses at Georgetown and Jessica is working on her law degree at Harvard," Abigail was informing

Tony as the waitress brought our drinks. "They're both a little frazzled, but they're maintaining they want to stay the course and finish." She glanced at me. "What university did you attend, Lacie?"

Was the question really that innocent or was she questioning whether I'd attended anything past high school at all? I shook off the notion. I was thinking too defensively.

"I received my Bachelor's from Columbia," I replied politely.

With a mocking expression that was meant for my eyes only, she goaded, "Oh, only your Bachelor's? How did you get employed at Ryan & Company?"

Ignoring the inference, I replied, "I started out as an intern and was working on my master's degree when Ryan & Company hired me full-time. They offered me a very generous salary that I couldn't turn down."

"In management?"

"No, as an administrative assistant."

"And you met my son…how?"

Tony put his arm around my shoulder and answered, "She was my administrative assistant."

"Oh, she was *your*…administrative assistant," Abigail stressed, eyeing both of us intently. "I presume that was quite controversial—you being her boss, Anthony."

Johnathan sighed and glanced at his wife momentarily before he took a drink from his glass. "Abigail, let's not make this an interview…"

But Abigail barely heard him. She looked past Tony and I and beamed all of a sudden. "Well, look who's here, Johnathan. The Sanders!" she said excitedly, waving to them.

*Didn't they just see them a day or so ago? How convenient.*

A nice looking couple around the Douglas' age and a younger woman approached our table. The younger, blond and green-eyed woman was pretty, but not striking and was of average height. Abigail rose from her chair. Johnathan appeared bothered by this interruption, but stood to greet them nonetheless.

Tony and I sat and watched as his parents and the new party chatted briefly. Then Abigail turned around happily and announced,

**91**

"Anthony, you remember Jeremy and Valerie Sanders and their daughter, Rachel."

*Hey, I'm here, too.*

Tony stood and shook all of their hands. When he reached for Rachel's, she held it a second longer and gave him a kiss on the cheek. After Tony broke the handshake, Rachel gaze lingered on him for a good moment before she turned back to the conversation at hand.

Oh, this was not cute!

Rachel had a huge crush on my man and this *spontaneous* meeting with the Sanders was not at all spontaneous. My feelings were confirmed further, when Abigail invited the Sanders to dine with us and signaled the waitress for more menus.

This surprised Johnathan, Tony, and I, but we made room and the waitress brought over more chairs. It was no shock when Rachel conveniently landed on the other side of Tony. I shook my head and smiled, amused by the calculated effort.

During dinner, Abigail and Johnathan talked amicably with Jeremy and Valerie while Tony, Rachel and I ate. Conversation turned when Abigail asked Rachel a question.

"Rachel, your parents told me that you're finishing your Master's at UVA. Have you been looking into any positions here in New York or are you planning to return to Connecticut?"

"I'm unsure at the moment. It depends on what they both have to offer. I'm beginning to look into settling down with someone," Rachel replied with a quick glance at Tony. I caught it, though.

"Oh? Anyone in mind?" Abigail asked devilishly.

"Abigail, you know very well that Rachel has had a crush on Anthony ever since high school. She really has, you know," Valerie said with a lighthearted laugh, looking at Tony.

"Well, that's flattering but I'm out of the market," Tony declared with a little chuckle and put his hand over mine on the table suggestively.

Valerie's face turned from surprise to mortification. "Oh...are you two...?" she gulped.

Tony smiled. "Yes, we've just made a month a couple of days ago."

Abigail took a deep breath, squinted at Tony in brief and then eyeballed me. "Excuse our rudeness, Jeremy and Valerie. Uh, this is uh… Leslie… uh…dear, what's your name again?"

"Lacie, Mrs. Douglas. My name's Lacie," I asserted, nodding to her smirk.

*Nice try, Abigail.*

I was glad when dinner ended, and when the Sanders were saying their good-byes, I snuck off to the bathroom. When I came out of the stall, Abigail was standing at the sink, putting on lipstick.

I felt a sense of déjà vu when I walked over to the basin. I hadn't even turned on the faucet when Abigail put the lipstick in its case and turned to look at me.

Her tone was calm and grave as she declared, "Don't get too comfortable being with Anthony. It'll be hell or high water before I let you into this family."

She retreated haughtily without leaving me any time to reply.

I took a deep breath and looked at my reflection in the mirror. Yep, just what I thought. It was going to be Simone all over again—only older.

Was a sista ever going to get a break?

# *Chapter 18*

# Dawn

I was going to hell. I just knew it.

I was also falling in love with Joe.

Since the surprising telephone call from Lacie that night, while Joe and I were in the midst of some heated foreplay, we'd been seeing each other continuously for four weeks.

We'd gone out every night and because Joe knew many celebrities in Miami, we attended every happening event in Miami. We wined and dined and took long strolls on the beaches hand in hand, talking and laughing. We talked on the phone constantly, checking the best time to schedule our next lunch or dinner date.

I was having an incredible amount of fun being with him and had never experienced anything of the sort. I found myself wondering if I were living in a dream. For in my eyes, Joe was the perfect man for me. He was the one that I'd been waiting for.

Still there was Lacie…

Every time her name wandered into my mind, this sickening, guilt wrenching, feeling would come over me and I'd get a headache. I knew it was wrong to continue seeing Joe, but still continued and tried to ignore the dishonor inside of me. More guilt came whenever I'd hear Lacie's messages on the answering machine.

Because of my busy work schedule and the time spent with Joe, I barely had a chance to talk with her. Quite frankly, I was thankful for that, because even thinking about her reminded me of my treacherous behavior. I'd finally gotten enough courage to speak to her one day when I saw her name on the caller ID, as I was about to meet Joe downstairs in the car. I realized then that the situation was about to get worse.

"*Dawn, we've got to talk!*" *Lacie expressed on the phone.*

"*Lacie, what's wrong?*" *I asked, slightly alarmed. She couldn't possibly know about me and Joe already.*

"*Oh, girl,*" *Lacie groaned. "I am headed for drama."*

"*What, girl? What happened?*"

"*I met Tony's parents and girl, was it awful!*"

"*What? Why didn't you tell me?*"

"*How could I, Dawn? You're never at home. I haven't talked with you in a month and I always wind up having a conversation with your answering machine instead of you. Don't think I don't know what's going on, either.*"

*Swallowing hard, I said, "You do?"*

"*Yeah, girl. You've hooked up with a man.*"

"*What makes you think that?*"

"*What makes you think that?*" *Lacie mimicked on the phone. "Girl, please. I know you. Now, who is he?"*

"*What?*"

"*Don't even try it, Dawn. You can't fool me because I've known you far too long. Whenever you're MIA, and I can't reach you, that's a clear indication that you've got some meat on the side somewhere.*"

"*Some meat, Lacie?*" *I laughed.*

"*Yeah, girl...meat,*" *Lacie asserted, laughing. "Look, we've got to get together because I need to have a heart to heart with my best friend. Tony and I are arriving early tomorrow morning so I'll give you a call right after we get our room in the hotel. And you'd better answer the phone, too.*"

She hit the nail on the head. The truth was that I really had been avoiding her calls. I'd been busy, but I'd known of her arrival for a few weeks and felt unprepared to face her knowing that I was keeping my relationship with Joe a secret from her. The bad part was that I hoped that she couldn't see through it. It wasn't that I didn't want to see Lacie, because I truly missed her. It was because Lacie had always been able to tell what was going on with me before I'd said it. She claimed that my eyes always gave me away. Frankly, I hoped they didn't this time, because I really didn't want to hurt my friend.

95

Friend. Huh. Such a strong word. It didn't even sound right coming from my lips.

True to form, Lacie called me early this morning and was now waiting for me to pick her up at the hotel. She was eager and I was angst-ridden. I sighed and sorted through my closet to pick something warm to wear. I knew of a nice restaurant where we could dine outside but the forecast called for cooler temperatures.

My cell phone rang. I smiled immediately, hearing the special ring that I'd assigned for Joe.

"Good morning," I answered softly.

"Good morning, gorgeous," Joe's masculine voice rang. "You're up bright and early. I'm just calling to let you know that our dinner date might have to be moved up."

"Why?"

There was a slight pause. "I'm going golfing with Tony this morning and then off to a business meeting. I don't know when it will end."

I inhaled deeply. "And I'm going to breakfast with Lacie. She called me at the crack of dawn. That's why I'm up so early."

Another pause. "How do you feel about seeing her?"

I sighed. "I've never hidden anything from Lacie before."

"I know." He blew hard. "Dawn, I'm sorry. I've put you in a tight spot, haven't I?"

"Joe, you didn't put me in anything that I didn't want to be in. We've gone out numerous times and I could have ended this a long time ago. But I didn't want to."

"I'm glad you didn't," he said softly. "I like being with you."

"Me too."

"Good. Why don't I give you a call once Tony and I finish our game and then we can look at hooking up after?"

"Sounds good."

"Great. I'll talk with you later, gorgeous," Joe said and then hung up.

Somehow talking with Joe made my worries fade away.

Lacie stepped off the elevator looking bright and fresh. She smiled instantly when she saw me. We rushed up to each other and embraced. We continued for a good minute, both squealing and crying with delight and paid no attention to the stares we were getting because of all of the commotion we were making in the lobby.

"Girl! It is so good to see you!" Lacie exclaimed, leaning back to look at me. "You look great."

"You too, girl. You too," I replied, enjoying the compliment. "Okay, where do you want to go?"

She looked at me with a dubious expression. "Dawn, I don't know this place. You pick the restaurant. I don't care where it is. I'm hungry, stressed out and I need to let everything out," she emphasized.

I laughed. "All right, girl. Come on. I know just the right place."

I felt as if I'd never left New York.

Lacie and I couldn't stop talking in the car or even after we arrived at the restaurant and sat down. As soon as our order came, she wasted no time in filling me in on everything that had happened in the past month with work, Mama and Reneé, her father coming, and what went down with Tony's parents.

"So look, girl, have you heard from Robert lately?" I asked. "He called me a while back and told me about his dad. I haven't heard anything from him ever since."

Lacie shook her head. "No, I haven't heard much from him either. I've called and left messages, but he hasn't called back. The last I heard, his dad wasn't doing well. But I guess no news is good news. That's the positive way to look at it, anyway. Plus, I kind of decided to give him some time to deal with things because he's got so much on his plate. If he needs us or if something happens, he'll let us know, I'm sure."

"Yeah, you're right," I said with a big sigh. "Oh, this is making me sad! Let's talk about something else." I shook my head quickly. "How do you think Miss Josephine is going to act when your dad comes?"

"Oh, there's no doubt Mama's going to be ticked," Lacie stressed. "Especially since I haven't told her. Dawn, they just don't get along and every time I think about them being together, I cringe. I've been so busy with everything and even though we've been working together on Reneé's wedding, I just haven't had time to tell her."

"Okay, but did you at least tell Tony what his mother said to you?" I asked. "Why not, Lacie?" I responded to her shaking head.

Continuing to shake her head she said, "Dawn, I am not trying to start something up and forget about me telling Mama, either."

"You didn't tell Miss Josephine?"

She looked at me incredulously. "Girl, are you crazy? You know Mama. She'd scratch Abigail's eyes out if she found out," she exaggerated.

"Yeah, you've got a point. Miss Josephine doesn't play," I agreed with a chuckle.

"Precisely. And I've had enough excitement," Lacie asserted, peering at me. "But I don't know, Dawn. I just feel like more is about to unfold" I gulped. She narrowed her eyes and looked upward. "I just feel it."

"Lacie, don't think so negative," I said quickly, sudden anxiety coming over me. "Just enjoy being here in Miami. I know you're here on business, but try to think of this as a vacation."

She looked at me and shrugged. "Yeah, I guess so. Honestly, I think Tony had the same idea because he went out with Joe this morning to play golf."

"He did?" I asked, pretending to be surprised.

"Yeah, Tony called him as soon as we got off the plane." Lacie exhaled. "Dawn, I am so glad they've maintained their friendship because I'd honestly thought I'd ruined it. But Joe, being the good guy that he is, forgave Tony and me. Joe even surprised me by saying that he didn't think he'd ever get over me."

I almost choked on my food. "What? He said that?"

Immediate concern appeared on Lacie's face and she exclaimed, "Dawn, are you okay?"

After taking a huge gulp from my glass, I nodded and waved my hand airily and said, "Yeah, yeah. I'm fine."

"You sure?" Lacie asked with a concerned frown.

"Yeah, yeah. I just swallowed wrong, that's all," I replied, clearing my throat. I put my glass down and looked at her intensely. "But Joe said that? He said he'd never get over you?"

Lacie nodded with a sigh after she was reassured that I was okay. "Yep. Sure did." She shrugged and smiled. "But you know, we'd just broken up and it was an emotional time for both of us so…"

*I bet it was.*

"Yeah…maybe you're right," I mused, holding back my aggravation at what she'd said.

Lacie eyed me closely. "You know, I've been so busy talking about myself that I haven't had any time to dip into your business," she hinted.

I looked at her fleetingly with a little irritation and shrugged with a thin smile. "There's nothing to dip about. My career is really taking off and I'm doing well. Mom is flying in tomorrow. She'll be staying with me for a good while, so I'll be entertaining her and showing her around. You know, that sort of thing."

"Yeah, I remember Mama telling me that. How is she doing? Has she gotten adjusted to you being so far away?"

"She's taking it in stride. I mean, I am an adult, right?" I snapped lightly.

Lacie frowned a little. "Dawn, are you all right?"

"I'm fine, why? And why do you keep asking me that?" I snapped again.

Lacie looked shocked and leaned back in her chair with a small shrug. "Your mood just changed a bit, that's all. Is something bothering you?"

Yes. I'm ticked off that the man that I'm in love with is still in love with you. That's what I'm upset about, I wanted to say.

*Watch it Dawn, Lacie's watching you very closely.* I checked myself.

I forced a smile and managed, "Girl, I'm fine. I just thought about all the things I have to do before my mom arrives, that's all."

Lacie snapped her fingers. "Hey, that reminds me, I've got to call Tony and find out when we're supposed to meet William Carr and

Trevor Weeks. He was supposed to call them after I left the hotel," she said, reaching in her purse for her cell.

*Did I hear her right?*

"Uh…Lacie, what did you say this guy's name was?"

She placed her phone to her ear and looked at me. "Trevor Weeks. He lives here in Miami and he's Mr. Carr's lawyer. Why? Do you know him?" Suddenly, she turned her head and spoke softly into the phone. "Hey, baby, how are you…?"

Astonished, I sat there, all at once remembering why I'd dreaded this meeting with Lacie. It was bad enough to learn that Joe was most likely using me. Now, I'd learned that Lacie was meeting with Trevor Weeks, the same guy Joe had introduced me to at a party a month ago.

This was too much of a coincidence and the web was getting tighter.

That's exactly what I get for dating my best friend's ex-man.

# Chapter 19

## Joe

"Man, what is up with you?" Tony asked as we walked toward the next hole on the green. "You've been walking on air ever since we got here. Your swings have even gotten better, too."

"Hey, don't be jealous because you're getting beat and you white folks ain't got golf to yourselves anymore," I ribbed, practicing my swing once we reached the hole. "You know brothas can't hold back their skills."

"All right, you got me," Tony chuckled with a nod. "But for real, man. Something's up with you. I've never seen you like this."

I took one good swing toward the hole that was a few yards away and the ball was in.

"Damn!" Tony exclaimed.

"Ha, ha, told you," I laughed, doing a little dance and moving aside.

"You're sick, man. Something is wrong with you," Tony murmured, shaking his head as he put his ball on the green.

"Man, if love is wrong for me, then I don't want to be right," I halfway sang out of tune.

Tony stopped his swing and held up a hand with a wince. "Hey, hey, hey, leave the singing up to me because I at least got you beat in that game," he laughed. "C'mon and tell me about this girl, man."

"It's like I told you before, man. I'm feeling her. *Really* feeling her," I declared strongly.

Seeing that I was serious, Tony asked, "Yeah?"

"Yeah, man." I nodded.

"Wow," Tony said, shaking his head and taking his swing. It was a good swing, but it grazed the hole. "Ooh, that hurt," he uttered with another wince.

"And that's also game," I said, laughing and giving him a pat on the back. "I told you. brotha's got skills."

"Whatever, man," Tony laughed as we gripped. "So what's so special about this one compared to the others?" he asked as we started heading toward the outside bar at the clubhouse, caddies strolling behind us.

I knew he actually meant compared to Lacie. "She wasn't looking for me," I said, simply, sitting on a bar stool at the bar. The man behind the bar, whose nametag displayed Louis, ignored me and continued wiping the counter.

"Huh?" Tony asked, taking a seat next to me. "What do you mean by that?"

Louis came over to him at once. "What would you like, sir?" he asked in a polite tone.

I scoffed and shook my head. It never failed.

Tony, irritated by the interruption and Louis' obvious disregard of me, shook his head. "He was here before me. Take his order first."

"Yes, sir," Louis said automatically. He turned ever so slightly my way but avoided eye contact.

"Spring water will do," I instructed Louis, then continued the conversation. "This girl's genuine, man. I've had just about every woman in Miami scoping me out and trying to land me. But this girl is not for any games and all she's looking for is love."

"All right, so when do I meet her?"

"You'll meet her…in time," I answered evasively.

Tony picked up on it. "What do you mean in time, man? What? You don't want me to meet her or something? You afraid I'll take her away from you?" he teased.

"Naw man, it's just…you'll meet her when you meet her, that's all." I shrugged.

Louis returned with our drinks and handed Tony's his first, and mine second. I took out money to pay for it.

"Naw, man…I got it," Tony objected.

"No, it's cool. I'll get it," I said, handing Louis a hundred dollar bill. "I'll pay since I beat you so bad," I chuckled.

"Hey, I *let* you win," he countered.

"Sure, sure. Keep telling yourself that," I snickered, holding out my hand for the change.

Louis overlooked my hand, put the change on the bar and started to walk off.

Tony's voice stopped him. "Uh, uh. Put the money in his hand."

"Excuse me, sir?" Louis asked, feigning innocence.

"You heard me. This gentleman placed the money in your hand. Now show him the same respect. *Hand* him his money or get punched out," Tony threatened.

Quickly Louis handed me my change.

"Thank you. Thank you so much, Louis," I joked Louis, chuckling as he walked away.

"Ignorance, man. Ignorance," Tony muttered, shaking his head. He looked at me. "Speaking of ignorance, I got a bad vibe from your man, Trevor."

I nodded. "Yeah, he's a little off, but he's a damn good lawyer and that's why William hired him."

"Yeah, Lacie and I are meeting with them in a couple of hours at William's condo and tomorrow we're going out scouting property."

"I know. I'm also tagging along."

Tony looked surprised. "Looking into making more cash, are you?" he asked.

"Yeah, Trevor roped me into it. He called me last night, saying it would be a good venture and I'd make a lot of dough." I shrugged.

"So I guess we'll be doing some more business together, huh?" Tony smiled.

"Yep, except this time, I'm *keeping* my woman," I gibed, chuckling.

"Whatever, man. Whatever," Tony chuckled.

Once Tony and I parted, I called Dawn's cell phone but there was no answer. Next, I called her apartment—still no answer. Reluctantly,

I left a message on both answering machines for her to call me back. Doing something absolutely unfamiliar to me, I called her back five minutes later on her cell and she picked up.

"Hello?"

"Hey, gorgeous," I greeted.

"Hey," she said. Her voice sounded distant.

"How was breakfast with Lacie?"

"It went fine," she answered with a curt tone. "We did a lot of catching up with each other."

"That's good," I said and glanced at my watch. "We're still on for the night, right?"

"You know what? Let's cancel and make it another time."

This was sudden. "Why?"

"No reason," she replied elusively.

"Did something happen between you and Lacie?"

"No. I said everything went fine," she replied in an aggressive tone. "Look, I've got a phone call. I'll call you later," she said quickly and ended the call.

I stood in the parking lot of the golf club looking at the phone, stunned.

She actually hung up on a brotha.

What the 'h' was going on?

# Chapter 20

# Lacie

It was like seeing an apparition.

Joe came in the lobby of the condominium smiling that gorgeous smile of his, with arms wide open. He walked up to me and lifted me up in a tight bear hug.

"All right, man, all right, that's enough. You're going to break her bones," Tony chuckled, teasing.

"Aw, man, I ain't gonna break her bones. She's got too much meat on her for that," Joe countered easily with a chuckle as he put me down.

"Talk about surprises. What are you doing here?" I asked, happy to see him. I looked at Tony. "What? Is he the surprise you were talking about?"

Tony nodded with a smile. "Yep. Trevor and Joe went to high school together and he invited him to be a part of this deal."

"Well, talk about coincidences," I murmured, smiling at Joe. "This is wonderful. Wait 'til Dawn finds out about this. She is going to trip." An idea hit me and I looked at Tony. "You know? All four of us should get together and go out for dinner or something."

Out of the corner of my eye, I thought I saw Joe flinch.

Tony glanced at his watch and shook his head. "That's a good idea, but we can get into that later. Right now, we need to go upstairs and handle business. William is waiting on us."

"Oh yes and so duty calls," I joked with a little sigh and started for the elevator.

On the ride up to Mr. Carr's floor, I looked from Tony to Joe, shaking my head at the irony of the situation. Once again, I was between these two fine men but the circumstances were different. Though it was inevitable that I'd see Joe again because of his friendship with Tony, now it appeared that we were going to work on yet another deal together.

The elevator door opened and we came to a door as we stepped off. A contemporary tailored butler opened the door and gestured us inside. William Carr walked up and greeted us at once and shook all of our hands.

"We were wondering about you guys," he remarked with a smile. "Come on in."

William led us to a huge sunken living room that overlooked the city of Miami and also gave us a view of Trevor Weeks, sitting comfortably on a tan suede chair.

The butler came over and took our requests for drinks before we continued with the formalities.

"Okay, Trevor, you're on," William said, once we'd had our drinks.

And he was. Trevor led us to an adjoining room with a large oak table that had everything laid out for our view. On the table was a map with impressive architectural sketches and models of a planned real estate venture to build luxury condominiums in Florida and Vegas, he explained. The venture also included plans for the rebuilding of run down homes in low-income neighborhoods.

Trevor continued by leading us back into the living room where he handed all of us an informative proposal that detailed all of the specifics involved.

"Well," Tony said, after reviewing all of the information. "This is pretty thorough and it almost seems as if you're doing our job. We're normally the ones that advise on investments," Tony said good-naturedly.

"I might be a lawyer but I look into all avenues of interest. It's my job to look out for my client and make sure that there are no stones unturned," Trevor answered.

"So what do you need us for?" Tony asked.

Trevor narrowed his eyes at Tony. "We don't *need* you for anything. It was my understanding that your company and William have a great relationship. Thus, he felt a need to have your company on board for consultation and a possible interest in this project."

William spoke. "This is new for me. You and Lacie both know my business. I'm an investor and I've made most of my money by buying up companies and many other ventures," William offered. "But I've made some bad financial decisions, with which your company's well aware and is graciously helping me out of. So I'm looking into new and better ways to broaden my business and my finances. When I hired Trevor, and he told me about the enormous profitability of this project, I liked the idea and wanted you to be a part of it. Having Joe on board with us, considering his success with real estate, is an added bonus."

That was Joe's cue to speak. He'd been eyeing the proposal the duration and looked at William. "William, this project suggests rebuilding homes in some of the poorest neighborhoods in Florida. What's going to happen to these people once the homes are rebuilt? Their property taxes alone will go up and most of these people are low income. Are they going to be pushed out so that the wealthy can come in and reside?

"I knew you were going to say that," Trevor offered with a nod. "The answer is on page thirty."

Page thirty proposed building a manufacturing facility for one of William's companies a few miles from one of the neighborhoods, which would include jobs for those living in the area.

"Impressive." I nodded. "You seem to have covered everything."

"That's what I do," Trevor said arrogantly, grinning at me. "This project may be ambitious, but it will be beneficial because it will grant lucrative opportunities for every income level."

"It will also involve a lot of money, research, footwork and gamble," Tony added.

I nodded in compliance, understanding Tony's point. The risk was big and William's estate and net worth couldn't possibly cover the costs of such an enormous project.

"Mr. Carr, this is a huge undertaking for you. Have you considered the risks involved?" I asked.

Trevor answered. "We've looked at all avenues as well as a few more investors that might be interested. Joe is one of them and the rest are good friends of William. They'll be with us when we meet again in New York. William just wanted you and Tony to have the first introduction, considering he and Tony's past." Defending his position even more, Trevor stressed, "As I've said, this is a huge opportunity for everyone concerned. William is adamant about working with Ryan & Company because of the good working relationship he has with you, not to mention the fringe benefits involved. This deal would generate more clientele for Ryan & Company, and broaden future possibilities of doing more business in other states and hopefully abroad. Once this project is done and word gets around, clients will come running."

Trevor wasn't a lawyer for nothing. His selling bid went on a few more minutes and was so convincing that he finally sold everyone in the room. William, Joe and Tony immediately started making calls. Joe went to one corner of the massive room to arrange to have his people at Monday's meeting and Tony went to another room to fill Richard in. I retreated back to the adjoining room to examine the plans and models again.

My peripheral vision showed Trevor, with drink in hand, strolling in.

"Still impressed?" he remarked, coming to my side.

I nodded, still eyeing the models. "Yes, I am."

"No. I meant about me," he said.

Slightly taken aback, I turned to look at him and said, "Excuse me?"

"You said a while back that you were impressed," he said. "What were you impressed about?" He took a swig from his glass.

"Oh, yeah," I said, flushing slightly. "You just had everything down. It seemed like you worked hard on your presentation."

"It's what I do." He smiled conceitedly. "I'm a business man and all business men have to work hard on their presentation. And I'm the kind of person that works hard for something I want."

"You sound just like Joe," I mused.

"Why do you say that?"

"He said something similar to me a couple of months ago when we were engaged," I blurted out unconscientiously.

*Lacie, you can really put your foot in your mouth sometimes.*

Unfortunately, Trevor hadn't missed it. "That's right. I knew I'd heard your name before," he said, snapping his fingers.

"Yep, there you go. That's me," I murmured with slight embarrassment.

"Yeah. Joe told me he'd found some sweet thing that he was planning to marry," Trevor said contemplatively.

"Sweet thing?" I asked, chuckling softly. "That's a 70s kind of lingo, don't you think?"

"Oh, it works on the women, now. Don't get it twisted," he said confidently.

"Maybe on some women, but not on me."

"So tell me what does."

I shook my head. I had to hand it to him. He was bold. "Mr. Weeks, I'm involved."

"It's Trevor." He nodded his head toward the living room. "You're involved with Douglas. I know that," he said. "But are you happy with him?"

"Yes, she is."

We turned around at the sound of Tony's voice. He and Joe were standing in the doorway. With a smirk, Tony immediately came over to me and put his arm around my waist possessively. For some reason I felt like he was staking his claim.

Trevor, being the smooth talker that he was said indifferently, "Hey, that's cool. It's good to know that a *sista's* being treated right. That's all."

I felt Tony stiffen.

Joe strolled in between the three of us. "Man, don't you have anything better to do than to try to make a play for someone else's woman?" he asked Trevor lightheartedly.

"Actually, I do," Trevor replied, taking a brief glance at his watch. "I've got to check out this jazz club that a partner of mine owns and wants me to invest in." He looked at Joe and then at me and Tony.

"Listen, why don't you all come down with me and check it out? Drinks are on me. Let this be a mini celebration of what's to come."

"You're quite confident even though the deal is not yet done," Tony said.

With a shrug and a sly grin, Trevor answered, "Hey, there's nothing wrong with confidence, especially if you know you're the best at what you do." His cell phone rang. "Excuse me. I've got to take this call and then I'll call the club to have them set up a VIP spot for us," he said and walked out.

&#8366;&#8578;

I heard Tony close the door hard behind me after we entered our hotel room. It wasn't a slam but it was enough to let me know that he was upset. I cocked my head at him as he strode past me toward the bedroom, mumbling.

"You know, it's really not a good idea to talk to yourself. People will begin to wonder," I stated casually, entering the bedroom.

He said nothing, jerked his tie off and walked into the adjoining bathroom.

"Tony, I know you know better than to act like the typical jealous boyfriend," I called out to him, taking a seat on the bed.

He came out. "I'm not jealous. I just didn't like him talking to you."

"That's…being jealous," I asserted candidly, nodding. "Tony, what are you going to do? Are you going to get jealous or upset every time a guy tries to talk to me?"

"No, it's not that," he said with a shake of his head. "You're a beautiful woman and I know that there are going to be men who see you and want you. That's a given. But it was how disrespectful Trevor was when he hit on you behind my back and then challenged my relationship with you that irked me. Honest men…*real* men don't do that, Lacie. If he'd have been someone else and he wasn't working with William to get this deal, my reaction would've been totally different," he declared. "And now we've got to go to this jazz club and I've got to

110

act cordial to him." He shook his head again. "I don't know, Lacie. It's just something about this dude that I don't like."

I nodded, recalling that I'd felt the same way about Simone. I stood up and walked over to him. "Okay, Tony, look. Nothing is set in stone yet. There's still a lot of formalities and research that needs to be done and that's why we've got such a good team back in New York." I put my arms around his waist and gave him a peck on the lips. "It's a lot at stake here and the bottom line is that we are really only here for William's interest. He's our client and we need to look out for him. Even though he won't be joining us at the jazz club, let's just be good sports about this and go there and try to enjoy ourselves. Listen, I'll even ask Dawn to come since Joe will be there. It'll be like a reunion of sorts. Okay?"

He blew out a deep breath. "All right, good idea," he said, smiling slightly with a nod. "It would be good to see Dawn again." He bent down and said, before he kissed me tenderly and headed back to the bathroom, "I knew there was a reason I fell in love with you."

I frowned at Tony's retreating figure, perturbed by how edgy he was. I grabbed my cell phone and dialed Dawn's phone number.

As soon as she answered I said, "Girl, I don't care what you are doing, but stop it and get dressed now!"

# Chapter 21

## The Jazz Club

### Dawn

It was a mistake to come.

Sitting in the VIP section of the club was Lacie, Tony, and...Joe. Why didn't Lacie tell me that Joe was going to be there? Aggravated, I blew out a small, exasperated breath as I viewed them from across the dance floor. I made eye contact with Joe briefly and saw the same look of surprise on his face.

Lacie spotted me and made her way through the crowded dance floor, and hugged me. "Dawn, thanks for coming. I owe you big," she whispered in my ear, then leaned back and checked me out. "Girl, you really went all out, didn't you? This dress is saying something!"

"Well, you did say to wear something nice—nice enough to catch someone's eye—I recall," I replied, raising an eyebrow. "So who is the victim?"

Lacie turned around and looked at the table to show me. Trevor Weeks suddenly came into view. Oh no!

"There he is," she stated. "Trevor Weeks. He made his move on me, girl, and Tony is mad! So please...can you just entertain him so that we can get through this night?"

I saw Joe walking over to us with that calm and self-confident smile of his. I was so ticked at him. A naughty notion came over me suddenly and I let out a soft chuckle. This'll teach his behind.

I gave Lacie a mischievous grin. "Don't worry, Lacie. I got it."

Joe approached us then. "Hey, Dawn, it's good to see you." He gave me a tight hug before releasing me and looked me over. "You look really nice."

I returned a tight smile and said, "Thank you. It's good to see you, too."

Lacie smiled as she looked at both of us. "I know. Isn't this great that all of us are together again?" she remarked. "Hey, look, we'd better get over there. The waitress is at our table taking orders for drinks." She started off, leaving Joe and myself to follow.

"I didn't know you were going to be here," Joe whispered.

"So? I gotta tell you what I do every minute?" I snapped.

With that, I left him and hasted to catch up with Lacie.

## Joe

What was that all about?

Dawn walked off, leaving me standing there like a chump in the middle of the dance floor. She was obviously mad with me about something. But what? Scratching my head contemplatively, I watched as Tony and Trevor stood up once she came to the table. Tony was frowning and Trevor's grin was a mile long as he took Dawn's hand, getting ready to go in for the kill

And...he'd also seen Dawn with me at the party!

I rushed through the thick crowd.

## Tony

"She's a beautiful woman, man," Trevor remarked to me coolly as I watched him ogle Lacie after Joe left.

"Yep. She is," I replied.

"So when did you two hook up?" he asked casually.

I gave him a blank look and said nothing. He turned his attention off of Lacie for once to look at me with a smirk.

"Yo' man, I already know about her and Joe. I'm just trying to figure out how you landed her, that's all."

"Man, what business is it of yours?" I asked. "You intimidated or something?"

His smirk didn't waver as he shook his head. "Naw, man. Not at all. I'm more annoyed than anything. It gets under my skin to see a fine black woman going to waste on a white man, that's all."

"Oh, she's not going to waste. I'm treating her real good. Believe that," I declared with a meaningful nod.

He didn't budge and neither did I as we stared each other down.

Then he grinned. "All right, man. All right. It's cool," he said, offering his hand. "You're all right."

I shook my head and gripped him anyway. This fool was crazy and I didn't like him. He didn't know it, but the waitress coming over had saved him from getting clocked on the jaw.


## Lacie


The waitress had left and Tony's expression was grim as he got up to stand when Dawn and I came to the table. I looked from him to Trevor, who immediately stood at the sight of Dawn.

"Are you men doing okay?" I asked casually.

"Yeah, yeah, we're fine," Trevor waved my question off impatiently. He eyed Dawn. "Hello, I must be dreaming! Where did this fine young thing come from?" he asked no one in particular, taking Dawn's hand in his.

"Hi, I'm Dawn," Dawn answered sweetly.

When Trevor bent to kiss the back of her hand, she looked at me and rolled her eyes upward. I stifled a giggle.

Joe came up suddenly and easily nudged Trevor away from Dawn. Smiling slightly, he said, "Hey, man, where'd the waitress go? I thought you brought us here for a celebration? Don't get cheap on us, man."

"Oh, man, cool it. I ordered a bottle of Courvoisier, so she'll be back. I told you I know the owner," Trevor replied as we all sat down.

It was boy-girl-boy-girl-boy at the table. I was between Tony and Trevor and Dawn was between Trevor and Joe. Tony and Joe were on the end and Trevor was in the middle.

After the owner of the club came over to talk with us, conversation immediately began with the project that we talked about in William's condo. Trevor continued his pitch and spoke highly about the investors that we would meet during the week, while cleverly managing to keep an eye on Dawn throughout the conversation. I was thrilled because it kept his attention off of me.

Conversation soon took a left turn when Trevor mentioned that he was interested in becoming a partner in the jazz club and wanted Joe to join him. During this time, I looked at Tony a few times curiously. He'd been sitting quietly, listening and seemingly brooding over something, while Joe and Trevor talked about the club.

Joe shook his head. "Man, I have no knowledge of running a club, let alone a jazz club."

"Man, you're not going to run it. You'll just be a silent partner. An investor, if you will," Trevor claimed.

"I don't know. I've got enough on my plate as it is," Joe said.

Trevor wasn't going to give up. "All right, look, just think about it. This place is in a good location and it's big enough to accommodate a large crowd if we can get some well-known acts in here. Also, I was thinking about looking into some new talent to broaden the scope, somewhat. There's a lot of undiscovered talent out there and this would be the ideal place for them to get their start. All we have to do is look for them."

"You know, that's a good idea. There is a lot of talent out there and people are always looking for ways to get into the public eye," Dawn offered.

"I really...*really* like this girl," Trevor said, looking at me and Tony. Then he gazed at Dawn wistfully. "I've seen you somewhere before, haven't I?"

Was it my imagination or did Dawn's eyes shift nervously?

Joe chuckled. "C'mon, man, you can't come up with a better line than that?"

"Naw, man, it's not a line." Trevor shook his head and pointed a finger at Dawn. "I've seen you before. I know it."

"Well, she is a model and doing quite well, I might add," I offered and Dawn gave me a meager smile. "She's been doing a lot of runway shows. You might have seen her in one of them."

Trevor shook his head again and said, "No, it wasn't there. It was somewhere else…maybe a month or so ago…"

I found it odd when Joe cleared his throat and spoke in haste. "Trevor, you were speaking of undiscovered talent. My boy, Tony, here is a serious pianist and singer. He can play the Ivories, believe me."

That got Trevor's attention. "He can, huh?" Trevor asked, casting a look at Tony with a raised eyebrow. "What do you play? I mean, you any good or what?"

"I can play anything. But I like Jazz and R & B," Tony replied confidently.

"Yeah, but are you any good?" Trevor goaded.

Tony's jaw clenched.

I didn't appreciate his insinuation either. "Oh, no doubt. Tony's very good," I defended.

Tony shot me a perturbed look and Trevor noticed.

Trevor scoffed in amusement. "Oh, this just gets better by the minute."

He signaled the owner of the club and he came over immediately. While he and Joe talked with the owner, I touched Tony's leg and searched his face.

"You okay?" I whispered.

Tony shifted uncomfortably. "No, I'm not."

"What's wr–" I started.

Tony shot me another perturbed look, but before he could answer, Trevor turned around after the owner walked over to the stage and dared, "All right, man. You're on. Show me what you got."

Without warning, the bandleader had gotten the crowd ready by introducing Tony. One small look at Tony and then at Trevor, who was grinning from ear to ear, and I knew that something was brewing between them and that Tony was incensed. Nonetheless, he stood up and strolled toward the stage with confidence. Joe went up with him and fixed the microphone while Tony settled at the beautiful black piano.

116

There were a few mixed laughs and low remarks, but he ignored them.

Right after Joe got off the stage to stand to the side, Tony did a short, funky, jazz piece with the keys and the crowd quieted immediately. Then he went into the beginning of *Overjoyed*, and spoke while he played softly.

"I know some of you may have your doubts about me being on this stage," Tony soothed on the microphone. Some of the audience laughed and nodded their heads.

"Excuse me, I've got to go to the ladies room," Dawn said suddenly, getting up swiftly.

I barely paid attention to her when she left and continued watching Tony.

Tony continued stroking the keys as he talked. "But you know, regardless of race, creed or color, one thing we all understand...is love. How many of you have been in love?" A few hands rose. "All right, that's good, that's good. How many of you are in love right now?" More rose and Tony nodded with an assertive smile because he had the audience's full attention now. "So you all know that love can be beautiful, but love can hurt, right?" A few of the women nodded and said 'yes'. "Especially, when you feel that the relationship you're in may be over or that maybe the one you're in love with is seeing someone else, right?" More heads nodded. "Well, here's a song that you all might remember involving that subject." He started playing the chords of *Lately* by Stevie Wonder and that did it. As soon as he started the first words, it was over. He had them.

I smiled proudly at my man who was singing with every bit of his soul. I glanced over at Joe who was standing to the side smiling. He was proud also. Oblivious to my surroundings, I sat there totally engulfed by Tony's mellifluous voice, when Trevor broke my spell.

"Shouldn't he be singing *Ebony and Ivory*?" Trevor whispered in my ear.

I turned around sharply, coming within inches of Trevor's grin. "That's not really a jazz song, is it?" I answered sarcastically, knowing fully what he was implying.

"Neither is this," he pointed out.

I turned my attention back to the stage and nodded with a smile. "Yeah, but it's working."

He moved closer to me and whispered again, "So you left Joe and went with the white man, huh? How could you do it?" He snorted sarcastically. "Tell me something, is being single really so terrible that sistas think they have no other recourse but to demean themselves by crossing over just to get a man?"

The jargon he used in the question was eloquent, but stupid.

I turned to look at him. "The only demeaning thing is when I get ignorant comments like the one you just made," I shot back. "And for the record, that's demeaning you, not me."

"Oh, so a brotha can't be upset?" Trevor asked, raising his eyebrow.

"Hella no," I replied, looking at him incredulously. "I don't have to answer to you and my relationship with Tony has nothing to do with you."

Trevor shook his head. "I just can't stand to see sistas with Whitey. Brothas like me hate to see our women crossing that color line. That's taboo."

"Oh, don't even go there," I expressed, holding up my hand. "That's such a double standard. There are plenty of brothas that forget their chocolate sistas once they start making money and start going for vanilla."

"But I'm not one of those brothas," he said.

"Hey, great. Maybe you'll find a sista for you then."

"I have," he said, staring at me intently.

I scoffed. "Trevor, weren't you all up in my friend, Dawn's face just a few minutes ago and now you're gonna try to give me some play?"

He grinned. "Hey, a player never stops playing the game."

I shook my head, irritated by his arrogance. "But this time the game stops here because I'm already taken and I'm happy too."

It was Trevor's turn to scoff. "How long do you think that's gonna last? How do you think his parents are going to react when they meet you and see that you're not white? Do you think his parents are going to like you?" He saw me flinch and studied me for a moment before he alleged, "Oh, so you've met them already, huh? Let me guess. His dad didn't like you." He searched my eyes for the answer and they gave it to him. "Nope, it was his mom." He shook his head again, still eyeing me. "What did she say?"

"None of your damn business!" I huffed.

Trevor hunched up his shoulders. "Hey, don't get angry with me. I'm just telling you like it is. Whitey don't want any parts of us, and the sooner you realize that the better off you'll be. You don't have to go through any drama with a brotha. I'm telling you."

"I've been with brothas before and it's never worked out."

"So you're going to cross just to see if Whitey's gonna treat you any better? Is that it?" He let out a little laugh. "Lady, you just haven't found the right brotha, that's all."

Leaning back, I peered at him and said, "And he would be you, right?"

The grin came back on. "That's right."

I sighed deeply, aggravated that I'd missed most of Tony's song because of this buffoon. "Listen, I'm gonna tell you right now before we continue working any further. *I'm not interested and I've got a man already.* Now, we came down here in Mr. Carr's interest and we are looking into this deal just because of him…not you. We've got a few meetings ahead of us and I don't want to have to go through this with you every time we're together. My personal life is none of your concern, so let's make this a pleasant venture so we can work together. Okay?" I asserted.

Amused, Trevor stared at me intently for a moment. Then he shrugged his shoulders and said, "Okay." He picked up his glass and took a swallow and put it back down. "But the door is always open."

I rolled my eyes and turned my attention back to the stage.

## Dawn

Tony was still on stage playing when I came out of the bathroom. Joe stood on the side with his eyes closed, nodding to the music.

Staring at him, I sighed in slight aggravation. How was I going to get over him and why couldn't he get over Lacie? I was so mad at him for being so fine and making me fall in love with him.

Suddenly Joe opened his eyes and caught my gaze. He gave me a friendly smile and my anger almost softened right there. Then I felt another pair of eyes on me and looked to my left to see a handsome tall light-skinned guy eyeing me fiercely. He started walking toward me. He'd gotten within two feet of me when Joe stepped in front of him.

"Hey, baby. I was looking for you," Joe said sweetly, coming to my side.

Light Skin walked away in defeat.

"Having a good time?" Joe asked once Light Skin was out of earshot. Standing beside me, he kept his distance while we observed the dance floor filled with couples, dancing to Tony's song.

Not really. But I answered, "Yes, I am."

"Good." He nodded. After a moment of silence, he asked, "So what's up? You've been giving me attitude and ignoring me and flirting with other guys in the club. You wanna tell me what's going on?"

"There's nothing to explain." I turned around and looked at him coldly. "I mean, it's not like we're exclusive or anything. Right, Joe?" I shrugged.

He didn't seem to like that comment. "So you're trying to play me, is that it?"

He had some nerve. "Don't give me that," I said heatedly. "Who's trying to play who here, Joe?"

He looked at me in disbelief. "Who's been up in Trevor's face all night?"

"Don't give me that! Who's been lying to me this whole time and stringing me along even though he's still in love with another woman?" I argued bitterly.

"What?" Joe asked, looking confused. He was about to say more when Tony, having walked off the stage amidst a round of applause, interrupted us.

"What's up you two? Everything all right, here?" Tony asked, glancing at us curiously.

With a final glare at each other, Joe and I muttered simultaneously, "Everything's fine," before we stalked off in opposite directions.

Joe dared to question me about playing him. I had to have been crazy to fall for him. Men can be such idiots!

Lacie, apparently going to meet Tony who had followed Joe to the bar, met me halfway as I headed back to the table.

"Lacie, look, I'm gonna go. Mom's coming in on an early flight tomorrow and after she gets settled I plan on taking her sightseeing. I want to make sure to rest up," I explained.

Her expression showing some concern, Lacie replied, "Sure, Dawn. Sure. I understand." She peered at me some more. "You okay?"

There was no way that I was going to tell her how ticked I was at her for being so beautiful and mad at myself because I had fallen for her leftovers.

Instead, I nodded and replied, "Yeah, girl, I'm fine. I just gotta go."

"Yeah, I'm about ready, too. Trevor's been hitting on me ever since you left the table. But listen, I'll call you soon and thanks again for coming and helping me out with Trevor," she smiled gratefully.

I smiled weakly in return. "Hey, girl. You know I got your back."

*Yeah. With the knife that I kept stabbing it with.*

## Joe

"You all right, man?" Tony asked easily, coming up next to me at the bar.

"Yeah, I'm all right." I nodded, signaling the bartender. "Wanna drink man? I feel like I need one."

"You sure you should do that? You've had a lot to drink already."

Ignoring him, I told the bartender what I wanted. It was a strong drink and I saw Tony raise his eyebrow.

"Look, man, I got it!"

"All right," Tony said defensively. He sat beside me and motioned to the bartender that he wasn't going to order. "Look, man, what was all that about with you and Dawn? You two seemed to be in a serious argument."

I shrugged. "Nothing, man. We just had a little disagreement."

"Is that all?"

"Yeah, man. Don't sweat it."

"I'm not. You just look mad and I've only known you to drink this heavily when you're mad."

"I'm not, man. Just cool it. Okay?"

A fine, slim, long-legged, dark chocolate, female tapped Tony on the shoulder and stood between his legs as if she'd already claimed him.

"I enjoyed your performance," she breathed huskily, placing a piece of paper in his hand. "Here's my number. Call me sometime," she said before she walked off with a switch of her hips to join the rest of her girlfriends who were standing a few feet away.

Tony and I looked at each other, grinned and shook our heads. He put the paper on the bar next to me. "Here man, I don't need this. This is for you."

I laughed. "Man, why is it that sistas are always falling for you? Why?" I saw Lacie coming over. "Speaking of which, here comes your girl."

"Hey, baby. You were great up there!" Lacie gushed, giving Tony a mean kiss on the lips. "You tore it up!"

"Well, Douglas," Trevor said, trailing behind her with drink in hand. "I admit. I doubted you. But I can't hate on you. You did all right...for a white boy."

"Well, you know. Something as beautiful and black as that piano has to be stroked smooth and easy. You've got to treat it like a woman. You know?" Tony shot back with a grin, putting his arm around Lacie's waist.

I shook my head and chuckled. Trevor was stupid for messing with Tony. Dude had no clue. There was a small twitch in Trevor's face after Tony's reply, but then he smirked.

"Yeah, man. I know," Trevor said.

Tony looked at Lacie. "You ready to go, babe?"

Lacie nodded. "Anytime you are."

Tony turned to me for a grip. "We're outta here, man," he said. He gave Trevor a fleeting glance. "Trevor, we'll see you tomorrow and thanks for inviting us," he said, before he and Lacie turned and walked away.

"Wanna be nigga," I heard Trevor mutter under his breath as his eyes followed Tony and Lacie.

"Man, will you chill out!" I exclaimed. "You've been on his case ever since he got here."

"And I'm gonna stay on his case. He ain't got no business with one of our sistas. That's just wrong, man." Trevor looked at me. "What are you defending him for anyway? He stole your girl from you."

"She wasn't mine to begin with," I declared. "She wouldn't have been happy with me because she was in love with him."

"If she'd been with me that wouldn't have happened," Trevor stated confidently.

"I'm telling you, man. Let it go. You don't want to mess with Tony."

"It's not him I wanna mess with."

Shaking my head, I said, "You're ignorant, you know that. Ignorant."

Trevor chuckled. "C'mon, man, don't get all bent. You know how I do. I'm always trying to shake people up when I do business with them. It's nothing personal." He put his glass on the table and the bartender immediately came over to refill it. "So tell me what's going on between you and honey dip."

"Who?"

"The long-legged model Lacie brought here to steer my attention away from her. Dawn. I saw you two arguing," he said with a smirk. "I also remember her from the party *you* asked me to have on the fly last month. Does Lacie know that you've been seeing her?"

I cursed silently. He hadn't changed since high school. "Look, man, you just keep your mouth shut, all right? It's none of your business."

"Don't sweat it, man. I won't say anything," he said, taking a sip from his glass. "You're playing with fire, though, man. Dating ol' girl's friend."

I glared at him hard. "Just so you know, Trevor. I'm no punk and I'm more street smart than you'll ever be. So don't try to run a game. I'll try my hand at this business deal that's about to go down, but just be sure that I'm going to be watching every move you make. Got it?"

I got off the barstool and left. As Trevor said, his game play had always been to shake up the person he was doing business with.

But I wasn't the one.

# Chapter 22

# Robert

It wasn't looking good.

Ma had already given me some detail about how bad it looked. But there was no way that I could have been prepared for what I saw. My father had so many tubes hooked up to him and it was only for a moment that I could stand to look at him in that condition.

My father, Reverend Nathaniel R. Payne, pastor of Mount Sinai Baptist Church, along with his many other health complications, had had another small stroke since he'd been in the hospital.

My mother, Ann, took the news hard at first. She'd cried her eyes out after we left the hospital. After we came home, and when she could cry no more, she sighed and said, "Whatever the Lord's will is, will be."

We'd been at the house for only a few minutes. Ma was sitting down in her chair, next to my father's favorite recliner.

"Ma, you gonna be all right?" I asked, kneeling in front of her.

"I'm going to be fine, Robbie," she replied, patting my hand. She took a deep breath and smiled at me fondly. "You were your father's pride and joy. Do you know that?" Not waiting for me to answer she said, "I know you and your father had your differences and that it was hard for him to accept your… lifestyle. But he still loved you, Robbie. Very much."

"He's not gone yet, Ma," I held, trying to sound encouraging.

She looked over to the living room window and shook her head. "No. I've never seen him this bad off. He's gone, Robbie. It's only a matter of time." She started to rise out of the chair and I helped her. "I'm going to start on dinner," she announced with a deep breath.

"Ma, I can do that. You need to rest," I offered.

"No, Robbie. Let me do it. It'll keep my mind occupied."

Though her words were an ominous prediction, deep down I had a feeling she was right.

My father, the man that I'd always looked up to, was probably going to die.

And there was nothing that I could do about it.

# Chapter 23

# Lacie

We were on the airplane heading back to New York.

Tony was sitting next to me with his eyes closed. He seemed tired, reasonably so.

We'd had an early breakfast with Joe, Trevor, and William and two more of his lawyers. After, we went for an aerial ride of the state over the proposed sites for the projects. On one of the sites, the land was miraculously untouched and covered miles of acreage. Trevor had revealed that there had been several severe bidding wars between two major corporations who were eager to embark on projects similar to William and Trevor's.

*"See, I'm telling you. This is a gold mine!" Trevor had stressed. "It's better to grab this opportunity while it's knocking at the door."*

*"What glitters is not always gold," Tony had muttered under his breath.*

*Trevor heard it and scoffed, looking at William. "I thought you said these two were good for looking at your best interest?"*

*"What—" Tony began.*

*Joe stopped him. "Trevor, don't worry, man. They've got their end covered."*

I had looked from Trevor to Tony and shook my head at the growing dissention between them. For the life of me, I didn't know how this deal was going to get through if they continued to go at each other's throats.

The meeting continued with dinner at one of William's favorite restaurants. A few hours later, Tony and I rushed back to the hotel, packed furiously and had barely made it in time for our returning flight.

I looked at Tony, took his hand and gave it a soft squeeze. "You okay?"

Tony opened his eyes slowly with a smile and squeezed my hand in return. "Yeah." He stretched and yawned. "What time is it?"

I looked at my watch. "It's almost ten o'clock."

The pilot announced over the intercom that we'd be landing at LaGuardia in approximately twenty minutes.

"You've been sleeping ever since we got on the plane," I stated.

"Yeah," he said, yawning again. "I'm just a little bushed. Have a lot on my mind, you know."

"What?"

He shrugged and shook his head. "It's not worth mentioning."

I nodded, looking at our interlocking hands briefly. "Listen, I'm concerned about this growing riff brewing between you and Trevor. It's mounting every time you're around each other. Are you going to be able to handle working with him?"

Tony shrugged coolly. "I have no choice, do I? William is pretty much set on this deal and I don't think my concerns are going to dissuade him." He shook his head. "I don't know, Lacie. This is baffling to me. This is unfamiliar territory for William and I'm having trouble understanding why he would want to take such a tremendous risk into something he knows so little about."

"Hey, I wondered the same thing, especially after this morning. But I think that's why William wants us around, because of the risks involved. He trusts our input and judgment and you've known him for a long time. He knows we're going to look out for him. We're just going to have to do our research and get our team working."

He nodded. "You're right."

Studying him, I said, "Tony, tell me something. Are your concerns with Trevor just business or more personal?"

He shifted his head and eyed me dubiously. "He continues to hit on my girl every time I turn around, cracks jokes about me being white and then challenges me to do an impromptu performance at a jazz club just because I'm a 'white boy.' Oh, no, Lacie, it's not personal," he said cynically.

I nodded, digesting what he'd said. "You handled it, though. And I handled him."

"That's the problem. You shouldn't have to," he replied.

The seatbelt sign lit up overhead.

I took a deep breath. "Okay," I said, abruptly removing my hand from his to unbuckle my seatbelt. "Enough said."

The limousine pulled up to my apartment building. I started to get out when the driver came around to open the door, but Tony stopped me and pulled me gently to him and kissed me.

"Hmm," I murmured after the tender kiss. "What was that for?"

"I'm sorry," he replied, taking my hand and kissing it. "I love you."

"And I love you, too."

"Are you mad at me?"

"Is that why you kissed me? Because you thought I was mad?"

"No, I just didn't enjoy the silence all the way over here."

"I didn't either and I'm not mad at you," I said, touching his chin briefly with a small smile. "Listen, let's just go to work tomorrow and concentrate on working to get this project moving. There's a lot to be done."

He nodded. "Deal." He leaned in for another kiss and I responded immediately and ran my hands through his hair. "You sure you want to go home tonight? My waterbed is nice and warm," he suggested softly after a heated moment.

I chuckled. "No, it's already late. We both need our sleep and we won't get any at your apartment."

"Good point," he chuckled with a nod and took my hand and kissed it again. "Listen, there's this wedding that I have to go to next month and I have to play at the reception. I'd like for you to come with me."

"Who's wedding?"

"Remember the Sanders?" he asked.

Remember? How could I forget? Abigail had practically pushed their daughter, Rachel on Tony.

Tony continued. "Their oldest daughter, Lauren, is getting married. Mom reminded me about it a while ago. Also, the next day is my twin niece's birthday and my mom's giving them a big party at their house."

"Tony, I didn't get an invite to either of these events," I stated simply.

"You'll be with me, so it'll be fine." He shrugged.

"It's more complicated than that, Tony. I don't think I'm going to feel comfortable going when I don't know anyone there. And why would I go to a wedding to see Rachel making puppy dog eyes at you?"

His expression was dumbfounded. "When did you start getting concerned about Rachel?"

"When your mom basically pushed the idea of you and her being an item in my face at that dinner, that's when," I stressed. "She doesn't like me, Tony, and she's itching for you and this Rachel to get together."

"I know she wants me to be with Rachel. But you know I love you, so don't worry about that," he assured.

Unconvinced, I shook my head. "Tony, I'm not going to know any of those people at that wedding," I repeated.

He shrugged. "And I probably won't know some of them either. The only reason I'm going is because I was asked to perform." He took a deep breath, seeing my reservations. "Listen, I definitely don't want to go to a wedding alone and as you say, have to deal with Rachel making puppy dog eyes at me either. And since we're already near my home you might as well meet more of my family."

I sighed. Tony still had no clue.

After his mom voiced her objection to me so clearly, I'd decided that I was going to stay away from her; at least until my relationship with Tony had become a bit more established. Yet when I looked into Tony's appealing and hopeful eyes, I couldn't disappoint him. Although I knew how Abigail felt about me, the only rainbow in the cloud was Johnathan, who seemed to be the opposite of his wife. That at least, gave me another reason to go.

I sighed decisively and smiled. "I'll go."

He lit up instantly and cupped his hands around my face and kissed me. It had to be at least a good three minutes that we sat there kissing in the limousine with the driver still holding the door wide open.

Finally, coming up for air, I said, "Now...can I go?"

Tony laughed as he climbed over me to get to the sidewalk. He took my hand and helped me out and took my suitcase from the driver.

"I really thought you were going to say no," Tony said while the elevator climbed to my floor.

"I did, too," I said, shaking my head. "But it's a month away and at least that'll give me some time to prepare."

"You won't have to prepare for anything," Tony said confidently, kissing my hand. "But hey, I want you to know that this means a lot to me."

"I know and that's why I decided to go."

The elevator door opened and instantly Tony and I looked at each other and frowned at what sounded like shouting coming from my apartment.

"Here, hold this," I said, handing Tony my purse as I fiddled with my key chain to pick out the key to open the door.

I didn't need to. The door swung open suddenly and Mama stood on the other side of the threshold with an irate expression.

"Well, I was wondering when you were coming home!" she yelled. "Look who just decided to drop by unannounced."

I was shocked by her anger, totally unaware of the source. The question in my mind was answered once Mama stepped aside and I walked into my apartment. Standing in the middle of the living room was my handsome, slender, six foot-three, salt and pepper, temple haired, father, Mason Adams.

Mama was saying something but my trance tuned her out.

Aware of my apparent shock, Daddy spoke first and opened his arms. "Well, is my only daughter going to welcome her father with a hug?"

I smiled. He had always been a smooth talker. I rushed into his arms without delay and was enveloped in that memorable daddy smell that I'd loved so much when I was a child.

"Hi, Daddy," I mumbled in his shirt.

"Ah...now that's my girl," he chuckled with delight, embracing me tightly.

"What the *hell* is going on?" I heard Mama yell again.

∞⟩⟨∞

From the corner of my eye, I saw Mama close the door after Tony came in and walk up to us with her arms folded. She cleared her throat and demanded, "Ah, excuse me. I hate to interrupt this touching moment, but there are other people here also and as I just said, what the hell is going on here?"

Filled with emotion and happy tears, I couldn't answer her question right then. I searched my Dad's face after we ended our embrace.

"Daddy, what are you doing here? I thought you wouldn't be here until next weekend."

He didn't have a chance to answer.

"Oh, so you knew about this?" Josephine asked, looking at both of us crossly.

I took a deep breath and looked at Mama. "Yeah, Mama. I knew."

"So when were you going to tell me?"

"I was waiting for the right time and I almost told you when we were at the Bridal Shop–"

She wasn't buying that excuse. "Right. And all you had to do was open your mouth and say, 'Mama, Daddy's coming.'"

"Mama," I struggled and closed my eyes for a second. I opened them and looked at Daddy and held out my arms. "See, I knew she was going to act like this."

Daddy wasn't listening. He was staring at Tony with a puzzled expression. "Uh…Lacie, who's this white boy with you?"

I saw Tony grimace at first, but then he smiled. With enormous respect, he walked up to us and extended his hand to Daddy. "I'm pleased to meet you, sir. I'm Anthony Douglas."

"Uh…he's my boyfriend, Daddy," I said, grabbing Tony's hand, while Daddy took the other.

"Uh…huh," Daddy uttered slowly, shaking Tony's hand firmly as he took in what I'd said. "Nice to meet you, too."

"All right," Mama interjected sharply. "Now that the formalities are out of the way, let's get to the real matter at hand." She pointed at Daddy. "Why is *he* here and where is he staying?"

"Daddy's just here for a visit. He called me a while ago and said he wanted to see me and…." I took another deep breath and stated, "he's staying here with us, Mama."

Mama's eyes widened. "The hell he is!" she burst out, shaking her head angrily. "Lacie, you can't expect me to go along with this. Not after you've sprung this on me."

"Are you intimidated, Josephine? You scared, Lacie…" Daddy started suddenly.

Mama turned to him sharply and raked him over with blazing eyes. "Don't bet on it, Mason," she interrupted in an acidic tone. "*Don't* go there."

The friction between my mother and father was disturbingly suffocating as they faced each other with equal determination. Mono y Mono.

Suddenly the front door sprang open and all of us turned toward the door. There stood a visibly upset and tear dripping Reneé.

"Lacie!" she cried hysterically. "Danny broke up with me. He says he doesn't want to get married and now the wedding is off!"

I had little time to react or say anything when Reneé ran over to me. She pushed Tony away with her body and almost knocked me over when she grabbed me and cried in my arms.

"Please! Can we *not* go through any more drama today?" Mama burst out with a frown as she shook her head and stomped toward the kitchen.

# Chapter 24

# Tony

It had to be a full moon.

Lacie looked as if she was going to crumble as she continued holding Reneé, who was sobbing uncontrollably.

I took the few steps over to her and whispered, "Lacie, you want me to go in there and talk to Josephine?" Lacie only shook her head and swallowed as tears ran down her cheeks. I brushed her tears away with one hand and nodded with a sigh. "Okay, how about if your dad stays with me tonight instead or whenever you get things worked out over here? Is that okay with you?" She glanced over at Mason who was now sitting down quietly. He nodded in compliance and she did the same. "All right, babe," I said softly, kissing her on the forehead. "I'm going to go. If you need me, don't hesitate to call."

ॐ

Mason's scrutinizing eyes had been on me ever since we got in the limousine. We stopped at a traffic light and I gave him a quick look.

"You're surprised that your daughter's dating a white guy, aren't you?" I asked directly.

After a good moment of silence, with steady scrutinizing eyes, he suddenly broke out in a soft chuckle, before turning to the window. "No, son. Life just has a funny way of repeating itself. That's all."

I tilted my head to the side, returned the same scrutinizing gaze, and wondered what he meant.

ЅᗝᏟᎡ

Mason was taking a good look around my apartment as I led him to the spare bedroom.

"This is nice, Anthony."

"Thank you, sir," I replied with a grunt, placing his suitcase on the bed. "And you can call me Tony. Everyone else does."

He nodded in compliance, sat on his bed and looked at me with a little less scrutiny this time. "That was a good thing you did—offering your home to me—with all of that turmoil at my daughter's house. Thank you."

"No problem, sir."

We eyed each other uncomfortably for a moment before he spoke. "Are you in love with my daughter, Tony?" he asked suddenly.

I nodded. "Yes, sir."

"And you won't hurt her, right?"

"No, sir," I declared.

"Good. That's all I needed to hear," he said with a satisfied nod. "We won't have any problems as long as you keep your word."

It was a short conversation but with a lot of meaning behind it. It was also the easiest interview that I'd ever had.

Mason Adams was definitely cool.

After leaving Mason's room, I went to the living room to wind down after all of the events of the day. I waited about an hour or so before I called Lacie to check on how things were at the house. She was still consoling Reneé in her room and said that Mama had barely said a word to her before she'd gone to bed in the guest room downstairs. I asked her if she wanted to take tomorrow off but she declined because of all of the work that needed to be done and said she'd explain everything to me in detail once she came to work.

Between her father's surprising arrival, met with Josephine's obvious anger and Reneé's outburst, Lacie was going through a lot in one night. Then again, everyone seemed to be going through a lot.

I'd come close to punching Trevor in the jaw, several times. Dude never stopped jabbing me with cheap vocal shots and his eyes continued to wander all over Lacie. Though I'd told Lacie I'd be able to deal with Trevor professionally, I seriously wondered if I could deal with his arrogance throughout this whole deal. It was clear that this venture would take several months before it went through and honestly, I didn't know if I could hang.

It wasn't Joe's day, either. While we went out scouting the locations for the projects, he seemed oddly aggravated throughout the day and was unusually quiet considering he was one of the potential investors. During one of the discussions on the size of the properties, he surprised me by getting curt with Trevor. He'd been that way ever since last night at the Jazz Club, and when he'd ordered a strong drink at the bar, my antenna went up.

Thinking back to what happened at the Jazz Club, I finally pulled him aside while we walked on one of the properties and questioned him.

"What's up with you, man?" I asked. "You've been uptight all morning."

With a nonchalant shrug and a slightly dazed expression, Joe replied, "Nothin' man. Just got a lot on my mind. That's all. Don't sweat it."

"You want to talk about it?"

He shook head his and shoved his hands deep into his pockets—a clear giveaway that he was stressing over a woman. It was his signature mark. He'd done it many times when we were in college.

I smirked. "Had a fight with your girl?"

Trevor came up to us and said loudly, "Yo', Joe, man... what was ol' girl's name again? You know, Lacie's friend?"

Joe frowned. "Dawn."

Trevor grinned. "Yeah, man, she is one hot one! Man, you've got to talk Lacie into giving me that girl's number. But first, William and Lacie want you two to look at something."

*It was odd to see Joe grimace, take his fist out his pants and then put them back in.*

*"All right, give us a minute, Trevor," I said immediately.*

*Trevor grinned wider and gave me a fleeting look before we watched him catch up with William, Lacie and the others.*

*"Man, what is with that dude? He's been on me all day and now he's got you riled up. What's up with that? I thought you two were cool?"*

*Joe shook his head. "Don't worry about that, all right? And I told you, we ain't that cool."*

*"But..."*

*"Look, just drop it, all right?" Joe interrupted sharply. He looked at me momentarily and then scoffed. "And why are you so surprised by him tripping on you, Tony? What do you expect? Brothas just can't stand seeing white men with their black women."*

*"But why? I see a whole lot of brothas with white women and I don't get offended by it."*

*"It ain't the same, man. You know that. White men have been taking our women and been doing everything imaginable to them since we were brought to America. Regardless of your good intentions, seeing that burns, man. You can't compare the two."*

*"Oh, so I've got to pay for what happened over four hundred years ago?"*

*"No, you ain't got to pay. You just got to deal with it, that's all." He shrugged. "You ain't never gonna get that brotha's acceptance, just because of your skin color and especially because you've got a sista as fine as Lacie on your arm. That's just the way it is," he repeated. "To him, you're always gonna be the white boy," he claimed, before walking away to join the rest.*

*I was always gonna be the white boy.*

That stung. Hearing it from Joe stung even more. It wasn't so much that he said it himself, it was when he'd said it and the circumstances involved, right after Trevor had mentioned Dawn.

Naw, something was up.

# Chapter 25

# Lacie

I woke up the next morning emotionally and physically exhausted.

I'd stayed up a good remainder of the night trying to comfort Reneé while she cried her eyes out over Danny until finally she went to sleep. Adding to that conflict was Mama's behavior. She was so mad over Daddy's surprise visit that she hadn't even bothered to check on Reneé before she went to bed and I didn't appreciate that.

I was also upset with Danny for treating Reneé the way he did. I was definitely going to have words with him.

Mama was flipping pancakes when I came in the kitchen for a quick cup of coffee before I left for work. While I poured coffee in my mug, she came up close to me and started.

"You know you're wrong, don't you? Not telling me that Mason was coming. What is wrong with you, surprising me like that?" she whispered anxiously.

"Mama, he surprised me as well. He wasn't supposed to…"

She nodded her head insistently with an accusing glare. "See there. You can't even finish the sentence because you know you're wrong."

I rolled my eyes upward. "Mama, please, not this early. I stayed up all night consoling Reneé, which is what you really should have done."

"I checked on her an hour ago and she's still asleep. I was too mad at you to deal with her last night."

"What for, Mama? He's my father."

She inhaled. "Lacie, you haven't seen that man in almost two years and he's been in and out of your life ever since you were born. Now all of a sudden he wants to play daddy and come here and stay with you. In this apartment, nonetheless!" she stressed.

"Mama, what is with you?" I said in exasperation. "What is so bad about him staying here?"

Mama shook her head vehemently. "I do not want him to stay here!"

I suddenly noticed little beads of sweat running down both sides of her temple and the rapid sound of her breathing. The nervous energy coming from her immediately piqued my curiosity because it was totally unlike her.

"Mama, is there something that you need to tell me?"

Caught off guard by my direct question, Mama took a hasty step backward and looked away. "There's nothing that you need to know. I just don't want him here, that's all." she replied.

I wasn't taking her word for it. She was definitely holding something back. "That's the only reason that you can give?" She nodded and I sighed. "Fine. But Mama, Daddy will be staying here. Just you not wanting him here is not enough of a reason for me."

After a small sip of my coffee, I poured out the rest and left the apartment, ticked and disappointed. Danny had broken up with Reneé, leaving her a nervous wreck, Daddy had come home and now Mama was hiding something from me. In addition, I had the displeasure of waiting a painful four weeks before I had to deal with Tony's mom.

And I was not looking forward to it.

Tony walked into my office five minutes after I'd flopped down tiredly in my chair.

"Good morning," he said.

"Good morning," I replied softly. He walked over and greeted me with a tender kiss. "How did everything go with Daddy?" I asked after the kiss.

He leaned against my desk with one leg and shrugged. "Fine. He had no problem making himself comfortable. This morning I ordered up some breakfast for him before I left."

"That was sweet." I smiled thankfully. "Listen, I appreciate you letting him stay over your house for the night."

"Hey, I was glad to do it," he replied. "How are Reneé and Josephine?"

I sighed and ran a hand through my hair and told him what happened after he and Daddy had left.

"Lacie, if your mother is that upset about your dad staying with you, he can stay with me," Tony offered after.

I shook my head. "No, Tony. That's not the solution. Mama's hiding something from me and I know it's got to do with Daddy."

"What?"

I shrugged. "I don't know."

He looked at me intently. "You sure you don't want to go back home?"

"No, I'm fine. I just have to get ready for all of the repair work that I have to do. That's all," I replied, giving him a small smile. He continued to look at me, unconvinced. "Will you stop staring at me? I'm all right."

"Okay, then," he said with a sigh and looked at his watch. "We have a meeting with Richard in a couple of minutes and it's probably going to be a long one. He was really excited about this venture with Mr. Carr, so we're in for a busy day. I'm going to gather up the rest of the team and meet you in the conference room." He leaned over, gave me another kiss and looked at me tenderly. "I love you and it's going to be okay."

"Thank you and I love you, too."

"That's my girl." He smiled. "I'll see you shortly."

Carrie came in with a cup of coffee right after Tony left. "I thought you might need this," she offered, placing it on my desk.

I gave her a weak smile. "I do need it. Thank you."

"Are you okay?" Carrie asked, peering at me. "This weekend must have been quite eventful because you look as if you haven't had any sleep."

"I haven't," I yawned, leaning back in my chair. "And yes, the weekend was eventful, to say the least." Carrie was still eyeing me.

"I'll tell you about it later. Right now, we've got a meeting to attend so let's get ready because as Tony just told me, it looks like we're about to become really busy."

Tony was right. Busy wasn't the word and the game was on. All of the details Tony had relayed to Richard about the development deal had strongly appealed to him and as a result, he didn't want the understudy team involved. Because of the seriousness of the deal, he wanted Tony and I directly involved with all of the research on the potential investors and their history. This meant many hours of investigation, phone calls, reports, statistics and correspondence that was needed to make sure that this was indeed lucrative. Mr. Carr and everyone involved were arriving Wednesday morning and Richard wanted us ready.

We were working under a demanding schedule—making calls, faxing information back and forth—and by the end of the day everyone seemed a bit wore out. After work, Tony and I picked up Daddy from his apartment and took him to mine. I'd been bracing myself for a big argument with Mama, but was surprised when we approached my apartment door and heard commotion on the other side of the door.

Hastily, I opened the door and saw Reneé and Danny in a heated argument. Daddy, Tony and I stood there momentarily, completely surprised by the scene at hand.

"Danny, do you know how much trouble I had to go through to even consider having this baby and now you want to break up with me because you're feeling a lot of pressure? And right before our wedding and Valentine's day, too!" Reneé shouted at Danny as they stood in the middle of the living room, face to face.

"Look, I said that I'd help you support the baby. But I just don't want to get married right now," Danny contended strongly. "I don't want to be tied down."

"Tied down? Tied down?" Reneé yelled with rage. "*This*," she argued, pointing to her protruding belly, "is being tied down, Danny!"

There was nothing like a woman scorned and Reneé's face showed every side of it as she glared at Danny. In a flash, her face changed from rage to a venomous blank stare. Recognizing the signs, I rushed to get in between them but was too late to stop the swift, thunderous and very hard slap that Reneé delivered to Danny's face.

Tony had reached them the same time I did and we got in between them. Tony pushed Danny away, who was now rubbing his face that had Reneé's hand imprint.

"You punk!" Reneé screamed through spiteful tears. She took off her engagement ring and threw it at Danny. "Get out! You hear? Get out!"

"Reneé, c'mon now. Get yourself together," I said, trying to soothe her. "Tony, take Danny in the hallway so that I can calm her down, please."

Tony was already a step ahead of me as he pushed Danny out the door and Daddy closed it behind him. Reneé flopped onto the sofa in hysterical sobs and I calmly picked the ring up off the floor.

Mama burst into the apartment then, looking anxious. "What's going on? I just saw Tony and your dad in the hallway holding Danny from coming back in here."

I pointed to Reneé. "Mama, just sit with her. I'm going outside to talk to Danny," I instructed.

Daddy came in. "Uh…I'm going with Tony to take Danny home," he said, eyeing Reneé uncomfortably, who was now blowing her nose. "Is she going to be okay?" he asked.

"She's going to be okay, Mason. Thank you for asking," Mama answered, glancing at Daddy fleetingly.

"Uh…you're welcome, Josephine," Daddy replied, looking at her slightly baffled. "I'm glad I was here."

"Daddy, I'll go out with you. I want to talk to Danny. Mama, I'll be back."

Tony was trying to calm down a pacing Danny when we joined them in the hallway. "Just take it easy, man. Reneé is upset, that's all," Tony was saying to Danny.

"And she had every right to be," I added sternly. "Danny, why did you come? You know she's already had difficulties with her pregnancy and upsetting her would only make things worse."

"She's the one that slapped me," Danny defended. "I just came here to talk with her calmly about the arrangements for the baby and everything and she started yelling at me."

"And you know why, don't you? Because she's hurt. She put her trust in you and you *emotionally* slapped her in the face. So don't get self-righteous on me, here," I asserted. "It was only just yesterday that she ran into my apartment crying and telling me that you wanted out of the wedding. You picked the wrong day to come and talk about arrangements, Danny."

"So how are we going to work this out?" Danny asked.

"I don't know." I shrugged. "That…is between you and her, Danny. You two are going to have to talk about it together but not today. Just give her a few days—maybe even a week—she's too emotional right now."

"She's right, man. Just let everything cool off," Tony added. "C'mon, Mason and I will take you home," he said, guiding Danny toward the elevator with a light hand on his back.

"Danny, before you get on that elevator let me ask you this question," I said, taking a step toward the elevator with them. "*Is* there another girl in the picture?"

Danny averted his eyes from me in answer.

I shook my head sadly. Reneé's intuition had been right all along.

"Let me explain…" he started.

I sighed tiredly. "Danny, right now I'm not in the mood for your explanation," I asserted crisply, placing the ring in his hand as the elevator door opened. "Just give Reneé about a week and then contact her."

I turned around to walk into my apartment and closed the door. It was disturbing to witness what was probably the end of Reneé and Danny's relationship. I'd really hoped that it was going to work out for Reneé considering that she was the third case of teenage pregnancy in my family.

In one day, Reneé's life had switched from being engaged, to a now sad and alarming statistic: a black, pregnant, unwed, teenage mother.

It was incomprehensible.

# Chapter 26

# Dawn

Joe was smoking.

He'd left several messages on my answering machine asking me to call him back. He was going to wait for a long time. He'd gotten one strike against him and I wasn't going to wait for the second. I'd been burned too many times to go through any more foolishness; let alone with him. So whenever the phone rang and the caller I.D. displayed his number, I'd let it ring. Let him feel what it was like to get played. I didn't know why I thought he would be different with me in the first place.

Sunday, I picked Mom up from the airport and took her around town. After a few hours of shopping, I took her out to lunch. Being with my mother was a nice distraction from all the turmoil that was going on in my head. The plan was to spend time with her and stay busy to keep my mind off of Joe. I intended on succeeding, too.

We'd gotten off the elevator and were busy talking as we walked down the hallway toward my apartment when my mother stopped short.

"What? Why did you..." I started. Then I looked down the hallway.

Joe was standing in front of my apartment door with an armload of the most beautiful colored roses I'd ever seen. I sighed deeply and shook my head. Didn't he know when to give up? I could feel my mother's inquisitive eyes on me, but didn't look her way. I was already ashamed that she'd found out—or at least had an idea of what was going on.

We continued toward the apartment and when we got closer, Joe said awkwardly, "Hello, Ms. Robinson. Hello, Dawn," as he stepped aside.

"Hello, Joe," Mom replied softly, ogling him intently. "It's interesting to see you here," she added. Then she turned to me with the same intense look. "Dawn, I'm quite tired. Can you open the door so that I can get settled in?"

"Sure, Mom," I said, unlocking the door with my key and opening it. "Just take a right as soon as you pass the kitchen. Your room is second on the left and the bathroom is directly across from it."

Mom nodded and walked into the apartment. "Don't take too long, now. You hear? You've got an early photo shoot tomorrow," she said before she closed the door.

Heated, I turned around to face Joe. "I can't believe you pulled something like this! I mean, this is ridiculous. This is on the borderline of being a stalker, Joe," I whispered anxiously.

"That's not my style. I don't have to stalk a woman to get a woman," he shot back.

"Why did you come here, Joe? My mom is here!"

"Hey, I didn't know your mom was coming. If you would have answered your phone then I wouldn't have come," he retorted. "Why haven't you returned my calls, Dawn?"

I sighed. "Joe, look, we're through. I've had a good time with you and everything, but I can't see you anymore."

"If you've enjoyed the time we've spent together why do you want it to end?"

"Because that's the way it's got to be," I maintained, avoiding his piercing stare.

He moved his head so he could look into my eyes. "That's it? You're not going to explain why you stood me up and then surprised me by coming to the jazz club with a chip on your shoulder? What's up with you?"

I'd had it. Here he was giving me the third degree and he was the one that wasn't being honest.

"Joe, why do you even care? You've been taking advantage of me and stringing me along ever since New Year's Eve. You're not interested in me. You're still in love with Lacie."

There, I'd said it. I'd been through too many guessing games with men. At least this time, I knew what was up before my emotions got anymore involved.

He nodded thoughtfully with dark brown eyes piercing into mine. "What? You think I'm trying to use you or something?"

"Tell me I'm wrong," I challenged confidently.

"And you think I'm still in love with Lacie, too," he stated, twitching his lips.

"You told her you'd never get over her, Joe. So don't act like you don't remember saying it."

"Oh, no. I said it, all right," he confirmed automatically, nodding his head quickly.

My heart sunk and I closed my eyes. "See. I knew it," I murmured softly.

I heard his footsteps move toward me and felt him touch my chin with his fingers.

"But I never said, I'd *always* be in love with her," he expressed with soft conviction. "I'm not in love with her anymore, Dawn. I'm falling in love with you."

I opened my eyes immediately to those words. Granted, they were sappy, but I'd already fallen for them.

"Joe, don't try to play me, all right," I continued, swallowing and trying to contain some dignity, while he rubbed my chin lightly with those magnificent hands of his. "You were only just engaged to Lacie about two or three months ago."

"Yes, but I have to move on with my life, Dawn. It's insane to continue loving someone when they're in love with someone else."

"But why me?"

"Why not you? Do you think so little of yourself that you believe you don't deserve someone that will finally treat you better than those fools before me?"

"You could have easily pursued someone else and not your ex-fiancée's best friend, Joe," I pointed out.

He sighed. "I know and believe me; I wrestled with that decision after our first date. But we just hit it off so well, Dawn. I mean, you're real, you know. You don't play games and I like that about you."

"And you're not playing games?"

His expression was serious. "No. I wasn't raised that way. I wouldn't have spent so much time with you if I were."

Our eyes locked intensely for an indefinite amount of time until he slowly lowered his head and brushed his lips against mine. With sheer smoothness and sweetness of honey, our kiss deepened when he dove his tongue into my awaiting mouth.

After a brief second, I jerked my head to the side and he buried his face in my neck. He slowly lifted his head and nodded, comprehending.

I glanced at Joe fleetingly as he looked down the hallway and took a deep breath.

"All right," he said. He looked at the roses in his hand and then handed them to me. "These…are for you."

"Thank you," I murmured.

"You're welcome," Joe said with a nod, still looking at the roses. "Dawn, listen, I know you've been through a lot and given the situation, you might find it hard to trust me or at least my motives, anyway. But understand this; I'm not a player. When I'm serious about something, you can believe it's real. And I'm serious about you. Take care of yourself, Dawn."

He planted one last kiss on my cheek before he turned around and walked down the hallway. He never looked back.

With a heavy sigh, I entered my apartment and headed toward the kitchen to find a vase to put the roses in. My back was toward the entrance when I heard Mom enter the kitchen. Ashamed, I avoided looking her way and said nothing while I continued arranging the roses in the vase. I braced myself for what was going to come next. Mom was a devout Christian, which meant that in any second, I was in for a sermon.

"How long have you and Joe been seeing each other?" she asked softly.

"We haven't been really seeing…" I started. Then I stopped and looked down for a second and took a deep breath. Who was I kidding? I was already lying to myself. Was I going to lie to my mother as well? I turned around and looked at her. "Since

New Year's Eve," I admitted and added quickly, "but I stopped seeing him."

It was a vain attempt because Mom saw right through the weak statement.

"But you're contemplating starting it up again. And let me guess, Lacie doesn't know," Mom assumed perceptively, shaking her head. "Dawn, you're asking for trouble, baby. Dating your–"

"I know, Mom," I said meekly.

"Then why are you doing it, Dawn? Why Joe when there are so many other men out there?"

*Very good question, Mom.*

"I don't know," I answered, voice breaking. "All of this just sort of…happened. I mean, I wasn't looking for this," I cried suddenly, putting my head into my hands.

"What were you looking for, then? You don't just *happen* to start seeing your best friend's ex-fiancé, Dawn." She sighed. "You know very well that you reap what you sow and if you play with fire, you're gonna get burned. You and Lacie have known each other since you were kids. You don't mess around with men that your best friend's been involved with," she voiced softly.

I lifted my head. "It's not what you think, Mom. He happened to be at the same New Year's Eve party that I was and he asked me out. Then it progressed from there…" I attempted, grasping for another futile excuse.

"Dawn, this is February…" she trailed off suggestively.

I hung my head again as tears started to trickle down. There wasn't much more to say after that and surely no way to justify what I was doing—or had done for that matter.

For a good moment, I felt Mom's eyes bearing down on me before she asked me the question that I didn't want her to know or admit to myself.

"Are you in love with him?" Teary-eyed, I looked up at her and nodded. She inhaled. "How does he feel about you?"

With a sniffle, I replied. "He says that he's falling in love with me."

"And you believe him," she said with a shake of her head. "If he is truly in love with you, Dawn, why would he risk putting you in this kind of position given your friendship with Lacie? What makes you think he's not using you?"

"Because he said it," I said simply.

Yeah, it sounds stupid to me too, Mom, I answered silently to her cynical stare.

"Is that enough for you?" she asked, resignedly.

I replied with a nod. My mind had been made up once Joe had said he was falling in love with me. There was no question. Seeing Joe and hearing him declare his love for me had stirred up a lot of emotions that I'd promised to bury for the sake of my friendship with Lacie. But the roses and the sincerity in his words only a few minutes ago was the defining moment for which I knew there was no turning back.

And I was going to hurt Lacie in the process.

Mom gave me a final nod. "Okay. Then you need to tell Lacie, Dawn. She needs to know," she said softly.

Her words hung in the air when she left the kitchen. She'd told me what I'd already known and what needed to be done. There was no question that I had to tell Lacie.

But how was I going to do it?

How could I tell her?

# Chapter 27

# Joe

There was nothing more aggravating than dealing with a woman.

I was temperamental and sulky at work and my employees were getting the brunt of it. Two days had gone by without me hearing a word from Dawn. She hadn't called me and I hadn't called her. After our last meeting, I'd decided that the next move was going to be hers. I had sucked it up and brought her all of those roses, and when she turned me down, I felt even more of a sucker. I'd laid out all of my feelings on the table and for what? Nothing. Not even a phone call. So I was done. I wasn't going to pursue her anymore.

Now granted, she did have a good reason to doubt any word that came out of my mouth after what Lacie had told her and because of my history with Lacie. But c'mon, I was a good catch. I had a thick, black, phone book filled with numbers of girls eagerly waiting for me to pick up the phone that I could call at any minute. But for some insane reason, I wanted Dawn. Even worse, was that I had fallen in love with her and was suffering from it because of her friendship with Lacie.

I was really getting tired of falling in love with the wrong women. I should have listened to the white figure on my shoulder when I had the chance.

As for business, Trevor was a snake.

If it wasn't for the huge potential of this deal, his jaw would be dislocated by now. Since he'd decided to open his big mouth and almost tip Tony on me and Dawn, I decided to get some of my people to do a little digging on the new project at hand. I didn't want to invest in anything shady and thus risk my reputation and business. Plus, if anything shady was found then that would substantiate me giving him a beat down. It was both personal and business. Fortunately, on his behalf, my sources found nothing shady about the deal, the land or the club. Everything was legit.

So it looked like I was going to go into business with Trevor. But my feelings about it were not good.

The intercom buzzed.

I pressed the speaker button. "Yes?"

"Mr. Mitchell, there's a young lady to see you. A Miss Robinson, sir?" Mrs. Henderson, my secretary announced on the intercom.

Ms. Robinson...Dawn. This was out of the blue. I sat thinking for a few seconds while holding the button. What was up with the untimely visit? Was she going to lay me out again?

"Sir, do you want me to let her in?" Mrs. Henderson asked.

"Sure, sure, let her in," I said, deciding quickly. "Also, Mrs. Henderson, be sure to hold all calls for now, please."

"Yes, sir," she replied.

A second later, Dawn walked in hesitantly, stopping at the threshold. She looked too good. I gulped, giving her a thorough exam with my eyes.

"Hey," she said softly.

"Hey," I returned, standing. "Come in and close the door."

When she turned around and closed the door, I caught a glimpse of her nice rear end. I gulped again.

*Stop it, Joe. Keep your cool, Bro.*

Dawn turned around and eyed me warily. "How are you?"

I gave her a casual nod. "I'm fine. You?"

She shrugged, still eyeing me. "The same," she said.

"Good," I said, jabbing my hands deeply into my pockets. "I'm surprised to see you."

Dawn nodded. "I know." Without warning, she took purposeful steps toward me, put her arms around my neck and kissed me hungrily.

We stood there with arms and lips on each other for a hot minute, before she stopped abruptly and stared directly into my eyes.

"Just so you know, Joe. My friendship with Lacie might end because of what I'm doing. I'm letting you know now, that I'm not for games. The second you try to pull some mess on me, I'm out. Understand?"

"Yes, Ma'am," I replied with a smile and then kissed her how I'd wanted to when she'd first walked into my office.

# Chapter 28

# Lacie

It was remarkable how tragedy always seemed to bring people together.

That big blow up between Reneé and Danny had bizarrely and thankfully distracted my mother's attention from my father staying with us, toward Reneé. The transition had gone pretty smooth and my mother was surprisingly kind enough to show my father where the spare bedroom was when he brought his bags into the apartment.

Although my parents had been cordial toward each other for the past three days, it was bittersweet, because Reneé had been a complete wreck. For two days, she hadn't bothered going to school and had stayed in her room. Mama had called me several times at work upset because she'd been trying to get Reneé out of her slump, to no avail. I was concerned about Reneé too, but told Mama that we'd have to give Reneé some time to heal. After all, she had a lot to think about and had been wounded by the punch that Danny had dealt her.

At work, Tony, the rest of the team and I had about finished getting everything ready for the meeting. I was elated because many man-hours had been devoted for this deal and fatigue was showing on everyone's face. Mine included. It was such a relief to be done by Tuesday and know that we were fully prepared for the next day's meeting.

Wednesday morning, Mr. Carr, Trevor, Joe and the rest of the entourage came into the office early, prepared to do business. After an amazing slide presentation, reports, negotiations and breaks in between, the deal was in motion by the end of the workday and all parties were ecstatic.

Richard and William invited everyone out to eat and to celebrate. Apparently reservations had been made ahead of time because there was already a large portion of the restaurant sectioned off for us, with an exclusive buffet and bar.

I was getting some food from the buffet when Trevor came up next to me with plate in hand.

"I just have one thing to ask you; did I come through or did I come through?" he asked, reaching for shrimp and putting some onto his plate.

I glanced at him quickly. "I never said you wouldn't."

"No, but your boyfriend over there doubted," he declared, motioning with his head toward Tony and Joe who were sitting at the bar. "He's been shooting this project down ever since I proposed it."

With a nonchalant shrug, I replied, "He just had his reservations. That's all."

"You sure about that?" Trevor asked, stopping to look at me. "You sure he's not feeling threatened?"

"By who?" I asked.

"By me, of course," he replied easily. "I'm successful, rich, and I came up with a project that's going to make this company more money that it ever dreamed. That makes for good competition. Oh yeah, I'm also after his woman."

I ignored his last statement. "You know, you are extremely self-absorbed, Trevor. Tony had no reason to be threatened by you," I said.

"Really?" he asked with slight sarcasm. "Listen, I've seen it and been through it a million times. White folks—especially white men—hate to see black men with the upper hand or with any kind of power."

To entertain him, I queried, "What about Joe? They're friends and he's not giving him any grief."

"Hey, Whitey's always gotta have his token."

"What!" I exclaimed a little too loudly, plate almost falling from my hands. He'd insulted Tony and Joe at the same time. Oh, he was such an imbecile!

From nowhere Carrie came to my rescue and took the plate from me. "Girl, watch it. You're gonna spill all of this food."

Trevor looked at Carrie briefly and walked away with a smirk.

Carrie and I stared at his retreating figure and shook our heads.

"He's just trying to push your buttons, girl. Don't let him get to you," Carrie soothed, handing my plate back to me. She started filling hers and added, "Especially since Richard just offered him the empty office next to yours."

"What!"

"Yep," Carrie confirmed with a definitive nod. "Joe's not the only one that's setting up temporary office in this department."

Damn!

# Chapter 29

# Tony

Trevor was at it again.

I observed Trevor slithering up to Lacie at the buffet line while Joe and I sat at the bar waiting for our drinks. I was tempted to go over there, but not wanting to look like the jealous boyfriend, changed my mind.

"Don't pay any attention to that fool, Tony," Joe remarked. "Lacie can handle herself."

"It's not easy, Joe. I know he's after her," I said.

"Can you blame him? Lacie's got them hips and luscious full lips and magnificent a–" Joe teased.

"Hey, man, you're talking about my lady," I interrupted, putting on a fake frown.

Joe chuckled. "Listen, Tony, all I'm saying is that you can't expect him not to try to challenge your relationship with Lacie. I already told you how brothas feel about white men being with black women. It's insulting." The bartender brought over our drinks and he took a swallow. He put his glass down and offered, "But look, you know I'm setting up a temporary office next to Trevor's, so I've got your back. I'll be watching him." He gave me a friendly punch on my arm. "Why are you so worried about him, anyway? Lacie loves you, man. Shoot, if anyone should know that it's me." He snickered.

"Yeah, you've got a point," I said, nodding. Relieved that we can now make light of the situation, I gave him a fleeting look before I led into my next question. "So Joe, are we cool or what?"

Joe frowned. "What kind of question is that, man?"

"I don't know." I shrugged. "Last time I saw you, you were in a real crusty mood and you flipped out on me."

He shook his head. "Naw, man, we're cool," he assured. "And look, I'm sorry about what I said to you Sunday. I didn't mean any of it. I was just tripping over a few things and you just caught me at a bad moment."

"I know. Right after Trevor mentioned Dawn," I remarked directly.

Joe shot me a quick, wary glance and laughed nervously. "Naw, man. He'd just said a few things to me after you and Lacie left the club that I didn't appreciate. It just rubbed me the wrong way and I was still ticked about it." He took a straight shot of his drink.

"So are you all right, now?" I asked, watching him closely.

He nodded, taking another shot. "Yeah, I'm straight."

I nodded my head. "I was hoping you were. I've noticed how much cheesing you've been doing ever since you came to the office. You've been quiet, too."

"So what's that supposed to mean?"

"Man, you're never quiet over money and business."

"Hey, I'm just happy," he said shrugging. "Happy to make some more money."

"And happy about that woman you're seeing," I concluded. "So, when am I gonna meet her, man?"

"Man, why do you want to see her so much? Why are you in my personal business all of sudden?" Joe asked.

I hunched up my shoulders. "Man, I'm just asking."

"Well, don't ask anymore, all right? I told you. You'll meet her when you meet her," he said and got off the barstool.

Watching him walk away with one hand holding his drink and the other hand jammed deeply into his pockets, I started getting a sickening feeling that my hunch was right. He was seeing Dawn. Suddenly, I saw Trevor smirking, apparently having witnessed the scene between us.

I glared at him with the unspoken words, "What are you looking at?"

He laughed and proceeded in the same direction as Joe.

I *really* couldn't stand him.

**157**

# Chapter 30

# Lacie

My life was drama filled—professionally and personally.

The two days of the beginning of a tumultuous two weeks alone, was evidence of that. But it didn't prepare me for it.

Trevor was in essence, an arrogant idiot. He was also our temporary partner and with an office next to mine, to my chagrin. Because the project was originally initiated by Trevor, Richard and William assigned him to oversee it along with Tony and myself. Trevor took delight in this appointment and was quite boastful about it. After the first meeting, once the deal was given its nod, Trevor had forewarned Joe, Tony, the rest of the team and I that this project was his idea and his baby. It was going to go through if he had to sell his soul to the devil. His uncompromising stance did not go without delivery, either.

While Trevor was shrewd, knowledgeable and made sure things were done promptly, he was incredibly condescending. He constantly barked orders to his staff and tensions continued to mount between him and Tony because of their constant bickering and prideful, male ego power trip. During one meeting when Trevor, Joe, Tony and I couldn't agree, Trevor played the charge card and said that he would make the final decision because it was his project to start with. Tony was enraged and his face turned red and thunderous. Trevor grinned, enjoying seeing Tony lose his cool.

My working relationship with Trevor wasn't working so well either and I'd get aggravated whenever he was around. Every second that Tony wasn't with me, Trevor would take the opportunity to make subtle snide comments about me and Tony and then flirt with me. Trevor was pretty slick about it, but somehow I felt that Tony had an idea of what was going on because he seemed so uptight. I was in a terrible position with the project going in full force. I didn't want to hinder the progress we were making, but moreover, I didn't want my relationship with Tony to be affected by it. I was feeling a load of pressure, but I wasn't alone.

Stress continued to mount and everyone was becoming short-tempered. Our office had never experienced such an unbelievable amount of discord before. And it was all because of Trevor. When Friday came, it was met with enthusiasm. Everyone was worn out from non-stop work and meetings and looked forward to their weekend so they could get away from the job—and Trevor.

Coming from an adjourned meeting, Tony and I were the first to walk out as everyone started to scatter and leave for the day. But Tony and I couldn't leave. We were due for a private meeting with Joe and Trevor to discuss a few more ideas and present the bids before we left work.

I was getting ready to tell Tony that Mama had invited him over for dinner after work as we headed to his office to get ready for the meeting, when a familiar voice suddenly rang out. Then the body that accompanied it came into view.

"Anthony, dear!" Abigail expressed loudly. She came up to him with open arms and practically pushed me out of the way in the process. As usual, she ignored me.

Bringing up the rear with broad smiles, were Rachel and her mother, Valerie Sanders. I gave them a brief and courteous nod.

"Mom?" Tony expressed with a curious frown and a wave to Rachel and Valerie. After Abigail finally let go of the vice grip around his neck, he asked, "What are you doing in town? I didn't know you were coming."

"Well, that's what surprises are for, Anthony," she answered airily with a little chuckle. In answer to Tony's puzzling expression she explained, "Your dad went away on a business trip and I just decided to come into the city to do some shopping and asked Valerie and Rachel to come along with me. We thought it'd be nice for all of us to go out to dinner."

Instinctively, I knew the plans didn't involve me. And didn't we have dinner with them last week?

"Mom, I'm in the middle of work and Lacie and I have to go to a meeting. I'm afraid I can't go," Tony said apologetically.

Abigail appeared to cringe a little at the sound of my name. Then she frowned. "Nonsense. You can go. I'm sure your boss won't mind if you left just a tad early to spend some time with your mother," she suggested confidently. "Valerie and Rachel wanted to go over a few things with you for the wedding. They came all the way over here to see you, Anthony."

*Dag, was it his wedding?*

Tony shifted uncomfortably and looked at me. I knew he was feeling pressured with Valerie, Rachel and Abigail looking at him expectantly.

"Mom, we're going to have to do it another–" Tony started out gently.

"Anthony, I won't take no for an answer," Abigail said loudly, standing her ground.

I looked around uneasily, conscious that everyone in the department had eyes on us. One of them was Trevor. I sighed. I didn't like what I was about to do, but nonetheless, decided to do it.

I felt Abigail eyes follow me when I put my arm on Tony's lightly. "Tony, go ahead. I'll do the presentation by myself. Spend some time with your mother," I suggested.

He looked at me with a small objective frown. "Lacie, I can't…"

I shook my head. "It's okay, Tony."

Uncertain, he asked, "Are you sure?"

Abigail didn't waste time. "Anthony, Leslie said she could do it herself. Now c'mon, son." With deft, she grabbed a hold of his arm and lured him to his office for his coat. Rachel and Valerie followed, leaving me standing alone.

Certain that eyes were on me, I didn't bother to look up and walked toward my office, suddenly feeling drained. Undoubtedly, Abigail hadn't changed her mind or her promise about me. Hence, the whole dinner ruse with Rachel and her mother. I was a bit irked by her purposeful shunning and slightly envious of Tony going out with them. I knew Abigail was going to use that as an opportunity to steer

Rachel and Tony together. However, I felt my point was made. I wasn't going to play along with Abigail's deliberate schemes. Someone had to be the bigger person.

"I saw what happened," Carrie said, entering my office after a few minutes wearing her coat and purse on her arm.

"Now why doesn't that surprise me?" I asked, giving her a faint smile.

She took a seat in front of my desk and tilted her head to the side. "You okay?"

"Yeah, I'm going to be fine," I replied, trying to sound cheerful. "Hey, Tony and I've been under each ever since we've started this relationship. It's okay if he goes out and spends time with his mother."

Carrie nodded with a sympathetic pout. "Right. And even if she is pushing Blondie his way, she's got nothing on you," she offered.

"It was that obvious to you too, huh?" I chuckled tiredly, running a hand through my hair.

"Very much so," Carrie stated. "But Tony loves you. Don't doubt that."

"Carrie, how am I going to contend with his mother?" I exasperated sullenly. "I mean, did you go through anything like that?"

"Are most black people Democrats?" Carrie bantered with a short chuckle. "Honey, what *didn't* I go through with my husband's mother, is a better question." She shook her head. "Lacie, you did right. Let *her* make a fool of herself. Ignorant people always do."

At that moment, Trevor walked in and took a seat in the chair next to Carrie. "All right, all right, time is precious. Let's get the show on the road," he demanded, snapping his fingers.

Carrie looked at him fleetingly then looked back at me and mouthed, "He's a prime example." I stifled a giggle.

She chuckled aloud and said, "Well, girl, I'd better get going so I can fix dinner and try to rest up from this week's madness. I'll see you later, Lacie." She stood up. "Mmm, hmm, you too, Trevor," she mumbled and walked out.

Trevor watched her retreating figure then looked back at me with a grin. "She doesn't like me, does she?"

"You're really asking me that question?" I asked sarcastically

His grin widened. "That's okay. I bet she'll like that fat check she gets from this deal."

I stared at him blankly. "Is money all you care about?"

"Uh…yeah," he said, with a brief nod and then chuckled at my expression. "Don't act like you don't. You wouldn't be with Whitey if you didn't."

My eyes narrowed at the sharp and deliberate attack. "Excuse me?"

"You gonna tell me that money isn't why you're with Douglas?"

"Do you *ever* think before you speak?" I stressed, gawking at him wondrously for a good moment. I restrained myself from reaching over to slap the grin off of his face. Common sense getting the better of me, I rolled my eyes and said, "Look, let's just not say anything else to each other until Joe comes."

"He's not coming," he said.

"What? Why not?"

"He left for a flight out to Florida," Trevor answered with a mischievous smirk.

I frowned pensively, not understanding the reason for Trevor's smirk. Florida? What was up with that? Joe knew about the meeting.

"So it looks as if it's just us. Shall we begin?"

"Fine," I muttered.

With a reluctant sigh, I gathered all the data Tony and I had and spread them out on my desk for him to view. In a short period, Tony and I had managed to get a list of contractors with their history and their bids. Trevor came over to my side of the desk to look over the documents.

"This is very good. Actually, it's remarkable that you were able to gather all of this information so quickly. You've got a sharp mind, Lacie," he said.

"So I've been told," I replied with a small sigh. I stood up and started to put all of the documents in my briefcase. "Anyway, Tony did a lot of research on the contractors and I just put all of the information together."

I was aware that he was watching me as he stood there for a moment silently.

"You just never quit, do you?" he scoffed suddenly. "It's bad enough that I have to see you two together and in each other's face all the time. Now you want to brag about what he's done."

Shocked by his unexpected statement, I slammed my briefcase closed and turned around swiftly. "What?"

"Why must you always put Whitey in a brotha's face?"

Man, he was constant with the Whitey bit. "Why must you hate on Tony so much?"

He ignored my question and came closer. "Is he really doing you so well that you're willing to be humiliated by his mother? Is he really that good?"

Stunned, I blinked. The conversation had made a complete left-turn and I was speechless by his blunt and crass comment.

He continued. "Didn't what happened just a few minutes ago make you realize that his mother doesn't like you? You shouldn't be going through this, Lacie. You deserve better."

I scoffed and folded my arms. "Oh, really? What?" His only response was a huge grin. I shook my head. "Huh. Not in this lifetime."

"Oh, don't knock it until you try it, now. I'll make you limber," he implied, inching closer.

"Get out of my way, Trevor!" I exclaimed furiously, grabbing my briefcase and brushing past him to get my coat and purse.

With a light chuckle, he asked, "What are you so bent about?"

I turned around heatedly to his amused expression. "Trevor, I am so tired of feeling that I have to justify my relationship with Tony to you. I am tired of having to deal with your snide remarks every time I turn around. And you know what? Basically, I'm just plain tired of you!" I professed vehemently, putting on my coat.

He was unmoved. "So what do you think is going to happen in the real world, Lacie? When he brings you home to his mother, even. Do you think you're going to fit in with his family? That they're going to accept you?" he expressed with sudden and unexpected seriousness. He strolled over to me slowly saying, "Lacie, I'm just telling you like it is.

I noticed the way his mother looked at you and she is not feeling you, girl. Why are you willing to put yourself through that kind of pain when you don't have to?"

"Why do you care?" I shot back.

"Because...I just do," he replied softly.

I stared at him in shock, surprised by his tender expression and what appeared to be sincerity. Without warning, he leaned in to kiss me but I turned my head and moved away from him.

"Uh, Uh. No. We're not going there," I murmured.

With haste, I grabbed my briefcase and purse and walked out. I didn't dare look back.

SOCR

I was moody and guilt ridden on the subway ride home. My row with Trevor had been really unsettling, considering my wounds were still healing from the shunning of Abigail. I hadn't thought twice about my decision to be with Tony since New Year's Eve, but now Abigail's antics and Trevor's constant vocal disapprovals were starting to get unnerving.

Trevor's comments had been quite rude, but in retrospect, they were good points. And that's what bothered me. Even more so, was the move that Trevor had made on me. Nothing had happened but I still felt as if I'd cheated on Tony. My bigger concern was whether to tell Tony. Would I be deceitful if I didn't tell him?

Deceit or not, I couldn't tell him. Trevor and Tony didn't get along as it was. Why pour gasoline on a burning flame?

Mama was in the kitchen fixing dinner when I arrived.

"Hey, Mama," I murmured, entering the kitchen and sitting down at the table.

"Hey, sweetie," she replied in a slightly drained voice. She looked up from the stove. "How was work?"

"Uh," I groaned. "You don't want to know."

"Long day?" I nodded. She looked toward the front door. "Where's Tony?"

"His mother came into town with a few friends, so he went out to dinner with them," I explained, running a hand through my hair tiredly.

"Why didn't you go with them?" Mama asked, turning around to look at me.

"I wasn't invited." She raised an eyebrow so I explained.

Mama shrugged. "Sounds to me like Tony didn't want to go either. Why did you encourage him?"

I sighed. "Because he needed some time with his mother."

"She just saw him last week, Lacie, and she had people with her this time."

"Yes, but that's fine, Mama," I uttered. It was far from fine and from Mama's expression, she knew it, too.

"Umm, hmm," Mama murmured, tilting her head to the side. "So then why the long face?" I didn't say anything. She folded her arms across her chest and gave me a penetrating stare. "You never told me what happened when you and Tony had dinner with his parents, Lacie. How did the white folks treat you and what are they like?"

I sighed and shook my head. She was always going to refer to them as white folks and that gave me enough reason not to tell her. She already didn't like that Abigail had assumed that I was a maid. If I told her how Abigail acted toward me and what she'd said to me in the ladies room, Mama would get upset. I'd also have to hear a whole spiel about white people from her and I didn't have enough energy for that.

I looked toward the entrance of the kitchen and asked casually, "Mama, where's Reneé and Daddy?"

Mama's quizzical gaze was still on me when I turned around. Then she gave a relenting nod. "Okay, I'll let you off this time, but we will continue this conversation. Sure as my name is Josephine, I know something's up. Because you know how I am, I'm assuming that you're not telling me because you don't want me to get mad." I said nothing. "Umm, hmm, that's what I thought," she murmured. She turned back around to the stove and motioned her head toward the kitchen door. "Mason's been out all day and Reneé is upstairs."

I frowned. "Still?"

"Yep," Mama said, backing away from the stove to sit at the other end of the table. "I'm down here cooking because I had to get away from her. I needed some peace of mind." She sighed and ran a hand through her hair, suddenly looking tired. "You're gonna have to talk to Reneé, Lacie. I think she is depressed. She hasn't left her room since that argument with Danny."

"At all?"

Mama shook her head solemnly. "I've tried talking to her. I even tried to get her out of the bed and take a bath but nothing I've said or done has seemed to help."

I suddenly felt bad. "I'm sorry, Mama. I didn't know this was going on. Why didn't you tell me as soon as I came in?"

"Because you looked like you were stressed and needed to talk." She shrugged. "I've spent so much time with her that I've missed out on time with you. Also, you have been very busy."

"I'm sorry, Mama," I apologized again.

"It's your job, Lacie. You've got to do what you've got to do." She threw up her hands helplessly. "I don't know what's wrong with this generation of girls. They get all caught up in guys and wind up forgetting who they are. No man is worth going through that kind of heartache. I learned that the hard way—believe me."

I had a feeling she was talking about Daddy. "Are you and Daddy still getting along okay?"

She gave me a weary smile. "We're not the best friends or anything, but we are dealing with each other."

"Mama, are you going to tell…" I started.

She held up a hand. "Lacie, what happened between your father and I is very painful. For your sake we are getting along and if you want us to continue, we don't need to talk about it. It'll just stir up old memories that I don't want to relive right now." She nodded toward the kitchen door again. "And since you just *conveniently* decided to ask me about your father and me, it's my turn to deliberately change the subject," she said wryly. "Go upstairs and talk to Reneé, okay? I couldn't get through to her. Maybe you can." Mama stood up and walked back over to the stove.

End of discussion.

After three unanswered knocks on Reneé's door, I opened it and was ill prepared for the sight before me. Reneé didn't even bat an eye when I walked in. She was lying on the bed, flipping the channels on the television with the remote. Hair unkempt, watching the television in a coma-like state and with a variety of snacks on the bed, she looked exactly as Mama described her—depressed. What energy I had, drained at the mere sight of her; no wonder Mama had seemed so worn out.

I immediately got annoyed with myself for being so busy and not being able to help Mama with this situation and with Reneé's pity party. What was she doing to herself?

"Uh, uh. I'm putting an end to this," I muttered, walking to the television and turning it off.

Immediately and without a word to me, with the remote, Reneé turned the television back on. In response, I unplugged it from the wall. That got her attention.

Bleak and gloomy eyes finally looked into mine. "Lacie, I don't want to hear any of your inspirational speeches, all right? I just want to be left alone," she pleaded softly.

"I know you do," I said, nodding and walking over to her. "But... unfortunately for you...this is my apartment and *I*...," I stressed emphatically, "am the only one that is allowed to feel sorry for herself. So you, my dear, are going to get out of this bed and take a bath."

"Lacie, I don't need a bath," she objected, inching away from me when I approached the bed and reached for her arm.

"I beg to differ, honey," I muttered, getting a whiff of her. I tried with all of my strength to get her out of bed while she resisted with all of hers. "Girl, you and I are going to have it out if you continue fighting me. Now stop it!"

While in the tub, Reneé experienced a serious melt down and let everything out. It seemed to have been what she needed because she'd obviously been holding it in ever since her breakup with Danny. She continued to cry while I helped her change into a new gown and back into bed. I let her carry on and remained strong while she sobbed. Crying never solved anything I knew, but after a good one, there usually came some sense of relief. Plus, a good cry never hurt anyone.

"Lacie, what am I going to do?" she sniffed after she'd finally stopped crying.

We were sitting on the bed and I was brushing her hair. Honestly, I was glad her rainfall had stopped because if she hadn't, I didn't know how long it would be before mine would start.

She continued. "I'm still in high school and I'm an unwed pregnant teenager."

I stopped brushing her hair to look at her. "What do you mean 'what are you going to do'? You're going to continue school, raise this baby and be a lawyer, just like you said you wanted to be. Honey, it's not the end of the world, you know."

"But I counted on him, Lacie. How could Danny do this to me?"

"Unfortunately, I don't have an answer to that," I replied with a shake of my head as I proceeded to brush her hair again. "But you don't need to concentrate on him. Right now, your focus should be on you and this baby."

"Did I do anything wrong, Lacie? I mean, he was the one that wanted this baby and for him to just love me and leave me like that, is just not right."

"I know," I sighed, finished with her hair. "You didn't do anything wrong, Reneé, and you can't control what someone else does or does not do."

"It just hurts so much, Lacie," she uttered. "What's worse is that I know you and Mama are ashamed of me."

"What? What gave you that—" I stopped abruptly, cupped her chin with one hand and made her look at me. "Listen, to me. No, stop crying," I commanded lightly, once I saw her lips tremble and her stream was about to begin again. "I am not ashamed of you and Mama isn't either. And I most certainly don't want you to be ashamed of yourself. We love you and more importantly we are here for you." I hugged her tight and instructed softly. "Now look, you've had enough time to feel sorry for yourself. I know your heart is broken, but you've shed enough tears. It's time for you to build yourself back up now. So I want you out of this bed, back in school on Monday and into civilization again." I released her and cupped my hand around her face again. "You can and will get through this. Okay?"

After a long pause and with our eyes locked on each other, Reneé finally gave me a glimmer of hope with a little smile. She wiped her face with her hand and said, "Okay."

"That's more like it," I murmured with a satisfied nod.

Yes, Reneé was young, unwed and going to be a mother. But did this put a limit on her future potential? Her future aspirations? No.

And I was going to make sure it didn't.

# Chapter 31

# Tony

I should have stayed at work with Lacie.

The instant we reached our table in the restaurant, Mom made sure that Rachel sat next to me. I shook my head and sighed. Mom was using my weakness for her and taking full advantage of it.

I was conscious of Mom and Mrs. Sanders making subtle but apparent plans for me and Rachel as if we weren't sitting at the table with them. They rambled on about the upcoming wedding and started talking about possible plans for a combined family trip. The ultimate goal, I surmised, was to get Rachel and I together.

Rachel tried her best to make lengthy conversation, but I couldn't entertain her. Instead, I talked with her in short sentences and ate my dinner silently. I was annoyed by the whole set up and that I'd left Lacie for this. Plus, I knew Lacie had been bothered as well by the disruption even though she'd put up a good front. This wasn't going to happen again and I had to let Mom know.

Right before dessert, Rachel and Valerie excused themselves and retreated to the women's room.

"Rachel's such a nice girl. Isn't she, Anthony?" Mom suggested, looking at me intently.

With a brief nod I answered, "Yes, she is."

She beamed immediately at my reply. "Rachel absolutely adores you, Anthony. She's expecting to dance with you at the wed–"

"Mom, what are you up to?" I interrupted her softly with a direct look.

Innocent eyes blinked. "Why, whatever do you mean, Anthony?"

I smiled thinly at her vain attempt. "Mom, why the sudden and unexpected trip in the city and why did you bring them with you?"

She didn't answer. "Mom?" I pressed.

"All right, all right, Anthony," Mom admitted tersely. "I planned this intentionally so you and Rachel could get reacquainted."

"Mom," I murmured in censure.

She put her hand on my knee. "Anthony, listen. Rachel is a good girl and she comes from good stock. She'd be perfect for you."

"You also thought Simone was perfect for me and look what happened," I pointed out dryly.

"And I still think you should have given Simone another chance," she asserted. "But never mind about her. Rachel is prime, dear, and she is just itching to get married. To you, I might add."

I shook my head. "I'm already seeing, Lacie, Mom. You know that," I contended frankly.

"And?" Mom brazened flippantly with a light chuckle. "Anthony, c'mon. You never close the door on all of your options, honey."

"What if I don't want any other options?" I suggested directly.

For a second, I thought her eyes flashed before she answered, "Anthony, don't be ridiculous." She waved her hand airily. "Do you really know this…Leslie?"

"Yes, I do know, *Lacie*, Mom."

"Really?" Mom said with skepticism. "Where does she come from? What's her background? Who are her parents and does she even have both parents in her life?" she asked candidly.

"You could have asked her all of that if you'd have invited her to come with us." She arched her eyebrows at that. "And Mom, c'mon," I said with a light laugh. "Does all of that really matter?"

"Yes…it does." Her expression was firm. "Money must always marry into money. Don't ever forget that." With that, she took a sip of her drink.

Astounded by the gravity of her statement, I cocked my head to the side and eyeballed her. Then with determination and with the same amount of gravity she used, I rebutted my last words.

"*Love* is far more important than money."

I called Lacie as soon as Mom, Valerie and Rachel got in the cab. I was irritated by the dinner and the conversation with Mom and needed to hear the sound of her soothing voice. It always seemed to calm me.

"Hey, you. It's so good to hear your voice," I said softly into the phone when she answered.

"Hey, you," she replied sweetly. After a small pause she asked, "How was dinner?"

"It was…okay," I said evasively, getting into my car.

Lacie caught on immediately. "Your mom pressured you about Rachel again, didn't she?"

I smiled. "How did you know?"

"Do you even have to ask?" she joked softly.

"No, I guess not." I took a deep breath. "Listen, I feel awful about my Mom and everything. I'm gonna make it up to you. I just want you to know that."

"Tony, don't apologize. Your mom is just being a protective mother. You don't have to make anything up to me."

"Ah," I scolded lightly. "You shouldn't be so quick to say that. You know Valentine's Day is Monday, now."

A slight pause. "On that note, yeah, make as much up to me as you want," she giggled.

"Bet," I chuckled. "Listen, I'm gonna let you go. I'll call you over the weekend instead of coming over so you can spend some quality time with your family. You're going to need it with the busy schedule ahead of us. But Monday you're all mine, so make sure you bring a change of clothes with you to work."

"Hmm," she murmured. "Can't wait."

I smiled at that. "Love you."

"Love you more."

A buzz came through as soon as Lacie hung up. It was Joe.

"What up, man?" I said, feeling better after having talked with Lacie.

He laughed. "What up with you? What are you so cheerful for?"

"Just in love, man."

"Hey, I know the feeling," Joe stated. "Look, I wanted to get with you on the bids. Did they look good or what?"

"What? You weren't there?"

"Naw, man. I had to jet back to Miami for pressing business," Joe said quickly.

"What pressing business? Dude, you've got to be back on Monday."

"I will, don't worry. Don't bust my chops. I just had some things I had to take care of, is all," he uttered vaguely. "Now give me the info."

I sat in the car pensively once I'd gotten off the phone with Joe after relaying the information to him. Joe's aloofness and sudden departure out of the city was niggling me. He hadn't mentioned he was leaving before and he'd been so restrained with his explanation. Furthermore, he'd also let it out the bag that Lacie had been alone with that jerk, Trevor.

Why hadn't she mentioned it to me when I talked with her?

*'Cause she knows you can't stand him.*

I shook my head, not liking that she was alone with him.

*Cool, it Tony. Don't act like a mistrustful boyfriend. You know Lacie loves you. Does her being alone with Trevor really matter?*

*Yes. When dude was after my girl, it did.*

# Chapter 32

# Dawn

Valentine's Day weekend was the best weekend I ever had.

On Friday, Joe had called me from New York and told me he would be flying back to Miami later that afternoon and wanted me to meet him at the airport. He told me he'd made special plans for us over the weekend since he couldn't be with me on Valentine's Day. I was excited and looking forward to seeing him again. Ever since he left to go back to New York and after I'd walked into his office with my bittersweet decision, we'd maintained continual contact via phone. It had only been a few days, but I still missed him terribly.

Clearly, he had missed me as well. He greeted me with a long lingering kiss outside of the airport before asking, "Your bag all packed?"

"Yep," I said.

"You ready?"

I smiled. "Ready as I'll ever be."

"All right, let's go," he said. He took my hand and started to lead me back inside the airport.

I pulled back. "Joe, aren't we going the wrong way?"

"Nope," he answered simply. "Just follow my lead."

His lead turned out to be on a secluded beachfront mansion in the Bahamas, I found out, as the small plane he'd charted landed on a private landing strip. I was fascinated in two ways. First, I'd never been to the Bahamas and had always wanted to go. Secondly, the mansion was out of this world! Massive and incandescent, it made a spectacular view from the beach, giving a supreme impression of luxury.

An entire staff greeted us at the entrance, and with utter hospitality, took our bags and showed us to our suites. The staff, Joe explained, was there for us to use at our utmost request.

Opulence couldn't even describe the adjoining suites when we entered. Both suites were beautifully decorated and lit with lavender scented candles. Even better, was the stunning view off the open-screened balcony that displayed the soothing waves of the beach. Joe chuckled while I walked around overwhelmed, inhaling every marvelous detail.

"C'mon, let's go for a walk," Joe said, taking my hand and dragging me away from my candle lit bathroom.

It was pitch dark and I had my reservations, being from the city and all, but Joe reassured me. It was well worth it. The walkway to the beach was lit and so was the beachfront. We strolled slowly and silently, hand in hand, enjoying the fresh air. The beauty of the place was something to behold and I was truly touched that Joe had initiated so much effort for me.

"You haven't said much since we got here," Joe commented softly.

I was so overwhelmed that my response could barely come out. I laughed thickly, trying to refrain from tearing. "I...I'm just speechless."

He stopped and turned to me, taking my hands in his. "You weren't expecting this," he stated perceptively.

"Nope," I admitted with a sigh. "I didn't."

He nodded. "This is better than what any of them other knuckleheads you went out with before me did for you, isn't it?"

I squinted at him and he laughed.

"You're enjoying this," I observed.

"What?"

"You're enjoying making your point."

"Yes, I like to be on top," he said.

That statement had a double meaning, I concluded, blushing.

"I'm sure you do," I returned devilishly.

He cocked his head and smiled. "Can I be on top tonight?" he suggested smoothly.

Despite his attempt at seduction, I wasn't ready. Not yet.

"Umm, not tonight, but I will give you this," I replied. With strong confirmation, I pulled his head down and kissed him with all the sweetness I could offer.

It was a good while before he pulled his head up from our kiss and brushed my cheek. "You are really making this hard for me." He shook his head and smiled. "C'mon, let's go back to the house," he said softly. "Dinner's waiting on us."

We strolled back toward the house wordlessly with his arm around my shoulder and mine around his waist.

This was surreal and terribly romantic. I was walking on a private beach in the Bahamas and staying at a fully staffed Mansion for the weekend, with a man that I was hopelessly in love with. For once, I finally felt my time had arrived.

*Could Lacie top this?*

*Stop it, Dawn*

# Chapter 33

# Joe

Why was I suddenly conscious of this now?

I looked at Dawn's fully clothed and sleeping frame in my arms and contemplated the issues at hand.

She'd made it clear on the beach that she wasn't ready and I respected her wishes. I wanted her, but didn't want to push her into regretting going to the next step. Although, after a night with me, I was sure she wouldn't. The biggest determining factor, however, was whether she'd be able to make such a step given my history with Lacie.

The other factor, was that I had a feeling Tony was getting closer to finding out about us. I should have never called him and told him I was back in Florida. I knew better than that. And he knew me all too well.

I was starting to slip.

Now that my relationship with Dawn was getting deeper, it was getting riskier by the minute. The deceit was bound to catch up with us, I knew. But I didn't care about myself. I cared about Dawn. I didn't want her hurt and I didn't want her relationship with Lacie to end.

On the other hand, I didn't want to lose Dawn, either. Dawn had me roped around her finger and I could see a future with her.

But she had to meet my mother first.

That was a given.

# Chapter 34

# Robert

Dad was home.

The doctors had sent him home a week ago and had arranged for him to have therapy and suggested twenty-four-hour care. Ma refused, claiming that we could take care of him.

Ma was glad Dad was out of the hospital, but hated seeing him in such a vulnerable state. Dad could barely talk and couldn't move his entire left side.

Ma and I did our best to take care of him, but eventually we were worn out. All of the equipment and tubes that he was hooked up to was too much and soon we had to relent to the twenty-four-hour care. Even though Dad was getting the best of care, I knew that I couldn't leave. Mama was physically drained and she needed a lot of help.

I called the show back in New York and informed them that my stay out of town was indefinite. They had to relieve me of my role, but thankfully, I'd had a considerable amount of savings to help with my responsibilities at home. I was sad that I couldn't return to the show, but my family was more important.

With everything changing, I realized that I had to call Lacie and give her an update on everything. It'd been a while since I'd seen her.

I wondered how she was doing.

# Chapter 35

# Lacie

Monday started out on a positive note.

Mama had called me at work and informed me that Reneé had gotten up for an early class and had gone to school. Her going to church with me and Mama on Sunday and my speech to her, seemed to be the reason for her brighter spirit. She'd also appeared more determined and told us that she was going to sign up for a program at school for teen mothers. The program prepped pregnant teens for college, work and parenting skills.

It was even better at work, for two reasons: Valentine's Day and Trevor was nowhere to be found. I couldn't have been more relieved. After the minor incident between us at work on Friday, I'd been apprehensive about seeing him, not wanting to relive it again.

The day seemed to go by smoother and faster than it had in a while and everyone was in a jovial mood. Squeals of delight filtered throughout the department as women received floral arrangements and chocolates and I was surprised by the numerous arrangements of roses being delivered to my office labeled: *from a secret admirer.* I was tickled, because I knew it was from Tony.

Toward the middle of the day, Tony told me he was taking me out for our first Valentine's Day, but was mum about the location. He still wouldn't tell me when he came to my office to get me after work. I was intrigued by this mystery because I couldn't grasp how he could possibly outdo all of the roses he'd had delivered to my office. That gesture had been an exceptional first for me, and in actuality, I felt he'd done more than enough.

But then he surprised me even further.

Waiting outside of the office building was a beautiful, white, horse drawn carriage. I looked at Tony in awed inquiry. Responding only with a smile, he put a finger to my lips and proprietarily helped me into the carriage where champagne and chocolate-dipped strawberries awaited on the back seat.

While the horse drawn carriage traveled in the midst of the Manhattan traffic, Tony pampered me with the chocolate dipped strawberries and sips of champagne. It was a good hour or so before the carriage stopped in front of one of the most expensive hotels in the city. The concierge greeted us at the doorstep. Then with grace and profession, he ushered us to a private elevator that took us to the top of the hotel and to two large double doors leading into a penthouse suite.

When the concierge opened the doors for us, I was blown away. Rose petals were intricately placed on every inch of the plush carpet and throughout the suite. I walked around in wonder and stopped to stare out the huge glass window at the city below.

Tony came up from behind and placed his arms around my waist and planted a tender kiss on my neck.

I put my hands on his arms. "This is so nice," I said softly. "You've done so much."

"No. If anything, I don't think I've done enough," he whispered in my ear in return.

I glanced down at my watch. "I guess I'd better call home…" I started.

"You don't have to do a thing," he interrupted. "That's already taken care of. They're not expecting you until tomorrow afternoon."

I turned my head slightly to look up at him. "You thought of everything, didn't you?"

"Yep, sure did," he chuckled. "It gets even better. Come with me."

He took my hand and guided me to the bathroom where a large whirlpool tub was filled to the brim with rose petals. Lit red candles were situated on every angle of the tub, giving off this magnificent mulberry scent.

"Wow," I said breathlessly.

He put his arms around my waist again and laid his head on my shoulder. "Tonight is all about you," he murmured tenderly. "We've been working non-stop and you've been going through a lot. So I want you to relax and enjoy this nice warm bath."

Mesmerized, I stayed unmoving while he slowly planted soft kisses down my body and took my clothes off gingerly, before guiding me into the awaiting tub. At once, the warm water absorbed and relieved my body when I submerged myself into it.

"How's the water?" he asked.

"Mmm," I murmured with a smile. "It's perfect."

He smiled in return and nodded. "Good. Just make yourself comfortable. I'll be right back," he said, before walking out.

He didn't have to tell me twice. I heeded his instructions and sunk deeper into the tub with the water to my neck and closed my eyes, all of a sudden feeling fatigued. Within moments he returned to the bathroom smiling, carrying a silver bowl full of chocolate covered strawberries.

"Again?" I raised my eyebrow. "You're not trying to seduce me are you?" I teased.

He grinned and winked. "Now why would I do that?" I couldn't help but laugh. He reached in the bowl and grabbed one of the chocolate covered strawberries. His expression was of adoration as his eyes locked with mine while he fed me a bite and then finished the rest.

"Umm, very sweet," I murmured, then yawned.

"Tired?" he asked.

"A little, yeah," I said, stifling another yawn and rotating my neck around. "My neck is hurting a little too."

Without a word, he came behind me and with a soft sponge, started washing around my neck with a little pressure. Then he proceeded down by my back and the rest of my body. After he'd finished, there was a knock at the door.

"That must be dinner," he said, leaning over to give me a soft quick kiss. I started to get out of the tub but he gently pushed me back in. "No. I'll get the door and I'll be back with a robe." I closed my eyes as he left the bathroom. I must have started a deep sleep when I felt him kiss my neck. "Wake up, sleepyhead," he said softly. "I was only gone for a minute and you're already asleep?" He tsked, tsked. He held out a white cotton robe for me with one hand and helped me out of the tub with the other.

"Sorry," I said. "I think the bath had an effect on me."

He chuckled. "That's okay. C'mon, let's eat."

He took my hand and guided me to the living room of the suite where an elegantly set table awaited. As I sat, he eased my chair up to the table and this time, poured me a glass of sparkling white cider.

"I figured one glass of champagne was enough," he explained.

"Good thinking," I said with a nod and a little chuckle.

We made good conversation while we ate dinner...rather he talked and I listened. For some reason, sleep had unexpectedly taken over me. I struggled not to yawn and keep my eyes open because of the effort that he'd made for the night, but couldn't fight it off.

"Lacie?"

"Hmm?"

"You're ready to go to sleep, aren't you?" he asked. I replied with a guilty nod. He smiled tenderly. "C'mon, let's get you into bed."

"No, Tony, that's all right. You've done—" I protested.

"Shh," he said, reaching across the table to take my hand. "It's all right. I told you tonight was about you. C'mon."

The bed, still covered with rose petals never looked so inviting. I couldn't wait to get in. With care, Tony disrobed me and I got in, instantaneously feeling the comfort of the satin sheets underneath. He laid on top of the covers and held me tight.

"I'm sorry, Tony," I murmured with a yawn.

He kissed my forehead. "Why?"

"I know you went through a lot to make this night special and here I am getting all sleepy on you."

"No," he whispered. "What's special is that I'm with you. That's what matters." He brushed my hair from my forehead. "Just close your eyes and dream about me."

I snickered lightly in response to his vain remark and did another yawn. "Yes, sir."

I smiled and closed my eyes, enjoying the intimacy we shared without sex and within minutes, I was asleep.

And coincidentally, as he requested, dreamt about him, holding a baby.

# Tony

Lacie didn't waste time.

I lifted my head to look at her and smiled at her sleeping form. Her breathing was soft and steady.

This was so perfect. Her and me. I wanted to be everything to her as she was to me. I didn't want her to be with anyone else.

It was ridiculous, but I was still perturbed about her having that meeting with Trevor alone. Call me jealous, but a man always knows when another man is after his woman. And Trevor was. That was for sure. It had only been a couple of days since he'd temporarily moved next to her office and already he seemed to take every opportunity to sit next to Lacie, and jab me with subtle negative comments. Lacie's love for me was without question, but Trevor was smooth, slick, rich, black and had a lot of woman eyeing him, despite his proud and condescending attitude. But, he was business savvy, which was grudgingly admirable.

I felt as if I was competing for my own woman. My mind wasn't fabricating this.

Thank goodness, Joe was working with us. He'd saved him from getting clocked a few times whenever Trevor would make a supercilious comment.

But honestly, Trevor wasn't my only concern.

Lacie was going through personal issues at home, Trevor was a constant pain in the behind, Joe was hiding something from me, and lastly, from the last conversation that I'd had with my mother, she wanted me to be with Rachel or get back with Simone.

Too much was going on and with the upcoming wedding Lacie and I were going to attend, I was starting to get a sudden foreboding feeling. I had a feeling that everything around us would crumble and fall to pieces and negatively affect our relationship. I didn't want that to happen.

I loved Lacie so much that it hurt and I wanted her to be my wife.

But would our love for each other be enough to withstand my premonition of the storm that I was sure to come?

# Chapter 37

# Lacie

I woke up the next morning rested and bright but feeling guilty about the night before. Tony, however, waved all of my concerns away when he came in the bedroom and greeted me with a breakfast tray. It was a great way to start the work day but when we arrived at the office, things immediately started to turn sour.

Richard had informed us that some of the deals with clients that Tony and I had attained, had hit a few snags in negotiations. It would undoubtedly affect the progress on the William Carr project. If Tony and I didn't take control and oversee the meetings ourselves, it would cost the company some serious money despite the lucrative possibilities of the William Carr project.

Tony and I went to work on it immediately. We entrusted Carrie, under our guidance, to work with Joe and Trevor on the William Carr deal for the time being, while we worked diligently and hastily to get our team and everything on track with the other deals.

This put an unbelievable amount of strain on us at work. It became more and more mentally and physically strenuous. Physically, the importance and beneficial aspect of the project entailed a great deal of work and the amount of hours spent on the William Carr project along with other accounts, was incalculable. Plus, the mental strain of dealing with contracts, bids and every kind of legality was draining.

And I was spending very little time at home.

One of the few days that I'd come home, I finally managed to tell Mama what happened during dinner with Tony's parents. As expected, she hit the ceiling and even more so when I told her about the wedding. She was unyielding in her vocabulary about me not going but once she realized that I was as equally unyielding about going, she relented.

Still, she never gave up in her warning. But I think there was more to her objections than she wanted to admit.

I found out through Reneé that there was still a little tension going on between Mama and Daddy, but they did try to remain cordial with each other. This was in part, I believed, because Mama was so preoccupied with helping Reneé. However, I did notice that whenever I'd get home I'd sometimes catch the tail end of a spat between Mama and Daddy. It would always end as soon as they'd see me. For this I was glad. There had been so much going on at work and even though I was seldom home, the last thing I needed was any more strain at home.

With every day that passed, Tony and I worked endlessly to correct the snafus with the other clients. Once we accomplished that feat, our workload commenced on the William Carr project. We were back on board, and so was Trevor's mind games and his constant jeers about me and Tony.

Tony and I dealt with him with a lot of strained patience; our consolation that we'd only have to deal with Trevor for the day and go to Tony's house. Our quality time was limited there though, because we'd wind up working when we'd get there as well. We knew that the end result would be rewarding, but we were clearly overworked. I was beginning to feel it more as February came to a close and March began. Fatigue and sleep were a constant battle as I struggled with every meeting or counsel at work.

Along with that. was the never ending anxiety I was feeling as the time neared for me to go to the wedding with Tony and face his mother again.

I wasn't looking forward to that day and didn't feel ready.

The day had come and and my uneasiness and exhaustion was at an all time high.

Tony and I were leaving work a half-day early to get a good start on the ride to Connecticut. I was putting documents in my briefcase when Carrie buzzed me and told me that I had an incoming call.

"Lacie Adams speaking, may I help you?" I said after I picked up the phone.

"Yes, this is Mr. Deutsch, Reneé Taylor's principal, calling. Is this her sister?"

My alarm went up. "Yes, it is. Is my sister okay?"

"You're sister's fine but we had a little incident at school today. I'm inclined to suspend her because of the fight she had with another one of my students. Is it possible if you can come to the school? I've tried to reach her mother but couldn't get an answer."

I couldn't believe what the principal had said and my mind started whirling.

My sister? In a fight?

"Uh, yes, sure. Certainly. I'll be there as soon as I can," I replied.

"Thank you."

I hung up the phone, dumbfounded. What was she doing fighting knowing she was pregnant? Tony came into my office and I didn't hesitate. Quickly, I closed my briefcase, grabbed my coat and purse and took his hand.

"Let's go. I'll explain everything in the car."

ℰℭ

"A fight, Reneé? A fight?" I scolded, glaring at her in the rearview mirror in Tony's car as he pulled onto the street. "Reneé, what is wrong with you? What possessed you to get into something like that in school and in your condition?"

I was incensed. The principal had threatened to suspend Reneé, but thankfully because of her excellent record at school, he'd changed his mind. That wasn't really what was disturbing. The principal showed me a quick glimpse at her grades. She was failing two courses and on the way to three, which might hinder her from graduating.

Reneé was adamant and glared in return with her arms folded across her chest. "Lacie, I already told you. I didn't start the fight. Danny's girlfriend, Angel, did."

"So what? Have you noticed your belly, Reneé" I paused effectively. "You're pregnant! How many times have I told you that you never, ever fight over the male species. Didn't you learn anything from seeing Dawn's battered and bruised face when she stayed with us? Do you know how much harm could have been done to the baby?" I exclaimed, turning around to look at her.

"Lacie, the girl *slapped* me. I wasn't going to just stand there and let her get away with it," Reneé asserted strongly. "It wasn't really a fight anyway because after my punch, she fell on the floor. What are you barking at me for, anyway? You were gonna give Simone a beat down if Robert hadn't stopped you."

Tony blew out a low whistle.

*Ouch!* Simone was still a very sore issue with me.

"Ho, ho, that was not cute, Reneé. And that's a moot point. I wasn't *pregnant!*," I hissed, shaking my head. "Where is this coming from? This is not like you. I thought you were doing so well and your confidence seemed to be building up and everything."

"Oh, I just acted that way so I wouldn't have to hear your lectures every time I turned around," she retorted airily with a wave of her hand.

Tony snickered. I shot him a hard look and he cleared his throat.

Turning back around, I squinted my eyes back toward Reneé in the mirror and rolled my tongue around in my cheek as I brooded over her statement momentarily.

"Okay. So you're just going to continue to feel sorry for yourself and let Danny and Angel win. Is that it?" I accused, nodding.

"I don't...feel sorry for mysef, Lacie," she muttered, welling up with tears.

"That's sure what it sounds like to me."

Tony pulled in front of my apartment building and Reneé hurried out of the car once it stopped. Tony got out of the car and came over to my side.

"Lord, she's upset with me," I moaned, rubbing my temple wearily as Tony opened the door for me.

He took my hand and helped me out. "It's going to be okay."

"Was I too hard on her?"

He shook his head. "No. Just a concerned big sister." He leaned his head down so he could look into my eyes when I heaved a deep breath. "You okay?"

No, I wasn't. I was tired from working so much, anxious about this weekend and disappointed in my sister.

"Don't worry about me. I'll be all right," I assured with a small smile. "Look, you'd better get over to your house and pack so we can leave soon. I'm going to go upstairs and clean up the mess I started. I'm sure Mama's gonna want to know what's going on."

"No doubt about it," he agreed with a slight chuckle. He looked down at his watch. "Okay, I'll see you about four o'clock? Does that give you enough time?"

"Yes, that's fine."

He planted a soft kiss on my lips. "Okay, see you then."

⧼⧽

Mama was waiting at the threshold of my apartment door when the elevator door opened on my floor.

"You don't have to explain. I already know what's happened. Her principal left a message on your answering machine." She gawked at me. "Goodness, Lacie, you look like you've been run over by a mack truck!"

I stopped in mid stride and raised my eyebrow at her. "Thanks, Mama. And where were you when he called?"

Her eyes dodged mine and she turned her head to the side. "I was out...with your father."

That brought both of my eyebrows up. "What?" I whispered in surprise, coming closer to her. "You went out with Daddy?"

"Oh, don't get so excited." She pursed her lips in annoyance. "I had to get a lot of groceries and it didn't make sense for me to bring them here all by myself," she explained.

A revelation suddenly came to me when she shifted uncomfortably and a hint of a smile appeared from under her set lips. I raised my hand and covered my mouth.

"Mama!" I exclaimed softly. "You're warming up to him, aren't you?"

"Shush. No sucha thing," she spat out. "And be quiet. Your dad's right in the kitchen putting up the groceries."

"Oh, you are, all right," I teased. "And you still have feelings for him, don't you?"

"Oh, shut up!" she spat out again. I giggled, still holding my mouth. "Feelings were never an issue. Just circumstances."

"So is it safe to say that all is well between you two?"

"Huh. Now you're *really* pushing your luck." She moved aside. "Go upstairs and talk to your sister. From past experiences, you've had better luck than I have. So go."

"Yes, Ma'am," I gibed with a small salute, dodging the hand she was trying to hit my arm with.

ဆဲလ

"Turn off the television," I demanded softly, entering Reneé's room.

"Don't you know how to knock?" she asked tersely but followed my instructions.

"Don't you know that this is my apartment?" I retorted, walking over to her bed. "C'mon, move your feet over so I can sit and talk to you."

She moved them and mumbled, "You sure are bossy today."

I shot her a look and was about to rebutt, but took a deep breath instead.

"Reneé, what's up with you?" I pleaded softly. "Huh?" The tears started instantly. "And I want you to be honest with me. Don't just give me something that you think I want to hear, either."

She grabbed me and let it out then. She was feeling a lot of pressure at school. Rumors were spreading about her pregnancy and she kept seeing Danny and his new girlfriend together. It seemed like every chance Danny got, he paraded Angel in front of her. Today, Angel had confronted her and that's when the fight started.

I inhaled, undersanding all too well what it was like to be betrayed and talked about. Being in high school made it worse. But I'd given her a pep talk already and I didn't want to pamper her anymore. She was going to be a mother in several months. It was time to grow up.

"Okay, so since you can't give her a beat down do you want me go to the school and do it for you?" I joked.

She let go and looked at me, confused.

I nodded, trying not to laugh. "I'm serious, girl. I've still got all of that pent up tension left from that argument with Simone and you know I'm nervous about this weekend. That would be a good stress reliever."

"Lacie?"

"What, girl? I'm serious," I contended and then winked.

Reneé burst out laughing and then I started laughing myself. "Listen, listen. All kidding aside," I said, gathering my composure. "I understand what you're going through, but I know that you know that you're more than petty and childish games. Hold your head high, baby, because you have nothing to be ashamed of. That baby inside of you is a blessing, not a curse. And let me tell you something else. That Angel girl is probably jealous of you because you're carrying her boyfriend's baby." Reneé looked at me in surprise and I nodded. "Yeah, girl. Baby mama drama goes way back. It's nothing new. So try to ignore her if you can but if she continues to harass you, let me know. I'll come down there and beat her tail myself." I shrugged simply and Reneé laughed again. I looked at my watch and said, "Look, not to change the subject, but I've got a small task for you."

"What?" Reneé asked.

"While I'm gone I want you to keep an eye on Mama and Daddy for me. If something goes down between them, call me on my cell."

Reneé frowned. "Why? They've been getting along fine."

"Yeah...but that's only because of me," I said. "That's what scares me. They went out shopping together today and I started to see a little light at the tunnel. The light was blocked though, when Mama warned me not to get my hopes up too high."

"You know, I think she still has a thing for him," Reneé remarked.

"Hey, so do I, but that won't stop Mama's mouth. She's been holding everything in and you know she has a tendency to blow up without warning because she's so sensitive. I feel it's coming too."

Reneé looked at me quizzically. "What *is* the issue between them?"

"Reneé, I wish I could tell you." I sighed, shaking my head.

At that moment, Mama knocked on the door and came in. "Everything all right?" she asked.

I looked at Reneé and she nodded at Mama.

"Thank God," Mama said. "You two surely have been in here long enough." She looked at me. "Lacie, Tony just called and said he'd be over in an hour or so."

I sighed. "Well, I guess that's my cue."

Mama peered at me when I stood up. "Lacie, are you okay? You don't look so good and you still look very tired."

"I'm fine, Mama," I said with a little yawn. I looked at her then, knowing what she was about to suggest. "I'm going, Mama."

"But why, when that woman was so nasty to you at that restaurant?"

"Because it's important to Tony and I can't hide from his family, Mama," I groaned softly.

"It ain't got nothing to do with hiding. It doesn't make sense for you to go there and have to deal with that uppity woman," Mama called after me as I started wearily out of Reneé's room and into mine. Both of them were on my heels.

"Wait, wait a minute," I heard Reneé say when I went into my walk in closet. "What's going on? What happened?"

Briefly Mama explained to Reneé what happened the night I had dinner with Tony's parents. "I've been trying to convince your sister not to go," she continued. "That woman doesn't want any part of

Lacie. She should have known that from the get go when his mama called her a maid."

"She called you a maid, Lacie!" Reneé exclaimed.

I came out of the closet with a few dresses on one arm and shoes in my hand. "She didn't know who I was, Reneé—not then, anyway."

"Hmmph, but she never apologized for it, did she?" Mama shot back.

I plopped my clothes on the bed in exasperation. "Mama," I said. "Let it go. I'm going and that's final."

"I should crash that wedding and go with you," Mama said suddenly.

"Oh, no! That is definitely out of the question," I said, shaking my head instantly as I walked to my dresser and took out some undergarments.

"Well, who's going to take up for you if that crazy woman starts something?" Mama asked.

"Mama," I said, turning around and eyeing her dumbfoundedly.

"Mama, I think Lacie can take care of herself. Not to mention, Tony will be there," Reneé obliged.

"Well, he'd better take care of her because if Lacie comes back here and I get any sense that something wrong happened, it's on. Tony's tail *and* his Mama's will be mine," Mama declared.

"I don't doubt that at all, Mama," I remarked dryly. "Now look, we can all sit here and talk about this 'til we're blue in the face, but Tony will be here soon and I've got to get ready. Are you two going to help me or not?" I asked pointedly, looking at them.

∽⊘⫷

Forty-five minutes later and after a soothing shower, I was fully dressed. Mama was putting a necklace around my neck and Reneé had finished applying my makeup.

"Well, what do you think? Do you think I'm too overdressed?" I asked, standing and looking at them warily. The dress I'd chosen was black, long, elegantly fitted and cut in a long V-shape down my back.

Mama smiled and said, "Girl, Tony is going to pee in his britches when he sees you. It's appropriate all right."

Reneé and I looked at Mama and started laughing. The words that left her mouth never stopped amazing us.

When we came out of my room, the view from the balcony showed Tony and Daddy sitting downstairs in the living room. Reneé closed the door behind me and Tony stood automatically and looked up. His jaw fell open when he saw me. He walked over to the stairs slowly and met us at the bottom.

"My God, you look amazing!" he exclaimed softly, easing my duffel bag from my grasp. "Nice necklace."

I was wearing the pearl necklace he'd given me for Christmas.

Pleased with his appraisal, I smiled broadly and nodded. "Thank you. I wore it just for you." With a wink, I added, "You don't look so bad, yourself."

Actually, Tony looked damn fine. The opening of his long black wool coat revealed a stylish and sharp black tuxedo.

He stood still, continuing to stare.

"What?" I looked down at my dress consciously. "Is something wrong?"

He responded by lifting my face with his hands gently to give me a lingering and breathless kiss. I suddenly became conscious that my parents—namely my father—could see us, and abruptly broke the kiss.

I blushed. "Tony?" I scolded, lightly.

He chuckled and said, "Does that answer your question?"

We stood gazing at each other, both forgetting that Mama and Reneé were behind me until Mama spoke.

"I declare. You two are like dogs in heat! I've never seen two people interlocking tongues the way that you two do," Mama expressed.

"Mama! Not in front of Daddy!" I whispered anxiously, as Tony laughed and took my hand in his.

**195**

"Lacie, this is nothing new to him. Do you think the stork brought you to us?" she asked cynically, motioning over to Daddy with her head.

I looked over at Daddy and he shook his head.

Mama continued. "Now, Tony, I want you to make sure that you take care of Lacie, now. You hear?"

"Mama, don't…" I started, stifling another yawn.

Tony frowned and put a supporting arm on mine when I came off the last step. "You okay? You look tired."

"I know, Tony," Mama said. "That's what I've been telling her. Lord knows how many times she yawned in our faces when Reneé and I were upstairs. I told her she needs to stay home and rest."

"I'm fine, Mama." I shook my head. "I didn't get all dressed up to just stay at home and neither did Tony." I stifled another yawn to Mama's raised eyebrow and Tony caught it also.

He searched my face. "Lacie, are you sure you don't want to stay here? I won't be upset if you do."

I smiled and shook my head. He was sweet to suggest it, but I knew he really wanted me to go.

"Lacie, you look stunning," Daddy piped in. He got up and came over to the stairs, studying me. "But maybe Josephine is right. It might do you some good to stay home and get some rest. You and I could use the time to talk and catch up on a few things—"

"You know what?" Mama interrupted swiftly, shooting my dad with a squinted glance. "Don't worry about what we've said. Go ahead and have a good time."

In that instant, Mama had changed from begging me to stay home to practically pushing me and Tony out the door. I eyed her, wondering what made her change her statement so quickly and then turned to look at my father. His face was now a bit grim. All of a sudden, the energy in the room had changed from pleasant to unsettling.

"Lacie?" Tony asked.

My mood suddenly broken, I took a deep breath and held my tongue. I wanted to pursue the matter, but now was not the right time.

"Let's go, Tony," I replied and started for the front door. While Tony hastily took my coat off the coat hanger as we approached the door, I took time to look back at my parents briefly. Mama wasn't looking at me and neither was Daddy. Both of them were tight-lipped. "Mama, Daddy. I'll be home Sunday evening some time. Reneé, remember what I told you. I'll see you later."

I was reeling from the swift and fragrant stillness between my parents as Tony and I left my apartment and waited for the elevator. Mama had some nerve to kick me out of my own house because Daddy mentioned that he wanted to have a talk with me. No. This was going to get settled as soon as I returned. I was already nervous about seeing Tony's mother again and having to go to a wedding where I would most likely be the only black person. Now I had all of this junk between Mama and Daddy hanging over my head.

The guessing games were going to end.

# Chapter 38

# The Wedding

*Lacie*

This was not how I wanted to go into unknown territory.

My nerves and thoughts immediately started to get a little panicky about the event ahead once we left Manhattan for Connecticut. As a result, there was limited conversation in the car ride. Tony wasn't talkative either, apparently into his own thoughts as well. However, our mulling didn't last long. Thirty-five minutes later, the beautiful church, rich with ancient architecture, came into view.

While Tony looked for a parking spot, I checked out the surroundings. Yep, just what I thought. I was going to be the only black person.

I sighed and shook my head when Tony finally found a spot. It was his first time bringing me to his hometown and to such a prestigious event such as this. I was sure that eyebrows were going to rise once people saw us together. There was no doubt about it.

Tony reached for my hand after he parked. "You okay?" he asked.

I faced Tony's stare. "Yeah…why?"

"You barely spoke to me during the ride over here," he stated.

"I've got a lot on my mind. You should know that," I replied. "Anyway, conversation does go both ways, Tony,"

"You're right. I've had a lot on my mind, too." He nodded thoughtfully with a deep breath and looked out his side window. A second later, he turned and looked at me warmly. "Listen, I know it took a lot for you to come here with all of the stuff that you're going through at home. I'm also aware of how uneasy you've been about coming to this wedding. But I want you to understand that I appreciate you being here with me."

He reached into the breast pocket of his tuxedo jacket and pulled out a long black box and handed it to me.

Flabbergasted, I hesitated, simultaneously staring at the box and at him in shock.

He smiled. "Are you going to open it or just continue to stare at me? The wedding is about to start, you know."

With shaking fingers, I took the box and opened it. My jaw dropped at the sight of the gorgeous diamond necklace and matching earrings on each side. Reflexively, my hand came up to my mouth while I continued to stare at the gift, speechless.

He chuckled in delight at my response and leaned over to take the necklace and earrings that I wore off. "Let's take these off, shall we?" he asked.

Still unable to utter anything, I sat there trembling slightly, overthrown by his generosity while he put on my new jewelry.

After, he gently took my hand and kissed it. "This is so you are sure of how much I love you and how much you mean to me."

"I never doubted—" I started to say.

"I know," he interrupted softly, "but I wanted to give this to you just the same." He cocked his head to the side and asked, "Does this make you feel better?"

"Oh, you have no idea!"

"I thought it would." He nodded and chuckled again. "C'mon, let's just go in there and let all of whatever we have going on in our minds, go. Okay?" he asked, giving my hand a comforting squeeze.

I thought for a moment before I answered. "All right, let's do this," I replied with a confident nod.

He smiled. "That's my girl."

৪৩৫

We held hands while we walked along the cobblestone pathway toward the church and up the stairs. I started getting conscious of the inquisitive stares we received from the rest of the guests entering the church, and the hosts as they offered us the wedding programs when we entered the hall of the church. Tony made small talk with some of them and introduced me to them, but not once did he acknowledge or entertain their whispers and curious glares. I saw in him an admirable sense of confidence and pride in his demeanor during the small talk, which helped give me a small amount of reassurance.

My reassurance automatically shattered when Abigail and I exchanged looks in the sanctuary when she turned around and saw the usher guiding us toward her and Johnathan. In slow motion, Abigail's facial expression went from shock to abysmal disgust and then to slight embarrassment as we approached nearer. This woman was *definitely* not happy to see me.

Abigail turned around stiffly and looked the other way when we reached their row. Johnathan, on the other hand, stood, embraced Tony after a brief handshake and then planted a kiss on my cheek. There were two couples and a woman that were sitting behind Tony's parents. Both males from the two couples were identical and the other woman who also resembled them, stood with beaming smiles.

Oh no! I was totally unprepared to be in the middle of a family reunion!

Tony and his siblings made a small amount of commotion as they embraced and greeted each other. Tony proceeded by introducing me to his brothers, Matthew and Mark, their wives, Joanne and Trisha, and his youngest sister, Jessica. I received warm and friendly handshakes from each with the exception of Matthew, who gave me a cool nod and sat down.

Suddenly, music started to play, giving us the queue to settle down.

I leaned over and whispered to Tony, "I didn't know I was going to meet your entire family today."

"You haven't. Jennifer isn't going to be here. She missed her flight," he whispered back with a smile.

"Oh, great," I murmured.

"Shh, the wedding's about to start," he said softly, putting his arm around me and squeezing my shoulder.

The procession of the wedding party began and strolled down the aisle to an accompaniment of classical music played by musicians toward the front of the church. After a slight pause, *Here Comes the Bride* rang out and everyone stood. The bride, accompanied by her father, beamed with happiness as she strolled down the aisle slowly, allowing everyone to get a good glimpse of her elegant gown.

The ceremony commenced to a few minutes of prayer and lighting of the candles before the priest announced Tony's musical performance. Tony walked toward the front with stride to the piano and began to play *Ave Maria*, and the other musicians joined in.

I sat in admiration and with tears streaming down my face as Tony's rendition displayed his harmonious voice. The bride, I noticed, was also affected and when Tony was done, she released her hand from the groom's to dab her eyes with a handkerchief. That touching moment only made my tears stream more and I took a tissue from my purse.

"Oh, please!" I heard Abigail mutter sarcastically beside me.

I gave her a fleeting glance, but she quickly turned from looking at me to stare straight ahead. Tony had reached our row by then and put his arm around me and gave me a soft squeeze.

"You all right?" he asked softly in my ear.

I nodded. "Yeah, I'm gonna be all right."

He gave me another affectionate squeeze and from the corner of my eye, I saw Abigail watching.

&#8286;&#8286;

When the ceremony was over, everyone started for their cars to the reception. While Tony and I were walking toward his car, Jessica trotted over to us and asked us for a ride.

"So, Lacie, by what small miracle did you start going out with my crazy brother?" Jessica asked me jovially, leaning between the two front seats. "I mean, you couldn't find a better guy than him?"

"You don't waste time, do you?" Tony chuckled, glancing at her briefly in the rearview mirror as he steered out of the parking lot.

"Hey, you know I gotta tease you. You're my younger brother."

"Well, tease or no tease, sit back and put your seatbelt on," Tony countered.

He gave her a playful push and I chuckled.

Not paying Tony any mind, Jessica continued to lean forward. She looked at me with a raised eyebrow and pointed at Tony. "You'd swear he was older than me. Wouldn't you?" The question was apparently rhetorical. She gave me a friendly smile and narrowed her eyes. "So tell me how he managed to snag a beautiful woman like you."

Tony looked at me quickly and rolled his eyes upward. "Lacie, forgive my sister. She's nosy, has no manners and has no idea how to be tactful," he joked.

Jessica opened her mouth to object but Tony interrupted her and continued to tease her. I watched with amusement as they continued their brother-sister good-natured fight for the duration of the ride. I giggled a few times when Jessica delivered some serious vocal punches to Tony's one-liners. She'd winked at me before she delivered them and that's when I knew she and I would have no problem getting along. She was good-natured like her brother.

They were still going at it until we crossed a bridge and arrived at the reception, situated on an island.

"In March?" I uttered with disbelief.

"Well, Spring is about a month away, you know," Tony offered reasonably.

"I'd be inclined to agree with you dear, brother of mine, but it's flippin' fifteen degrees outside and snow is on the ground!" Jessica sighed as she looked out the window. "Trust Lauren to do the most outlandish by trying to out-do everyone in this town for her wedding. This had got to be the stupidest…" She shook her head. "Let me be quiet. Dad already gave me a warning to behave myself. C'mon, you two, let's go," she said, opening the car door.

I giggled. I was really beginning to like Jessica.

We got out the car and followed the rest of the guests toward a massive, incandescent white tent, elegantly decorated in nothing but white on the inside. Better still, were the large heaters that were neatly tucked away on each side, emanating instant warmth as we entered. The rest of the Douglas' hadn't arrived but there were already a sizeable number of guests inside. The guests mingled, helped themselves to the appetizers offered on two elongated tables and some had even formed a line at the bar.

The three of us started walking over to the tables with the appetizers, but as we approached nearer, Tony was abruptly blocked by a gentleman with a woman on his arm. Tony motioned for me to proceed with Jessica. I hesitated but Jessica put a light hand on my shoulder.

"You don't want to meet them. They are two of the many snobs you'll see walking around, putting on airs," Jessica uttered softly. "If they wanted to meet you, they could have easily walked up to both of you," she reasoned. "I'm hungry. C'mon, let's get some grub," she said, taking my hand and leading me toward the table.

While Jessica and I helped ourselves to the appetizers, my eyes kept wandering over to Tony. I saw that the woman who had been with the man had left his side and he and Tony were alone. They seemed to be in earnest conversation and for a second, I thought I saw Tony grimace. Suddenly, Tony, as if feeling my eyes on him, looked in my direction and smiled warmly with an encouraging nod.

Reassured, I turned my attention back to the table and continued to put more appetizers on my plate and make light conversation with Jessica. A few people came over and greeted Jessica briefly but never said a word to me. They only nodded at me warily. But Jessica made sure to introduce me to everyone of them. That, in itself, was flattering.

I looked back at Tony and saw that he was now in what seemed to have turned into a heated exchange with the male from the couple that had interrupted him. His brothers, Matthew and Mark, had joined them and Mark was steering the man away from Tony, but not very discreetly as some of the guests watched.

Jessica shook her head, having witnessed the whole scene as well. "It figures that Jeremy would start something with Tony. He's always been envious of him."

With a sigh, I turned my attention back to the table and suddenly noticed a familiar looking woman watching me intently. I tried to ignore her gaze and moved over to retrieve the utensils and napkins but my peripheral vision showed her continual stare. When I'd decided that I'd about had enough of her scrutiny and was about to say something, Jessica beat me to it.

"Liona, why are you staring at this woman so much? Is there something wrong with your eyes, honey?" Jessica asked facetiously, her eyes never looking up as she grabbed her utensils, too.

"Not at all, darling," Liona remarked casually, her eyes never leaving mine. "I noticed you arriving with Tony at the church," she said to me. "Your name is Lacie, correct?"

How did she know my name?

I tilted my head to the side. "Yes, it is. It's a pleasure to meet you," I replied with a smile. Sure that she was trying to be cordial, I extended a free hand, but she shunned it and her eyes turned cold.

With a curt nod and tight lips she said, "I thought so. Simone is my sister."

Oh, crap!

If this wasn't soap opera drama, I didn't know what was.

## Tony

"So, Tony, who's the girl?" Jeremy Barrett asked, nodding toward Lacie and Jessica at the buffet table, once his wife strolled away after light conversation.

I should've kept walking. I peeked at him carefully, instantly aware of his real reason for stopping me. His family and my family were slightly close, having attended many functions together and Jeremy and I'd gone to the same high school. Still, we were only casual acquaintances. In all honesty, I always thought he was a jerk.

With composure, I smiled. "Her name's Lacie Adams," I replied, as we watched the buffet line get longer.

"She's stunning. Where did you meet her?" he asked straight-forwardly, still eyeing her.

"At work," I replied evasively, taking a glass of wine from a tray offered by one of the servers walking around.

"No kidding," he murmured, helping himself to a glass as well. "Is this serious or—"

I nodded proudly. "Yep."

He turned to me swiftly with a look of surprise. "Really?" he stated. He took a swig of his champagne, shook his head and chuckled. "I didn't know you were into that kind of thing."

"What kind of thing?" I asked coolly, but I was already getting annoyed.

"Into black women. Oh, excuse me, the proper term now is African-American, isn't it?" He shook his head again. "You've certainly got nerve, Douglas. A lot of nerve," he remarked.

"What do you mean by that?" I asked.

"You know everyone's surprised that you brought her here, especially after Simone." I grimaced from his statement and even more so when he looked back at Lacie with lust in his eyes. "But hands down, Douglas, she is hot. I will give you that."

I had to get away from this buffoon. This was a wedding and I didn't want to spoil it by pushing the glass that he was drinking from all the way down his throat.

Instead, I gave him a hard slap on his back. "Thanks a lot, Jeremy," I said sarcastically. "Look, I'm going to get something to eat. Take care and enjoy the wedding, okay?" I started walking away but he blocked me.

"Oh, no you don't, Douglas," he said, putting a hand on my chest briefly. "You can't leave without letting me know if what they say is true." I stiffened in annoyance as he leaned in and asked, "Are colored women really that much better in bed than white women?"

"Colored?" I asked, glaring at him incredulously. He nodded with a smirk and it set me off. "What the—" I began but was interrupted when Matthew and Mark approached us.

At once, Mark put his arm around Jeremy and steered him away swiftly, saying, "So, Jeremy, tell me about this case you're working on." Mark's voice faded as they moved further away.

"Jerk," I uttered bitterly.

"That's Jeremy for you. Always has and always will be," Matthew concurred. "We saw that he was getting to you and decided to relieve you."

I nodded. "Good looking out," I remarked dryly, still fuming.

"Hey, I'm your big brother. That's what I'm supposed to do," Matthew asserted strongly. Then he drew in a deep breath and nodded over to Lacie and Jessica. "So, that's her, huh?" he asked.

"Yep," I said.

"Well, you certainly know how to make a statement. I give you that," Matthew murmured.

I frowned at him. "What the hell does that mean?"

He shook his head. "Nothing. Don't worry about it. We'll talk about it when we get to the house."

I scoffed. "As far as I'm concerned, there *is* nothing to talk about..." I started. A commotion at the appetizer buffet line suddenly caught my attention.

What the? Was that Simone's sister, Liona? What was she doing here?

"Oh, hell, Matthew. It looks like I'm not the only one that's going to need rescuing," I murmured, giving him a slight pull as we headed toward the buffet table.


## Lacie

"Is that supposed to mean something, Liona?" Jessica inquired casually.

Liona glanced at her briefly and replied, "Yes, I want her to know that I'm aware that she's the one that stole Tony away from my sister."

Jessica scoffed. "Liona, honey, Tony wasn't Simone's to begin with. You know that."

"Yes and you made sure of that, didn't you?" Liona replied.

Jessica let out an exasperated breath and voiced a little loudly. "Liona, this is your best friend's wedding, okay? Let's not turn this into a catfight. I kicked your butt in high school so don't let me do it here because you know I will."

I stood there rooted, amazed and slightly uncomfortable with their heated exchange as everyone had suddenly stopped putting appetizers on their plates to watch Jessica and Liona.

Liona wasn't affected by Jessica's threat. She countered with, "No wonder your parents put you in boarding school. You just never had enough class."

"Lacie, hold this for me..." Jessica began. She was getting ready to give me her plate to go after Liona when out of nowhere, Tony and Matthew appeared. Matthew took Jessica swiftly by the hand and steered her away.

"Hello, Liona," Tony said calmly, coming to my side.

Liona glared at Tony, turned, and walked away.

Tony took me to the side and asked with concern, "You all right?"

Everyone else continued with the buffet but I was well aware that prying eyes were on us.

"You should be asking Jessica that question," I said matter-of-factly, letting out a deep breath. "But yeah, I'm fine. Jessica came to my defense, anyway."

He nodded. "That's Jessica, for you," he said, smiling.

We both observed Jessica still mouthing off while a calm Matthew politely held the chair out for her to sit at the table with the rest of the Douglas'.

I searched Tony's face. "How about you? Are *you* all right? It looked like you got into a little confrontation with that guy back there a minute ago. You want to tell me about it?"

He shook his head quickly. "Nothing to worry about," he answered evasively with a taut smile.

"Okay," I said with a small sigh. Clearly he was bothered by something and didn't want me to know about it. But there was something that I did want to know. "Listen, I'm already surprised to find out that Simone has a sister and that she's at this particular wedding. Is there any chance that Simone is going to be here, too?"

Tony hardly got a word out before I heard a female voice behind us say, "Hello, Tony."

The hairs on my neck automatically prickled at the familiar voice.

I winced as Tony and I turned around, not wanting to believe the circumstances. Yet, there stood Simone wearing a beautiful white fur-lined dress.

Damn it! I spoke her up.

Tony instinctively put his arm around my waist and I saw Simone's eyes follow as he did. I was glad he put his arm around me because at that moment, I was feeling lightheaded, troubled by the weird coincidences that were happening. Shoot, we had only arrived about fifteen minutes ago.

"Hello, Simone," he replied evenly. "What are you doing here?"

Responding with a thin smile and opening her arms out a little she said, "I'm a friend of the bride and her family. Shouldn't I be?"

He shrugged nonchalantly. "I guess I can't argue with that."

Those famous eyes flashed crossly for one second before she gave him another thin smile. "No, you can't. Anyway, it's good to see you, Tony." She looked at me and her eyes dropped to the new diamond necklace on my neck and then to my earrings. She pursed her lips tightly with a small indifferent nod and muttered, "Lacie," before she walked away.

Tony and I stood there in silent stupefaction. Finally, he took a deep breath, looked at me with both eyebrows raised and asked, "Okay. You ready to go to the table?"

I took a deep breath also and looked up at him with a nod. "Yeah, that's a good idea because I need to sit down."

He laughed softly. "I know what you mean."

With slight haste, we walked over to join the rest of the Douglas' at the table, hoping that the remainder of the reception would be without incident. Immediately, I noticed Abigail's chagrined expression when Tony, in a gentlemanly manner, pushed my chair in. Home girl was ticked! Thankfully, the bridal party entered the tent at that moment, taking her attention off of me, at least, for the time being.

The bride and groom's face lit up as people stood and took pictures. They were without a doubt, very happy and very much in love. I felt Tony's arm come around my shoulders and him kiss my shoulder. I turned to look at his tender expression and smiled. Kindred spirits.

The reception ensued as we sat and watched the series of events that occurred. Shortly after, perfectly suited waiters and waitresses lined in sequence, came to each table and set the main entrée in front of each person. Each plate was nicely decorated with a large lobster tail, rice pilaf and steamed vegetables.

As we ate, I listened to most of the Douglas' make small talk and banter with each other. They even took time to engage me in the conversation. Abigail, however, remained silent at the table. She ignored my presence and didn't make any effort to introduce me to the throngs of curious people that came over to the table that were clearly wondering about the strange new member at the table—me.

Abigail's standpoint was made perfectly clear when one guest asked her to introduce me to them. Her face immediately turned red, but Tony, with an affectionate hand around my shoulder, answered for her by politely introducing me as his girlfriend. That seemed to do it for Abigail. Without a word and without excusing herself, she stood up, left the table and headed straight for the bar. Matthew got up also and went after her.

I tried not to get aggravated by Abigail's attitude and her total disregard and enjoy the reception, but once I saw the cunning grin Simone was slyly giving me while she pulled a shy and bashful Rachel Sanders toward Abigail, I started to tense again.

This was absurd!

Here I was, the only black person at a wedding, didn't know any of the people here, and I had to deal with Abigail's cantankerous attitude, a snobby Simone again, and a schoolboy crushed, Rachel.

Irritated, I breathed deep and pushed my plate away roughly. My appetite was spoiled.

It didn't get past Tony.

"What's wrong?" Tony murmured in my ear.

"Nothing," I fibbed.

. "Are you sure?" He gave me a skeptical look before taking a glance at my plate. "You've barely touched your food and you just pushed your plate away like you're upset about something. Is it the food?"

"No, it's not that. I guess my stomach's filled from the appetizers."

"Uh, huh," he uttered, still looking skeptical.

"What?" I asked, hunching my shoulders.

A slow instrumental ballad suddenly engulfed the tent, giving the cue for the newlyweds to have their first dance. They walked hand-in-hand onto the dance floor and with loving expressions, encircled their arms around each other and danced. A few minutes later, the bride and groom switched to dance with each other's parents and soon other couples started for the dance floor.

Tony looked at me and I shook my head as soon he held out his hand. "Nope," I said. "Don't even think about it."

"C'mon," he said with a mischievous wink. "You scared?" he teased.

Hell, yeah, I was! Tony was out of his mind for asking me to dance, knowing that people were going to be staring at us. Still, he kept his hand out, despite the mean glare I was giving him.

"Might as well, Lacie," Jessica said supportively. "Because I am. I'm going to walk right to that table over there and ask that guy to dance." She leaned over to me and pointed to an attractive guy a few tables over from us who was smiling back at her. "I don't know who he is and have never seen him in my life. But he's good-looking and we've been eyeing each other ever since Matthew steered me to this table. This is the twentieth century and gone are the old-fashioned ways. I'm going in for the kill!"

Jessica did just that, too. She strolled over to the man and after a brief conversation, they walked onto the dance floor with the rest of the crowd.

"Well, I'm going to take that as a hint and find my wife before the song ends," Johnathan announced with a smile, getting up from the table. "Excuse me."

"How about it?" Tony asked softly. We watched Mark and Trisha get up and make their way to the dance floor and Joanne leave to find Matthew. "C'mon, Lacie," Tony encouraged.

*Here goes, Lacie.*

Nervously, I took a deep breath and took his hand as he guided me gently onto the floor. I was fully aware of the eyes and whispers that followed us.

"Just concentrate on us. Don't be concerned about whether people are looking," Tony murmured as we walked onto the floor.

"I'm trying not to," I replied, wryly.

"But not enough," he shot back. With a grin he pulled me into him abruptly with one hand and held my hand to his chest with the other.

"Show off," I hissed softly, surprised by his assertive strength.

"Oh, you haven't seen anything, yet," he murmured.

In that second, he led me into a slow and romantic dance and soon everyone else around us became non-existent. This was our first dance together and because Tony could do everything else well, I shouldn't have been surprised by how well he danced.

Rhythm was definitely not lost on him—in all aspects!

His steady affectionate gaze never left mine as he held me in his arms and moved me around the dance floor in a slow and perfect tempo. My anxiety quickly disappeared and I relaxed, laying my head on his shoulder. I was in perfect bliss and wanted to stay in his arms.

"You feel better?" he whispered in my ear as his hands caressed up and down my back. Another slow tune came on and most of the couples remained on the floor.

I looked up at him with a smile. "Much better."

"Good. I knew something was wrong and figured this would brighten your spirit some."

"You did, huh?" I asked, raising my eyebrow.

Laughing softly he said, "Once you were in my arms and dancing with me, I knew you would."

"Aren't you arrogant?" I gibed softly.

He shook his head. "No. Just wanting to take care of my girl, that's all."

I gushed at his statement and replied with, "Remember a while back when I was so overwhelmed by your skills on the piano and your voice?" He nodded. "Well, I've got to tell you. I'm not at all surprised at your skills on the dance floor."

"Oh, no?" he asked, his turn to raise an eyebrow.

"No." I grinned devilishly and added in a husky tone, "Because you've got skills in bed."

He looked at me flabbergasted for a second and then shook his head. "That," he chuckled, "was very bad."

With a wink and a wider grin, I whispered in his ear, "I know. Payback for what you said a few minutes ago."

"Oh, all right," he said in amusement. With a nod and a smirk, he added, "Wait until we get to the hotel."

I was about to make another comeback when Abigail came up to us, with Rachel behind her, interrupting our dance.

Ignoring me, she said, "Anthony, would you mind giving Rachel one dance? She didn't know you'd be bringing a guest along and had been looking forward to dancing with you." She didn't even wait for him to reply. "Thank you, darling. You're such a good son." She smiled lovingly as she placed Rachel's hand in his and gently pushed me out of the way while Matthew, simultaneously and conveniently came up to me.

He took my hand and said, "Lacie, c'mon and dance with me."

The ruse had been cunning, deliberate and smooth, giving Tony and myself no time to react or protest. Like torn lovers, we eyed each other disturbingly while both of our new partners steered us away from each other. Tony's expression was taut and annoyed but he continued with Rachel proprietarily and kept a safe distance from her while she swooned like a lovesick puppy. Embarrassed, I looked around and momentarily locked eyes with Johnathan. He was standing by the sidelines with a wry expression, clearly having witnessed the brief exchange, no matter how cleverly done. From the looks on some of the other guests, it had not been missed by them, either.

"My mother's not happy that Tony brought you to this wedding," Matthew stated coolly, steadily steering me away from his brother.

ACROSS THE COLOR LINE

I looked up at him. "Really?" I said, sarcastically. "No! I would have never guessed."

He gave me a small, tight grin. "Just so you know. If my mother's upset about something, I will do anything I can to alleviate the problem," he shot back in a meaningful tone.

Aw, man! Now him, too?

Abruptly and before the music stopped, he released me and said with a smirk, "Thanks for the dance."

"Thank you," I said crisply, as he walked toward his wife and left me alone on the dance floor.

Slightly depleted of all energy and all at once feeling a little queasy and lightheaded, I walked toward the back of the tent. Someone slid next to me. It was Simone.

She had to come up to me, didn't she? Damn, this woman didn't know when to stop!

"They look good together, don't they?" she remarked, looking at the dance floor.

I blew out a tired breath. "Simone, I'm warning you now. Don't start."

She let out a little laugh. "I just asked you a friendly question."

"You know very well that you're not trying to be friendly, Simone," I stated evenly. "And no—they don't look good together—she's not his type."

"And you are?"

"I'm here with him, aren't I?" I retorted.

"But to stay?" she shot back, laconically.

Wincing and feeling the queasiness intensifying, I noticed a few people glancing our way curiously and decided to not say anything. I'd been insulted by the insinuation and did not trust what would come out of my mouth next.

Taking my silence for an opportunity to get another jab in, Simone started again. "That's a gorgeous necklace you have on," she remarked dryly. "Tony must have given it to you, because you obviously couldn't afford it yourself." She tsked, tsked. "It's a pity something so nice has to go to waste."

"Evidently Tony doesn't think so because he gave it to me, didn't he?" I struggled heatedly, feeling a little faint. A few more people looked our way again, but I didn't have a care in the world. She'd plucked my nerves. "When was the last time he gave you anything?" I looked up and pretended to ponder briefly, before I looked back down and glared into her cold eyes. "Oh yeah, it's been a while, hasn't it? 'Cause he's *my* man now, Simone. Remember that."

"So," she shrugged nonchalantly, immune to my retort. "Do you think Abigail's going to let you into the family? You will *never* be accepted in Tony's family. You are way out of your league, Lacie, and you will never fit in because you don't belong. It would completely ruin Tony and his family's reputation in this town to have a black–"

Wedding and reception completely forgotten and with a great deal of effort, I braced and balled my fist. Despite how sickly I was feeling, I was determined to get her and this time Robert wasn't here to stop me.

Then I heard a voice behind me say forcefully, "Simone, shut up. Just shut up and leave Lacie alone! I've been watching you ever since you arrived. Don't you know when to give up?" Jessica came to my side.

Relieved, I put one of my hands on her shoulder for some support and the other on my stomach. Nausea was rising in my stomach and I was getting more lightheaded.

Jessica waved her glass of red wine airily. "Tony doesn't want you."

"Because of you." Liona marched up to us angrily, coming to her sister's rescue.

"Hey, a slut, is a slut, is a slut," Jessica said matter-of-factly.

"Oh, you, bitch!" Liona yelled.

We got a few more glances our way.

I held onto Jessica tighter as the room seemed to spin slowly in and out of focus.

"Liona, that's all right," Simone said calmly, stepping up to Jessica's face with a devious grin. "Jessica's just letting off some steam, is all. You know she's always been that way. Despite her wealth, she's just

214

never had enough class. You can't expect any manners from this piece of white trash."

*Ouch!*

I winced for Jessica and myself as I felt nausea getting ready to come up any minute.

Jessica took what Simone said in stride and eyed her glass as she swiveled the red wine around. "You're one to talk about manners, Simone. Don't you know it's considered improper etiquette and insulting to wear white at a wedding? Only the bride is supposed to wear white. Here, let me give you a hand!" Jessica voiced calmly and dashed the wine in Simone's face.

The look of horror and embarrassment on Simone's face, along with the red wine dripping on her expensive white fur-lined outfit, was priceless and definitely overdue. Adding to that, was the exorcist like stream of vomit that suddenly protruded out of my mouth and onto Simone's outfit, taking place of the laugh that it was originally intended for. Reflexively, a small giggle seeped out of me when I eyed the peculiar mixture I'd made to go along with the red wine stain. With effort, I put my hand over my mouth, struggling to maintain my poise and not let another giggle loose or anything else for that matter. But the damage had already been done.

Simone's eyes widened and she screamed, "You, bitch!" As she lunged after me and Jessica moved me out of the way and slapped her, I wondered if this was what really happened at rich people's functions, before my world suddenly became black.

## Tony

"Your girlfriend is beautiful," Rachel remarked a few minutes into our dance.

"Thank you." I replied stiffly, uncomfortable with dancing with her.

I noticed Mom trying to steer Dad toward us while they danced and chuckled silently when he responded by purposely turning her in the other direction.

"I'm in love with you," Rachel confessed with sudden boldness, searching my face for a reaction.

Her statement made me feel even more uncomfortable. The only thing I could think of to utter was, "Rachel—"

"I know you're in love with Lacie, Tony," Rachel soothed, quickly. "But I still had to tell you. I've felt this way about you ever since high school and was so afraid to tell you. Then you went off to college and when you came back you got engaged to Simone. After I heard that you and Simone broke up, I figured I'd finally have my chance. But after dinner in New York that night and seeing how you are with Lacie and the way you look at her…" She shook her head. "I've never seen you look at Simone or anyone else the way you look at her." She chuckled softly. "Lacie is an extremely lucky woman."

"No, I'm the lucky one," I declared.

"Ah, ever so modest you are, Tony," she said tenderly. She reached to touch the back of my head and I moved it. She smiled thinly and let out a small sigh. "Right. I told your mother and Simone that this was useless." She released her grip from mine and said thickly, "Excuse me."

I stood still, watching Rachel walk through the crowd swiftly. Mom noticed Rachel leaving and stopped dancing with Dad. He followed slowly behind her as she approached me with a concerned expression.

"What happened? Why did Rachel leave?" she asked.

I raised my eyebrow and with a straightforward expression said, "We need to talk."

"What do you mean?" Mom asked innocently.

"You, bitch!" I heard a familiar voice scream. The scream was potent enough for the music to stop and everyone to look in the direction it had come from.

In the back of the tent, were two male guests trying to hold Simone and Jessica while they grasped at each other and nearby, was a limp Lacie getting ready to slump to the floor.

"Oh my, God, Lacie!" I yelled, rushing to her.

# Chapter 39

# Tony

"Are you sure she doesn't need to go to the hospital?" I queried Dr. Rosen a third time with concern, twenty minutes later in my old bedroom in my parent's house.

Getting up from the bed where a sleeping Lacie lay, Dr. Rosen shook his head, and took off his stethoscope.

"No, I've checked all of her vitals twice. When she immediately stirred after I put the smelling salt under her nose at the wedding, and after I checked her pulse, I figured it was nothing to be concerned with. But I'm glad I followed you in the car over here to be sure."

I breathed a sigh of relief and shook my head. "I don't know what happened. After she came to I put her in the car and then she went back to sleep."

He frowned at Lacie thoughtfully. "Has she been tired a lot lately? Have there been any changes in her appetite—that kind of stuff?"

It was my turn to frown. "We've been working a lot of hours and she's been yawning a lot recently. As far as her appetite, I don't know. You're going to have to ask her."

As if he had a sudden revelation, Dr. Rosen smiled and shook his head.

"What, Doctor?"

"Nothing. Nothing at all, Tony," he said with a slight chuckle. He gave me a pat on my arm. "Just make sure she gets plenty of rest and tell her that she must follow up with her primary physician when she gets back home. She needs to find out the cause of her upset stomach. If anything changes, call me. You've got my number. She should be fine, though."

"Thank you, Dr. Rosen," I said, shaking his hand.

Once he left, I walked over to the bed and with care took her vomit stained gown off and undergarments. She stirred only slightly and with eyes still closed, gave me a small smile when I pulled the covers over her. I sat down and looked at her and tucked some hair behind her ears. She looked peaceful while she slept, but my God, did she scare me half to death!

I'd reached her in enough time to catch her falling body and panicked when her eyes rolled in the back of her head and saw the color leaving her face. Thank God, Dr. Rosen was at the wedding. He acted promptly despite the other guests gathering around us and the chaos between Simone and Jessica. Once Lacie came to and I was assured by Dr. Rosen that there was no need to take her to the hospital, Dad insisted that I bring her to the house instead of going to a hotel. He would take care of the damage.

I shook my head, feeling culpable for pressing Lacie to attend the wedding with me in the first place. Too many incidents had happened and the sheer fact that Simone had been there when she should have been out of the country, had me concerned about the strange happenstance.

I glanced at my watch when I heard the rest of my family entering the house with a lot of commotion. I took one last look at Lacie before I tiptoed softly to the door and went downstairs.

&#8365;&#8359;&#8360;

"Jessica, it was supposed to be a wedding, not a brawl!" I heard Mom voice loudly when I entered the family room. "I have never in my life seen a wedding go so awry! Do you know how embarrassed I am and how many calls I'm going to get because of that commotion you caused? I'll have to apologize to just about everyone who attended that wedding!"

"Mom, you don't have to apologize to anyone. Everybody there was snobbish enough as it was, thinking they were better than everyone else just because they have money and Simone got exactly what she deserved! Lacie was getting sick and she was getting ready to go after her," Jessica defended.

"Because she vomited all over her outfit!" Mom stressed, before suddenly noticing my appearance. "Ah, the man of the hour. I'm so glad you decided to join us, Anthony."

I took notice of how odd it was that both of my brothers were there, considering the late hour and that they both had homes of their own to go to.

Mom explained why. "We've been waiting for you to come down so we can have a family meeting."

"A family meeting, huh?" I asked with a cool nod. "Sounds serious."

Everyone was in their usual spots. Matthew and Mark were sitting in upright chairs by the picture window. Dad was in his easy chair. Mom was in her chaise and Jessica was across from her on the sofa.

Dad looked at me with concern. "How's Lacie, Tony?"

"She's fine, Dad. She's upstairs asleep in my bedroom," I replied and strolled over to Jessica and sat down next to her.

He nodded, satisfied with my answer.

"Why couldn't you take her to a hotel?" Mom asked abruptly.

"Abby," Dad warned softly.

I cocked my head and squinted at my mother, surprised by her brusque tone. She didn't look my way.

"A comment like that is exactly why I guess we need to have this *sudden* family meeting," I said, taking a fleeting glance at everyone in the room. "I'm at a loss by what happened today and the convenient incidents that occurred. Two questions: Jessica, why were you scrapping with Simone and Mom, what was Simone doing there? Actually, scratch the first question. I have a slight idea of why you and Simone went at it Jessica, but Mom?"

Mom avoided my eyes. "I'm not Simone's mother, Anthony."

"Yes," I said slowly. "But I know for a fact, that Simone wasn't due to return to the states for at least another year. Did you have something to do with that?"

"Why are you asking Mom, Tony?" Matthew asked, always the first to defend her.

I gave him a momentary look, hating that everyone always seemed to have to answer to him. "Because I know how upset Mom was when

Simone and I broke up and I'm concerned about the convenience of it all," I replied tersely.

"It wasn't convenient, Anthony. I heard your mother tell Simone on the phone that you were going to be at the wedding and she almost begged Simone to come," Dad answered for her.

"Johnathan!" Mom said hotly.

"It's what happened, Abbie," Dad said matter-of-factly, shaking his head.

"Mom," I said, disappointingly.

Mom's face changed color the way it normally did when she was embarrassed—red. She stiffened in her chair. "Anthony, you have to realize that Simone would want to be there because she's Lauren's friend. There was no reason why I couldn't let her know that you were going to be there as well." She leaned over to look at me earnestly. "Do you know how many people came up to me asking me why you and Simone broke up? You know Simone wants you back, Anthony."

I sighed exasperatingly, not even wanting to go there. "And that whole fiasco with Rachel, Mom? What was that about?"

Her expression was apathetic. "You were supposed to be there alone, Anthony. You knew Rachel was looking forward to you being at the wedding and that she wanted a dance with you. I told you when we had dinner in New York. So I saw no harm in giving you two a moment alone. That way you might consider..." she trailed off shrugging her shoulders.

I looked at her dubiously. "Where did you get that idea, Mom? I'm not interested in Rachel and you had to know I would bring Lacie with me," I scoffed. "How could you expect me to be able to get with Rachel and try to rekindle a relationship with Simone at the same time?"

"It's not impossible," Mom claimed. "I told you. Always keep your options open, Anthony."

"Mom, you put Tony in a complicated position, by putting him in between Rachel and Simone, knowing that he was with Lacie. And you might as well give up hope that Tony and Simone are going to get back together. It's a lost cause," Jessica remarked, shaking her head.

Mom looked at her sharply. "And you, young lady, are skating on thin ice. That fight you started with Simone was uncalled for! She is a major celebrity in this town and is on her way to being the highest paid supermodel ever."

"That doesn't give her the right to be cruel, Mom. She was very mean to Lacie and when she started in on me, that's when I had to take matters into my own hands," Jessica defended. "That is why Tony shouldn't be with her in the first place, because she's a cold-hearted b–"

Mom, always hating any kind of expletive, interrupted Jessica with a shake of her head. "Lisa is a grown woman. She couldn't defend herself?"

I gritted my teeth at the mispronunciation of Lacie's name. "Her name's Lacie, Mom."

"Lisa, Leslie, Lacie, it doesn't matter," Mom said defensively with clear aggravation. "Anthony, *you* were the only one invited. When you brought that girl to that wedding, all of a sudden I was besieged with all kinds of questions and comments and was totally unprepared to give explanations to everyone around me. Who's that girl with Anthony? Where is she from? I didn't know he was into that sort of thing. How long has this been going on? *Oh...I feel so sorry for you,*" Mom stressed. "It was embarrassing, Anthony! *All* of our friends and a lot of important and influential people were there."

I stared at my mother blankly.

Matthew straightened up in his chair and peered at me. "And just *when* did you start dating African-American women, Tony? C'mon, couldn't you have chosen a Chinese woman instead?"

Annoyed, I raised my eyebrow. "There wasn't any *choosing* involved," I corrected quickly. "By the way, Matthew, you don't have to be so politically correct by saying the term, 'African-American.'"

He looked at me skeptically. "Oh yeah? *We* always have to be careful about what we say around black people at work. If we say the wrong thing or make them mad, they'll be quick to file a lawsuit against us or call the NAACP."

I grimaced and wondered when my brother became so ignorant. "Matthew, Lacie is not a 'they or them.' She's an individual," I snapped. "And watch what you say!"

He was unperturbed. "Still…we need to know; are you trying to fulfill some sexual fantasy or—" he started, but my hard glare stopped him.

Mom answered for me. "This *has* to be something he's trying. It's nothing serious. It can't be."

I looked at my mother calmly. "No, that's where you're wrong, Mom. My relationship with Lacie is very serious."

There was dead silence in the room.

Catching on quickly, Mark finally spoke up. "Tony, you're not thinking about marrying her, are you?"

I nodded. "That's why I wanted her to come, so that she could meet all of you."

"But she's black!" Mom shrieked, shaking her head furiously.

Her statement tore into my soul.

"Abbie!" Dad exclaimed.

"You did not just say that," I said angrily at Mom's remark. "You did not just say that."

Mark smiled at Matthew. "I told you, Matthew."

Matthew ignored Mark and shook his head with a deep sigh. Out of the corner of my eye, I saw Mom holding her face in her hands.

"Tony, you *cannot* expect Mom or any of us for that matter, to be okay about this, considering everything that happened today. You've always been the eccentric one, but we've never known you to be interested in African-American women. You can't be serious about this," Matthew contended straightforwardly.

"Oh, I'm very serious," I said dryly.

Matthew squinted at me for a good second before he said, "Is she pregnant? Is that why you're considering this? Is she blackmailing you?"

"No, she's not pregnant and the last question is just ridiculous. I love her, man," I snapped, defensively

"I just don't believe it," Mom uttered stupefied, as she ran her hands down her face.

I shook my head. "Mom, I told you—" I started.

She shook her head violently and cried, "But you've always dated white women, Anthony! *Always!*"

"Why didn't you tell us about this sooner, Tony? We could have discussed this so we wouldn't be so embarrassed and caught off guard," Matthew piggybacked Mom crossly.

"Oh, I made *you* uncomfortable by bringing the woman that I love to an event where my family and friends would be," I said sarcastically. "I've never had to *discuss* any other women that I've brought around before."

"This is different, Tony," Matthew argued.

I took a composed look around the room. My dad in his chair, forearms on his legs, leaning over. Mark sitting quietly, expression calm and Jessica, frowning and shaking her head. Then I turned and looked at my mother and oldest brother. I loved them both but at that moment, I couldn't stand them. The actuality that I was slowly and painfully starting to comprehend was very hard to swallow.

I shook my head and scoffed, my anger starting to manifest. "I've just got to ask this question directly to make sure that I'm not losing my mind because of all that happened at the wedding and the comments that have just been made; but do you all really have a problem with me being with Lacie? And would we even be having this meeting if Lacie were white?" I stressed looking at Mom and Matthew, who were avoiding eye contact with me.

There was no response, which triggered more anger. "*No one*, besides Dad and Jessica has even bothered to ask how Lacie was doing or has come to her defense after all she went through tonight, seeing Simone and being literally pushed away from me by my own mother. And the only focus in this family meeting is the fact that I'm dating a black, oh—excuse me, Matthew, *African-American* woman?" I voiced bitterly, raking him over momentarily.

"I don't know what's going on here, but all of this stinks to high Heaven and some of you'd better check yourselves!" I asserted harshly. "We have all in some way been around and associated with black people—really all different races of people. But all of a sudden when I find a woman that I truly love and seriously intend to marry it becomes an issue? Because of her color?"

"Tony, remember how upset you got with Jeremy Barrett? You were ready to punch his lights out because of the comments he made,"

Matthew contended. "Do you want to go through that all of your life, having to defend your position every time you turn around?"

"I'm defending it now, aren't I? To the people—my *family*, mind you—who I thought would stand by me no matter what the cost," I retorted.

"Anthony, listen, we're not prejudice. We don't have anything against black people or any other race for that matter. You know we have some black friends. But we just didn't think either of you would get involved with one of them!" Mom blurted.

She gasped, covered her mouth and looked at me, but it was too late. The words had already come out and had sliced right through me.

"Whoa," I uttered, standing up. "One of them? One of them?"

"All right, let's all just calm down and discuss this in a mannerly fashion," Dad intervened calmly.

His request went unnoticed because I was already incensed.

"I'm sorry, Anthony...I," Mom started.

I didn't even want to hear it. I started heading out the room saying, "You know what? We're out of here."

Matthew stood up and blocked my way. "Tony, sit down and don't go off the handle. Let's talk this out."

I snarled at him and clenched my teeth. "Matthew, back up. Right now," I threatened.

His eyes widened in surprise and then he moved.

I was furious. If it took carrying Lacie down the stairs with our luggage—we were out.

Dad and Jessica caught up with me before I went up the stairs.

"Son, son, listen to me. Not everyone feels the way your mother and Matthew do," Dad said, grabbing my arm. "I don't want you to go. I don't want either of you to go."

"Yeah, Tony, don't leave," Jessica pleaded softly. "Don't pay any attention to Matthew, either. You know how pigheaded he can be."

Dad spoke quickly, seeing my hesitation. "Listen, Abbie's just upset right now because of the wedding and all. Tomorrow, she'll be in a better mood."

I shook my head and blew hard.

"Son, it's okay, really," Dad's eyes implored.

With a decisive nod, I said, "Okay. She'd better be."

Muttering under my breath, I continued up the stairs to the bedroom with reality and a lot of disappointment sinking into my skull at every step. Lacie had been so worried about what my parents and my family were going to think.

And damn if what she'd been so concerned about hadn't come true.

# Chapter 40

# Dawn

I loved Joe's family.

As soon as Joe came off his flight he had called me, saying that he wanted to take me somewhere. He didn't tell me the place, only told me to dress comfortably.

*"Where are you going?" Mom asked casually, coming into my room.*

*I paused, reluctant to tell her. "Out with Joe," I replied quickly, avoiding her eyes while I put on my shoes.*

*"You're going out with him again even though you haven't told Lacie yet?"*

*I could hear the displeasure in her voice and decided not to say a word. She already knew the answer anyway.*

*"Dawn..." she began.*

*I looked up abruptly, aggravated by my own guilt and what I knew was getting ready to come out of her mouth. "Mom, I know. You don't have to say it."*

*Mom sighed. "All right. Just so you know; that there is always a consequence for this type of behavior."*

*She still had to say it. Didn't she?*

When Joe came to pick me up, I couldn't have been happier. Happy to see him and elated to get away from the unfavorable looks by my mother.

"I'm taking you to meet my parents," Joe said immediately as he pulled onto the street. "They've invited us over for dinner."

"What?" I exclaimed.

He smiled and patted my hand. "Yep, so get ready."

"You sneaky son of a–" I voiced.

"Hey, watch your mouth!" he teased, grinning.

Joe's parents, Barry and Margaret Mitchell and sister, Jade, were nothing but welcoming and embraced me as soon as we entered their massive but comforting house. Joe had spared no expense in making sure that his parents had had a nice spread.

Barry was of medium height and thin—the antithesis of Joe. Margaret, Jade and Joe were like identical triplets. While Joe and his father conversed in the living room, Margaret showed me around the house like a proud parent, showcasing all of Joe's high school and college trophies and awards. Jade continued with dinner in the kitchen.

I giggled at one of Joe's baby pictures on the refrigerator that showed him with a little afro, as we joined Jade in the kitchen.

Joe surprised me by coming up behind me and grabbing me around my waist. "What are you laughing at, huh?" he asked.

Still giggling, I looked up at him and teased, "I'm not laughing at you. I'm laughing with you."

He raised his eyebrow. "Oh yeah? Let's see who's laughing now," he remarked, and reached for me.

I tried to get away from him, but he was too quick. He took a hold of me and started tickling me and all I could do was laugh.

Margaret smiled and shook her head at us with her hands on her hip. "Joe, stop tickling that girl. You know I don't like that foolishness in my kitchen. Go do that somewhere else," she complained. "My goodness, you'd swear he'd never brought a girl home the way he's acting," I heard her say to Jade as he walked me out of the kitchen with his arms around me.

The rest of the visit continued with a delicious dinner and great conversation as Joe and his family caught up with what was happening in each of their lives. I listened, enjoying the warmth of the atmosphere. And then…

"Dawn, I must thank you. I don't know what you've done to my son, but I've never seen him so happy," Margaret remarked, giving Joe an affectionate glance. Her expression turned suddenly weary and she shook her head, reminiscently. "You should have seen him at Christmas. He was so sad and his heart was just broken from that last girl he was with. He just wasn't himself." She turned to look at her husband. "What was that girl's name, Barry? Lina, Liza…"

"I think it was Lucy," Barry said contemplatively.

"No, it was, Lisa," Jade said self-assuredly.

"You're all wrong. Her name was Lacie," Joe intervened, with an uncomfortable smile.

"That's right, Lacie. That was her name." Margaret nodded and shook her head again. "I can't tell you how painful it was for me to see my boy so hurt; especially when I found out how she jilted him. Oh yeah, I was upset, all right."

From the corner of my eye, I saw Joe shift uneasily.

"Frankly, I was ready to kick her a–" Jade said.

"Jade, please, don't be rude," Margaret interjected, giving Jade a sharp look.

Ill-affected, Jade commenced with spooning more macaroni and cheese on her plate.

Margaret continued with an apologetic smile, looking at me. "But you see, Dawn. We didn't raise our son to hate or to get even. We raised him to respect women and treat them right. And my son is a good man," she said with conviction. She raised her arms and shrugged. "So this Lacie has missed out on a good man to be with another man."

"And a white man at that," Barry added, shaking his head.

"That's not the issue, Barry. You know you like Tony," Margaret contended, looking at him briefly before turning her eyes on me again. "Now although Joseph was badly hurt by Lacie's rejection, it's alright because now my boy is very happy and has clearly acquired a rare gem," she remarked with a warm smile. "After seeing how my son's face lights up with you, I know that you are that treasure."

Margaret reached out for my hand and I grasped hers with tears forming in my eyes.

"Thank you for making my son so happy," she said, tears welling up in hers as well.

I swallowed and dabbed my eye with a napkin with my other hand. "Thank you for making me feel so welcome."

She nodded. "From now on, our home is your home."

Jade cleared her throat. "Hey, not to spoil the moment, but just *how* did you meet my brother anyway, Dawn. Was it love at first sight, or what?"

Yeah, she spoiled the moment, all right. I breathed in deep and looked at Joe uneasily, who was equally flabbergasted at the unexpected question. Everyone was waiting patiently for my answer.

"Ooh, it must have been something sinister how they met. Look at them. They're both blushing," Jade bantered, giving Joe a slight punch on the arm.

Joe chuckled and shook his finger at Jade. "You know you're going to get it, don't you?"

"Jade, you've embarrassed them. It's not important how they met. They're together now." Margaret squeezed my hand comfortingly.

Suddenly bold and surprising myself, I declared, "I'll tell you how I feel about Joe instead." I had Joe's attention now but I couldn't look at him as I spoke. "Notwithstanding that he is by far the most handsome man I've ever met. But he is like fresh warm spring air after a cold winter, waiting for me to slowly step into and be engulfed by. My dream man deferred, but now presented to me in the most perfect and amazing gift-wrapped package."

"Wow," everyone exclaimed at the table in unison.

"So, I'm a gift-wrapped package, huh?" Joe chuckled softly, looking out the window of his car as we sat in front of his parent's house.

We'd not moved and had been sitting in his car for fifteen minutes.

"Yep," I confirmed with a small sigh, looking out my side of the window. I shouldn't have said what I'd said. I'd revealed too much, making myself vulnerable.

"Did you mean what you said?" he asked.

I took a deep breath, deliberating whether I should be so truthful. Why not? I'd already exposed my deepest feelings to him and his family. Might as well go all the way.

I turned to look into his eyes and said softly, "Yes. Of course, I did."

His eyes replied with the same love and compassion that I had for him. He swallowed hard and said, "I guess we'd better get going. My parent's have been looking out the window ever since we got in the car. They'll be out here any minute if we don't leave."

His statement wasn't suggestive in any way, but for some reason—whether it was because of the time spent with his family or that I hadn't had any sex in a while or that he was looking so damn fine and was making me incredibly aroused—boldness was my theme for the night.

Maintaining eye contact with him, I murmured resolvedly, "I guess you'd better get me over to your house then."

Without a word, he started the car and pulled onto the street.

⚮

His house was everything I'd imagined it to be.

Perfect, masculine and very large—just like him, I determined.

I heard him close the front door behind me as I walked toward the middle of the large great room.

"You like the house?" he asked.

I turned around, ready to reply and saw his awaiting, intense and rather speculative, glare.

"Why are you looking at me like that?" I asked with a nervous smile.

"You know why."

I did, but it was still amusing to ask. "You surprised?"

With only a nod, he walked closer to me. I stood still and paralleled his passionate energy with mine. Reaching me, he pulled me to him with one hand with moderate force and looked down into my eyes. It was already over. He had me and he knew it.

He smiled warmly before he brushed his lips softly with mine. I was ready to take all of my clothes off right then. I weakened even more when he took my hands and started seducing me with small kisses. His kisses moved to my neck and toward my chest while he slowly undid the buttons of my dress with one hand. With smooth efficiency, he reached under my dress with his other hand and lifted one of my legs, wrapped it around his hips and began rubbing my behind with deliberate and slow movements.

With little effort he picked me up and carried me into his bedroom.

His mouth came on mine hungrily as soon as he brought me in the room, laid me on the bed and skillfully took off my dress. I met his lips just as feverishly, while my fingers moved hurriedly to undress him so I could view his magnificent body. Within seconds, we were both naked, pleasuring each other with rapturous foreplay, before we slowed down to kiss each other softer, enjoying our flesh pressed together.

When he stopped to look into my eyes and smooth my hair, we understood. He reached into his nightstand with one hand, while still smoothing my hair down with the other. He took a condom out and sheathed himself easily. He entered me gently and slowly moved in perfect rhythm while my body responded to his movements. Masterfully, he moved his body with mine into every position imaginable on his king-sized bed, until lastly, and exhaustively, we came to our fulfilling end.

# Chapter 41

# Lacie

*"Abigail's not going to let you into the family."*

"Lacie," the voice was saying.

*"You will never be accepted into Tony's family."*

"Lacie," the voice said again. I felt a finger brush my hair from my forehead.

*"You are way out of your class, Lacie. You'll never fit in."*

"Lacie, I love you, honey." The voice was more earnest this time. "Wake up."

The voice became a face when I slowly opened my eyes and saw a worried looking Tony staring down at me.

A relieved smile came on his face. "I was just about to call Dr. Rosen," he said.

I felt a bitter taste in my mouth as I looked around the room in confusion, realizing that I wasn't in a hotel.

"Where am I?" I asked. "And who's Dr. Rosen?"

"You're in my bedroom at my parent's house. Dr. Rosen attended to you last night after you fainted."

"Huh? I fainted?" Little by little, I started to recall last night's events. The wedding, Simone and Liona, Tony's mom, Simone yelling "you, bitch," to Jessica and then darkness. "Aw, man, I threw up on Simone and fainted," I groaned, putting a hand on my forehead as I started to sit up.

"Hey, hey, easy now," Tony cautioned softly, easing me back down.

"It's okay, Tony. I'm all right." I took a deep breath and looked at him. "Tony, I'm sorry. I didn't mean to be any trouble, especially in front of your family and friends. Your family must be so upset with me."

"Hey," Tony said firmly. "Don't worry about them. I'm just concerned about you. How are you feeling?"

I yawned. "I don't know. Still a little tired, I guess."

He peered at me. "Dr. Rosen said you should get plenty of rest and follow up with your physician at home."

"Yeah, like that's going to happen," I murmured. "We've got a lot of shopping to do, Tony. Rest is not on the agenda," I said, getting ready to pull off the covers.

"Shopping? What for?" He stopped me gently with his hand. "The last thing you need to do is shop. You need your rest."

I looked at him dubiously. "Tony, it's your nieces' birthday. They need something from us—if not me. I feel very bad about all the trouble I caused. I don't want to anger your family anymore by not having something for the twins."

"Lacie, they don't expect–" he started, still holding me with his hand.

"Exactly. That's why it's important that I do this," I said firmly and he let me go.

"All right, but you don't have to do this," he said, shaking his head.

"I know, Tony." I started to get out of the bed but stopped when I realized that I had no clothes on. "How did you..." Tony answered with a grin. "Never mind, I already know the answer. Where's the bathroom and where is my suitcase?" I said, getting out of the bed unashamedly. He didn't reply. He gazed at me in a stupor as I stood stark naked in the middle of his bedroom. "Tony!" I snapped my fingers.

"Huh," he said blinking and shaking his head. "I'm sorry. I just thought of doing something really naughty, that's all."

"Tony!"

"But I'll be patient." He grinned. "Your suitcase is in the closet and you're standing right in front of the adjoining bathroom." He stood up from the bed and started for the door. "I'll go downstairs and let you get dressed."

I stopped him with my voice. "Oh, yeah, Tony? What time is the party?"

233

"Three o'clock," he said and closed his eyes while he stood at the door. "And will you *please* put some clothes on," he pleaded before he walked out.

I giggled and shook my head, then looked at my watch. It was ten o'clock. How long had I been asleep? I brushed that aside. No time to think about that. I had only about four and a half hours to get some gifts.

After gathering some clothes from my suitcase, I walked toward the bathroom suddenly feeling nauseous again.

What...was...wrong with me?

# Chapter 42

# Tony

Mom, Matthew and Jessica were in the kitchen when I entered. Mom was standing by the stove and Matthew and Jessica were seated.

"Good morning," I greeted politely. Despite remembering the conversation last night, I kissed my mother on the cheek and gave one to Jessica also.

"Have a good night sleep, son?" Mom asked, cheerfully.

"Could've been a little better," I replied. There was a fresh pot of coffee made, so I walked to one of the cabinets and took out a mug. "Where's Dad?"

"He's out with the horses. Your brothers were helping him but Matthew just stepped in for a cup of coffee," Mom answered. For a good minute, there was pin-dropping silence until Mom started. "Anthony, we need to talk," she said abruptly.

"What about, Mom?" I shook my head as I started pouring coffee into my mug.

"Are you really planning on marrying this girl, Anthony?" Mom asked solemnly.

I took a sip of my coffee and looked at Matthew who was waiting for my answer. I swallowed and smiled grimly. Here we go again, back to the same old drawing board.

I looked at Mom directly and corrected her with, "Lacie, Mom. Lacie."

"Okay...Lacie." Mom smiled thinly. "But are you really considering this?"

I nodded my head quickly. "Oh yeah, I meant what I said."

Matthew looked at me in disbelief. "He's completely lost his mind, Mom."

"Oh, Matthew, stop it. There's nothing wrong with his intentions," Jessica asserted strongly. "Frankly, anyone's better than Simone and I, for one, am happy for Tony."

I winked at Jessica.

"You would be," Matthew retorted.

"You're making a terrible mistake, Anthony," Mom murmured, shaking her head.

Fresh, clear-headed and ready for debate, I leaned against the counter. I cocked my head at my brother and mother, seeing them both in a different light.

"What's so terrible, Mom? And just what is your opposition to this whole thing, Matthew?" I queried.

Mom shook her head indignantly, as she clenched the edge of the stove tightly. "Anthony, you have no idea what you're getting into. You don't know enough about this girl to be considering marriage."

"And you don't know anything about her to have such a strong objection," I returned, irritation starting to fester again. "So far the only reason you've given me is that she's black."

"Isn't that enough of a reason, Tony?" Matthew added.

"Hell no," I rebutted sarcastically.

"Look, Tony. We're just concerned about you. We want what's best for you and we see the trouble that can arise with this situation," Matthew huffed.

"Trouble for me or trouble for you?" I asked directly.

"For everyone involved if you want the truth. It's just not natural," Matthew said frankly.

"What?" Jessica and I exclaimed together.

"Hey, it's in the Bible. God separated the races in the beginning and told them not to mix and it was for a reason. The confusion it would cause," Matthew claimed.

I looked at my brother in absolute stupefaction, uttering, "You're actually saying those words," while he continued.

"Hey, I have no problem with African-Americans. It's okay to have them as friends, go out with them in groups, but dating and marriage...no. Out of the question," Matthew expressed.

ACROSS THE COLOR LINE

"How big…of you, Matthew," Jessica uttered in a condemnatory tone.

"Jessica, that's enough!" Mom cried disapprovingly.

Jessica stood up abruptly and shook her head. "I'm going outside. I need some air," she muttered and walked out the back door toward the porch.

I looked at Mom after Jessica left. "Is that how you feel too, Mom?"

"You know where I was raised, Anthony, and Matthew has a point. You shouldn't take this personally," Mom expressed strongly. "We have friends in this town that are very influential and we have a certain status to maintain. *You* have a status to maintain. Do you want to have to deal with the trouble that can arise from this and be considered an outcast because of her?" She shook her head. "I have lived a long life, Anthony, and one thing that my father always stressed to me, that is still in me today, is that I was to never bring a black man home. If I did, he would disown me. That was the ultimate treason and I *never* forgot that."

I squinted at my mother. "Is that a threat?"

"No," she said, not backing down. "I'm just making you aware of the enormity of this situation and how *concerned* we are."

Overthrown by her subtle attempt at intimidation, I scoffed and put my hands over my face and tilted my head upward as she continued. This couldn't be my mother. This couldn't be the woman that raised me.

"Anthony, did it ever cross your mind that she might be after your mo–" Mom began.

My head came down immediately. "What?" I cut her off sharply "She's not after my money."

"Are you sure?" Mom raised her eyebrow and I blew hard. She put a hand on my arm lightly. "Listen. There are so many other women out there, Anthony. You need to reconsider, son. Consider how your children will be affected by this. Do you want your kids to be torn about whether to mark white or African-American on applications? Do you want them to be confused about who they are?"

**237**

I'd just about had it with this conversation.

"Do you want them to be teased at school?" Matthew added.

I remained silent, overburdened and disgusted by the onslaught of berating questions.

"They'll be called mongrels," Matthew continued.

I gritted my teeth.

"And half-breeds," Matthew pursued.

My fist started to ball into a knot.

"And nigg…" Matthew stopped as I dashed toward him swiftly.

"Anthony, no!" Mom yelled.

It was too late. I grabbed my oldest brother by the collar and pulled his stocky frame out of the chair.

"They…will…be…people!" I barked furiously. "People!"

"Tony, you need to let me go," Matthew demanded. He struggled to break free but my grip was too strong for him.

I ignored Matthew's command and continued to glare at him. The only sounds that I could hear was the back screen door opening behind me and heels coming down the stairs from my right. I was so enraged that I took no notice of Dad, Jessica and Mark coming in from the back door.

"Anthony, let him go, son," I heard my father say calmly. "Let him, go. It's okay."

I didn't heed to Dad's plea and still held Matthew up while he continued to try to break free. Then there was Lacie's voice—my calm in the storm.

"Tony," she uttered softly.

Matthew dropped heavily onto the chair when I finally let him go.

"You better watch who you put your hands on," he said thickly as Mom came to his side.

I said nothing, grabbed Lacie's hand and headed out the front door.

## Chapter 43

# Dawn

The man had rocked my world.

I smiled at the sun shining through the curtains, signifying a bright new day. A brand new day indeed, because Joe was holding *me*. Joe was holding *me*.

Placing my hands across my face, I giggled softly, enjoying the complete and fulfilling bliss that was in my heart. I took a sideways glance at Joe and let out a contented sigh. No wonder Lacie had been so confused. Joe was an incredible artist in the bedroom.

There I go again.

*Dawn, did you have to mention Lacie's name?*

I shook the weird feeling off, determined to enjoy my day of happiness. The squeeze I got from Joe came at the right time.

"Good morning," he murmured.

"Umm, good morning," I replied.

He squeezed me again and whispered in my ear softly, "Any regrets about last night?"

"Mmm," I murmured. "Not at all."

"You just don't know how happy I am to hear you say that," he chuckled softly, putting his head in my neck. "I love you, Dawn."

I realized it at the same time and replied, "I love you, too."

There was no turning back now.

# Chapter 44

## Joe

*"I love you, too"* she'd said.

Hmm. Dawn's words were music to my ears.

I'd been ready and patiently waiting for what I'd considered a long time, wondering if we'd ever make it official.

Then she met my parents and as soon as she walked into their house, it was no question that she was the one. My parents took to her instantly. The icing on the cake was when Dawn told me to take her to my place. I didn't waste one second as I pulled onto the street and arrived in record time at my house. It had taken her so long to decide, I didn't want to risk her changing her mind.

She didn't. There was no doubt about it. The fire in her beautiful brown eyes was convincing enough and that was all I needed. There was no time to worry about Lacie or the risks that we were taking. I didn't care at that moment. I wanted her.

My pent up desire had been stored up for her and was ready to be released and I took full advantage of it. I wanted her to never forget that night.

I knew I wouldn't.

# *Chapter 45*

# Lacie

The honeymoon was over.

Speechless, I shook my head sorrowfully, seeing Tony's clenched jaw and how white his knuckles were from holding the steering wheel in such a death grip. Disappointment, fury, frustration, hurt and what looked like a little bit of defeat, were only a small number of words that could describe the expression on his face.

What could I say to ease the amount of pain I knew he was feeling? How could I have prepared him when I literally had to brace myself for a moment like this, noticing all of the signs? Could it have been possible? I doubted it. He'd had so much faith and trust in his family, and had been confident that my color and our relationship would not matter. Yet, it had been altered dramatically in less than twenty-four hours—all because he loved me.

"You hungry?" he asked briskly.

"Uh…yeah," I managed to say.

He nodded. "All right, I'll pull over to this restaurant and we'll eat there."

Tony and I could care less about the stares and whispers that we got as the hostess led us to our table. I shook my head. Nothing like a big upset at an affluent family's wedding in a small town to get people gossiping.

We continued to sit in silence after our waitress, Theresa, took our order. Honestly, I didn't know what to say. What could I say? I told you so? This was to be expected?

I took a deep breath and decided to say something—anything to lighten the atmosphere. "So, how old are the twins? I guess I'd better know how old they are before I get their gifts, huh?" I said, trying to be cheerful.

"Ten," he muttered swiftly.

More silence.

I nodded. "What are their names again?"

"Amber and Alicia."

Still more silence. I inhaled. He wasn't even trying to have a conversation.

I glanced around the restaurant and out the window awkwardly for a few minutes until I couldn't take it any longer.

"Tony, are we just going to sit here and not discuss what happened back at the house?" I asked softly.

He shook his head. "I don't want to talk about it."

"Are you mad with me?"

He shot me a dubious look.

I nodded. "Okay. So you're not mad with me. Fine. But this," I pointed at him and then at me, "is not going to work if we don't communicate," I stressed and took a deep breath. "Tony, listen, I know what happened. Shoot, I heard a lot of it when I was dressing upstairs. Let's talk about it. Please."

His face turned solemn and he sighed. "Lacie…you don't under—"

"What?" I interrupted him softly. "What don't I understand? You don't think I realize that your family is upset that you're involved with a black woman?" I leaned over the table and peered at him. "Tony, this isn't beyond my comprehension. Discrimination has been a factor in my life ever since I can remember. It's just going to be a bit more challenging now because I'm involved with you, that's all," I said, matter-of-factly.

He shook his head furiously. "No, that's not all, Lacie," he said with soft anger. "I feel…I feel as if I don't know my own family anymore," he declared somberly, stumbling to get out the words. "I'm so sorry, Lacie. I didn't expect this kind of reaction."

*Dear Lord, this was really weighing heavily on him.*

I reached over the table and put my hand over his. "Tony, I know. It's obvious that you didn't." I rubbed my forefinger over the back of his hand in slow circles. "I'm just worried about you," I said, searching his face. "You were holding your brother up by the collar in mid air. You surprised me."

He looked down at our hands. "I know. I've never done that to him before."

Now it was my turn to feel bad. He'd been defending me—us—our relationship and because if it, the discussion he had with his brother had turned into a violent confrontation.

"I'm sorry, Tony. I didn't mean to start a fight between you and your brother."

"Hey, hey, hey…don't," he said, immediately reaching out to touch my face lightly. "You didn't start anything and Matthew was wrong for what he said, Lacie." He took a deep breath and nodded his head decisively. "But I was wrong for what I did to him. When we go back to the house, I'll apologize to him and we'll get it straightened out. It'll be okay. I'm sure of it," he said confidently.

"Excuse me," an older blonde-haired woman who'd approached our table delicately interrupted, looking at me. "But you're the girl that fainted at the Sanders wedding last night, correct?"

I groaned inwardly and exchanged a weary glance with Tony.

"I'm afraid so," I answered with a thin grin.

The older woman clapped her hands together softly and whispered anxiously, "I thought so. My friends over there and I saw you two enter the restaurant and were just wondering how you were doing. Are you feeling better?"

Not at all prepared for what she'd said, I couldn't utter a word and looked at her with my mouth agape. Tony seemed shocked also but answered immediately.

"She is, thank you," he replied for me.

The woman took that as an opportunity to pat my hand lightly. "Well, I'm glad to hear that, dear. I just wanted to check to see if you were okay," she said. She made a half turn as if she was about to walk away, but stopped and looked back at us. "By the way, you two make a handsome couple," she remarked, giving me a last little pat on my hand. "You take care of yourselves and may God bless you two," she said, before she rejoined her friends at the table.

I looked at Tony and smiled.

"Well, I'll be darn," I murmured.

ℰℭ

The woman coming over to our table seemed to be what we needed to lighten the atmosphere. Tony and I were able to make simple talk after she left, but we never returned to the conversation beforehand.

"All right," I asked Tony, while we stood in front of the restaurant. "Where is the nearest shop where I can get something for young girls?" I asked, glancing up and down the street.

"Hmm," he said thoughtfully. "I'm afraid you won't find much around here. These are primarily specialty shops in this area. Why don't we go back into the city and go to FAO Schwartz? They'll have more of a selection."

I peeked at my watch and shook my head. "No, that's too much trouble and it'll take too much time. You know how difficult New York City traffic can be—even on the weekend." I suddenly caught sight of a store across the street. "You know what? Let's try that one," I said, getting ready to pull him across the street.

He pulled back a little. "Listen, you go on in and I'll meet you in there in a minute. I want to check something out."

I cocked my head. "Why? It'll only take a moment," I suggested.

He smiled and shook his head. "You know better than to say that. Women take the longest time to shop." He chuckled when I raised my eyebrow at him. "Seriously, though, go ahead on in and I'll catch up with you."

"Are you sure?"

He nodded and winked. "Yeah, go ahead."

244

Still a little reluctant, I started walking across the street and said, "Okay, don't take too long, now. You know I don't know my way around this town."

𝕤𝕠𝕔𝕣

The shop was cute, quaint and nicely arranged, I noticed, stepping in. It was sort of an upscale novelty store. After a short greeting to the two female clerks inside, I started looking around, taking my time. I soon understood why Tony wanted to drive back into the city. I'd no idea how I was going to find anything in this store for ten-year-old twin girls.

I continued my quest, eyeing everything the store offered that would be appropriate gifts. As I wandered around, I noticed one of the two female clerks that were in the store, following me. She was doing a poor job at being discreet about it, too. This was quite amusing because the two women hadn't bothered to reply to my 'good morning' when I entered the store. They'd only responded with a brief nod and now one of them was following me.

*Calm down, Lacie.*

Maybe I was imagining things. After all, there were a couple of customers in the store as well. But as soon as the rest of the customers had left and the clerk continued to follow my every step. I passed by a mirror and double-checked my appearance. I looked well-dressed, with my long black leather coat and nice black boots.

*Relax, Lacie.*

I sighed. I'd seen so many scenes like these in movies and had encountered them in real life many times, but c'mon, this kind of thing was getting tired. Couldn't my apparel and the way my face and hair looked be sufficient? Why must I continually validate myself when I'm the only minority in a room, restaurant, wedding or anywhere? Why couldn't I stay out of these situations? Why couldn't Tony's family accept me?

And *why* in the hell was this woman *still* following me?

*Damn it!*

Aggravation got the best of me and I turned around swiftly to tell her off, when my eye caught a large glass display case. In it were two dolls, neatly encased in glass-shaped boxes. Stylish and perfectly detailed with hand stitched embroidery, the porcelain dolls were beautiful, curly, dark-haired and brown eyed. On the inside of each box was a doll-sized fur coat hanging beside the dolls, with the label reading genuine fur. Oh, this was too much! Ever since I was a little girl, I'd wanted a porcelain doll.

"These dolls were made in France. They are very costly," the woman clerk who'd been on my heels ever since I'd entered the store, obliged.

Not wanting to accept what her statement subtly implied, I gave her a good-natured smile and said, "I see. Would you mind opening the case so I could get a better look, please?"

"Well, I would have to…find…the key…" she trailed off, glancing at the other clerk with surprise.

I shrugged with an even broader smile. "That's perfectly fine. I can wait. I'm waiting for my boyfriend, anyway. I have time," I said, enjoying the look of displeasure in her eyes.

Tailcoat pursed her lips and said, "I'll be a few minutes," and walked to the back of the shop.

I instantly became aware of another pair of eyes on me and turned to the other clerk at the register with the same smile I'd given Tailcoat. She quickly looked away and I chuckled softly. Oh, was this fun!

The bell in the shop rang, indicating someone entering. It was Tony.

"Hey, baby," he said pleasantly. "Did you find anything?"

His mood seemed to have changed as he planted a kiss on my forehead and put his arm around my waist.

"Well, I think I did," I answered happily, pointing to the display case. "I was thinking about getting them these dolls for their birthday. Do you think they'd like them?"

Tony looked at the dolls in the display case and nodded. "Very much so. They're beautiful and they would be a great addition to their already extensive collection."

"Great! Then I've made the right choice."

"Tony?" Tailcoat said with surprise, suddenly reappearing from the back of the shop. "What are you doing here? I didn't know you were in town."

She came over to him instantly and got in between us to plant a kiss on his cheek. I didn't particularly care for that gesture, especially since she'd been tailgating me ever since I walked into the shop.

She stepped back and looked at him affectionately. "It's good to see you."

Tony returned a friendly smile and responded with, "Hi, Diana. It's nice to see you, too. I just came for Lauren's, well actually, we," he said, squeezing my waist and pointing at both of us, "just came for Lauren's wedding."

I smiled up at Tony sheepishly and he winked. When I looked back at Diana, there was disgust in her eyes.

"Oh," Tailcoat...Diana muttered.

"Oh, I heard about that wedding. It's all over town. You must be the girl that started that fight and fainted at the wedding," the other clerk piped up.

"I forgot how quickly things spread around this town," Tony mumbled grimly.

Tailcoat Diana turned toward the other clerk. "Of course she is, she was the only—" she started and stopped in mid sentence. Her shoulders lifted up and down as she took a deep breath and turned back around. She avoided looking at me, though, when she said, "I'm sorry. But the two dolls you wanted have been reserved. They've already been sold to another customer."

I heard a soft gasp from the other clerk and glanced at her. She looked flabbergasted.

I raised my eyebrow at the suspicious statement. "They're not labeled 'sold' on the boxes. Why are they still showcased?"

Not expecting a dispute, her eyes flashed.

Here it comes, the crappy explanation.

Tailcoat Diana fumbled, "We...we continue to keep our merchandise out in the open until we get another shipment. It...it's just what we do."

I took another glance at the other clerk and saw her frown.

Tony spoke in a composed voice. "Diana, why didn't you let her know they were sold before you went back there? She was really looking forward to getting them for my nieces."

Her eyes moved down and to the side, a clear sign that a lie was about to come out of her mouth. "I just happened to see the sales receipt on my desk in the back."

Tony nodded slowly and glared at her as he stressed, "You just *happened* to see—"

Tailcoat Diana continued to look down as she added, "There's another shop down the block where I'm sure you could find—"

"Diana, I know. I used to live here, remember?" Tony interrupted her sharply. "Good-bye," he said with a curt nod. He took my hand and led me out the store without a backward glance.

We went to a few other stores but were unable to find anything that could replace what I'd originally wanted to purchase for the twins. Lastly, Tony took me to a jewelry store where we settled on a matching pair of necklaces with diamond-lined lockets. The gifts were nice but my heart had been set on the dolls. They'd just seemed more thoughtful.

Tony and I rode back to his parent's house and talked about the job this time. We were in silent agreement not to discuss what happened because we didn't want to relive the incident in town.

As soon as our car approached the driveway and stopped, we were accosted by two, young, curly, dark-haired girls in matching outfits. They swarmed the car when Tony walked over to my side to let me out.

"Uncle Tony! Uncle Tony! What did you get us?" they exclaimed, hugging him and almost pulling him down.

He beamed at once. "Okay, girls, okay," he laughed. "Calm down, Calm down. You'll get your presents when it's time to open them. None sooner," he teased, holding the bag with their presents above their heads. "Meanwhile, I want you two to meet someone very special." He extended his hand to me and helped me out of the car. "This is Lacie," he said, putting his arm around my waist.

Two sets of identical sparkling blue eyes looked at me and smiled. The one with braces smirked and asked forthrightly, "She's your girlfriend, isn't she?"

An uncle unprepared for such a direct question, Tony strained out with a nod, "Yes, she is, Alicia."

Amber piped up with, "Are you going to marry her?"

"Uh," was all Tony said.

"You said she was special, Uncle Tony," Alicia reminded him innocently.

"No, Alicia. He said, 'very special'," Amber corrected.

Tony was speechless and I couldn't help but giggle.

"That's enough, you two. Go back into the house and join the rest of your guests. Go on, now," Matthew instructed in a fatherly fashion, as he and Jessica appeared on the front porch of the house. "They're about to start some more games."

"C'mon, girls, you heard your dad. You've got guests waiting. Lacie, c'mon in the kitchen and help us with the party," Jessica said, waving me inside as the girls ran by her.

Tony handed me the package and kissed me softly. "Go on inside, babe. I won't be long."

Knowing that he was getting ready to talk to his older brother, I hesitated toward the house. I kept looking back one or two times with uncertainty when Matthew passed by me as he walked over to Tony. With a deep sigh, Jessica came down the steps of the porch and put her arm through mine and hurried me up the stairs.

"You ever heard of slow as molasses? Well, you're certainly walking that way," Jessica teased gently, taking the package from me. "Tony's gonna be all right, Lacie. He's a big boy," she assured with a wink, when we entered the house.

I wasn't prepared to see the number of kids when Jessica and I walked into the huge recreation room. There had to be at least twenty children, running around, shouting and playing. They were clearly having a grand old time. Matthew's wife, Joanne, and Mark's wife, Trisha, looked a little overworked while they struggled to get some games going. They looked relieved when Johnathan and Mark came into the room and announced that it was time for the children to ride the ponies.

Despite how cold it was outside, the children wasted no time. They rushed toward the back of the house, almost tripping over each other in the process. Joanne and Trisha followed behind them tiredly, shaking their heads.

Jessica laughed. "C'mon, Lacie. I think they've got it under control now. Let's go and help Mom in the kitchen."

That was the last thing that I wanted to do. Everything that had happened so far had given me every instinct to know that Abigail did not want me around, and knowing that a kitchen was every woman's treasured domain, that was the last place she wanted me in.

My instinct was right.

Abigail hardly said a word to Jessica or me when we entered the kitchen. That's the way it was the entire time when I helped Jessica make the cookie dough and place them on the sheets to bake. If it wasn't for Jessica initiating conversation, I think I'd have gone crazy from all of the negative energy that I was getting from Abigail.

I was thrown when Jessica suddenly got up from the stool next to me and said casually with a soft pat on my back, "Lacie, I'm gonna abandon you for a second and take the baked cookies out to the table on the porch. I won't be long."

Abandon was an understatement. I'd have felt safer if she'd left me in the company of wolves.

She had to be crazy leaving me alone with her mother!

I looked at Jessica longingly, wanting to escape with her, as she walked quickly out to the back porch. With slight anger, I flicked a spoonful of dough on one of the cookie sheets, which in turn made a small speck flick back onto my nose. Huh. 'I won't be long,' seemed to be the phrase of the day. Tony hadn't appeared since I'd left him and now Jessica had jetted on me.

I suddenly felt Abigail's eyes on me from across the counter and looked up. She was staring at me hard, too. I swallowed some pride and responded with a small, friendly smile. Her response was to quirk a brow, shake her head and look back down to spread icing on the twins' birthday cake.

Okay. Lacie, she's obviously not going to make any attempt at any conversation. Why don't you give it a shot?

I cleared my throat. "Uh, Mrs. Douglas, I want to thank you for letting me stay in your home."

She nodded her head, still spreading icing on the cake. "You weren't invited, but what's done is done. You'll be leaving today, anyway," she said curtly.

O…kay. Lacie, take a deep breath and try again.

"You've planned a wonderful birthday party here and Amber and Alicia seem to be enjoying—" I began again.

Her head came up swiftly with a stone expression and she surprised me with a blaring, "Do you really think this is going to work? I mean, honestly?" She paused. "Understand that I'm terribly dissatisfied with what has occurred in the past twenty-four hours since you've been here. You've managed to instigate a fight at a prestigious wedding, vomit on a guest and then faint, which turned everyone's eyes from the bride and groom onto yourself, my son had to leave, and because of you, I watched two of my sons almost get into a brawl!" She put her head down to continue with the frosting. Her application was more vigorous now along with the shaking of her head.

Not an "Are you feeling better?" or any kind of concern for my well-being. Only accusations. Then again, from my past experiences with her and from the stunt she pulled last night, should I even expect her to have a change of heart?

I took another deep, but this time, nervous breath. "Listen, I apologize about what happened at the wedding. I just got sick all of a sudden and I'm deeply sorry about the row between Tony and Matthew. It took me by surprise as well because I've never seen Tony so upset before. I don't know what happened."

Her head shot back up. "*You* are what happened. That type of chaos has never taken place in this town or in my home. Not until you came."

I swallowed more pride along with the lump in my throat that started to form. "Mrs. Douglas, I told you that I'm very sorry about everything, but the onus is not on me."

"Oh?" She raised a cynical eyebrow. "This family has always been close and peace has always been in my home. My children did not fight with each other because it wasn't tolerated and for the first time in all of these years I had to get in the middle of a near fist fight between my oldest and youngest son because my youngest was defending you."

Was that such a bad thing? So, it was my fault that Matthew was making such bigoted remarks that Tony felt compelled to knock him out for it? I was to blame because her oldest son was prejudiced?

Amazed, I shook my head as the knot in my throat tightened and watched her resume her task again. I was trying to make amends, but she was making it incredibly hard. Yet, she was Tony's mother and I had to give it my best shot. In any conflict someone has to be the peacemaker. My dad had always told me that.

I inhaled and tried, "Mrs. Douglas, I'm really trying to make peace here. What can we do to fix this problem because we've got to find some way to get along with each other?"

She didn't even look up when she replied with, "Nothing as far as I'm concerned. It's too late."

The lack of concern in her voice struck a nerve and I couldn't contain some of my aggravation. "So you don't even want to try, despite how Tony feels about me? Despite what he wants?"

"You think he wants you?" she queried and paused to look up with a speculating glare.

She went there. This woman was too much. She was actually challenging me.

Without hesitation, I rebutted with strong conviction, "No. I know he wants me, Mrs. Douglas. He wouldn't have brought me here if he didn't. Or don't you know your own son?"

My sarcastic comment had slipped out but my reward was the slight glimpse of doubt in her eyes and the spreading knife slipping from her hands onto the counter. She hadn't been prepared for my argument and I'd gotten to her. In the process, I believe I'd started something, too.

All the same, she managed to reply with a calm, "Oh, I know my son very well, dear, and wanting and needing are two different things. This affair is just what it is—an affair, nothing more."

Dismissively, she took the cookie sheet that I'd been putting the cookie dough on and turned to put it into the oven.

I shook my head again, trying to ignore the discomfort of her insinuation and responded with soft assurance. "I believe that Tony would beg to differ with that statement, Mrs. Douglas. He's happy and very much in love with me."

Her back straightened up immediately and she turned around with an arched eyebrow and icy glare. "He just thinks he does."

I managed a confident smile despite shivering slightly from the cold breeze that came with her icy glare. "No, Tony *knows* he's in love with me, Mrs. Douglas."

"Are you certain?" she taunted. She turned toward the oven again, took out a different sheet of cookies, turned back around and then placed them onto the island countertop. She sighed. "I don't know. Rachel and Tony were dancing pretty close and he even seemed to reacquaint himself with Simone. Actually, I always thought he and Simone would make beautiful children if they got married," she said whimsically, giving me a fleeting glance, before she reached for a spatula to take the cookies off and place them on a serving dish.

The mentioning of Simone's name had opened a barely healed wound and I fell for her trap. "But they're not, Mrs. Douglas. Tony and Simone are over and he is not interested in Rachel. Your plan didn't work," I snapped heatedly. "You might as well get used to the idea, Mrs. Douglas. Your son loves me and wants me in his life."

*This is Tony's mother, Lacie. You are in her house. Stay calm, don't get sick and don't let her get to you.*

She stopped abruptly and looked at me with a mocking and satisfied smile. "Dear, you've only seen just a measure of the lengths I will go to for my son and my family's best interest. Whether it's Simone or Rachel or anyone else for that matter, he will be with someone acceptable. And you are not acceptable. So what my son *wants* is irrelevant. What he doesn't need is trouble and turmoil in his life and you are full of it, Lisa, Leslie, or whatever your name is. The incidences—despite the obvious—have all but proven my immediate opinion from when I first set eyes on you; you're not good enough for my son. Therefore you and Anthony cannot stay together," she stated.

"But we're together now and I'm not going anywhere," I declared. I glared back at her with every bit of anger and frustration in the pit of my stomach and struggled not to break down in front of her.

Tony had to be adopted. There was no way that this bitter, calculating woman had given birth to him. I was so ticked with her big spiel—"despite the obvious"—which really meant that I was black. Even worse was her statement that I wasn't "acceptable." Yet, she would rather have a conniving spoiled, racist like Simone be with Tony, simply because she was white. That ripped right through me, which is what she wanted. But I wasn't going to let her see me cry. I didn't want war, but I wasn't going to surrender, either.

Her eyes widened with apparent surprise and then narrowed with malice as she immediately recognized my unwavering defiance. Yep, the war was on, all right.

Abigail leaned against the counter. "You wanna play hardball? Fine, I'm going to be upfront with you. This dialogue has gone on long enough and I want you to understand exactly where I'm coming from." I saw the cloud of cool wind coming from her mouth as she stated with hostility, "I...don't...like...you."

*Lacie, girl, hold on. Don't you let them tears roll. Stick out your chin and hold it up high.*

"There's no reason to sugarcoat it anymore. I am strongly opposed to interracial relationships and I will not stand you being with Anthony. Your kind belongs to each other and our kind belongs to each other. I believe that's the way God intended it and that's the way it's going to be in *my* family."

254

It would have been simpler if she'd waved the Confederate flag in front of my face. I sat there feeling very emotional all of a sudden. Tears threatened to roll down any minute because of the words that were flowing from the mother of the man that I was in love with. I was in her house and was desperately trying to respect her because of Tony and trying to maintain some composure, but her words continued to wound as they flew out of her mouth.

"Your attendance at the wedding and at this party does not give you a free pass into my family nor a chance at weaseling your way into it. Regardless of how well some of my family has befriended you, you will not be a part of this family. I'm giving you fair warning; I will do everything in my power to cause trouble and strife between you and Anthony." I bit my lip to stop it from trembling at her blue eyes that became black with hate as she commenced. "Do not consider challenging my relationship with Anthony either, for that will be a grave mistake. He's been my son for twenty-nine years and he loves me very dearly. If he has to choose between me, his mother, and you, who do you think he's going to choose?" she asked bitterly. She didn't wait for me to reply as she sneered, "Anthony will *never* forsake my feelings for the likes—"

That was enough. I dropped everything that was in my hand onto the counter, got off the stool and rushed upstairs to Tony's bedroom to pack and jet. I'd done my best to play nice and respect Abigail and even with some reluctance, had stood up for myself. But that woman was too wicked. No. It was best to leave now before I did something that I would really regret.

Furious tears fell at length upon entering the bedroom and I silently cursed myself for staying too long to listen to Abigail's verbal abuse. With promptness, I started gathering my clothes. I was ready to get out of the house and leave this doggone town. I didn't need any more of a hint and I wasn't going to continue being disrespected.

"Damn it!" I exclaimed angrily, shaking my head as I tried through the haze of tears to look for my suitcase. "Where did I put that thing?" my voice shook.

"Lacie, what's wrong?" Jessica came in swiftly looking concerned.

My stream came down uncontrollably at the sight of a friendly face and I shook my head in answer. I finally found my suitcase and started throwing my clothes in. I noticed Tony's bag sitting on the bed. I should have packed and told him I wanted to go this morning.

Jessica came up to me and put her hands around my shoulders, stopping me momentarily. "Lacie, talk to me. Did Mom say something to you?"

I shrugged her hands off and with another shake of my head, strained out tearfully, "It doesn't matter, Jessica, because I'm outta here," while I continued packing in haste.

Jessica sighed deeply as she took everything in for a moment and then rushed toward the window. "Tony! You'd better get up here. Now!" she yelled.

It didn't stop my progress. Even if Tony wasn't coming with me, I was out of there.

It seemed like it was only a second when Tony rushed through the door.

"Hell," he muttered at once, obviously seeing me packing and Jessica standing at the foot of the bed with her arms folded. "Lacie, what's wrong?" Tony asked immediately, coming to my side.

I didn't trust myself to say anything, especially to him.

"Tony, she won't tell me, but my guess is that Mom said something to upset her. She wasn't like this before. We were just in the kitchen making cookies," Jessica informed him, swearing softly under her breath. "I knew I shouldn't have left her with Mom. But she told me she'd be on her best behavior," she contended.

Fat chance of that, I thought grimly.

Tony took a hold of my shoulders and turned me to face him. "Babe, what did Mom say to you?" he asked softly. I hesitated and he looked deeper and more compassionately into my eyes. "It's okay. Just tell me what happened, honey."

It was Tony's turn to swear softly as I broke down silently and fell into his arms. I was so glad only he and Jessica witnessed that scene.

"Jessica, my keys are on that nightstand over there. Go downstairs and get my car started, please," he instructed firmly, while he held me and caressed my back. "Lacie and I are leaving…now."

Without a word, Jessica heeded her little brother and left the room.

Everything was a blur as I continued to weep and blow my nose while Tony sat me gently on the bed and finished packing for me. Whether it was the statement that Abigail had made, or that I'd kept everything in, my rainfall was unstoppable.

Eager to leave the house and the bad memories with it, I barely heard what Tony was saying to his parents while Jessica ushered me out the door and into his awaiting car. Seconds later, I saw Tony storm out of the house and rush toward the car. The last impression in my head would be of Johnathan and Mark rushing to catch up to us, and Jessica holding her head down with arms folded as Tony spun out of the driveway, with gravel and dust flying behind us.

Again, Tony's jaw was clenched and grimly set while he gripped the steering wheel with white knuckles and spun the car around with purpose and headed out of the gate of the Douglas' residence.

What had I done?

I shook my head sadly, closed my eyes and laid my head back, feeling depleted of energy with nausea rising in my stomach again.

God help us both.

# Chapter 46

# Tony

You can pick your friends but you can't pick your family.

It was an old adage, but it had now become a devastating fact for me.

I continued for a good two or three miles as I drove from my parent's house with blood boiling through my veins, vividly recalling everything that had happened.

*"You really love her, don't you?" Matthew asked, leaning against the car with me as we watched Jessica and Lacie enter the house.*

*"With every inch of my soul," I replied with conviction.*

*Matthew sighed and shook his head in reproach. "I don't know, Tony. I just... don't know."*

*I looked at my brother fleetingly. "Matthew, do you remember how you felt about Joanne when you started dating her? Remember how lovesick you were and how you used to keep me up all night talking about her? I used to tease you about that, remember?"*

*He responded with a grudging nod. "Yeah, I do."*

*I nodded. "That's how I feel about Lacie."*

*"But how long will your feelings last for her, Tony? Are you going to feel the same way about her when you're getting teased and taunted. Or discriminated against?"*

*"Do you still feel the same way about Joanne, the way you did when you first started going out?"*

*"You can't compare the two, Tony."*

*"Yes, I can."*

*"Tony, I'm telling you as your oldest brother; I see problems heading your way and I don't want you to have to go through that. You're living in a dream world if you think this relationship is going to be a bed of roses."*

*"Even if the roses have thorns on them, I'd want to go through them with Lacie."* I shook my head. *"Matthew, just imagine all of the trouble Lacie encounters by being a black woman alone or what the black race has gone through just because of their color? Are they the only ones that can go through hardships? Are we above any pain or suffering in this life than blacks? Just because I'm white does that exclude me from any burdens and tribulations in life?"* I paused and scoffed.

He shrugged. *"That's just the way things are, Tony."*

*"But that doesn't make it right."*

*"Tony, listen, you can't change the world and why do you have to be the one to make a statement?"*

I turned to him in aggravation. *"Damn it, Matthew. It's not a statement! I... am...in love with Lacie,"* I stressed. *"I don't care what I have to go through to be with her. I want her in my life and I want to marry her. I want her to be the mother of my children. I want to grow old—"*

*"All right, all right,"* Matthew uttered, holding up a relenting hand. *"You've made your point."* He sighed. After a moment of silence, he added dryly, *"I should have known that when you pulled me out of my chair this morning."*

I nodded. *"Matthew, you were making bigoted remarks and insulting Lacie and me. You just kept pushing. And Matthew, I know that there will probably be incidences where I might have to deal with prejudice and bigotry. Hell, Lacie and I just experienced it at one of the shops here in town. But I didn't expect this from you and especially Mom. I didn't expect this from any member of my family, not as close as we are. And that hurts, man."*

Matthew lowered his head down for a moment. Then with a defeated sigh, he looked at me and said, *"Look, this is hard for me, here. You already know from the comments I made this morning and last night that I have strong opinions on this."* Another sigh. *"But you are right. We are family. I can't promise that my opinions are going to change overnight, but I will give you my word that I'll try. And I'll talk with Mom, too. I'll make sure to apologize to Lacie before you guys leave, also."* He extended his hand. *"All is forgiven?"*

"Yeah, man. We're cool." I took his hand and held it. "But Matthew, if you ever say anything contrary to Lacie, about Lacie, or to me, about me and Lacie, we're boxing," I stressed.

"Hey, point taken," he replied, raising his hand in surrender. "Now can we kiss and make up?" He chuckled and didn't wait for my answer as he grabbed me into a bear hug. "I love you, man," Matthew said, patting me on the back.

"Love you, too," I replied, patting him as well.

Matthew glanced at his watched once we parted. "C'mon, let's go to the back. I think the kids should be riding the ponies now.

જીભ્ય

Mark came up to my side as I stood on the deck and watched Matthew help Dad put some of the children on the ponies. I chuckled as Joanne and Trisha tried to hold off the other children who were pushing each other trying to cut in line for their rides.

"Did you and Matthew settle your differences?"

"Yeah," I replied. "We squashed everything."

"I'm glad." Mark nodded. "You know how protective he is. Even though he's a minute ahead of me by birth, he still stands by the whole big brother bit."

I glanced at him briefly and took a deep breath. "What's your opinion as the other older brother?"

"You love, Lacie. You want to marry her and I accept that." He shrugged. "Life is too short for all of the garbage the world offers. And sometimes you have to say, 'to hell with what everyone thinks'." Jessica came out carrying a tray of cookies. "Just ask our dear sister, here. You know she doesn't care."

"Huh? What?" Jessica murmured, putting the tray on the picnic table.

Mark put an arm around Jessica and squeezed. "I was hinting to Tony about that altercation you had with Simone at the wedding. You really let her have it."

*Jessica shrugged. "Hey, she was going after Lacie when she got sick and she called me white trash. I had to," she said, shaking her head. "Simone and her crowd were always so mean and self-righteous in high school. They'd constantly tease me because I wasn't part of their 'in' crowd and because I was in and out of boarding school. They were just so arrogant and I guess what she'd said brought back up those bad memories and my temper."*

*"Yeah, I remember how Mom used to have to come to school because you'd wind up in a fight with one of them," I said.*

*She smiled wistfully. "Yeah, those were the good old days. But hey, I'm over it now," she said lightly. "But oh, was it funny to see the look on Simone's face when Lacie vomited all over her," she said, bursting out with a laugh.*

*I shook my head when Mark joined her. "Trouble, that's what you two are." I started heading inside. "I'm going in the house to check on Lacie."*

*Jessica walked in front of me. "No you're not. You're going to stay out here. Lacie's fine. She's been helping us in the kitchen. Give Lacie some time to get to know us instead of her being under your watchful eye. Leave us women alone so we can get the food prepared for the party," she suggested.*

*"So what are you standing out here talking to us for? Go back in there, then," I teased exasperatedly, giving her a little push toward the door.*

*She stared at me for a second, shook her head and then retreated back into the house.*

*Mark and I burst out laughing.*

It wasn't long after that when Jessica called me to come up to my room. When I saw Lacie standing there in tears packing her bag, I was immediately concerned, wondering what had happened. And when she broke down in my arms, I lost it. Once Jessica confirmed my suspicions that Mom had said something to make Lacie upset, I knew it was time to go. I didn't want Lacie to go through any more than what she'd already been through.

*"Anthony, honey, wh…where are you going?" Mom asked earnestly as I pulled Lacie down the stairs with me in haste.*

*I looked at Jessica, who'd just come in from starting my car. "Take her to the car for me."*

*Jessica put a supportive arm around a tear-stained Lacie and they quickly exited the house.*

*I turned to my mother. "What did you say to Lacie, Mom?" I asked tersely. She didn't answer. "Mom... answer me," I strained out angrily. Still no answer. "What did you say to her?" I bellowed out in frustration.*

*That was the first time I'd ever yelled at my mother. It had caught her off guard also, but she remained tight-lipped.*

*Dad came in, followed by Matthew and Mark. "What is going on in here?" He glanced at the suitcases at my feet. "Tony, where are you going?"*

*"Ask Mom," I snapped, glaring at her.*

*"Abigail?" Dad turned to her.*

*Mom took her time answering as everyone's eyes were on hers, waiting. She stuck her chin out and shrugged. "I just told that girl the truth. I told her that you didn't need any trouble in your life therefore you two couldn't be together."*

*"Abigail!" Dad exclaimed.*

*"Mom?" Matthew and Mark exclaimed simultaneously, looking at her in shock.*

*"Wh...what gave you the right to say that to her?" I uttered through clenched teeth.*

*"Just be quiet, all of you!" Mom snapped heatedly, raking all of us over with scornful eyes. "Do not act surprised! I told you how I felt last night and my feelings have not changed." She looked at me firmly, eyes never wavering. "As far as my right, Anthony. I am your mother and you cannot expect me to just stand for you being with that...that girl!"*

*Oh, it was like that? I stepped back.*

*I nodded and glared at her and cocked my head to the side. "You're right, Mom. I can't expect you to and I won't. Good-bye."*

I was hopping mad!

After the incident at the shop, I had desperately prayed and hoped that once we came back to the house, being the twins' party and all, Lacie and I would have a chance at some reprieve with all of the turmoil that had recently happened and spirits would be brighter. It had been too much to ask for.

I glanced over at Lacie sleeping and shook my head. Even though she'd been apprehensive about this weekend, I knew she really wanted everything to work out right. Now tearstains were on her face and she was worn out; all from what I did.

God help me, I didn't know how Lacie was going to forgive me.

This whole weekend had been a joke.

An absolute joke.

# Chapter 47

# Dawn

"You had sex with him, didn't you?"

My mother's straightforward question stopped me in mid-stride. I'd walked past her after entering my apartment around two in the morning and that was the first thing that came out of her mouth.

She scoffed when I stopped, confirming her suspicions. "I knew it. You just looked like you had sex." She held up her hand and shook her head when I turned around to face her. "I don't want to hear it," she said in a flippant tone.

Spasms of guilt ran through my chest as I looked down and twirled my keys in my hand. Shoot! I couldn't even look my mother in the eye as she sat on the sofa. How was I going to tell Lacie?

"I've got a few auditions this week in New York, so I'll fly back with you on Monday. I'll tell Lacie, then," I uttered.

Mom looked at me with cynical bewilderment. "What for? Might as well continue on with the deceit and not tell her at all. The damage is done."

"I owe it to her."

"What you *owed* is long gone, Dawn. You shouldn't have gotten involved with that boy in the first place and now that you've gone to bed him, it makes matters even worse," Mom voiced disapprovingly. "Were you really thinking about what you were getting ready to do, Dawn? Haven't you learned anything from your past mistakes? What goes around comes—"

"I know, Mom," I interrupted her loudly, finally looking at her. "You don't have to say anymore," I said tearing. "But I love Joe and he loves me. I've never felt this way about any other man before."

"So you say," Mom uttered.

What?

My expression must have said it all when Mom answered the silent question.

"Dawn, every time a good-looking man comes around, you always say that you never felt that way about any other man before. You've just been through so many men, Dawn," she suggested.

"And that's the issue you have with me, isn't it, Mom? Your daughter, the slut. Is that what you want to say? Is that it? I can't possibly be in love with a man like him, because I go through too many men to name them all?" I exclaimed bitterly.

Mom said nothing and shook her head sadly.

"You don't think I deserve a man like Joe? Do you?" I accused.

"Dawn, I don't know Joe from Adam." Mom looked at me tiredly. "I don't know anything about him. But what I do know is that he was involved with Lacie, *first*. And that he was in love with her, *first*."

"But he's in love with me *now*, Mom," I said with conviction. "And believe me, when I say that I *am* in love with him."

"Okay," Mom softly understated, nodding her head with skeptical eyes. "What about your love for Lacie? Shouldn't you have a sense of loyalty to her?" She paused. "Is your *supposed* love for Joe so strong that it's worth taking a chance on your friendship with Lacie?"

I couldn't believe it myself when I said it.

"Y...yes," I strained out.

Mom stared at me in disbelief before she uttered, "Well, for your sake, Dawn, I hope that Lacie can forgive you. Because she's the best friend you ever had."

# Chapter 48

# Robert

My father had had another stroke. This time it was massive.

It was my parent's anniversary and we were in the hospital in the emergency room. My father had always been a strong man, but I honestly didn't know if he could handle another one.

I knew my mother couldn't.

I shook my head sadly and looked at her while we sat in the waiting room. This was really taking a toll on her. She looked ten years older and though having always been a petite woman, she was now rail thin.

Dad's doctor came out with a haggard expression and gave us the update.

Dad was being admitted back into the hospital. This stroke had affected a good portion of his brain, leaving him to rely on life support. The outcome did not look good, the doctor said and most patients in that condition rarely bounced back.

All of a sudden, Ma let out a strangled cry and fell into my arms tearfully. The doctor, having known Dad since he was a young child, touched my mother's arm sadly and walked slowly down the hall.

I swallowed angry tears, knowing that there was nothing I could do to stop the inevitable.

I was going to lose my father.

# Chapter 49

# Lacie

There's no place like home.

Dorothy, in the Wizard of Oz couldn't have said it better.

Despite having spent the majority of the ride sleeping, I awoke immediately when Tony pulled up to the warehouse apartment building. I must've sensed I was home.

The weekend had been seemingly very long and tiring. Nothing felt better than to see my apartment building. Anxious to get out of the car and into my apartment, I grabbed the door handle. I didn't care to wait for Tony to be a gentleman and open the door for me.

Tony put his hand on mine and stopped me.

"Lacie...let's talk," he said softly.

I sighed. Couldn't he take a hint? Didn't he know that all I wanted was to go into some familiar territory, regardless of how it had been when I'd left it, see my own family and not worry about trying to make any impressions on anyone?

Reluctantly, I sat back in the seat and looked at him and immediately felt bad when I saw the unmistakable pain and sadness in his eyes.

"I'm sorry, Lacie," he said with a ragged breath. "You warned me about this and I didn't listen."

Yeah, I'd told him. But nothing I could have said or done would have prepared him. He had to find out for himself and that was what was so painful about it—for me, even. I hated seeing him this way—so despondent and so wounded. Yeah, I was hurt, mad and tired because of all of the mess that had happened. But so was he.

Prejudice was nothing new to me, but as far as I knew, this was *his* first time dealing with it; with his flesh and blood, to boot. So it had to be more devastating for him to see that some members of his family did not want him with me, nor approve of our love for each other. So I was not going to kick a man when he was already down. We'd been through enough in one weekend.

I took a deep breath and mustered a small encouraging smile. "Tony, you wanted me to meet your family and there's nothing wrong with that." I shrugged. "I know you're upset with the way your mother reacted–"

"I'm more than upset," he interjected swiftly.

I squeezed his hand, remembering Abigail's words, and let out another deep breath. "But the reality is that sometimes we can't change people's feelings or ideas." I shook my head sadly. "I hate to break it to you, Tony, but your mother might be one of them."

He nodded with compliance. "Yeah, I'm starting to realize that too," he said sadly. His voice was thick with emotion as he added, "I want you to know that it was not my intention for you to get insulted and hurt this weekend. I didn't want that. I wanted…" he said, breaking off.

I touched his face tenderly. "I know you wanted it to go better than it did. I know that," I whispered and leaned over to kiss him on the cheek. "But don't worry about me. I'm a big girl and I can take care of myself."

He grabbed me swiftly with all of his strength and lowered his head on my chest. "I love you so much, Lacie, and I'm so sorry."

"I know. I love you, too," I soothed.

We sat in the car for a few moments holding each other. Both of us were depleted emotionally. He broke the embrace slowly and glanced out his window as he tried to conceal the tears welling in his eyes. I shook my head again, imagining his pain.

"C'mon," I said, opening my door. "Let's go upstairs and see if my mom and dad have been able to get along this weekend.

⚜

"Mason, I don't want to hear it. I don't want to hear it!" Mama's scream welcomed us when I opened the door to my apartment.

Oh, c'mon! This was getting ridiculous.

My stomach had already sunk and the nausea had risen when the commotion could be heard from the hallway. Yet, here they were arguing again. I turned to Tony for a silent answer to my question: Was it that difficult for me to return to my own house for a little bit of peace and tranquility? Tony shook his head and put a supportive arm around my shoulder.

I suddenly noticed Reneé who was sitting on the sofa with her hands over her face.

"Josephine, you're going to have to tell her. Lacie and I have to know!" Daddy demanded loudly.

That sparked my interest. "What is he talking about, Mama?" I uttered, moving closer to them. Intuition was telling me that this was very serious. My stomach started to churn, nausea moving closer to my mouth.

Mama shook her head crossly. "After all of the crap that I've taken from you, you have the nerve to think—"

I got in the middle of them with Tony trying to hold me back. "Think what, Mama?"

"How am I supposed to be sure, Josephine?" Daddy voiced indignantly. "You were with that Hudson boy when we were together!"

"Daddy?" I asked.

Tony was still holding my arm lightly while I looked from Mama to Daddy. Neither of them seemed to care that I was standing in between them.

"It was one time Mason and I was already pregnant with Lacie then! How many times have I explained that to you?" Mama defended vehemently. "You...were the one that was fooling around on me. Messing around with all of them women. The whole town knew except for me! I loved and trusted you, Mason, but you took every ounce of dignity that I had for myself and just threw it in the garbage." She blinked back tears. "It was the first and only time that I found solace in another man, Mason, and I acted on it. But we couldn't be together and you know why. He never took the place of you. Never." She stared

269

him down and pointed her index finger up, expressively. "It was just one little discrepancy out of I don't know how many times you were unfaithful to me and you have the gall to point a finger at me? You bas—"

"Mama!" I exclaimed.

Daddy shook his head. "One little discrepancy is all it takes to make a child. How am I supposed to know that she's my daughter, Josephine?"

What the? I wasn't his daughter? I covered my mouth instantly at his words.

Infuriated, Mama's eyes widened and she screamed and pointed at me. "Mason, look at Lacie! Look at her! She has your nose, your eyes. Your complexion!" She pointed to her heart. "I loved you, Mason! And all you've ever had to do was count the months, you idiot!"

"Will you two stop it? Just stop it!" I shouted angrily, tears flowing profusely from my eyes. "You know, I am so *sick* of you two arguing! It's like dealing with two children. This is ludicrous and I have just about had it up to here…" I managed to utter before the nausea raised to its height, threatened to escape my mouth. I covered my mouth instantly and hurried to the bathroom. I had reached the commode in time before a steady stream of vomit flew out of my mouth and into the bowl.

# Chapter 50

# Tony

"See what you've done!" Josephine had screamed when I hurriedly followed behind Lacie to the bathroom.

Mason and Josephine were still arguing when I closed the door and locked it. Lacie didn't need to hear any of this. I knelt beside her and rubbed her back while everything imaginable came out of her and spewed into the commode. I put my hand to my mouth, shaking my head at the outcome of events. This was too unreal to imagine, and very untimely.

Once she started heaving, a clear sign that she was about done, I grabbed a tissue with a free hand and wiped her mouth. I felt her head. She didn't feel hot, but she was sweating. She gazed up at me with tears and exhaustion in her eyes. She opened her mouth to speak, but I shook my head.

"Don't say anything. Just let me take you up to your bedroom," I said softly. I stood and picked her up.

She went limp in my arms and cried softly against my neck when I carried her out. Reneé met me in the hallway as Mason and Josephine's argument ensued.

"Is she okay?" she asked.

"I don't think so," I replied. "Where to?"

"Upstairs, second one on the right. But I don't think it's a good idea for you to carry her all the way up there," she suggested.

"It's quite all right. I can manage."

Reneé looked at me as if I was crazy, but followed me up the stairs while I carried her sister.

"You are definitely in love with my sister, I tell you that," Reneé remarked once we were in Lacie's room. She pulled the covers back so I could lay Lacie on the bed.

"That," I grunted, lifting Lacie up slightly to arrange the pillow under her head. "I most certainly am," I finished.

With very little resistance from an enervated Lacie, I deftly and quickly got her straight for bed. Reneé stood by, watching me with an inquiring expression as she handed me Lacie's nightgown.

"I've had practice this weekend. Believe me, you don't want to know," I explained dryly after Lacie was tucked in, task completed.

"Can you believe this?" Reneé asked with a despondent whisper, looking down at her sister's lethargic and sleeping form.

"No, I can't," I whispered in return and sighed. "But after the events this weekend, I shouldn't be too surprised."

We turned toward the door, hearing the synchronized sound of two slamming doors.

"I guess they're finished," Reneé remarked candidly.

"Thank God," I whispered in relief. "I thought it would never end."

"Tell me about it. It's been brewing ever since you two left and I've been in the middle of the secret war that's been going on between them. I didn't dare call Lacie, though. She had too much on her mind with this weekend and all," she said. She nodded at Lacie. "Things didn't go so well, huh?"

"No, they didn't," I replied briefly, not wanting to relive it. "Listen, Reneé, I'd like to stay up here for a little while and make sure she's all right. Do you think Josephine is going to mind?" She replied by giving me an incredulous look. "Right."

"Do you think she's going to be okay?" she asked.

"I don't know and I'd rather not have her come in to work tomorrow until she sees her doctor. I think she might be coming down with a virus or something. The same thing happened last night. Matter of fact, we might want to put a bucket by the bed just in case." A small smile crept onto Reneé's face suddenly. "What?"

"Nothing." She shook her head, walked toward the bathroom and came out with a bucket. She put it right by Lacie on the floor, before heading out the room. "Look, stay as long as you like and if you need anything just let me know. I'm a door down."

I laid on top of the covers next to Lacie, holding her for a good portion of the night. She tossed and turned a few times, but not once did she wake up. A few times, I heard someone downstairs in the kitchen, but other than that, the apartment stayed quiet.

It was nearly three o'clock in the morning when I left. I was reluctant to leave Lacie, but didn't want to overstay my welcome.

I realized I'd left my cell phone in my car when it vibrated in the middle console. The caller I.D. displayed my parent's house phone.

I hit the 'end' button without a second thought, started the car and pulled onto the street.

Mother or not. I wasn't ready to talk to her. Not yet.

# Chapter 51

# Lacie

I had to vomit.

I jumped out of bed, hurried to the bathroom and did something awful to the commode. After what seemed an eternity, I stood up and looked in the mirror, feeling a little relief.

What…was…wrong with me?

Following a thorough cleansing of my mouth, I returned to my bedroom and sat on my bed. Then slowly getting my bearings and remembering the scene with my parents last night, I covered my face with my hands and started to cry silently.

Then I got angry and the tears stopped.

What the… Mason Adams, might not be my father? This was some soap opera, talk show, Maury Povich crap.

Heated, I sat on the bed for a while, before I glanced at the clock on my nightstand. With purpose, I got up from my bed, strode to my closet, picked out some clothes, went to the bathroom and started the shower.

I had to get out of this house.

Regardless of how early it was and how miserable I was feeling, I didn't want to stay at home. I didn't want to see my mother and didn't want to see the man who I'd thought was my father.

I needed to get away.

The queasiness started up again before I even made it to work. I stopped at a twenty-four hour deli at the corner and purchased a bagel with cream cheese with the hope that once I ate, my stomach would settle. Hope became despair. The smell of the bagel in the elevator alone got to me and as soon as the elevator stopped and opened on my floor, I threw it in the wastebasket.

I groaned when I walked by Trevor's opened office door, hearing him on the phone. Why'd he have to be here so early? I strode by swiftly, not wanting to say anything to him—or anyone for that matter.

I walked quickly to my office, closed the door behind me slightly, put my belongings on the chair and with relief, crossed my arms on the desk and laid my head down.

Tap. Tap. Tap.

What?

Startled, I jerked my head up to see Trevor's merry grin spread across his face and his knuckles tapping on my desk. He was too happy this morning.

"What up, Sleeping Beauty? You've been asleep for a while. Long weekend, hmm?" he bantered. I glanced at the door. "It wasn't closed, so I just took it as an invitation and walked in," he explained.

"What do you want, Trevor?" I said unkindly, yawning and sitting up.

With a triumphant smile, he slapped a piece of paper in his hand. "I've got good news."

"What?"

"You look terrible," he remarked abruptly, fixing his eyes on me for a brief second before he pointed to the paper in his hand. "I just got one of the best contracting bids we've ever seen. I want you to sign off on it."

I sighed gravely. "Trevor, you know we're not supposed to sign off on any of the bids unless all of us agree to it. And I've already given you the list of contractors we researched already. We were supposed to go into consultations this week," I replied wearily, queasiness coming over me.

He smirked. "Yeah, but this one beats them all. Not to mention, this is my project and I have the final say so."

"And so you keep reminding us," I retorted dryly.

He squinted at me. "You know, you should think about going to a doctor. You look pale." My mean glare didn't faze him as he smirked and started explaining, "Look, an associate of mine advised me on this guy. I just got through talking with him and he faxed his resume over to me. He's handled all kinds of jobs like this. You really need to look at this."

"It's so early in the morning, Trevor," I groaned, leaning back in my chair and running a hand through my hair.

"Lacie, you know the crunch time we have on this project. We need to jump on this," he persisted. "I'm sure Tony and Joe will sign off once you have."

Would he…just…leave my office?

I eyed him with a mixture of misery and annoyance. "Look, Trevor. I'm not feeling so well right now and I'm definitely not fit to make such a decision so early. Let's just wait until the rest of the team gets here and go over it." I put my head back on my desk.

He still stood there, unmoving.

I raised my head. *"What?"* I asked, irritated.

"He's got other jobs pending," he hinted. "I doubt Richard and William would be happy if we passed up on a chance to save some money in this deal when the budget has already gone over."

With an exasperating sigh, I thrust out my hand. "You know what? Just give me the paper. Give it to me!" I demanded in annoyance.

He passed the document to me eagerly. It was filled with all kinds of jargon that my unfocused eyes were not ready for. Yet the second page did show an impressive resume of jobs the contractor in question had done. After a quick, but thorough review, I signed it and handed it to Trevor, ready for him to get out of my office.

"Thanks. It's good to know that Tony doesn't have you so whipped that you don't have a mind of your own," he said with a wink, walking out. "Make sure you get to a doctor."

"Uh, huh. Get out, Trevor."

I shook my head and laid it back down on my desk. A few seconds later, I heard Carrie tap on my door and come in. What was it with everyone coming in to work so early—and in my office?

"'Morning, Lacie," she greeted cheerfully.

I raised my head up slowly. "Mornin'," I strained out.

She halted in mid- stride. "Ooh, girl!" she said with a frown. "You look tore up. What happened to you over the weekend?"

"Everything," I moaned. "Carrie, I'm not feeling good."

Worry came over her face. "What's wrong?" she asked, walking over to me and putting a hand over my forehead.

"Carrie, I don't know. I just feel very nauseous and weak."

"It doesn't seem as if you have a temperature." She looked down at me after she took her hand off my forehead. "How long have you been feeling this way?" she asked, pensively.

"All weekend. I've been throwing up since Saturday night and I even fainted at the wedding." Carrie put a hand over her mouth, hiding a smile. "It's not funny, Carrie." I shook my head and ran a hand through my hair. "I don't know what's wrong with me. I must have the flu or something. Whatever it is, I just want it to go away."

Carrie smiled and gave me two soft pats on my back. "Honey, I think whatever you have won't be going away for a very long time," she chuckled.

I looked up at her sharply. "What?"

Tony walked in before Carrie had a chance to answer. "Good morning," he said briefly. "I wasn't expecting to see you this morning," he remarked.

"Why not? I work here, don't I?" I snapped.

He stopped short and raised his eyebrow.

"O…kay," Carrie uttered softly, taking a deep breath and walking away from me. "Lacie, I'm going to fix you a cup of tea. Better yet, I'll get you some ginger ale to help with that upset stomach."

Tony came over to me and brushed a strand of hair away from my face with his finger. "Still not feeling well?" he asked sympathetically, planting a kiss on my forehead.

"No." I shook my head. "I'm sorry I snapped at you," I mumbled.

He sighed. "You really should have stayed home, you know. Or at least gone to the doctor."

"No. I was angry when I woke up and all I wanted was to get out of the house before anyone else awoke." I gave him a weak smile. "But thanks for everything last night."

"I'm glad I was there," he murmured, leaning against the desk to look at me. "You want to talk about it?"

"No."

"And you're sure you don't want to go home?"

"Yes."

He nodded. "Thought so. But I figured I'd ask anyway. Okay," he said with a sigh standing up. "You already know what's ahead of us today, so needless to say, we're going to be very busy. If you change your mind, I'll take you home. You know Richard won't mind."

I regretted not taking Tony's offer.

Meeting after meeting, I struggled to get through the middle of the day, the queasiness never leaving me. Tony and Carrie kept watchful and concerned eyes on me and at one time, without realizing it, I'd nodded off, until I felt Carrie elbow me in the side.

When the meeting adjourned and everyone broke for lunch, I declined to go out with them to stay in my office. Thankfully, Carrie offered to go out and bring back take out for me from a local Chinese restaurant instead. After all, I hadn't had anything to eat all day. Maybe some food would help.

The Won-Ton soup that I'd ordered seemed to settle my stomach a bit, while I ate alone in my office. The shrimp and broccoli lunch deal didn't. It tore my stomach up, bringing the queasiness back with full force.

What now?

The meeting reconvened shortly after lunch and my stomach would not give in to my silent prayers. I kept thinking to myself, "*You're not going to throw up, Lacie. You're not going to throw up.*" But my stomach didn't agree and my digested lunch started to rise into my throat.

Oh, no, I groaned inwardly. This was not happening.

Soon, I wasn't able to stand it anymore and hastily but silently, snuck out of the room. Once the door closed, I dashed to the bathroom, which, to my relief, was a few steps away. I rushed into the closest stall and vomited all of my lunch in the commode.

It was a good while before I felt confident enough to get up from the commode. When I came out, drained and with a little perspiration on my forehead, there was Carrie leaning against the bathroom counter facing me with an amused smile, holding out a paper towel. I noticed her purse hanging on her shoulders.

"Finished?" she asked easily, reaching to hand me the paper towel.

I took it gratefully and patted my forehead. With a slight nod, I walked at a snail's pace to the counter and leaned on it for support. "I think so." I took a deep breath and turned on the faucet.

"Here. I want you to do this first," Carrie said, turning around to look at me in the mirror. She reached in her purse and took out a box labeled "EPT" and pushed it toward me.

"Carrie…girl, are you crazy? Put that away!" I exclaimed, pushing the box from me and looking at the door nervously.

"Don't worry, I locked the door. No one's going to come in," she explained easily as she pushed the box toward me again. "I bought this when I went to get your lunch. You've got all the symptoms, so you need to take this test." I shook my head insistently and she let out an exasperated breath. "Lacie, c'mon, girl. You've been tired, nauseous, vomiting and not to mention you look a mess! Now do this so that I can see if my hunch is right."

"No," I said, shaking my head more insistently as I looked at her reflection. "I'm not doing it." I pushed it back to her.

"Lacie, just check and see," she coaxed. "It's no harm done. If you're not, you're not."

"I'm not pregnant, Carrie," I said decisively.

She folded her arms. "And you know that because…" she murmured skeptically.

I shrugged and rubbed my stomach with a wince. "I just know that's all."

"Right, umm, hmm," she said more skeptically. "Have you had your 'friend' recently?"

"What?" I exclaimed, looking at her dubiously. "C'mon, Carrie. We're both grown women. We can say 'period' to each other."

"Well...have you?" she insisted.

Frustrated, I stared at her blankly through the mirror, immediately realizing that I couldn't answer the question.

"Uh...yeah. That's what I thought." She thrust the package toward me again. "Girl, if you don't take this test," she argued.

"Carrie?" I objected.

"Ah...do it!" she demanded crossly, pointing her finger at me.

Annoyed, I twisted my lips, snatched the box from her, returned to the stall, and followed the directions.

"Come back out when you've finished peeing on the strip," she instructed on the other side of the stall. "I want to see the results, too."

I couldn't believe her. *Well, Lacie, she did pay for the test.*

After I was done, I came out, grabbed a paper towel and placed it on the counter with the EPT tube on top of it. Then I washed my hands.

"All right, now. It says we've got to wait three minutes," Carrie said.

"Carrie, I've done this before," I said crisply, looking at her as I turned the faucet off.

She turned to me with a raised eyebrow. "Lacie, you'd better not be one of those hormonal, out of control, pregnant women that stay mad all the time. Because if you do, I swear I'm going to ask for a transfer," she jeered good-naturedly.

"I'm not...pregnant," I spat back through clenched teeth.

"Fine," she shot back imperturbably with a couple of taps on her watch. "Time will tell. We've got two and a half minutes."

"Stubborn woman," I muttered under my breath.

"Hey, I'm right here," Carrie retorted. "I *can* hear you, you know."

⊗⊗⊗

Time crept by slowly while Carrie and I paced the restroom floor, restlessly waiting for the two and a half minutes to pass.

"All right," Carrie announced finally, signaling that the time was up. "Are you ready?"

"No," I gulped, shaking my head. I pointed at the tube as if it was foreign. "You look at it. I can't do it."

With an exaggerated sigh, Carrie stepped over to the counter and looked at it, with me watching her every movement. She turned around and looked at me with a reserved expression before her mouth slowly curved into a very broad and very revealing smile.

No!

# Chapter 52

# Tony

"Richard, William, we have found the perfect contractor for the job," Trevor was saying confidently.

Stunned, I eyed him swiftly. When did this happen? I glanced at Joe and he had the same expression. And where did Lacie run off to?

Trevor proceeded to pass out a document around the table. "You all have the list in front of you of the prospective contractors that we had originally considered," he said. "But," he asserted, holding up a single document. "This is the one that I'm certain we should go with and I'm ready to go into formalities." He returned to his chair triumphantly.

"Excuse me, but this is the first time this has been presented to us," Joe said after looking over the document momentarily. "We had no knowledge of this company or its history."

"That's quite all right. Everything is spelled out in black and white on the sheet," Trevor replied smoothly.

William and Richard glanced over the material carefully.

A minute later, Richard looked up with a satisfied grin. "Well, Trevor, you hit the nail on the head with this," he remarked.

William nodded in compliance. "The figures are very good."

"Yeah, Lacie and I thought so, too. All we have to do is get Joe and Tony to sign off and we can move forward," Trevor added with a blank face.

*Say what?*

Richard turned to us. "What's the problem, guys? You didn't like the figures?"

I couldn't even reply because I was stunned at the way Trevor's hand was played.

Trevor answered quickly. "No, sir. I spoke with the contractor this morning and jumped on it. Joe and Tony were not here this morning when Lacie and I talked it over."

I was fuming. He was trying to get all the credit and in the process was trying to make us look like we weren't on top of our jobs.

Richard glanced at me and then at Joe with a smudge of reproof. "All right. But let's make this happen. I don't want this guy to get away from us." He straightened the papers on the desk and said, "Okay. Meeting's adjourned."

I glared at Trevor, who smirked at me in return.

"You know," I murmured to Joe, as I stood up. "I'm gonna knock him out before this project is done. I swear I am. After all of that research we did he's just going to knock it out of the box without letting us know?"

"All right, all right. Just chill out, man. I got it," Joe said calmly, with a slight chuckle. "Let me talk to him and see what's up."

I pushed my chair in a little too aggressively, watching Joe walk over to Trevor who was putting all of his stuff in his briefcase.

William walked over to me. "Exciting weekend, Tony?" he hinted.

I returned a brief nod. "You heard about the incident between Simone and Lacie."

He shrugged. "I might have been on the other side of the country but word travels fast and you know that town. No one sneezes without people knowing about it," he said. "But yes, Simone did mention it."

"Look, I'm so—"

William shook his head. "Simone's a spoiled brat, Tony, and she probably deserved what she got," he said, waving it off. "She should be the one apologizing to Lacie and your sister. But...from experience we both know that won't happen." He sighed. "I don't know when she'll grow up. I didn't raise her to be that way," he said. "But look, I just wanted to talk to you about it and make sure that there were no hard feelings involved. I didn't want this to get in the way of our business."

"No. Of course not," I replied.

"Good." He nodded and shook my hand. Before he started walking out the room, he said, "Tell Lacie, I'm sorry about what happened."

I frowned. Where exactly was she, anyway?

I heard Trevor and Joe talking when I came out the conference room.

"I'm just telling you, man. You need to relax. We know you're good at what you do. It just wasn't cool the way you have handled it. That's all," Joe explained to Trevor.

"Man, look, I saw a chance and took it. How many times has Whitey taken advantage of us and we were left looking stupid?" Trevor defended candidly.

I grimaced. Every time I heard him utter the word, 'Whitey', I literally had to restrain myself.

"Man, I've just about had it with you and that word. As educated as you are, can't you think of anything else?" I interceded.

Trevor looked at me blankly. "Was I talking to you?"

"No, but I'm talking to you. What is with you, man? What in the hell were you trying to pull back in there? Do you know how many hours were put in to get that list up? We worked our butts off! We're supposed to be on the same team, man," I contended.

"Why so angry, Tony? A brotha can't play the same game as Whitey?" he taunted.

*Oh, so he was stepping up?*

Impulsiveness got the best of me. I walked up to him to determine which side of his jaw I was going to sock him on, when Joe got in between us. "Man, we looked like idiots in there!" I said furiously, glaring at Trevor. "We're all supposed to agree on everything before we sign off on it. You know that."

He shrugged. "Business is business, man."

"But there's a way to do things, man. Especially in *business*," Joe disputed.

Trevor shrugged again and with a smug smirk said, "Hey, Lacie thought it was a good idea. That's why she signed off without question." His smirk turned into a satisfied grin, when I grimaced.

"What, Tony? Are you upset that Lacie took the initiative and moved on with the better man?" He tsked, tsked before he turned and strolled off.

"Okay, okay, cool it, man," Joe said, holding me back as I was getting ready to go after Trevor's retreating figure. He patted my shoulder, chuckling. "Why are you letting him get to you? You know he's only doing that because he's jealous of you and Lacie."

"Yeah, but what he did was underhanded and what he just said had a double meaning," I said grimly, trying to cool off, still looking down the hall. I looked at Joe. "Why do you think he did that and why so quickly? We're on a deadline but we were getting ready to decide on it this week." "I know," Joe said with a little frown. "I don't understand it, either. Looking at that bid, though, I've got to be honest. I'd have gone for it, too."

"Thanks a lot, man," I said sarcastically.

"C'mon, man, lighten up. I mean, is this really worth it?" Joe asked, holding out his arms. "You know from all of the meetings that we've had, that Trevor ain't got any sense. But he's here to make William, Richard and all of us bank. That's why he's rolling with us."

"Yeah, but at what cost?" I muttered.

Joe shook his head and looked at his watch. "Look, man, I'd like to sit here and listen to you brew, but I've gotta get out of here. You gonna be all right?"

"Yeah, I'm cool," I replied, looking at him fleetingly. "Listen, Joe, we gotta talk and it's long overdue," I said in a serious tone.

Joe frowned with concern, recognizing the tone. "Sure, man. What's up?"

I shook my head. "Man, some real ill stuff happened this weekend at my parent's house and there are some other things that have been on my mind. But I don't want to talk about it right now because this isn't the place or the time."

He nodded thoughtfully. "Okay, you want to hook up for lunch tomorrow, then?"

"I was hoping we could discuss it today. How about we meet after work and go out for some beer?"

"No, man. Can't," he said quickly, looking away. "I've got a few things I need to take of. I'll be out all night."

My radar hiked up instantly and I pressed the issue with a hard stare. "I'm not asking for all night. I got a life, too, you know. What's up? You can't spare an hour or two with your buddy?"

"Nothing's up," he said, tightly. "Just got things to do, that's all." He shrugged. "Look man, I gotta go. Let's do lunch tomorrow and we'll talk then. All right?" he asked hastily. "Peace, man. I'll see you later." He gave me a pound and shoved his hands deep into his pockets and walked away.

I brooded at his walking figure, putting all of the signs together. He'd been in an incredibly good mood, hadn't barked about that whole mess with Trevor, was evasive about his love life, avoided eye contact with me and of course, the tell-tale sign—had shoved his hands deep in his pockets.

I had a feeling he was seeing Dawn, but he couldn't be sleeping with her? Or could he?

For Lacie's sake, I hoped for the contrary.

Still mulling, I started toward Lacie's office and was stunned to see her door closed and apparently locked. I saw Carrie walking over with a mug of coffee in her hand and in intense conversation with Lisa, one of the other members of the team.

"What? Girl, you're kidding! Oh, you have got to give me all of the info!" Carrie was saying when I came up to them swiftly.

"Excuse me," I said, interrupting them. "Uh, Carrie, where did Lacie go?" I asked, putting my hand on her arm lightly as she staggered with surprise.

"Oh, hey, Tony." She turned to Lisa. "Girl, I'll talk with you later, okay?" She turned back around to look at me. "Uh...Lacie's gone, Tony. She wasn't feeling very well, so she decided to leave," she informed lightly as she put her cup of coffee on her desk.

"What? I told her I'd take her home. Why didn't she come and get me?"

Carrie shrugged with a hint of a small smile. "I guess she didn't want to interrupt the meeting," she replied.

I sighed. "I hope she's gone to the doctor. I told her she should have stayed at home," I said rhetorically, looking at her door thoughtfully.

"Oh, I'm sure she's gone to the doctor, all right," Carrie blurted out abruptly. I turned around to witness her put her hand over her mouth with wide eyes before she put it back down swiftly. "Uh…I mean, I *think* she went to the doctor." She looked away quickly and covered her mouth again. Only this time, it looked like there was a huge smile underneath.

I peered at her wistfully for a moment before I uttered, "Thanks, Carrie." I gave her a brief nod and started for my office.

I heard the phone on my desk ringing when I entered my office and hurried to answer it. "Ryan & Company. Tony speaking."

"Hello, son," Dad's voice answered through the other end of the line.

I inhaled and sat down heavily. His voice brought the incidents from the past weekend into memory again. "Hey, Dad," I replied, running a hand over my face tiredly.

"Son, we need to talk about this weekend," he started easily.

That was a no go for me. "Dad, I don't want–"

He cut me off. "Son, you're mother's been upset ever since you left so angrily yesterday. She really didn't want you to leave."

"Dad, *she* was the reason why I left," I defended. "The way she treated Lacie was inexcusable. There was no way I was going to let Lacie stay there—not after what Mom said to her."

"I understand, son." He sighed. "Listen. Despite everything that's happened, you must know that your mother loves you. She only wants what's best for you. We all do."

"Lacie is what's best for me. I love her."

"Point taken. But it was clear the moment I first saw you two together."

"You mean at my apartment?"

"Yeah, at your apartment," he chuckled. "Listen, son, you're mom's a southern woman, born and raised. She's stubborn and has her beliefs. Yet, she married a Yankee with different ones. I guess that's what attracted us to each other." He sighed again. "Son, this is your life. You have to live it the way you choose. I just want you to know that I'm behind you one hundred percent. I'll keep working on your mother and we'll go from there. Okay, son?"

"Thanks, Dad."

"I'll talk with you later, son. I love you," he said.

"Love you, too, Dad."

"Hey, look," he added hastily before I was about to hang up. "Tell Lacie that I'm deeply sorry for what happened. Okay?"

His concern for Lacie brought on a smile. "Sure, Dad. I will."

That was the perfect way to end my workday.

# Chapter 53

# Joe

Tony knew. I could feel it.

I grumbled as I pulled up to the passenger pick up section of LaGuardia Airport and waited. Dawn was returning to New York with her mother and she'd called me earlier at work with her arrival time. I was slightly early, so I had a short wait. I couldn't wait to see her and be with her, but hated to give her a heads up about Tony.

Thirty minutes later, we were in Jamaica, Queens in front of her mother's house.

"You gonna stay with me, Dawn or are you going with him?" Rose asked her daughter, while I pulled her suitcase out of my trunk.

Rose said it like I was some disease.

"I... I'm going to stay with Joe, Mom," Dawn replied quickly, giving her a kiss on her cheek on the front porch of her house.

"Umm, hmm," Rose muttered, eyeing me disapprovingly as I set her suitcase on the porch.

"Would you like me to take this in the house for you, Mrs. Robinson?" I asked politely.

"No, thank you," she said curtly. She turned and looked at Dawn. "I'll be speaking with you later." She looked back at me. "Thanks for the ride, Joe,"

I gave her my best charming smile. "It was my pleasure, Mrs. Robinson."

"Umm, hmm," Rose muttered, with the same disapproving glare.

"I take it that your mom doesn't like me," I remarked to Dawn in the car, five minutes after I drove off from her mother's house.

Dawn exhaled as she stared out the window. "It's not that she doesn't like you. She just objects with how we got together."

I nodded, understanding the silent implication. "From the way she was glaring at me through the rearview mirror on the way over to her house...she thinks that I'm using you. Am I right?"

"Yeah...that's about right," she said, still looking out the window.

"Dawn," I said softly. "Look at me."

She shook her head. "Joe, don't. I'm all right uptight as it is and it's too late to go back. Much too late."

"You know I love you, right?"

She only turned her head and stared at me for a good second, then turned back to the window.

℘℘℘

"So this is it," Dawn remarked, looking around while I pulled her suitcase into the apartment.

"Yep," I said, closing the door. "Do you like it?"

She stood in the middle of the living room and nodded, looking at the fireplace. "Very nice," she said softly.

I noticed her melancholy tone when she replied and walked up behind her and put my arms around her waist. "What's wrong?"

She broke away from me easily and turned around. Her eyes were wary and questioning. "Did you and Lacie ..."

"No, we never..." I struggled momentarily, trying to find the right word to use. "We were never intimate here," I finished.

Dawn replied with an unconvinced nod and walked over to the fireplace in silence.

"Dawn, Lacie and I never slept together in this apartment."

"Sure." Her eyes were brooding and accusing.

I took a deep breath and walked over to her. "Look, I'm not going to lie to you, here. This was where Lacie and I had our first date. It was a memorable night, but we never slept together here."

"She helped you pick out this apartment."

I was unsure whether she was asking me or whether it was a statement. "Yes, she did."

She shook her head decisively. "You know, I'm going to go. I should have never come over here."

She was already at the door and had opened it by the time I realized what she was doing. I caught up to her quickly, put my hand above her head, and shut the door.

"Hey, hey, hey," I said, taking her hands and pulling her back into the living room.

Tears were in her eyes when she looked up at me. "Joe, I shouldn't be here. This whole place reminds me of Lacie and what you two had."

"*Had*, is what it *was*, Dawn," I asserted. "Lacie and I are over. You and I are together now."

"And that's the problem, Joe. I feel like such a traitor!" she exclaimed softly. She glimpsed around the room. "I don't know whether it's because I'm back in New York or what, but...I just don't feel...right." She sighed. "I'm so nervous about seeing Lacie again and I don't know how I'm going to tell her, Joe."

I had to let her know. "You might not have to." She looked at me in sharp inquiry. "I think Tony knows about us."

"What?" Stunned, she removed her hands from mine and went to sit on the sofa. "How could he? Did you tell him?"

"No," I said quickly, sitting next to her.

"What do you think he knows?"

I shrugged. "I'm not sure, but he's been asking a lot of questions about my love life lately."

"Wonderful. This is just terrific," she murmured sarcastically. She leaned back on the sofa and put her hands over her face.

Feeling quite guilty and responsible, I took her in my arms while she cried softly. Was I being too selfish here and unrealistic of the situation? I was dating my ex-fiancée's best friend and this was tearing her apart. Was my happiness worth seeing Dawn in this way?

Hell yeah, it was!

I was in love with her and more importantly, she was in love with me. There was no way I was going to give her up.

Thoughtlessly I started rubbing her arms and her back. In response, she put her arm around my neck and started rubbing my nape. Then her hands went to my ears and without a second thought, I started to kiss her, enjoying the sweet taste of her lips. Our kiss deepened when she responded with a willing and eager tongue as mine. Oh, her body was soft! I took my hands and started rubbing her buttocks slightly, squeezing it with every rub. She moaned in response and pressed herself against me in earnest. Our heated exchange intensified and I was about to pick her up to carry her to the bedroom when her cell phone rang in the outside pocket of her purse. With deft, she reached over and grabbed her phone as we continued giving each other little kisses. She opened her flip cell phone and her eyes got wide.

She showed me the caller I. D. It was Lacie.

I blew hard.

Lacie sure knew how to wreck a man's groove.

# Chapter 54

# Dawn

"Girl...I am so upset!" Lacie yelled into the other end of my cell phone.

The sound of the distress in her voice immediately cooled the heat from my body and I sat up. I looked at Joe uneasily as he stood and went into the kitchen.

"What, girl? What's wrong?"

"Dawn, I'm pregnant!" Lacie declared in anguish.

"Whaaat?" I exclaimed loudly. Joe came out of the kitchen with concern on his face.

"Dawn, what am I going to do? I wasn't expecting this," she grumbled.

"Okay, okay, just take it easy, Lacie," I said calmly, suddenly overwhelmed with a ray of hope. "Have you told Tony, yet?"

"No, girl. I just found out this afternoon." She sighed. "Dawn, I'm telling you. I don't need this right now. There's just too much chaos going on in my life and this is going to make matters worse."

"Okay, okay, okay, listen," I soothed. "Are you at home?"

"Yes."

"Do you want me to come over?" I blurted.

"What do you mean come over? Are you in New York?" she asked excitedly. "Dawn, why didn't you tell me you were coming?"

"Uh... that's a long story," I said, looking at Joe warily with a shrug of my shoulders. "Look, I'll be over there short—"

"No, girl, don't come over. I already told you there's too much confusion going on. I don't want you to be in the midst of it," she said swiftly.

Concerned again, I said. "What? What's going on?"

"Dawn, I'll tell you about it when I see you and when I do you're not going to believe it," she said wearily.

"Okay, look. How about we go to lunch tomorrow and you can tell me all about it then?"

"Yeah, girl, that's fine. I can't wait to see you. I just need my best friend, right now," she implored.

I gulped. "All right, girl. I'll come by your job around noon. Then we can talk."

She let out a relieved sigh. "Thanks, Dawn. I'll see you tomorrow."

"What's up?" Joe asked once I flipped my phone over.

I looked at him, dumbfounded. "You're not going to believe this. As a matter of fact, I don't even think I should tell you."

He frowned. "Is something wrong?"

I shrugged. "Depends on how you look at it." Not being able to keep it in, I said. "Lacie's pregnant."

He didn't respond at first, only stared at me blankly as he took a seat next to me. "Whew! Talk about coincidences!"

Stunned, we silently grasped this information as we sat on the sofa. The news about Lacie's pregnancy gave me a weird sense of liberation. I somehow felt that this would validate me being with Joe because she couldn't possibly be preoccupied with us, now that she was expecting. Then, I recalled the last statement Lacie made. *"I just need my best friend, right now."*

Huh, best friend, indeed.

I shook my head angrily.

*Dawn, being with Joe is starting to make you twisted.*

# Chapter 55

# Lacie

If the story of my life were in a book, it'd be a bestseller.

That's how dramatic and tumultuous my life was going. I closed my cell phone in anger after speaking to Dawn and telling her the news.

I was so mad at myself! How could I have let this happen—again?

After a miserable experience with Tony's mother and finding out that after twenty-seven years, Daddy was questioning the legitimacy of his paternity, now I was pregnant. It was too inconceivable.

Huh, inconceivable.

And yet, Tony and I had conceived. What a metaphor; except it wasn't.

I shook my head and thought of Carrie. She'd been too happy and grabbed me in a tight hug while I stared in shock, my heart sinking at the color of the EPT stick.

*"I knew it! I knew it! Lacie, girl, you are going to be a mama!" Carrie laughed excitedly after letting me go. "This makes the fifth pregnancy in this department! One thing's for sure. I am definitely not going to drink any of the water in this building."*

*"Don't joke, Carrie," I shook my head again. "This is serious."*

*She frowned lightly. "What?" She paused. "You're not happy about it?" she asked.*

*"Carrie, you don't understand. I can't be pregnant. I just can't," I said, still looking at the stick in disbelief.*

*"Well, it says so right there…" Carrie began.*

*"I know, Carrie," I cut her off. "I see it too, but this can't be. This is going to cause problems." Carrie looked at me confused.*

*I didn't want to tell her the real reason why I shouldn't be pregnant. It was too shocking to me. So instead, I told her what happened in Connecticut.*

*Once I'd finished, Carrie sighed and put her hands on her hips. "Okay, I understand and sympathize with you about the weekend and his mother and all. But this doesn't change the facts. That test is pretty accurate and it looks like you and Tony are going to be parents. So what are you going to do? Are you going to tell Tony?"*

*I paused. Then with quick decision replied, "No," and hastily started gathering all of the wrappers from the package from the counter.*

*"Lacie!" Carrie exclaimed. "He has to know!"*

*"No, Carrie. He doesn't. Not until I know for sure," I declared. "I'm going to leave right now and go to the doctor."*

*"But, Lacie..." Carrie sputtered in protest, watching me in disbelief.*

*"C'mon, Carrie, help me clean up this mess. Will you?" I interrupted swiftly, beckoning her with my hand. "I don't want any evidence of this laying around." Then I thought of something as she began to help, mumbling in disagreement. "And Carrie, you'd better not breathe a word..." I threatened.*

*"Lacie, c'mon, who am I going to tell?" Carrie asked, stopping to look at me.*

*"Everybody!" I snapped automatically.*

*Carrie shook her head and resumed with a sarcastic, "Pregnant women, I tell you."*

*"Whatever," I reciprocated. "But believe me; This EPT test will not have the last word."*

My doctor did.

*"Well, one thing is certain, Lacie: You are very, very fertile. Very," Dr. Jones chuckled, returning to the exam room with the test results.*

Yeah, yeah, Dr. Jones. I get the point. I'm fertile.

*It was a one in one-thousand chance pregnancy, which occurred—despite me being on birth control pills—he explained to my horror. I stared at him blankly, not amused at all that he was chuckling, while I was struggling with an extraordinary amount of bewilderment.*

*"Dr. Jones, are you trying to tell me that I got pregnant on birth control pills?" I didn't even wait for him to reply and burst out irately, "How is that even possible? That's what birth control pills are for, to control birth!"*

*Doctor Jones was unruffled by my outburst. "Oh, it's possible, all right. Not very common—but possible," he confirmed and looked down at his chart. "And from the time frame you've given, you're approximately two months."*

*"But I've taken them religiously, never forgetting one pill!" I objected, still in denial. "I mean, what's the use of taken them if they're not even effective."*

*He looked at me as if I was a little child and explained patiently, "Lacie, they are effective. They're just not one hundred percent guaranteed. There is always that one percent chance and the only sure way for it not to happen is abstinence or either tubal ligation."*

*"Oh, no, no, no, no, no!" I groaned, covering my face with my hands. "This can't be happening. This is not happening!"*

*Dr. Jones patted my leg with a fatherly touch. There was a kind smile on his face when I removed my hands and looked at him.*

*"Relax, Lacie," he soothed. "I do believe that there is a Divine reason for this. So you'll be okay." He gave me another pat on my leg and sighed. "Now I want you to start drinking plenty of liquids immediately because you're slightly dehydrated. This might explain your fainting spells. I'm going to give you a prescription for the nausea and prenatal pills. Try to eat in small amounts..." he continued while I blocked him out.*

Troubled tears welled up in my eyes.

Oh!!! Was I in a mess!

As the cab pulled up to my apartment, I glanced down at my watch and saw that it was still early from the usual time I'd come home from work. Prayerfully, no one would be home.

My cell phone buzzed in my pocket as I took the elevator to my floor. The caller I.D. showed that it was Tony, but I didn't want to talk to him. Dawn was the only one I really wanted to talk to and I was glad that she happened to come back into town at the right time. She'd help me get through and help me figure things out. She'd always been in my corner whenever things got rough.

I rubbed my forehead as the elevator door opened. My head was throbbing from stress, my stomach ached, I was tired, and all I wanted was to walk in the door and face complete silence. A bit queasy and with so much tension in my head, I didn't want to see anyone because I was an emotional roller coaster.

I sighed with relief when I realized no one was home. Yes! My prayers were answered.

Reneé was attending an afternoon program that counseled pregnant teenagers and I didn't know where my mother and supposed father were. Truthfully, at that moment, I didn't care. I was too upset with either of them to be concerned. Not to mention, myself. My mind instantly started to go into a melancholy whirlwind of everything that was going awry in my life.

*The constant bickering between my parents. My dad might not be my dad.* Wearily, I dropped everything on one of the chairs in the living room. *Reneé and her problems with Danny.* I slowly headed for the kitchen. *The wedding and what Simone said to me.* I looked in the refrigerator and grimaced. *The incident at the boutique.* My stomach churned at the sight of food. *I was unwed and carrying Tony's child. Great Lacie. Just great. What a superb role model you are!* Something to drink, maybe? *Oh, ol' Abigail will really be thrilled about this! She couldn't stand me as it was.* Nothing but caffeine-filled sodas in sight. *I don't like you, she'd said.* Water maybe? *You are not acceptable, she'd said.* I got out a glass from one of the cabinets and put it under the faucet and let the water run. *You're not good enough for my son, she'd said.* I took a small sip of water and instantly got nauseous. *Your kind belongs to each other and our kind belongs to each other, she'd said. You're not good enough for my son. You're not good enough for my son!*

Angrily, I threw the glass in the sink, not caring that it had shattered into pieces, as I put my face into my hands and burst into uncontrollable sobs from the weight of the stress.

"Lacie?" I suddenly heard Mama's voice as she and Daddy entered the kitchen. I hadn't even heard the front door open. "Lacie, honey, what's wrong?" Mama asked as they both came to my side immediately.

I backed away and turned my back to them. "Nothing, Mama. Just leave me alone. Okay?" I exclaimed tearfully.

"Baby girl, c'mon, now. What's going on?" Daddy tried to soothe.

For the first time, his soothing voice didn't work. I shook my head, not wanting to speak for fear of exploding.

"No, Lacie," Mama expressed, turning me around to face her. "You're scaring me, now. What's wrong?" she asked with a frightened expression. I still shook my head with tears falling profusely. Her eyes widened and she gently shook my shoulders. "Lacie, tell us! C'mon, now, tell us!"

"I'm pregnant, Mama! Okay? I'm pregnant!" I finally exploded. I nodded my head to her shocked expression, wiped my face, and spread my arms out wide. "Yep, that's right, Mama." Mama tried to embrace me and Daddy inched toward me, but I moved away and continued my hysterical spiel. "Tony's mother hates me and now your oldest daughter has gotten herself knocked up again! Can you believe it? Aren't you proud of me? I've messed up my life—again!" I expressed with a maddening giggle.

Suddenly Daddy and Mama rushed up to me and took me into their arms. That one harmonious act and the strength of their embrace made me sob even more. I had to look like a complete twenty-seven year old mess of a baby, sobbing as my parents tried to calm me down. But I couldn't help it.

A sista was stressed.

෨ඏ

"I'm gonna to break that woman down!" Mama exclaimed vehemently after I'd finished telling her about the weekend.

We were upstairs in my room and I was lying on the bed with a cool washcloth on my forehead. Daddy and Mama had helped me up the stairs and Daddy had gone to the store to get my prescriptions and a few items to help with my nausea.

She handed me a glass of water and then reached for the portable phone by my bedside and pressed the talk button. "I'm gonna call Tony and get her phone number."

I didn't want to drink any water. Whether it was from my breakdown, hormones or anxiety, my queasiness was in full force.

I put one hand over the washcloth on my forehead and groaned, "Mama, no. That's not going to help."

"But it'll sure make me feel better," she countered, starting to dial.

"Mama, please, okay? I don't need any more drama. I'm already stressed out as it is," I pleaded weakly.

"Yeah and that's because of Tony's mother!" Mama objected.

"No, Mama, it's because of everything that's been going on. Did you forget that I just found out that I'm expecting?" I said excitedly. Some water spilled out of the glass onto the bed while I tried to sit up. "I mean, I don't need this."

Mama pressed the talk button again with one hand and pushed me back down with the other. "Okay, calm down, Lacie," she said easily, taking the glass of water from my hand. "You're right. We don't need another episode. Hormones, I tell you." She shook her head and put the glass of water to my lips. "Lacie, c'mon, now. Drink this water." I made a face and pushed it away. She raised her eyebrow with an exasperated sigh and said, "Listen, Lacie, you've already had a meltdown and you're dehydrated. Regardless of how hormonal you are right now, you're still my daughter. Now drink!" She pushed the glass back to my lips and I took a little sip. "That's better." She took the washcloth off and dabbed my forehead with it. "Now what was all that about downstairs? What did you mean when you said you messed up again?"

I let out an exasperated breath. "Mama, I wanted to be married before I had another child. I didn't want to repeat the same mistake over again."

"Why are you calling this a mistake?" she asked sharply, pushing the glass at me again.

I took another small sip and replied, "No...it's not a mistake. You're right. But this wasn't my plan. I'm not a teenager anymore. I'm grown, educated and a professional working class woman with a good career."

"And that means you shouldn't get pregnant?" Mama punned. "Lacie, no matter what your plan was—God had another."

"Obviously," I said dryly.

"Lacie, listen to me. There is nothing new under the sun and you are not the first case of an unwed professional woman."

"But I'm also black, Mama. I'm falling right into that stereotype."

"Are you because of what society says? Because what man says? No. Because the white man says," Mama insinuated.

I groaned and rolled my eyes upward. I had started her off and mentioned color.

To support her theory, Mama proposed, "When that 'Material Girl'... uh...uh...what was her name?" Mama asked, snapping her fingers to recollect.

I smiled wryly. "Madonna, Mama."

Mama eyes lit up, glad that the answer was found. "Yeah, yeah, that's right. Madonna. When she got pregnant, did everyone make a big stink about her not being married?" I shook my head again. Mama shrugged. "Mmm, hmm. Why is that? And she's rich. Now, professional....that's questionable." I let out a small giggle and Mama chuckled. "Neither you nor Reneé are a statistic. Just like STDs, pregnancy does not discriminate. So no one is above anything happening to them and no one is above anyone else." With one nod she added, "And Miss Abigail is going to find that out real fast when I invite her and her husband over here for dinner."

"No, Mama." My eyes widened with alarm.

"Yes, Lacie," she countered with another nod.

I put my hand on my forehead again and strained, "Mama, the only reason you want to invite her over here is so you can break her down."

"That's what I said, didn't I?" Mama quipped. "She says she doesn't like you and that you're not acceptable? Okay. Let her come over here so she can experience how it is to feel uncomfortable and mistreated since she didn't think twice about your feelings or her own son's."

"So we should stoop to her level and play right into her hands? Her scheme to have Tony choose between her and me?" I shook my head. "That not the way to handle this, Mama."

"And what way is, Lacie?" Mama argued. "That woman insulted you and threatened you! No, Lacie. We've got to get this settled now, because if we don't then it'll continue and you'll get more stressed. You don't need that."

"Mama, we're not talking about just anybody here. This is Tony's *mother — his blood.* I don't want him to be in the middle of a war between us. I don't…"

"Lacie, will you get some backbone?" Mama cut me off, frustrated. "After all of the arguing and fighting we did over the past few months, now all of a sudden you want to get soft. Child, even Tony had enough wisdom to stick up for you!" Mama declared strongly.

"But that's the problem, Mama," I maintained. "Don't you see? Even though Tony defended me, it wasn't without consequence. He was hurt and upset to see his mother behave that way. Now that I'm expecting it's going to complicate things further."

Mama studied me for a moment before she sighed. "Okay, listen, this dinner needs to happen and we're not getting anywhere." She closed her eyes tightly. "I hate to admit this, but Tony defending you this weekend…" she choked up and nodded her head. "It…it…it really said a lot. Now, I really see how much you two love each other. So…" she inhaled and opened her eyes. "I will try to be on my best behavior. Okay?"

That meant a lot because that was a huge step for Mama. "Thank you, Mama," I said, smiling gratefully and tearing up some.

"Lacie, if you don't stop with all of that crying," Mama warned lightly and I chuckled. "C'mon, girl. Drink some more water."

While she continued pushing water on me, I studied her and after a few minutes decided to ask the question that had been on my mind ever since last night. "Mama, is Daddy…?" I asked suddenly, trailing off.

"I knew that was coming up next." She stopped with the water, inhaled and looked at me with intensity. "Lacie, Mason *is* your father." I put my hand to my chest in relief and she smiled wryly. "We are not on TV and this is not the soaps. Deep, down Mason knew. After you screamed your head off at us last night and left so early this morning, we figured that we needed to bring everything out in the open. So we went out for lunch and had a good, long, talk."

ACROSS THE COLOR LINE

"Finally!" I said breathlessly.

"We just went through so much when we were together." She heaved a big sigh. "Girl, you just don't know. Love can make you lose all of your common sense sometimes and I loved your father dearly." She closed her eyes tightly and reopened them. "Oh, Lacie, it was hard — very hard, loving him."

"So Mama, what was dad talking about when he mentioned some Hudson...?" I started, but she put her hand on mine and stopped me.

She nodded. "I know where you're going with this so let me start from the beginning." I sat up and looked at her intently as she opened up. "Your Dad and I were seeing, dating or whatever kind of slang you young kids use today for when a guy and a girl gets together. He was just eye-candy with the naturally curly black waves and those light brown eyes. And so tall. Oh! I was crazy about him and so were a lot of the other girls, which caused a huge problem, even though, I was the one that caught his eye. I kept hearing rumors that he was going with other girls even though we were supposed to be with each other and...he was my first, Lacie. I was hurt. So..." she swallowed, looking at me warily, stopping.

"Yes...so?" I urged her.

She swallowed again, "I...I uh, had a job working as a baby-sitter after school for this family and they had an older son. He was very kind to me, showing me all kinds of att–"

A knock interrupted her.

"Come in," I said, slightly irritated by the interruption.

Daddy came in carrying a tray with my medicine, a bowl of chicken noodle soup, a pack of saltine crackers and ginger ale. To my surprise, Tony came in behind him. Mama's face flushed with a little embarrassment as she stood up so Daddy could sit next to me.

"How's my baby girl?" he asked tenderly, placing the tray over my lap.

I rolled my eyes upward with a little smile and he chuckled.

"This should make you feel better. Your mother gave me explicit instructions on what to get you, so your pantry and refrigerator is stocked with everything you need. Okay?"

I gave him a warm smile, remembering that whenever I did visit him and happened to get sick, he would take very good care of me. "Thank you, Daddy."

Mama cleared her throat and said, "Tony, let me talk to you outside for a minute. Let Lacie alone with Mason for a while."

Without waiting compliance from Tony, she put her arm through his and steered him out my room.

I sighed. "I guess she's going to talk to Tony about this weekend."

"Well, you know your mother," he stated simply, looking at the door. Then he turned to me. "Lacie, I'm sorry about all of the arguing Josephine and I have been doing. I didn't realize we were putting so much strain on you. When you went off on us yesterday, that's when I knew that the bickering between us had to stop."

I peered at him. "Daddy, did you really doubt that I was your daughter?"

He blew hard and swallowed. "I was a dog, Lacie. A true dog and I was also very young." He shrugged. "I was scared and didn't feel ready to be a father. I don't know how your mother put up with me, but she did. I cheated on her with every girl that I could find, but she still held on. So when the other guy started eyeing your mother...as hypocritical as it was, I got jealous and adamant. I believe that's what made me feel justified about leaving her, because I was so scared — among other things."

"So...what made you claim me as yours if you had so many doubts?" I pressed.

With a proud smile, he answered simply, "When I saw you in that hospital after you were born." He shook his head. "You were the prettiest baby I'd ever seen."

"But why didn't you and Mama get back together?"

"Because we couldn't get along and there had been too much damage done—on both of our parts—to go back to where we were. We knew it couldn't work. And when a man's woman gets with another man, it wounds the male ego. I'd also gotten seriously involved with another girl at the time, so..." He trailed off. "Lacie, I know that you are mine. I think I knew it a long time ago, but was just so hurt by what your mother did..."

"Is that why you came? To find out the truth."

"Yes and no." He sighed. "You've suffered so much, Lacie, because of the mistakes and misgivings between your mother and me. And I was never really there for you as a father." He shrugged. "I figured that the time had come to finally confront the past and somehow make up for it." He put his hand over mine and looked at me tenderly. "I love you, Lacie and I'm so sorry for all of this."

I smiled and said softly, "It's okay, Daddy and I love you more."

"My baby girl." He leaned in and gave me a kiss on my cheek, then cleared his throat as he straightened up. "So...I hear I'm going to be a grandfather."

"Yeah, that's what the doctor said, anyway," I confirmed wryly.

He looked at me closely and deduced, "You're concerned with how Tony's going to react."

"Yes, but more so about his mother." I sighed. "Daddy, his mom was so rude to me. I mean, just cruel."

"Hey, hey, hey," he soothed. "This baby is your concern now and so is Tony and I want you to know that I'm glad I'm here to have my first experience as a grandfather," he said proudly.

"I am too, Daddy."

I really was.

# Chapter 56

## Tony

"How's she doing?" I asked Josephine once we were outside Lacie's bedroom.

She narrowed her eyes slightly and looked back at Lacie's door. "She's uh…okay. She uh…went to the doctor and found out she's got a little situation with her stomach and all, but I think she's going to be all right."

I breathed a sigh of relief. "Good. I was really starting to worry about her. She's just been so sick lately."

"She's going to be fine, Tony," Josephine assured with a smile. "Now, let's get to the reason why I brought you out here." She held up a hand when I started to speak. "Before you say anything, yes, I know what happened this weekend. I want to thank you for taking up for her the way you did."

I shrugged. "It's no need to thank me, Josephine. It's what I was supposed to do."

With a somewhat stunned expression, she said, "This is true, but still, I feel I should…given the situation. I know how difficult it must have been for you." She tilted her head to the side, studying me. "It *was* hard, finding that out, about your mother, wasn't it?" she asked directly.

Ashamed, I blew hard and held my head down for a second. "Uh, yes…it was," I admitted, looking back up at her.

Her expression turned incredulous. "You really didn't know?"

"No," I replied grimly, clearing my throat.

She digested this information for a brief moment and then smiled. "Oh, you're so lucky I like you." I chuckled. With a deep breath, she clapped her hands together and said, "Okay, Tony…here's the deal. I want you to tell your parents that I'm inviting them over here Saturday evening for dinner."

I looked at her skeptically. "Are you sure about this?"

Her smile widened and I caught a little twinkle in her eyes. "Oh, I've never been so sure about anything in my life. Everyone needs to meet and sit down and have a good conversation." She turned around and started going down the stairs. "All right. Saturday at five o'clock. When you go back in Lacie's room, tell Mason I said to come down here and stop bothering Lacie. He can't hog up all of her time."

In that instant, Mason came out with a broad grin and said, "You're next." He slapped me lightly on the arm and proceeded down the stairs.

Lacie was sitting up when I entered. She looked at me warily. Why did she look so nervous?

"Hey, baby. Are you feeling any better?" I asked softly, walking to her bed to sit beside her.

She gave me a weak smile and tucked her hair behind her ears. "Actually, I am. Guess the soup and crackers worked. Having my daddy feed it to me helped a little, too," she answered with a light giggle.

"Josephine told me what's wrong," I said gently, taking her hand.

Her eyes widened. "She did?"

"Yeah," I replied with a shrug. "She said it was a little something with your stomach, but that you'll be fine." I sighed. "I guess you've got that stomach virus that's been going around, huh?"

She stared at me blankly and with a light nod, said, "I guess so." She sighed and moved her hand from mine easily. "So...enough about me. How did everything go at work after I left?"

I inhaled and looked at her suggestively. "Well, Richard and William liked the contracting..."

"Oh, Tony. I'm so sorry. I completely forgot to tell you and Joe." She put her hand over her mouth suddenly. "Look, I know we had agreements about the bid and signing and everything. But I took a good look at the information when Trevor came into my office, this morning and everything looked legit. I was feeling so terrible this morning and he wouldn't leave until I signed it..."

I put a finger to her lips. "Hey, it's okay. It's fine."

She yawned and then looked at me with dubiously. "You're not mad?"

"No, not at you anyway," I admitted. "It's just that Trevor showboated in front of William and Richard. We looked like complete idiots because we didn't know what was going on that's all."

"I'm sorry," she said, closing her eyes and wincing. She'd suddenly looked ill.

I peered at her. "Lacie, you don't look good. Are you all right?"

"Stomach's just queasy again, that's all," she murmured, holding her mouth. "Pass me the bucket, please."

I picked up the bucket and held it in front of her while she put her head over it.

"Lacie, are you sure that the doctor diagnosed you correctly and that it's not something else?"

She looked at me with apprehension. "There is a little something..." she trailed off softly.

"And?" I coaxed softly. "What is it?"

Suddenly a loud squeal emanated from downstairs in the living room. The squeal distracted her and she looked at the door. She looked back at me and gulped with nervous eyes. "He said that I uh..." Her attention turned back to the door as we heard "I knew it!"

I frowned and waved my hand in front of her face, suddenly getting more worried. "Lacie, what is it?"

She looked back at me with a pensive frown and then shook her head decisively. "It's nothing, Tony. Don't worry about it right now," she managed, wincing and breathing in deeply.

"No, I'm not buying that–" I started.

Reneé suddenly burst through the door and I turned around, a little perturbed. "I knew it, Lacie. You're...oooh," she said suddenly, looking at Lacie. Her eyes widened as she hastened to the bed. "Tony, watch–"

Catching on quickly, I turned around and pushed the bucket in front of Lacie in time before she heaved right into it.

# Chapter 57

# Lacie

I'd have almost thrown up on Tony if it hadn't been for Reneé's fast observation and Tony's quick hand. His swift response didn't stop it from getting onto my nightgown, however. He told Reneé to get a towel and another washcloth as he continued to hold the bucket under me.

I could feel Tony's eyes bearing down on me as he said, "Something's not right, Lacie. You're not telling me something. Now what is going on?"

I looked up at Reneé for help when she came back from my adjoining bathroom. Her eyes were wide and she gestured with a push of her arms to tell Tony, but I couldn't. I just couldn't. Meanwhile, Tony was still looking at me expectantly and I started tearing.

"Lacie…what is up?" he asked a little more sternly.

Mom saved me from answering when she burst into the room. "What is–" She started, but stopped when all of us turned to look at her. She took one look at me and then at the bucket in front of me. I shook my head slowly at her. Immediately, she understood and rolled her eyes ever so slightly. She inched Tony out of the way, as she sat down on the bed.

"Tony, why don't you go downstairs and help Mason set the table while Reneé and I get Lacie cleaned up, okay?" When he didn't budge, she put a light hand on his arm. "Tony, it's all right. Lacie's going to be fine. Go on downstairs, now," she urged in a gentle tone.

Tony sighed and kissed me on the forehead before he walked out, muttering under his breath.

"You didn't tell him, did you?" Mama said, turning to me once the door closed. I was too weak to answer. With my head now leaning on the side of the bucket, I barely managed to shake my head. She heaved a sigh. "Reneé, please look in Lacie's drawer and get out another nightgown. This child is a mess."

"Yes, Mama," Reneé obliged, doing as she instructed.

Mama pushed my shoulders down gently so I could lay back with my head on the pillow. "I don't know how I'm going to handle two pregnant girls at one time," she muttered.

⊱⚭⊰

"That is the most stupid thing I've ever heard come out of your mouth, Lacie Adams!" Mama exclaimed, standing in front of me with both of her hands on her hips.

It was a few minutes after my incident and Reneé and Mama had helped me get cleaned up. I was sitting on the edge of the bed, feeling a little better.

Mama continued. "You need to tell that boy now, that he's going to be a father. Don't leave him out like that. He needs to know what's going on. And did you see the concern on his face? He's worried about you, girl!"

I sighed. "Mama, please. I'll just feel better about telling him after dinner on Saturday, that's all."

"What difference is that going to make if you tell him today or then?"

"The difference is that I'll have a better idea on how to handle this whole pregnancy thing and where I stand. I'll know what to do then."

Mama misunderstood my answer and her eyes widened. "Lacie! Are you seriously thinking about…"

"An abortion, Lacie? C'mon, you can't be serious!" Reneé finished Mama's sentence.

"I'm not saying that. You're both jumping to conclusions." I ran my hand through my hair. "Listen, right now, I'm too worn out to think about anything. I want to have a clear head and I've had no time to adjust to any of this," I stressed. "This matter is much more complex than me telling Tony, 'hey, honey, I'm pregnant'. There are serious factors to consider, here. Tony and I've only been in this relationship for a couple of months, his mother is prejudiced and hates my guts, and I just got pregnant on a technicality! I mean, c'mon! This was not supposed to happen. I wasn't prepared for this!"

Reneé sat next to me, and acting much older than her age, put her hand over mine. "Lacie, this is totally different from your first pregnancy. You're older, more educated and you have a lot more going for you now."

"Reneé, it's a little more than that," Mama concluded softly, studying me. "I think your sister is afraid and convinced by Miss Abigail's threat that Tony would forsake Lacie's feelings for her. Am I right, Lacie?"

I looked at both of them and shrugged meekly. "She didn't hold back any words, Mama."

"And neither will I," Mama huffed without hesitation and strode over to the door. "Ya'll come on downstairs, now. I've had enough of all of this sappy stuff for today."

"Mama..." I started.

She turned around to look at me. "Lacie, you look much better and the color has come back on your face. You can come downstairs and have dinner with us. Reneé, you too." I started to object, but she held up a hand. "Nope, c'mon. Now for the life of me I don't know why Tony hasn't figured out what's going on with you by now, but if you don't come downstairs, you best be sure he's going to find out!"

She didn't have to tell me twice.

೮ಾ෴

"How are you feeling?" Tony asked, immediately meeting me at the bottom of the stairs when Reneé and I came down.

I gave him a small smile. "Better."

"Maybe I should take—," he started.

Mama interrupted him as she came out of the kitchen with a crock-pot. "Tony, stop worrying Lacie and come over here and sit down at the table and eat with us. Lacie's doing all right."

Distracted, he turned around and said, "Oh, that's okay, Josephine. I've got to get going and—"

"Do what? Sit at home all alone?" Mama raised her eyebrow and put a hand on her hip. "Don't you know that it's impolite to refuse an invitation to dinner when someone asks you? Now get over here, before I get offended."

"You know better than to argue." I smiled at him. "So you'd better do what she says."

"Yep," he said with a deep breath. "C'mon, let's go," he said, taking my arm proprietarily when I started walking over to the dining room table.

I stopped and looked at him tenderly. "Tony, I *do* know how to walk."

"Yeah, but—", he started again.

Mama interrupted him again. "Oh, for crying out loud! Will you two get over here? Everyone else is ready to eat. If you two continue making goo-goo eyes at each other, the food is going to get cold. Now, c'mon!"

We chuckled and hastily joined the others.

I was glad Mama made me come downstairs. Not only was her good old fashioned potato soup, baked fish, creamy corn bread and green salad tasty, but the meal had miraculously settled my stomach. Adding to the meal was the merry conversation at the table and the joy of having Tony with us for dinner.

"Thanks for inviting me to dinner, Josephine. It was delicious," Tony remarked politely after dinner when everyone started getting up from the table. "I'm glad to see that it seemed to have had an effect on Lacie as well. She looks so much better than she did when she came down earlier."

"But of course, she would. A mother always knows what's best for her daughter, Tony," Mama punned good-naturedly. "Tony, you keep hanging around us and eating our food, you'll soon have more color than you do now," she chuckled, scraping the food off the plates and piling them onto each other.

"Mama!" Reneé and I protested in unison. We stopped helping to clear the table enough to look at her in shock.

"What?" Mama asked innocently, shooing us with her hand. "Tony knows I'm teasing him. Don't you, Tony?"

She turned to Tony and I followed her gaze. Tony was chuckling softly and so was Daddy. Mama looked at me with a triumphant expression. "See? Tony's not taking what I said seriously. Plus, he should know by now that if he plans to be around us—or me anyway—he'd better be able to take a joke. Now come on in here with me and Reneé and keep us company while we clean the kitchen," She commanded lightly and proceeded with dishes in hand toward the kitchen.

All I could do was shake my head as Reneé and I followed.

ຂາ)ແ

Daddy and Tony remained talking in the living room while we were in the kitchen. I'd offered to help Mama and Reneé, but they objected and instructed me to sit and rest while they cleaned up everything. Curiosity killing me, I'd get up a few times, amidst Mama's objections to look out the kitchen door and peek in on Daddy and Tony. They seemed to be in earnest conversation as they stood looking out of the window that overlooked the village.

The kitchen was about cleaned and dishes put away when both men entered. With a last 'good bye' to everyone and a kiss on Mama's cheek, Tony took my hand and pulled me up gently so I could walk him to the door.

"So…did you have a good conversation with Daddy?" I asked while he put on his coat.

He grinned. "You just couldn't help yourself."

"What?" I asked innocently.

He chuckled. "It's eating you up wondering what we talked about, isn't it?" I nodded and he put a hand on my arm. "Relax. It was just

**313**

man talk. I just had a few things I wanted to talk to him about, that's all."

"Like what?"

"Lacie!" he exclaimed softly.

"Well…you know how I am, Tony," I claimed.

"Exactly and that's why I'm not going to tell you," he said. He gave me a quick but soft kiss on the lips. "Look, I want you to get plenty of rest. You still look a little tired and now that a decision on the contractor has been made, the project will be even more demanding.

I winced. "Yeah, and look, I'm so sorry–"

He stopped me. "Hey, what's done is done. Anyway, Joe reminded me so eloquently that the main objective really is to make the company money. So maybe you and Trevor's signing off on it was the best thing after all and…maybe I let my personal feelings get in the way. Ryan and William seemed to like the idea so…" he trailed off with a shrug.

"You're really not mad at me then?" I queried again.

He touched my nose lightly with a forefinger. "No. I'm not," he said, smiling. He gave me another kiss. "I'll see you tomorrow. Tell your mom again how much I loved dinner. Love you."

I heard Daddy come up behind me once Tony closed the door and left. "Tony…he's a good guy. I like him."

I turned around. "You do?" I asked.

"Yes." As I was about to open my mouth, he pointed a finger and added, "Don't ask me what we talked about, either. It was man talk."

What was up with all of the man talk?

# Chapter 58

# Tony

Whew!

I let out a huge sigh of relief and took out a handkerchief to wipe my face once I got in my car.

Mason had said yes, thank God. He approved of me proposing to Lacie, but he'd made me sweat for it…a little. We'd been talking in the living room for a good while when I took a chance and asked him.

*"You…want to marry Lacie," Mason stated, eyeing me incredulously.*

*"Yes, sir, I do," I asserted, glancing toward the kitchen nervously.*

*As Josephine had done a couple of months back, Mason was doing the same thing—taking his time to stare at me without a word. I'd never been so nervous in my life. The fact that he was a man—and Lacie's father—made it so much more intimidating and important.*

*He continued to ogle me before he finally spoke. "Are you ready for that, son?"*

*I took a guess at what he meant and tried not to get annoyed considering I'd heard this question before. "I don't feel I have to ready myself for anything. I love her and I want to spend the rest of my life with her. It's as simple as that," I confirmed.*

*"Um, quite bold," But Mason was on to me. "That whole deal with your family is just the tip of the iceberg, Tony."*

*I nodded decisively. "I know, sir."*

*"Your parents don't know?"*

*"No, sir. I mean, I told them my intentions, but I just recently decided."*

*"What do you think they're going to say?"*

*I shrugged indifferently. "I don't care. That's not my problem."*

"Really?" he asked, appearing impressed. "And you still want to marry her, son?"

"Yes. Very much."

He continued to study me. "Did you get a ring already?" I nodded.

"Yes, sir. This weekend." I took another look at the kitchen. The coast was clear so I took out the box from my left jacket pocket and handed it to him.

He whistled softly while he studied it and then looked at me. "This weekend, huh?"

"Yes, sir."

He handed it back to me. "When are you planning on asking her?"

I hastily put the ring back into my pocket. "I haven't decided. She's been so sick lately and I wanted to make sure she was feeling well before I asked her, but I wanted to ask you first."

He swallowed hard. "I appreciate that." He sighed. "I haven't been much of a father, but I'm here now and that's what matters."

"How long are you going to stay?"

"I'm retired now and I've got plenty of time on my hands," he replied with a shrug. "It really depends on Josephine and Lacie," he said. "But," with a twinkle in his eye, "I have a feeling I'll be around for a while."

"May I marry your daughter, sir?"

He took a deep breath and after a short pause said, "Somehow, I feel unworthy to answer that question, but...yes, you may." He offered his hand. "I see nothing but good in you, Tony. Just make sure that you take care of my baby girl."

"Of course, sir. Thank you, sir."

He smirked and pulled me closer to him with his hand and whispered, "For the record, I wasn't questioning whether you were ready for any flack that might come your way, but rather if you were ready to marry a black woman. It's a lot of work loving any woman — but a black woman?" He chuckled. "Whew! That's a whole different ball game."

# Chapter 59

# Lacie

I woke up early with no nausea and more energy than I'd had in weeks. I was happy that I was feeling better, but my mind was still pondering my dilemma as I walked through my department at work.

After putting up my belongings, I decided to do something I'd not done in a while, since Carrie had not yet arrived—get coffee. But when I walked into the kitchen, it hit me. I couldn't have caffeine.

Darn it!

I sucked my teeth and looked through the cabinets aimlessly for any sign of decaffeinated coffee but it was hopeless. Our department stayed too busy for that and the stacked cabinets filled with regular cans of coffee was proof that caffeine was a necessity.

All of a sudden, my eye caught a very small can of instant decaffeinated coffee. Amen! Happily, I turned on the water boiler, took out a spoon and went to work. I didn't hear the footsteps when they came in a moment later.

"Decaffeinated coffee? What's up with that?" I heard him ask.

Grabbing a few small packages of sweetener, I avoided his question and struggled to reply with a purposefully distracting and sunny, "Good morning, Trevor."

"Mighty spry, aren't we?" he taunted, peering at me from the side with an arched eyebrow. "Feeling better, I see. You're just a glowing. What happened to change you from looking so terrible yesterday?"

I looked at him and forced a smile. "Is there something I can do for you, Trevor?"

My politeness seemed to take him by surprise and he stammered, "I...I...just wanted to let you know that we got the go ahead for the contractor."

Nodding, I turned around when I heard the water heater machine click off and poured water in my mug. "I know. Tony told me."

He sighed in exasperation. "That means the project is well under its way now. That's good news, you know?"

I turned back around with the mug in my hand. "Depends on how you look at it. You put me in a bad position, Trevor. You manipulated me into signing off by pulling the charge card on me. That was a good one you pulled. But I'm letting you know that if anything goes amiss with this project, knowing that my name is signed on it, then it's going to be me and you."

"Ooh, I like that — me and you," he said with a grin.

I ignored him and walked out the kitchen.

Carrie met me on the way to my office. "All right, all right. Tell me what happened when you told Tony?" she whispered anxiously.

I stopped in front of my office door and looked at her. "Carrie, you couldn't wait until you took your coat off?"

She gave me a simple look. "I know you're not asking me that question," she huffed. "I've been waiting–" She stopped and pointed at my mug with wide eyes. "What are you doing drinking coffee? You know you're not-" she started loudly.

"Shhhhh!" I put my finger to my lips and looked around nervously. "Get in there," I ordered through clenched teeth, motioning with my head at my door. I closed the door. "See," I said, pointing my finger at her as I walked to my side of the desk, "how you just let stuff out?" I flopped into my chair.

Carrie wasn't affected. "Girl, please. No one heard me. Now tell me what happened. Are you…?" I nodded slowly. "Lacie, that's great!" she exclaimed. I shook my head. "What now?" she exasperated and plopped down on the chair across from my desk.

I'd told her everything and all of my concerns and Carrie looked at me perplexed. "Saturday? I have to wait until Saturday?" I gave her a blank look. "Lacie, do you *know* how many women in this company have been in your exact position? Some without anyone else knowing?" I knew she would know. "Lacie, don't let these people fool you. Everybody has had a bone in their shoe at some time or another.

I can give you a rundown of every one of these so-called 'professional' women—some very high up. Lacie, you don't have anything to be ashamed of," she asserted.

"Right, but in just one day, from one simple test, my life has changed drastically. So will Tony's," I said. "That's why Tony needs to be told methodically and at the right time."

Carrie stood up with her hands on her hips. "So you mean I really have to wait until after this weekend to tell everyone?"

"I'm afraid so, Carrie."

"Lacie, that's not fair. I've been itching to spread the news ever since yesterday, but respected your wishes. Do you know how hard that was for me? How am I supposed to keep that quiet until then?"

I couldn't help but tease her. "Simple. You see this," I gestured by twisting my fingers on my lips. "That's how."

She gave me a good-natured squint. "I see now that these next nine months are going to be long and difficult. But you're lucky I love you."

"Yeah, I love you too, Carrie," I giggled as she went to my door and walked out. Tony strolled in with a raised brow. "What's so funny?"

"Just something between me and Carrie, that's all." I gave him a soft kiss on his lips when he came to my side. "Good morning."

"Good morning to you," he replied, pulling me into his arms. "Feeling better?"

"A little," I said.

He nodded. "I'm glad. That bug you had really seemed to take its toll on you and I was beginning to get concerned."

*If he only knew what kind of bug.*

He caressed my back with his hands. "I'm glad you're better, babe."

"Me too, because now when I go out with Dawn I can order a good lunch."

"Dawn?" His hands stopped abruptly. "Dawn's in New York?"

"Yeah. I spoke to her yesterday."

"How long has she been in town?" he asked.

"She came in yesterday, I think." A thought came into my mind. "You know what? Why don't we all go out to lunch together? That would be nice, wouldn't it? I mean, the last time all of us were together, it wasn't the best of circumstances with Trevor and everything. This time it would be just the four of us." He didn't reply and was obviously mulling over something. "Tony?"

"Yeah, yeah," he replied quickly, snapping out of his reverie. "That would be good. It'd give us time to catch up on a few things." He cleared his throat. "What time?"

"She should be here about noon. I can hardly wait."

"Yeah," he said slowly. "Me too."

☙❧

It was a good fifteen minutes before lunchtime when Carrie knocked on my door and opened it with a smile. "Guess who's here?"

She moved out of the way and Dawn walked in smiling.

We ran into each other's arms and started squealing and hugging each other.

"I'm going to leave you two alone," Carrie chuckled. "Lacie, I'm leaving for lunch. You girls have fun and behave yourselves," she said and closed the door.

Dawn and I stood hugging in the middle of my office for a good while before I let go. "Oh, Dawn," I exasperated, wiping a tear from my eye. "Am I glad to see you!"

"Well, here I am, girl. In the flesh," she said in a sassy tone, wiping hers also.

"You're looking good too, girl. Look at that suit!" I complimented, noticing the nicely cut suit. We sat down in the two chairs in front of my desk. "The Florida sun is doing you justice and your modeling career must really be taking off."

"Oh, don't even go there. You're not doing so bad, either," she shot back with a chuckle. She looked at her watch before she clapped her hands once and inhaled. "All right, girl, we've got about fifteen minutes until lunch, so let me have it. I'm all ears so let it all out," she commanded.

And boy did I light her ears up! The words came out of my mouth so fluidly that I was sure her ears had to be burning by the time I'd finished.

"Well, I'm glad that whole issue between your parents has been somewhat resolved. At least that's once less thing you have to worry about, with your condition," Dawn remarked after.

"Speaking of my condition; can you believe it, girl? Can you believe the chances?" I asked, looking at her with a perplexed expression.

Dawn peered at me after a brief pause. "Lacie...*how do you* feel about being pregnant? Are you happy about it?"

"Dawn, I haven't had time to think about it. I think I'm still in shock. I was just so careful."

"Lacie, listen, mist—well, not mistakes, but these things happen sometimes and maybe this was just meant to be. Maybe there is a purpose for this," Dawn suggested tenderly.

I sighed. "Yeah, so I've been told."

She leaned back. "How do you think Tony is going to react?"

"I don't know, Dawn." I shrugged. "I mean, this is really life changing. Tony and I've talked about children in brief and even marriage, but nothing serious. Our relationship is still so fresh." I took a deep breath. "I'm worried about dinner this weekend."

"Do you think his parents will come?" she asked.

"I don't know. I don't know if he's asked them yet." I ran a hand through my hair. "Part of me hopes they won't Dawn, because if they come, something's going to go down. I can feel it. This whole dinner thing with our parents has got me on edge. Mama did not like what happened this past weekend and I just know that she's going to let Abigail have it. You know how she is."

"Maybe that's what Tony's mother needs, Lacie." Dawn put her hands over mine. "I'm glad you stuck up for yourself this weekend, but that wasn't enough."

I looked at her dubiously. "Dawn, I couldn't curse that woman out in her own house."

"No, you couldn't," she agreed with a nod. "But Miss Josephine can this weekend." She and I burst out laughing. Then she said, "Seriously, though. You've tolerated that woman too much and now that you're expecting, it wouldn't be a bad idea to have Miss Abigail told off. Honestly, Lacie, after everything that you've told me about his mother and what she said to you, I wouldn't mine putting foot in her—"

"Okay, Dawn. Okay. I've got it," I chuckled, interrupting her. I glanced at my desk clock and stood up. "C'mon, girl, let's finish this conversation at lunch."

"Okay," she said, chuckling to herself as she got ready to stand. "Not that you asked me, but I've got to agree with Miss Josephine. You need to tell Tony."

"What does she need to tell me?" I heard Tony say.

I looked up to see Tony and Joe in my doorway, surprised that I didn't hear them come in. Dawn was surprised as well. She was apparently so surprised when she turned around, that she almost fell backward from her seat.

I caught her arm and was slightly baffled to see how fast Joe came to her side, catching her other arm.

"Dawn, are you okay?" I asked when she stood up.

She shrugged both of us off of her a little too quickly and with a shaky voice, replied, "Just lost my footing a little, that's all. I'm fine."

"Good," I heard Tony say tersely as he came to my side and helped me put on my coat. "Let's all head out to lunch. There's a table waiting for us," he said. Unexpectedly, he took my hand and hastily led me out my office and through the department, leaving Dawn and Joe back in the office.

"Hey, hey, hey, Tony. Wait a second," I said when we reached the elevator. I was wondering why he was pushing the 'down' button hurriedly. "We're leaving Dawn and Joe behind."

"They'll be all right," he said.

The elevator came and opened.

"But..." I started to object.

"We'll meet them downstairs," he said dismissively. He took my elbow gently and guided me onto the awaiting elevator.

"What... is...up with you?" I asked. I looked at him questioningly, but his jaw was set tight.

I folded my arms, turned to face the elevator door, and glimpsed Trevor standing in my office doorway, talking to Dawn and Joe before the elevator door closed.

# Chapter 60

# Dawn

"Are you sure you're all right?" Joe asked, touching my arm again.

"I'm fine," I hissed softly, swatting his hand away. "Don't touch me. Not here." I looked at the door nervously before turning on him with a cross look. "I thought you were going to lunch with Tony."

"I was, but Tony suggested that we get Lacie for lunch so we can go over a few things about the project."

I put my hand on my hips. "You forgot that I was going to go to lunch with Lacie today?"

He looked puzzled. "No...I didn't forget."

A sudden revelation came to me and he seemed to pick up on it as well.

"Then...this was planned," we said in unison, looking at each other's wide eyes.

"Damn!" Joe muttered explosively. "Tony knows."

"Hell!" I said, equally explosive. I looked up at him suddenly, another thought coming to me. "Lacie...Joe," I implied fretfully.

"All right. Come on, let's go and catch up with them," he said quickly, taking my arm and leading me to the door.

From nowhere, Trevor came in the doorway. He blocked our way and leaned against the side of the doorpost casually with one hand in his pocket. "Tsk, Tsk, Tsk," he said, wagging a finger with a smirk. "Very naughty—and very, daring, I might add."

Joe's tone was not meant to be argued with. "*Move*, before I make you."

"Certainly," Trevor countered, stepping aside leisurely.

I still felt his eyes on us as we walked swiftly through the department toward the elevator. As we came to it, Carrie came out.

"Hey, you two. Tony and Lacie are downstairs—" she started.

"Yeah, yeah, Carrie. We got it," Joe said in a rude tone, as we stepped in the elevator.

Surprised by his tone, Carrie's friendly expression immediately turned into an inquiring and curious frown. I smiled at her apologetically but then lowered my eyes in guilt when I saw Trevor still smirking and standing in the distance in front of Lacie's office. Carrie turned and followed my eyes.

The last thing I saw before the elevator door closed was Carrie turning back to look at me with an arched eyebrow.

# Chapter 61

## The Awesome Foursome

### Tony

"My…everyone is certainly very quiet," Lacie remarked casually, glancing around at all of us quizzically at the table. "The four of us haven't been together in a while and no one has anything to say?"

I sure didn't. I was incensed.

We'd been sitting at the table silently ever since the waitress had left with our order. That had been almost ten minutes ago.

I glanced at Dawn and then at Joe. She was avoiding looking my way and Joe was cool and calm, stirring his drink.

Remembering how quickly Joe went to Dawn's aid in Lacie's office, it was plain as day to me, now.

Man, I was angry with them!

### Joe

I felt Tony's reproving stares, but ignored them and drank from my glass unperturbedly, rationalizing.

All he had were suspicions, really. Nothing concrete. So until then, I was keeping mum.

I cast a quick sideways glance at Dawn. She looked as if she was going to break at any moment.

I sighed inwardly and took another gulp.

This secret between us was getting annoying. I was tired of sneaking around, lying and hiding my relationship with Dawn.

Dawn didn't want to hurt Lacie and that I understood.

Still, it was inevitable.

But our secret coming out had to be on our terms and no one else's. If Trevor kept pushing, he was going to see the hood come out of me. No doubt.

## Lacie

No one was talking.

Ever since we'd arrived at the restaurant and sat at the table, conversation had been minimal. In addition, the atmosphere had changed from when we'd left the office.

I sighed and glanced around the table fleetingly, then observed Tony sitting next to me. His jaw was as set as when we'd left the office and he was frowning and drumming his fingertips on the table. Joe seemed calm and was taking casual, but frequent gulps from his glass. Dawn was sitting up straight, staring and fiddling with her napkin and was…quiet. Oddly quiet.

I had to say something. The silence was driving me crazy.

"So Joe, I hope you're not upset with me going along with Trevor on the contracting bid. It was a good bid and as he put it, the contractor had other jobs in line. We had to jump on it."

I hated to talk about business, but I had no idea what else to say.

Joe shook his head coolly. "No problem. You made a good decision and I can't say that I wouldn't have jumped at the chance myself."

"Right. And Joe is an expert on jumping on the closest thing that comes along, aren't you, Joe?" Tony quipped gruffly.

I shot him a swift look, dumbfounded by his tone.

"That's right. I never miss out on a good deal," Joe said evenly.

I looked at both men and was not comfortable with the locked glares they were giving each other. I exchanged quick questioning glances with Dawn but her eyes were as wide with surprise as I felt mine were.

"All right, here we go." Our waitress, Susan, came over cheerfully, carrying our orders on a large tray. "Now you ordered the filet mignon entrée, correct, sir?" she asked, looking at Joe.

Slowly Joe pried his eyes away from Tony and with a thin, but polite, smile answered, "Yes, I did, thank you."

"And I ordered a *bloody* T-Bone," Tony stressed, emphasizing the word bloody.

While Susan gave Joe his plate, I leaned closer to him and muttered, "Tony…what is wrong with you?"

He put his arm around my shoulder and squeezed comfortingly. "Lacie, don't worry about it. It's just an old joke between friends," Tony replied. "Right, Joe?" he asked, turning his attention back to him with a mocking smile.

Joe didn't even look up as he said swiftly, slicing into his steak with vigor, "Umm, hmm, yeah, Lacie. Don't worry about it. It's all good."

There was unnerving friction in the air while Tony continued to glare at Joe. I knew that the tension between them wasn't my imagination when I noticed the waitress eyeing them uncomfortably as she passed Dawn her plate.

I felt Dawn's eyes on me. When I looked at her, she looked away swiftly, thanked the waitress and started in on her food.

What in the world was going on?

## Dawn

Thank God, the food had arrived!

It was an uncomfortable moment and I felt Lacie's eyes on me. She was wondering what was up, but I couldn't bear to look at her and started eating my lunch.

After a good moment, she finally turned her attention to her food. I cast a sideways glance at Joe and then back at Lacie, who was thankfully eating her shrimp fettuccini,, her curiosity gone for the moment. I continued with my lunch. It might as well have been rubber because that's what it tasted like.

When I looked up from my plate to reach for my glass, Tony's eyes were raking me over. He knew and his eyes showed it. Fretfully,

I took a gulp from my glass and was surprised to feel someone pat me on my back.

"The awesome foursome at it again. Well, well, well!!" Trevor's voice rang in my ear.

The liquid almost spewed from my mouth at the sound of his voice.

"Trevor, what are you doing here?" Lacie asked immediately.

"Just picking up my order. I saw the four of you over here and thought I'd come over to see how my favorite people were doing," he replied casually. He gave me a slight squeeze on my shoulder and looked down at me with a smirk. "Dawn, it's so good to see you and how odd it is for you to be back in New York. Things not going so well back in Miami, hmm?"

I swallowed and looked up at him quickly with a tight smile. "Things are going very well, Trevor. Thank you," I replied.

"They are? So what brings you back if things are going so well?" he pressed with a wink. "Are you ready to rekindle what we started back in the club?"

I saw Joe's hand ball into a fist under the table and trying to be inconspicuous, patted it. Trevor's eyes didn't miss a beat. He narrowed his eyes at me when I looked back up. I put my head back down and looked at my plate.

"No, Trevor. Just thought I'd stop in and see Lacie," I replied softly.

"That's right. Because you are Lacie's *best friend*, aren't you?" he asked. He put his hands on my shoulders again and caressed them. He leaned in and whispered in my ear. "Listen, if you change your mind about me…"

"Yo, man, didn't you say that you were here to pick up your order?" Joe interrupted sharply, shifting in his seat to look at him.

Trevor raised up and snickered lightly. "You know, you're so right, Joe. My bad," he said, giving Joe a pat on his shoulder. "But look, I sincerely came in peace and to remind you and Tony to sign the bid once you get back. Richard and William are anxious." He looked at Lacie. "Kudos, Lacie, for having enough guts to take a chance." He glanced at his watch. "All right, I'm gonna go pick up my order and head back to the office. I'll see you guys in a minute." With one last pat on my arm before leaving he remarked, "By the way, you four make such good couples."

I swallowed hard with his last statement. I didn't even have to look at Joe to see him cringe. I looked at Lacie who was frowning as Trevor walked away and then I made contact again with Tony's accusatory eyes.

I shook off the tears that were getting ready to fall and grabbed my purse. "Excuse me. I'm going to the ladies room." I stood up abruptly and left the table in time before one tear fell down my face.

The four of us having lunch together had been a very bad idea.

## Lacie

I watched Dawn walking hastily toward the women's bathroom.

Yep, he'd done it again.

Trevor never ceased to bring a load of negativity wherever he went. He couldn't stop putting his hands on women that didn't want him.

With a sigh, I put my fork down and stood up. "I'd better go talk to Dawn, and make sure she's okay."

Tony put a hand on my arm lightly as soon as I'd said it. "You sure you want to do that, babe?"

Then Joe added quickly, "Yeah, maybe you should leave her alone. I'm sure she'll be all right."

I looked at both of them with slight bewilderment. "Yes, I'm sure," I said to Tony. "And no, I'm not going to leave her alone," I said, turning to Joe. "When something bothers her it bothers me." I pointed at both of them. "Now while we're away, you two get whatever it is that's going on between you settled, because this here…is not cute. This was supposed to be a lunch between friends and it's turned into a lunch filled with drama. What kind of drama, I have no idea, but whatever it is, you two squash it before we come back." I leaned over and gave Tony a quick peck on the lips and commanded, "I mean it," before I walked away.

## Tony

Joe looked at Lacie as she left, then finally turned around and caught my glare.

"What, man? What?" he asked defensively, holding out his fork and knife.

"You gonna keep up this charade or what, man?" I asked.

He turned his attention to his steak and started jabbing the knife and fork into it. "What charade, man? I don't know what you're talking about," he said.

I scoffed. "You're gonna sit here and lie to me in front of my face and act like we both don't know what's going on?" I asked calmly. "Shoot, Joe, even Trevor's on to you two. Look at you, man. The veins are virtually popping out of your neck from Trevor making moves on Dawn and putting his hands on her. And you're butchering that steak."

The sign came again when Joe put his knife down, grabbed his glass and took a huge swallow of his drink. Then he ever so slightly slammed the glass on the table. "I don't know what you're talking about, man. There ain't no two."

"Oh, really?" I asked. "Give me the name of the girl you've been seeing and have become so head over heels in love with, then. You know the one you mentioned in *Miami*?" I stressed.

"Tony, man, I told you. I'll let you know when I let you know." Joe's mouth tightened as he picked up the knife again. "Man, just let it go," he voiced strongly, turning his attention back to the steak and cutting another slice into it.

I sat back in stunned aggravation for a good moment and observed the butchery he was doing to his steak before uttering, "So, it's like that?"

He looked up with a small scowl and gave one nod. "And that's the way it is."

I nodded repeatedly, absorbing his words. "I'm imagining things, then?"

He shrugged. "Your words, not mine," he stated finally, putting a piece of steak into his mouth with his angry glare, never leaving mine.

I took a deep breath and relented, "Fine." I stood up. "I'm going to go pay the tab. Lunch is on me."

I muttered a soft curse and walked toward the front of the restaurant.

Joe was lying to me right in my face and I didn't like it. This conversation wasn't over. He was getting a visit from me this evening and we were going to settle this.

Lacie's feelings were at stake and I'll be damned if she was going to get hurt.


## Joe

Hell! I jabbed another piece of steak into my mouth furiously.

Tony was sore with me.

Admittedly, he had a right to be. He knew what was going on and was trying to protect Lacie. But because I'd promised Dawn I wouldn't say anything, I had to lie to him to try to get him off our trail. Still, Tony looked convinced. Trevor's actions and comments led Tony's strong sense of smell right to Dawn and me, again.

No doubt, Trevor making moves on Dawn had been intentional. It had also been a grave mistake on his part. Very grave.

He thought he knew a game, but he didn't.

My background check on Trevor hadn't gone as deep as it could have, because I'd liked his pitch for the project. I also thought it would be a good opportunity to make money and work with Tony and Lacie again.

This time, however, the stakes were high and he'd gone too far.

Though I liked the bid that Trevor got and was going to sign off on it once I got back to the office, I didn't like the way he'd handled it. It was too underhanded and too sudden. That, along with the stunt that he'd just pulled, gave me more of an incentive to get even.

All I had to do was make a call as soon as I got back to the office.

## Dawn

I was dabbing my eyes with a tissue when Lacie came in the bathroom. I turned my back to her so she couldn't see, but it didn't work.

She came around to face me. "Dawn, honey, are you okay?"

I nodded. "Yeah," I uttered, sniffling and blowing my nose.

Lacie sighed. "Dawn, don't let that idiot Trevor get you upset. He made a move on me too, so don't even sweat it," she revealed.

I looked at her in surprise. "What? He did? When was this?"

She waved her hand. "Oh, girl, this was about a month ago in my office. He just moved in for a kiss and I dodged it."

"You think he's interested in you?"

Lacie looked at me dubiously. "Girl, didn't you just experience him feeling you all up?" She shook her head. "No, I think he just likes beautiful women and you know we're both hot," she added and we both giggled.

I sniffled and asked, "You didn't tell Tony what he did?"

"It wasn't even worth mentioning because nothing happened. Besides, I had too much going on to even be worried about his sorry behind." She poked her finger at my chest. "And you shouldn't be worried about him, either."

"Yeah, you're right."

Lacie peered at me thoughtfully. "Dawn, things are going okay with your career, right?"

Her question threw me. "Yeah, why do you ask?"

"You just look as if you've had some serious rainfall. I was just wondering if you got so upset because there might be some truth in what Trevor was saying. I mean, you have been very quiet ever since we left the office."

I waved my hand airily. "No, girl. Everything's fine. I just have a few things on my mind, that's all."

"Anything you'd like to tell me?"

The question wasn't whether I'd *like* to tell her, but *how*.

I gulped. "No, I'm good."

"You sure?" she pressed, eyes bearing into mine.

"Yeah, girl, I'm sure."

Unlocking her gaze, she sighed resignedly and looked at the door. "All right, I guess I have to accept your answer," she said. "C'mon, let's go back to the table with the guys and finish lunch. They should have gotten their issue squared away by now. They'd better."

As I followed her out of the bathroom, I instantly realized how good I'd become at deception. I'd never been able to lie to Lacie with a straight face before.

It was a very painful first.

## Lacie

They hadn't gotten it straight. That was for sure.

It was quite obvious once Dawn and I'd returned from the ladies' room. Tony's jaw was still tight and Joe's mouth was set in a grim expression.

With all of the tension from the beginning of lunch, Trevor's untimely and unwelcoming visit, Dawn getting upset and my food getting cold, I was relieved when we all got up to leave the restaurant. Dawn said her good-byes to the three of us, promised she'd get with me later and got in a cab.

Leaving the restaurant didn't help the mood any as Tony, Joe and I rode the elevator to our department in silence. Even worse was when the door opened and there stood Trevor with his irritating smirk.

"Enjoy your lunch, guys?" he mocked with fake concern.

"Shut up, Trevor," Tony, Joe and I murmured as all three of us exited the elevator and went our separate ways.

Carrie got up from her desk swiftly to meet me halfway and followed me into my office. "Lacie...are you all right?"

I barely paid attention to the slight anxiety in her voice, flopped down in my chair exhausted and looked at her standing figure in wonder.

"Carrie, you know, I was so elated to see Dawn today and even happier that we were all going out together," I murmured pensively. "But it had to be the most nerve-racking experience I've ever had with them. There was hardly any conversation at lunch. It was just…" I turned my attention to the wall, struggling to find the word. "absurd." I sighed. "Then Trevor came and you know he didn't make the situation any better."

I turned to look at Carrie and noticed an array of expressions on her face. She was staring at the huge glass window behind me, frowning with hesitation, strain, and worry all at once. Then she looked at me and opened her mouth and closed it just as fast as she'd opened it.

"Carrie?" I asked. "Are you okay?"

It took her a second before she came to, took a deep breath and then cleared her throat, with only a hint of a reassuring smile. "Yeah, I'm fine." Her smile disappeared quickly and she motioned with her thumb toward the door and spoke slowly. "Uh…I took the liberty of getting you some decaffeinated tea," she gulped. "It's…uh…in my… drawer. Do you want me to uh…fix you some?"

I just stared at her momentarily, perplexed with her actions.

"Tea, Lacie. Do you want me to fix you some tea?" Carrie snapped.

"Sure, Carrie," I answered, jumping out of my skin slightly to her brusque tone. "Thank you."

She uttered with a nod, "Okay…I've got to take care of something first and then I'll be right back with it," and turned and walked out my office.

I sat back in my chair, staring at the door.

Everyone was going crazy.

# Chapter 62

# Joe

I'd just hung up the phone after making my call when the document landed on my desk with a hard slap.

The guilty party, Carrie, stretched out her fingertips and pressed them hard on my desk as she leaned over and gave me the meanest scowl I'd ever seen on a black woman.

"Here's the bid for you to sign you nasty, slimy son of a–" she began in a low murmur.

"Wait a min—" I began defensively.

"No," she cut me off sharply. "Don't even try it, Mr. Joseph Mitchell. I *know* what's going on between you and Dawn and don't even try to deny it 'cause it ain't going to work. The guilt is all in your eyes." She nodded insistently. "Yes, I'm coming to you first, because you are the culpable party here. You knew before you started that it was wrong and it's obvious that you didn't care."

"You're wrong I do care," I objected. "I care about Dawn and–" I stopped, annoyed that I was defending myself to her. "You know what, Carrie? This is none of your business."

"Oh, it's my business all right," she shot back without missing a beat. She pointed toward the door. "That girl, a few doors down, is a very good friend of mine. I work with her five days a week—more than eight hours a day—so our relationship is more than casual, Joe. Therefore, I'm not going to excuse myself or apologize for being concerned for her well being, especially since she's…" She stopped herself as if getting ready to blurt out something. "…not been feeling well." Then she continued just as strongly. "So you and Dawn better be very careful with how Lacie finds out about your little thing. Got it?"

Carrie waited for no response and swung her body around swiftly and started to walk out. She stopped short before she reached the door and turned around. "Oh, and if you want to find out something on Trevor and this contractor, I've got a contact that might be able to help you out. The number will be under your door tomorrow morning," she added before she walked out.

Stumped by what she'd said, I watched her as she walked out until my cell phone rang. It was Dawn.

"Hey, gorgeous. How are you?" I asked softly.

"Oh, I've been better," she groaned. "I'm in a cab, waiting outside my mother's house. I decided to call you before I went in since she doesn't approve of us." She sighed. "Joe, how are we going to tell Lacie? I mean, it was a close call today at lunch with Trevor coming over and everything."

"Yeah, it was. But Trevor wasn't going to say anything."

"How do you know?"

"Because he's not stupid," I replied bitterly. "But we do need to tell Lacie soon, Dawn, because our little secret is coming out little by little."

"Let me guess. Carrie?" she assumed.

"How did you know?"

"We left quite an impression on her when we walked passed her to get to the elevator," she replied. "From the expression she gave me, I'm certain she's on to us. She sure has an uncanny way of finding out things."

"Hmm, tell me about it," I muttered.

"What?"

"Never mind, it's not important." There was a long silence before either of us spoke. Then I asked, "Okay, so when do you want to tell her?"

"Tony's parents are having dinner over her house, so this weekend is out. I doubt that will be a good time to tell her that I'm sleeping with her ex-fiancé," she replied tersely.

I didn't like how she put it. "Did you really have to say it like that?"

She scoffed. "How else was I going to say it? It's the truth."

Before I replied, I breathed in deeply, understanding. Dawn was angry with herself.

"Okay, listen," I said, glancing at my watch. It was twenty minutes to two. "I'm getting ready to sign a few papers and then I'm heading out of the office. Why don't we meet at my apartment around three so we can discuss this in person?"

Her voice was detached. "I don't know how long I'll be over here at Mom's. Actually, I'm thinking about staying over. I'll give you a call later when I make up my mind."

That hit below the belt but I kept my cool. "Okay, if that's what you want. You know how to reach me."

A pause and then, "Okay," she said briskly. "Talk to you later."

"Talk to you later."

I waited 'til after she'd hung up to slam the phone down and started muttering angrily.

She didn't want to come over? Fine. She could stay for the duration for all I could care. If she didn't want to see me again, that was fine, too.

*Joe, who're you trying to fool, brotha?*
*You know you're whipped.*

# Chapter 63

## Tony

My parents were coming to dinner.

Mentally exhausted after speaking to my mother on the phone, I leaned back in my chair in my office and recalled the conversation with her only a moment ago.

*"Hello, Mom," I said politely.*

*"Anthony... I was wondering when I would hear from you again," Mom breathed into the phone with a small sigh. "I'm so glad that you called. I knew you'd forgive me and understand my concerns. Now, we'll be able to move on and Rachel is— "*

*"Wait, wait, wait a minute," I interrupted. "Nothing's changed, Mom. I'm still upset with the way you treated Lacie this weekend."*

*"Oh," she uttered. She paused and then more coolly said, "And your reason for calling is...?"*

*I got right to the point. "Lacie's mother has invited you and Dad over for dinner this Saturday."*

*"For what purpose?" Her tone was distant.*

*I gritted my teeth, resisting the urge to be sarcastic because I knew she was being this difficult on purpose. "She wants to meet you and get to know you."*

*"Anthony, that is quite useless, don't you think? I don't see a reason for this meeting."*

*I put my fingertips on my forehead, feeling the intense mental strain of the struggle. Then I thought of a different approach.*

*"Mom, you've always had a good sense of etiquette. I've never known you to decline a dinner invitation," I suggested smoothly.*

*"This is diff—"*

*"Okay," I interjected smoothly. "I told her mother I'd ask and I have. Whether you're up for the challenge of a simple dinner is up to you and Dad. I'm only the messenger."*

*It was a last, desperate attempt but I figured it would work. A proud woman, Mom never resisted a dare. After all, I'd challenged her manners and her nerve.*

*Fine," she answered tightly. "I'll inform your father. What time are we expected?"*

*"Five o'clock."*

*"Fine," she said again.*

I ran my hands over my face tiredly. This weekend was going to be very interesting indeed.

"Here are the papers for you to sign, Tony," Carrie announced, walking into my office after one sharp knock on my door.

"Thank you, Carrie," I replied, sitting up and relieving the stack from her hands. I flipped through the stack swiftly, noticing that Joe had already signed off and then caught an oversight. "Is Joe still in his office, Carrie?"

"No, he left for the day."

"He left?" I asked.

"Yep, about ten minutes, ago. Why?"

"There's a page that he missed," I replied, tapping it thoughtfully.

She raised her eyebrow. "Richard and William want this matter taken care of as soon as possible," she implied.

"I know. I'll run this by his house tonight so this can go through early tomorrow morning."

"Okay," she said. "We've got a short meeting in ten minutes."

After Carrie left, I sat back in my chair and thought about the tense conversation with Joe at lunch, remembering that during the rare times that we ever got into an argument—it had always been because of a woman.

Enough was enough. I was taking that document over to his house and he was going to have to own up.

୫⃝୧

I was driving Lacie home, mulling and agonizing about how I was going to approach Joe again about my suspicions. Lacie kept looking at me curiously a couple of times, but there was no way that I could tell her. Not yet.

Finally, she exhaled. "Okay, Tony. What's up? What's going on?" she asked.

I knew she'd ask sooner or later. I glanced at her quickly with a small smile and turned my attention back to the road with a shrug. "I've just got some things I'm working out in my head, that's all."

"I've noticed. I've also noticed how edgy you've been ever since lunch. Do you want to tell me what going on between you and Joe?"

"No. It's just something Joe and I have to work out. When I take the documents over his house for him to sign, we'll talk then. I'm sure it'll be okay."

Was I really?

"Let me guess, it's a man thing?"

"Something like that," I replied, glancing at her with a quick laugh. Deliberately, I switched the subject. "Listen, I called my mother earlier today and told her about dinner. They've accepted the invitation."

She stiffened. "Mmm, hmm," she said, holding in her breath.

I cast a quick encouraging look at her and took her hand in mine. "Don't worry; everything's going to go fine."

*Was it really?*

I was beginning to wonder myself.

# Chapter 64

# Joe

I was glad to see her when I opened the door.

But I didn't want Dawn to see how relieved I was, so I kept my cool.

"I'm surprised to see you," I remarked casually, closing the door and taking a quick glance at my watch.

Elated was more like it. It was seven o'clock and she'd really made a brotha sweat! And did she always have to look so good? I winced at the way Dawn switched when she walked and stepped down into the living room.

She turned around and looked at me warily. "Yeah...I had a lot of thinking to do and just wanted to clear my mind."

I folded my arms and joined her in the living room, careful to maintain a safe distance between us.

"How is your mind now?"

She shrugged. "I don't know. Seeing Lacie again wasn't easy, Joe, and the comments Trevor made certainly didn't help, either. It hurt, you know?"

"I know. But what does this have to do with us? And why were you so cold to me the last time we talked?"

She sighed. "Joe, this is very hard. I mean, c'mon, you can't expect me to be comfortable about this whole situation and what we're doing—the deception and what I'm doing to Lacie.

"Hey, I understand that, but you're forgetting that I'm in this with you. You're not alone because I'm going through the same thing you are."

"She's not your best friend, Joe."

"No, but she was, as you have pointed out time and time again—

my ex-fiancée and Tony is my friend. So I'm lying to both of them just like you."

Dawn winced. "Thanks a lot, Joe. Thanks for reminding me. That really helped," she uttered, stepping away and walking over to the window with her arms folded.

I held out my arms helplessly. "Dawn...I don't know what you want me to say...or, or, do, here. No matter how you look at it, this is just a bad situation all around and the bottom line is that feelings are going to get hurt. You knew this Dawn, when you decided to be with me. Not much has changed since you saw Lacie in Miami, Dawn."

"A *lot* has changed, Joe. I wasn't sleeping with you then," Dawn retorted, still looking out the window.

"But you made a choice so accept it and stop reliving it," I countered quickly. "I hate to be so blunt, but life goes on and Lacie and I broke up more than two months ago. Why do we have to keep going over this...again...and again...and again?"

"Because she's my *best friend*, Joe!" she repeated loudly, turning around with tears.

"I *know* this!" I bellowed. "But I happen to be in love with you! Do you understand that?"

We locked frustrated eyes. Tears were streaming down her face. But oh, did she ever look so sexy. It was a warped notion, I know, but that's how much I loved her.

I swallowed hard. "Dawn, I need to know where you stand because I refuse to constantly debate this issue with you. We haven't even told Lacie and we're already arguing. I hate to argue, so we're either in this together or we're not together at all, because I can't keep going through this."

Her eyes widened in unbelief and she wiped the tears off her face with one sweep. "Okay, then. I guess we're not," she declared, marching past me with purpose.

I grumbled.

*Joe, man, you know better than to give a black woman an ultimatum. And, a sexy one at that. Man, are you crazy?*

**343**

Yeah, I was crazy. I was crazy in love and didn't want to see her walking out that door. I rushed toward it before her hands touched the knob. More tears ran down her face as she swatted my hand away when I moved between her and the door. She backed away with her doe eyes blazing into mine.

I held out my hands. "Look, look, I'm sorry," I apologized quickly, pulling her to me and wrapping my arms around her. "I'm sorry. I'm so sorry," I whispered in her neck continuously until I felt her body go limp in my arms after a few moments of her struggling. "I don't want you to leave. Don't go."

She didn't answer, but broke down and wept into my arms.

I cupped my hands over her face to make her look at me. "I didn't mean what I said, okay? I don't want us to be over. I love you." I groaned tenderly between numerous, short, sweet kisses on her tear stained lips. "I'm so sorry. I love you so much."

"I'm sorry, too," she murmured, returning my kisses passionately. "And I don't want us to be over either."

I stopped and looked at her earnestly. "So...are we back on?"

When she answered with a smile, I took her mouth hungrily and longingly, my tongue probing and enjoying the savory taste of hers. Within a second, my hands took over by taking her clothes off and throwing them in the air without a care of where they landed.

Hot blood ran straight from my head down to my private anatomy when she moved her lips to my earlobe and licked them with fervor. I took one of her breasts in my mouth, tasting her delicious body oil, while my hands ran over her body and succeeded in finding the sweet spot between her legs. She moaned and jumped onto me, straddling her legs around mine in response.

Without hesitation, I started toward the sofa, making record time in taking my clothes off as we kissed each other hungrily. With deft and care, I laid her on the sofa and we went at it. Our foreplay was euphoric and frenzied as we kissed and touched each other with increasing intensity. It was such that we paid no attention to the doorbell when it rang the first time, but commenced,, not wanting to interrupt the pleasure, we were giving each other.

Within seconds, it rang again.

"Oh, hell, who is it!" she exclaimed breathlessly.

"Did you really say that?" I managed, looking at her with surprise.

"Something wrong with your ears?" she derided lightly. I laughed and started to get up but she tugged on my arm. "Joe don't go. C'mon, whoever it is can wait or come back some other time," she reasoned.

Yeah, I felt that way, too.

I kissed her tenderly. "No, honey, I ordered pizza and that might be it," I said. I stood up and put on my boxers then took my wallet out of my pants. I chuckled when she pouted. "I promise it'll only be a second." I picked my T-shirt off the floor and tossed it to her. "Here, honey, put this on." She didn't budge. "O...kay, here's something to tide you over."

I bent over and ran my tongue over her stomach tenderly. She responded instantly with a little whimper and I stopped myself. The door was never going to get answered if I continued. Right away, it rang again.

"Come on, babe, put on my shirt, because you're killing me, here," I pleaded in a raspy voice.

She answered with a tantalizing smile, quickly opening and closing her legs enough for me to see her goods. I dropped my wallet.

"There's more where that came from," she purred with a wink.

I raised my eyes up to the ceiling and uttered, "Help me, Lord," then proceeded to the door, hearing her giggle.

Before I opened the door, I looked back to make sure she had on my shirt. She did, but had that same cat smile and was sitting on the sofa with bare legs crossed. I shook my head and opened the door.

"Okay, man, how much do I owe–?" I started, but stopped when I saw that Tony was not the pizza guy.

With a friendly chuckle Tony said, "Thought I was your order, huh?"

"Uh...yeah, I ordered pizza," I said in a soft cool tone, raising my arms higher on the door to shield him from the view in the living room. I pulled the door slightly closer to me and leaned out to the hallway some, pretending to look for the delivery guy.

Tony backed away a little with a small puzzled frown. "How long ago did you call it in?"

"Uh...about an hour ago," I said offhandedly. "I told security to go ahead and let him up. So I don't know," I said, completing my act by looking at my watch.

He nodded with a slight smile. "You're in Manhattan, man. Not Miami and traffic is no joke."

"You're right, you're right," I said.

Tony took a deep breath and said, "Look, Joe. I came over here to see if we could talk. I really didn't like what happened at lunch today and..."

His voice trailed off when I felt Dawn's body come up to mine as she opened the door a tad wider. "Joe, honey, you forgot your wal–" she started.

I looked at her wearily with the unspoken words that said, *Dawn, honey, why didn't you just stay in the living room?*

Her eyes widened in panic when she saw Tony. I glanced over at him and was not surprised by the brooding expression on his face. I looked down at the threshold floor and sighed.

"I guess, I'm not imagining things now, am I, Joe?" Tony muttered sarcastically. I pulled my head back up and didn't back down from his reproving glare.

Dawn's voice was thick with emotion as she tried to explain. "Tony, listen we–"

I interrupted her softly. "Dawn...leave us alone for a second, okay?" I turned and saw that her eyes had already filled with tears and my heart went out to her. I touched her cheek lightly. "It's okay, honey."

With a small gulp, she nodded, walked to the living room to retrieve her clothes and started walking slowly toward the bedroom. I moved away from the door and saw her turn around to look at me before she closed the bedroom door.

Eyes not moving from the bedroom door, I said, "Come on in, Tony."

# Chapter 65

# Tony

"You son of a–" I began with anger, slamming the door close behind me after entering.

Joe held up a finger. "Hey, I almost got called that today already, so…," he said, turning around to face me. "lay off."

"You lied right to my face," I accused crossly. "How long has this been going on, man?"

"Since New Year's Eve," he muttered, avoiding looking at me.

"Since New Year's Eve," I repeated, nodding my head in disbelief. "Why'd you lie, man? I thought we were cool."

"Look, Tony, this has nothing to do with you, all right?" he returned.

"Say what?" I asked him incredulously, coming up to him. "You're sleeping with Dawn, man. Dawn, Lacie's best–"

"Friend!" he cut me off sharply, turning around to look at me. "Man! I'm so sick of hearing that word! I know."

"Do you realize what kind of position this puts me in—especially now that I know?"

"Look, Inspector Gadget, if you weren't so busy asking me questions and coming over here to check up on someone, you wouldn't be in this position, right?" he returned cynically, turning to step down into the living room.

"This…!" I asserted, holding up a manila envelope with the documents that had been in my hand the whole time. "Is why I came over!" I stepped down into the living room. "You missed a place in these documents and the bid can't go through without your signature. I already told you the other reason why I came." I stared at him hard. "Man, what is wrong with you? Don't you realize how bad this situation is? Or are you so whipped that you don't care about anybody but yourself—as usual?"

"When it comes to not caring about anyone but yourself, you're number one, Tony," he snapped back.

"What?"

"You weren't being self-centered with what went down with Lacie?"

"That was different, Joe," I asserted.

"There's no difference in what you and Lacie did to me," he said. He walked further into the living room and started to pace back and forth.

"You're actually going to bring that up again? Or are you just trying to grasp at straws in an attempt at justification?"

He didn't say anything. Just stared, pacing.

A thought came into my mind and I narrowed my eyes at him. "Are you using Dawn to get back at Lacie?"

That stopped his pacing. "Naw, man. I love her!" he bellowed.

"Oh, I get it, now. You're showing your love for her by placing her in the middle of Lacie and you," I mocked, scoffing. "But you know I can't really put this all on you, man. Dawn is a grown woman and she had a choice. I guess she made it." I smirked. "But I bet you didn't make it hard for her, did you?"

He said nothing and stared into the fireplace with a stone expression.

"Answer me, man!"

His face was livid when he turned around to face me. "Don't let the doorknob hit you in the back when you leave."

I nodded in cool fury. "Okay. I'm out." I threw the envelope toward him and it landed on the couch. "Make sure you turn this in early tomorrow morning."

The delivery guy was getting ready to ring the bell when I opened the door to leave. I looked over my shoulder casually and remarked with a terse, "Your pizza's here. Enjoy your meal."

I heard Joe bark, "Man, what took you so long?" to the delivery guy as I strolled toward the elevator in the hallway.

How in the hell was I going to tell Lacie?

As if in answer to my question, a fully dressed Dawn rushed up to me a moment later as the elevator opened on the floor.

"Tony, listen," she started, holding me back from getting into the elevator. "Please don't tell Lacie," she pleaded tearfully.

I sighed. "I don't know, Dawn..."

"Tony, look," she implored hastily, wiping her face with one hand while she held my arm with the other. "I...I...don't want Lacie to find out from anyone else. I want to tell her myself. Please..."

I looked at her with remorse, hating that she was asking me to hide something from Lacie. I was being put in a tight spot. Then again, should I be the one to tell?

With a fleeting glance, I noticed Joe standing in the hallway outside his door. I looked at Dawn and with a resigned sigh, asked, "When are you going to tell her?"

A small smile of relief came on her face. "As soon I can, but I thought it would be best to wait until after this weekend with your parents coming over and...everything..." she said, trailing off.

I understood what she meant and nodded in agreement. "Okay. You can tell her...but this can't go on much longer."

She hugged me gratefully and whispered in my ear. "Thank you, Tony. This means a lot."

I returned her hug. "Yeah, you're welcome," I murmured grudgingly, looking down the hallway at Joe. "Do you really love him that much?" I whispered.

"Yeah, I do," she returned softly and let go. "Thanks again."

I nodded my head down the hallway and with a little wink uttered, "Go on. Joe's waiting for you."

She replied with a peck on my cheek then walked hastily down the hallway to Joe.

The elevator came as soon as I pushed the 'down' button. I went in, punched the 'lobby' button hard, leaned against the wall and banged my head against it once in aggravation.

Now that I knew, I wish I didn't.

# *Chapter 66*

## Lacie

I was sweating.

Tony's parents were due to arrive in less than ten minutes. It had already been a strange week—the strangest I'd ever been through.

No one around me had been acting like their normal selves.

First, there was Trevor's jovial mood. His mood was too jovial and he'd been that way ever since the project had been set in motion with the contracting bid. He was halfway decent to deal with in the meetings and seemed to treat the rest of his team better than he had since the beginning of the project. Even stranger was how courteous he was toward Tony.

Second, Joe and Tony were barely speaking to each other. With the project going full speed ahead, they carried on with the routine of handling business, but the peculiar friction between them in the meetings was quite obvious. I'd tried to squeeze it out of Tony several times, but he'd shrug it of, refusing to tell me.

Lastly, Dawn had been acting quite odd. I hadn't seen her and had barely spoken to her ever since that fiasco of a lunch. She'd been very quiet and though I'd managed to talk with her a few times, it was only briefly and her demeanor had been very aloof. I was starting to wonder if she was avoiding me deliberately.

But why?

With all the peculiarities happening, I had a sickening feeling that dinner wasn't going to go well, either.

"Lacie, will you leave the table alone?" Mama exclaimed, slapping my hand away lightly with a dishtowel. "It looks fine. Why are you messing with it?" she asked, putting her hands on her hips.

I wrung my hands together nervously. "I...I...I...just want everything to be perfect. This will be Tony's parent's first time over here and I want to make a good impression."

"Lacie, I've cleaned this house spic and span from top to bottom and have been decorating all week. Not to mention, I've been slaving over a hot stove all day and still managed to put on one of my Sunday's best and makeup. What more of a good impression do you want?" Mama asked.

"I...I...don't know. Everything's just got to be right," I claimed.

"Girl, that woman really did a number on you," she uttered, staring at me in awe. "I can't wait 'til she brings her uppity behind in here."

I groaned. "Mama, you said..."

"Yeah, I know what I said," she declared. "But I didn't promise."

"Mama, please–" I started nervously. I felt a hand on my shoulder.

"Take it easy, baby, girl. I'm sure Josephine isn't serious–" Daddy began.

"Huh. Wanna bet?" Mama stressed, before walking into the kitchen.

I put my hand over my forehead and heaved a big sigh. "Daddy, this is going to be so bad," I cried softly, leaning into his chest.

"It's going to be okay. Stay strong now," he soothed, rubbing my arms.

"You're right," I murmured, pulling my head off of his chest. "I've–" I stopped, noticing the way he looked. "You have on a suit and tie," I said in surprise.

"Well, you wanted us to look our best. Right?" he winked.

I chuckled. "Right, Daddy."

Reneé came down the stairs then, with her pregnant belly protruding through her navy blue dress. "I look like a big blue whale!" she pouted when she reached the bottom. "Lacie, why do I have to be down here for this dinner? I look terrible!"

**351**

"Nonsense," I encouraged with a smile, walking over to put my arm around her shoulders. "You look cute with your round belly showing. You're glowing!"

"Cute? Glowing? That's it," she said. "This was the wrong outfit. I'm going back upstairs to change." She turned back around to the stairs.

"No, Reneé. C'mon, you look fine," I assured, steering her into the living room with a small chuckle. "You really do."

"Are you sure?" she asked. "I know how much this means to you and I don't want to be a distraction."

"Be for real," I said dismissively. "Just sit down and relax."

The doorbell rang. Reneé, Daddy and I looked at the door hesitantly. I checked my watch. They were on time, but I couldn't move.

Mama came out of the kitchen and stared at us. "Are you three going to just stand there and let the doorbell continue to ring?" When we didn't answer or move, she started walking toward the door, mumbling, "This doesn't make any sense."

"I'll get it, Mama," I said with sudden boldness, stopping her.

"Well, c'mon, then. We don't want to be rude or give Tony's mom any reason, now," she commanded.

I hasted toward the door and smoothed my dress over and nervously patted my hair.

"Lacie...if you don't open the door..." Mama scolded, coming up behind me.

"Okay, okay. I am," I said, waving her off.

Inhaling a courageous breath, I opened the door and was greeted by Tony's tender expression and Johnathan's friendly smile. Lagging behind was Abigail, taking purposeful, little steps from the elevator toward us. Her expression was pure, unfriendly, steel.

"Wench," I heard Mama utter low enough so only I could hear.

*Lord, please let Mama behave.*

# Chapter 67

## The Dinner

### Tony

Lacie was nervous.

It was all over her face when she opened the door.

"Hey, you," I said immediately, stepping over the threshold to embrace her and plant a kiss on her lips. "These are for you... and you, Josephine," I said smoothly, handing each a bouquet of roses.

"Thank you, Tony," Lacie replied softly.

"Thank you, Tony," Josephine said gratefully, taking the bouquet and leaning over so I could plant a kiss on her cheek.

I stepped aside. "This...is my father, Johnathan."

"Pleasure to meet you, Josephine," Dad said pleasantly, shaking Josephine's hand.

Pleasantly, Josephine returned, "You, too, Johnathan."

"And..." I looked behind me and saw Mom standing remotely behind us — not even two feet from the elevator. I left Lacie for a moment to get Mom and brought her to the door. "my mother, Abigail," I concluded.

"It's a pleasure to meet you, Abigail," Josephine murmured with a small smile, offering her hand to Mom.

Mom barely shook Josephine's hand before she quickly removed it. Josephine raised her eyebrow and looked as if she was about to say something when Mason came over then and introduced himself to Dad and then to Mom. Mom responded in the same way, but it didn't seem to bother him.

Josephine clapped her hands together and inhaled. "Well, let's all go into the living room so that we can get acquainted," she stated, turning around to lead us in. "This is my youngest daughter, Reneé," she introduced once we entered the living room.

Reneé stood up and smiled. "Hi," she said with a little wave.

"Hello," Mom returned. She looked at Reneé's belly with wide eyes then shot me a meaningful, sideways glance.

"May I take your coats?" Josephine offered.

"That won't be necess—" Mom started abruptly.

"Abigail, here, let me help you," Dad interrupted, taking her coat off smoothly and quickly.

He ignored the look Mom gave him and handed both of their coats to Josephine. Mason took the coats from Josephine and retreated to the hall closet.

"O…kay," Josephine said with a mysterious twinkle in her eye. "Can I offer anyone something to drink? We have Pepsi, lemonade, punch and bottled water."

"No, thank–" Mom began again.

Again, Dad interjected. "I'll have some lemonade and Abigail…" He turned to her. "What would you like?"

"Water will do," Mom replied stiffly.

Josephine turned to me. "Tony?"

"I'll have a Pepsi," I replied.

"I'll have one too," Mason added.

"Okay." She nodded and turned to Reneé. "Reneé, come in the kitchen with me and help me with the drinks, will you? You all have a seat and make yourselves comfortable," she said.

While she and Reneé went into the kitchen, the rest of us stood in awkward silence for a good moment.

"C'mon. Let's all sit down," Mason said at last, motioning toward the sofa.

Lacie's hands were shaking slightly when I took them and led her to the loveseat with me, giving them a comforting squeeze.

The awkward silence continued as we sat, taking fleeting looks at each other. I noticed Mom and Dad taking in the apartment. They appeared impressed.

Finally, Lacie asked, "So…how was the drive from Connecticut,

Mr. and Mrs. Douglas? Did you run into much traffic?"

Dad smiled at her gratefully, relieved by her initiative to break the silence. "Actually, it was a pretty smooth ride and hardly any traffic once we came over here."

Lacie took a satisfied breath. "Good. I'm glad."

"I must say," Dad said, leaning forward to look at her. "This is an amazing apartment, you've got here. The décor is outstanding," he complimented, taking another sweep before he continued. "I noticed all of the African artwork you have displayed. Is that a hobby of yours—collecting African art?"

Lacie chuckled softly. "I haven't really thought of it as a hobby much. I just like art — well…"

"Any kind of art," I jumped in with Lacie.

We both chuckled and briefly exchanged surprised glances before I turned to my parents to explain. "Lacie said the same thing to me during my first visit here, so I've heard this before."

"And thank you for the compliment," Lacie added. "I've been told this many times so I guess I'm doing something right."

"Mmm, indeed," Mom murmured, nodding and gazing at Lacie wistfully. "This *is* a very beautiful and spacious apartment. It's also in a pricy area which I'm sure must have cost you a great deal. How is it that you're able to afford such luxury?" she asked bluntly. "You can't possibly be living this well on your salary."

Flabbergasted, I cleared my throat nervously and shook my head at Mom in disapproval, which she ignored. I looked at Lacie peripherally and saw her stiffen and blink, taken aback.

"And why in the hell not?" Josephine said calmly, as she and Reneé came beside her with drinks in their hands.

Dad, Mason and I exchanged uncomfortable looks. Then I ran my hand over my face and flinched. We hadn't even been in the apartment ten minutes and already Mom had started.

Mom didn't back down and looked up at Josephine with a cool glance. "Manhattan is known for its high priced real estate and attractive apartments," she said in a dry tone. "A place such as this with expensive furniture could not have come by cheaply. Also, I do

**355**

know a few people that live in this area and they are very well off."

"What are you insinuating?" Josephine asked directly, still holding Mom's glass in her hand.

Reneé's eyes shifted uncomfortably when she walked passed Mom. She handed Mason and Dad their drinks, who, along with Lacie and I, were quietly observing the tense dialogue between the two older women.

"I'm not insinuating anything," Mom replied immediately.

"Mmm, hmm, sure you aren't. Here's your drink, Abigail," Josephine murmured quickly, handing Mom her drink and mine. Then she took a seat next to Mason in a chair.

Mom continued her defense. "I'm just aware of where Lacie is employed, that's all. She couldn't possibly afford this by being just a secretary."

"I believe the term I used was administrative assistant, Mrs. Douglas. In fact, I was one of the *top* administrative assistant in the company," Lacie informed Mom calmly. "Just recently I was promoted to Director of Accounts."

"And even if she was *just* a secretary, would her income be any of your business?" Josephine added crisply.

"It was just an observation," Mom replied in an airy drawl.

"Mmm, hmm. Would you even be wondering that if Lacie were white?' Josephine said bluntly.

I felt Lacie tense up as she murmured, "Mama."

Mom's eyes flashed with a tight smile on Josephine. "Are you accusing me of something?"

"Not at all, dear. I was just *observing*," Josephine countered with unmistakable sarcasm.

Josephine and Mom exchanged unfriendly glances while the rest of us sat in discomfort. No one said a word; the air was so thick with contention.

All of a sudden, Mom lifted up her glass and inspected it.

"Is something wrong, Abigail?" Josephine asked.

Mom gave an airy shrug. "No, nothing at all." Then she looked at Josephine suggestively. "I *always* inspect a glass before I drink from it. Just to make sure if it's clean."

356

I squirmed, embarrassed by my mother's statement.

"Woman, you have got some nerve..." Josephine started.

Lacie stood up abruptly. "Uh...Mama, let's go into the kitchen and check on dinner. It should be just about ready. Don't you think?" She looked at Josephine fretfully.

Josephine, catching the earnest tone in Lacie's voice, nodded decisively with wide eyes. "You know what, Lacie? That's not a bad idea. As a matter of fact, I think I'm going to pour myself a drink. Maybe with some liquor in it," she remarked before she stood up and strode in haste toward the kitchen with Lacie following.

"I'll help you," Reneé offered anxiously, getting up as well.

I heard Mason draw out a deep breath and ask with tactful and deliberate diversion, "So, Johnathan...what kind of sports do you like?"

As Mason and Dad started to talk, Mom deliberately avoided eye contact with me and calmly took a taste from her glass.

I just sat back and gawked at her.

## *Lacie*

"Mama...I know what you're going to say," I said as soon as we entered the kitchen.

Mama turned around and looked at me with wide eyes. "Oh! You have absolutely no idea." She leaned and spread her hands over the counter. "Lacie, I'm telling you. I feel like I'm in the Twilight Zone," she brooded calmly.

"Tell me about it," Reneé remarked. "Tony's mother is a trip. I've never seen someone be so cool and offensive."

Mama went to the oven to check the roast while she muttered, "She thinks Lacie's not good enough to have an apartment like this and then hints that I'd actually give her a dirty glass. Uh, huh. I see where this night is going."

I studied Mama. She was too calm.

I walked over to her and put a hand on her shoulder. "Mama, are you all right?"

"Child, yeah. I'm fine," she claimed, standing up straight to look at me. "I'm just trying to keep my composure, because what I really want to do besides be here in this kitchen is to go back in there and pluck out her fake eyelashes."

"Mama, no..." I said.

"Oh, Lacie, don't worry, honey. It's gonna be all right," Mama promised, nodding her head several times. "Miss Abigail's claws came out sharp and quick, but mine are longer. Huh. She hasn't met her match, yet. She's lucky I'm not the way I used to be or else she'd get cut!" she declared and turned around swiftly to the refrigerator to take out the green salad and dressing.

"Mama!" I exclaimed. Reneé burst out with a loud laugh and I looked at her sharply. "Not funny, Reneé!" I went over to Mama as she eased over to the cabinets for the serving bowls. "Mama...please... just calm down," I beseeched softly. "This was your idea to invite them here for dinner. Let's not turn this into a battleground. It won't solve anything."

Mama turned around and looked at me dubiously. "Lacie, I know this was my idea, but I also know that that woman has never been told off before. She's got a superior attitude and thinks she can talk to anyone in any kind of way."

"Mama..."

Mama closed her eyes tightly. "Lacie, stop. That's enough. I've got this handled. Now you know that I'm not one to take no mess. Believe me, that woman came here for a fight, honey — not for peace. I saw the challenge and the determination in her eyes." She opened her eyes and looked at me sternly. "Lacie, all I want you to do is sit back and be quiet so she won't have any leverage against you. I know how to handle her so let me do it. Lord, knows I don't want you to get into it because you might get upset with your over emotional and hormonal self," she said with exasperation. "Now, if you will, help me get the food onto the table." She turned back around and continued what she was doing.

The battle had begun and it was out of my hands.

## Tony

"Why did you come, Mom?" I asked her crossly, moving to sit beside her.

Dad and Mason were standing by the window, talking.

"You wanted me here, didn't you?" she asked simply.

I put my arm over the back of the couch and leaned in close to peer at her. "Yes, but not to start an argument with Lacie's mother and definitely not to insult them."

"Oh, please, Anthony. There was no harm done."

"You really believe that, don't you? You really believe that you weren't insulting when you belittled Lacie's position and then questioned the amount of money she makes?"

"No," she said straightforwardly, shrugging her shoulders. "She shouldn't feel insulted—unless she has something to hide."

"You're determined to make this an uncomfortable situation," I stated rhetorically. "Dad's showing some effort with all of this, but you...you're not even willing to try—"

"No, Anthony. I'm not!" Mom declared, eyes flashing. "Why should I try when I am totally against this relationship?"

"Because...I...love...her," I stressed, gritting my teeth. "It's not about you."

She looked down at her glass in her hand. "Anthony, I just don't know how to say this any—"

"Mom, unless you're willing to give in at least a little—there's nothing else to say," I cut in.

She pursed her lips. "I guess not."

I guess not.

## Lacie

Mama had outdone herself for dinner.

An entrée of roast beef, homemade scalloped potatoes, freshly cooked garden greens and her homemade biscuits were a few items on the menu. I'd definitely gotten my love and good cooking skills from Mama.

Dad, Mason and Tony were eating heartily, laughing and talking about sports and the news. The bad news; all four of us women had barely uttered a word from the moment prayer was said.

Mama watched Abigail silently, noticeably aggravated and feeling disrespected by her picking at her plate. Reneé and I exchanged uncomfortable and knowing looks a few times while we ate. One thing we were certain of; Mama was and had always been proud of her cooking because she knew she was an excellent cook. Mama considered it an extreme offense when someone picked at the food that she had so diligently prepared. Plus, it didn't help matters that Abigail had ticked her off.

Reneé and I ate slowly, cringing and waiting — waiting for the explosion to detonate.

Mama started on cue. "So...Johnathan, Abigail...what did you think of my daughter when you first met her? It was quite a shock, hmmm?"

What? Why'd she start of with such a direct question?

Abigail tensed up instantly.

The Three Musketeers, who had been having a grand old time talking, stopped and looked at Mama as soon as she'd dished out the question. I glanced at Mama curiously because she'd taken a whole different route than what I'd expected.

Johnathan grinned and glanced at Tony quickly. "Yes. It was quite a shock, given the untimely and awkward circumstances. Your daughter and my son were clearly not expecting us. Nor were we prepared to catch them in such a compromising position. I believe it was quite embarrassing for all of us," he chuckled.

*Hmm, tell me about it.*

Johnathan continued. "But save for that incident and after having dinner with her and Tony a couple of days later, I took an immediate liking to your daughter." He glanced at Daddy and then back at Mama. "She truly is an adorable person."

360

Mama looked at Johnathan in surprise. Daddy smiled with pride.

"So...you don't have an issue with Lacie and Tony being together—despite the differences in color?" Mama asked.

"No," Johnathan replied with a shrug.

Abigail jabbed a fork and knife into her roast. Tony frowned at her.

"Really?" Mama asked again.

Johnathan shook his head. "Josephine, I'm a retired Navy Captain. I've traveled all around the world and have seen all kinds of races and cultures getting along in other countries. It baffles me that this country still has problems with race. It's a shame really, and people in other countries make fun of the United States because of it."

"Amen," Reneé agreed softly.

Again, Abigail jabbed her fork and knife into her roast.

"So you're not concerned with whatever backlash your son may get because of other people's perceptions?" Mama continued her inquiry.

"Anthony's a grown man and he can fend for himself," Johnathan asserted. "This might sound cliché but as long as he's happy, so am I." He smiled at me. "In all honesty, I've never seen him so in love with any other woman."

"Oh, honestly, Johnathan! You're being ridiculous!" Abigail burst out, throwing down her knife and fork on the plate. "This is so like you Johnathan — always trying to be diplomatic but never reasonable. Anthony's life will be ruined if he continues to be with her!"

I looked up at the ceiling. *Here we go.*

"Abigail!" Johnathan said, turning to her sharply.

"Mom!" Tony said, just as sharply.

"Why is that?" Daddy asked Abigail calmly. "Is my daughter not good enough for Tony?"

*Oh, she told me that already, Daddy.*

All eyes were on Abigail and she glanced around the table quickly, showing slight discomfort with being put on the spot. She sputtered with her answer.

"I...I...just want my son to be happy," she defended.

"Mmm, hmm, and he couldn't possibly be happy with my daughter. Isn't that correct, Abigail?" Mama dared.

Abigail returned Mama's penetrating stare. "Anthony and your daughter have only been together for a few months. That's not a lot of time for him to be rational about his feelings. His senses are blocked and he's unaware of what he's in for by being with her."

"I am aware of everything, Mom and my senses couldn't be any clearer," Tony contended adamantly, looking at his mother. "Rationalizing is not a factor."

"Abigail, if your son is so sure of about his feelings, why do you have a problem with his decision?" Daddy asked simply.

*She doesn't care about his feelings, Daddy.*

"Because his relationship with her can have an adverse effect on his career. My husband and I have toiled for Anthony to be a success. We invested a lot of money into his future — and all of our children's. We sent them to the best schools and colleges. They've received and been nominated for countless awards–" she explained

"Mom, you're being paranoid," Tony objected with a sigh.

"Exactly," Mama added. "Abigail, what does his career have to do with their relationship? How will that affect him being a success?" Mama asked. "You and Johnathan investing in Tony's future was what you were supposed to do Abigail, because, as my daughter has explained to me, you're his parents. But let me point out some facts since you've assumed so much already. Lacie attended a prestigious private school, was elected class president twice, and received several scholarships—one in particular to Haaar-vaaard," Mama stressed dramatically. "So what's your point?"

*You tell her, Mama.* I smiled and put a piece of roast in my mouth.

Abigail exclaimed heatedly. "My point…is that I don't want Anthony to risk his future just to be with a–"

"Abigail, don't," Johnathan interrupted quickly.

"No, that's okay, Johnathan. Abigail, go ahead. Speak your mind." Mama put her fork down and held out her arms emphatically. "I mean, this is why I wanted to have this dinner. So, let's lay it all on the table," she challenged with a nod toward Abigail. Mama folded her hands and leaned across the table with a scrutinizing expression. "What were you going to say? African-American? Black? Negro? Nig–"

I winced while I chewed the roast and Tony shifted uncomfortably.

"Don't go there, Josephine," Daddy interrupted her.

I swallowed the roast and murmured, "Mama."

Not backing down from Mama's stare, Abigail spoke through tight lips. "You have no right to judge me," she muttered in defense.

"Why not?" Mama raised her eyebrow, giving me a momentary look. "Isn't that what you've done to Lacie? Judge her and make her feel uncomfortable just like you feel right now? You told her that it'd be hell or high water before you let her into your family and that she'd never be good enough for your son without even giving her *one* chance."

Tony looked at me and exclaimed, "Lacie, why didn't you tell me?"

Too nervous to answer, I stared at him.

"Abby?" Johnathan asked his wife. "Did you say that to Lacie?"

Abigail narrowed her eyes at Mama briefly before she turned to look at her husband defiantly. "Yes…I did."

Mama nodded satisfactorily and sat back. "Ah…and so she admits it."

Reneé sighed deeply and uttered a soft, "Oh, boy."

Tony shook his head. "You really shouldn't have said that, Mom."

"Why not, Anthony?" Abigail voiced. "Don't I have a right to be concerned about your well being?"

Johnathan blew out a weary sigh and put a finger on his temple. "Abigail…Anthony's a grown man—"

"You've already said that, Johnathan," she spat out angrily, eyes fixed on his. "If you think for one instant that I'm going to apologize for anything that I've said or done to that girl, you're terribly mistaken!"

" *That girl's* name is Lacie," Daddy spoke with a firm tone.

Mama said sadly, "No matter how well we do as black Americans, it's people like you that still have that same type of mentality that hinders this country from healing from its terrible history of racial injustice. Why is that? All we want is to be treated fairly and equally. Is that too much to ask for when we were brought over here to a foreign country against our will in chains and lost our heritage, language, free—"

Abigail rolled her eyes upward and interrupted with a sharp, "Spare me the slavery speech because it's been over four hundred years! I'm sure the next thing you're going to tell me is that racism still exists and that there's no equality–"

"There isn't, Abigail! The chains from racism are still there—mentally and emotionally. Not just in us but in *everyone!*" Mama expressed, holding out her arms across the table. "The fact that we are even arguing over two people who are in love and happen to be of a different color confirms how far we have to go as a people! As a country! Blacks can't even move into a predominantly white neighborhood without being gawked at, scrutinized or stereotyped. *'Oh, they're black; they can't possibly afford that nice big house. That Mercedes, BMW or Cadillac can't be theirs. Oh, they must be drug dealers!'"*

"I did not say that! I never said that!" Abigail defended vehemently.

"But you implied it and that's bad enough!" Mama blared in return. "As soon as blacks move into a nice neighborhood white people are ready to move out because they're afraid the value of their property will go down. I mean, c'mon! Who are we kidding here? Racial prejudice is still out there. It's just not as noticeable as it used to be because the white sheets are no longer over certain people's heads!"

Abigail lifted up her chin. "How dare you insinuate that I'm prejudiced when I'm merely trying to look out for the best interest of my son? We've always treated you people—"

"You people?" Mama, Daddy and Reneé exclaimed in unison

Tony and Johnathan lowered their heads sadly and I sighed in exasperation.

Abigail sputtered as she looked around the table. "I...I...I'm not prejudice, just a realist."

Daddy offered a simple shrug and said with light sarcasm, "Right, right. We're black, and you just want us to get back. That's all." He nodded. "I understand very well."

Reneé, Tony and I snickered.

Abigail narrowed her eyes and glowered around the table. "You all think you're so smart, don't you? Trying to make me look like the bad guy, as if I'm the culprit in this sordid affair! Well, I will not apologize!

I stand by my beliefs; and will say it again to everyone here at this table. Yes, I am against interracial relationships. It is immoral and a sin. Too many children end up emotionally and physically scarred because of such a union. And that's not going to happen in my family. It is unnatural and is not what God intended. It says so right in the Bible. God made the races unique and intended them to remain in their distinction. He never intended the races to be together."

"What?" Mama exclaimed. Then she looked at Johnathan in stupefaction. "*How*...did you two ever meet?" she emphasized.

I glanced around the table uneasily and saw Reneé and Daddy staring at Abigail open-mouthed. Tony had his hands over his face.

"Abigail, let's not get into a debate about religion or the Bible. People are always twisting and using the Bible for their own personal ideals," Johnathan advised peacefully.

Mama wasn't letting it go so easily. She was an avid church-going woman and studied the Bible regularly. "Abigail, what Bible did this come from?" she asked, looking at her in awe. "You must not go to church for you to use God's Word in an attempt to validate your idiotic viewpoint. There is nothing in the Bible to suggest anything against interracial relationships."

Abigail sat up straight, haughty and defensive. "I was raised in a southern Baptist church and coming from the south, my belief has always been that blacks stay with blacks and whites stay with whites."

"'Your belief' is the operative statement, because it sure isn't God's," Mom retorted.

It was my turn to put my hands over my face and try to maintain some composure. This was useless and the scary and ominous part was that the conversation hadn't even reached its peak.

"We're in the twenty-first century, Abigail, and we're no longer in the south. Things have changed since when you were raised," Johnathan pointed out.

"Nevertheless, my views remain the same," Abigail maintained.

"Wow...you still can't let that flag go, huh?" Mama wisecracked.

"The nerve of you to insult my heritage!" Abigail voiced bitterly.

"What about American heritage, Abigail!" Johnathan said immediately and Abigail gave him a hard look.

Mama looked at Abigail and spoke with angry fervor. "Abigail, your belief and that kind of statement keeps people segregated—physically, mentally and emotionally." She nodded her head insistently. "I'll admit that I did have a problem with Lacie being with your son at first." Abigail nodded in satisfaction, liking what she'd heard. "But," Mama pointed a finger, "the difference is that my feelings were based on my experiences with Jim Crow and segregation laws when I grew up. Dealing with racism and prejudice is painfully demoralizing and because Lacie's been through a lot in her life and I didn't want her to have to go through any more pain than she already has. But when I saw the love that she had for him, I realized that I couldn't stand in her way of happiness based on *my* feelings. She has to live her own life and I had to give Tony a chance. I'm so glad I did." She glanced at Tony briefly with a smile, before looking back at Abigail. "But not once have I said anything to belittle him." She shook her head at Abigail. "Since you laid eyes on my daughter you've been unjustly hostile toward her, disrespecting her time and time again by your words and actions." She narrowed her eyes at Abigail. "What are you afraid of, Abigail?" Mama taunted. "Or are you just insecure?"

Abigail responded with a thin smile and with an air of arrogance. "That was a very nice speech you did, dear. It was ineffective, nonetheless. My reasons are not because of insecurity for I am only defending the welfare of my family and my son."

"By what? By being abusive and spiteful to the woman he loves?" I burst out abruptly in frustration.

From the corner of my eye, I saw Mama shake her head at me and felt Reneé's hand on my arm, but I ignored them. I was overwrought and had gotten increasingly perturbed with how the conversation was going. Everyone had been taking up for me and Tony except me, and I couldn't suppress my silence any further.

My voice shook with emotion. "I *know* you've seen the love in your son's eyes when he looks at me and how well he treats me. You saw it at the wedding and yet you still refuse to be blinded by our difference in color. Why can't you just let go of your stupid ideologies and let your son live his life? He loves me! Me!" I exclaimed, looking at Abigail.

Her expression was frosty when she turned to me and batted her eyes. "Lacie, you are living in an unreal world. Do not mistake experimentation for love. I told you before that you're not good enough for him."

"That's not something for you to decide, Mom!" Tony snapped suddenly. "*I* feel that she's enough for me — more than enough. And I've had enough of trying to convince you of that."

Everyone looked at Tony, stunned.

Abigail's eyes flashed slightly from Tony's rejection of her and his defense of me. She gave me a fleeting look of embarrassment.

Mama clapped her hands and chuckled lightly. "I guess he told you," Mama teased, then attempted peacefully, "C'mon, Abigail, can't you see that they're in love? Why do you insist on being so objective?"

Abigail's mouth tightened, seeing that the entire table seemed to ask the same question as we appealed to her for some surrender. It didn't work.

She glared at me in distaste for a second before she took a look at both Daddy and Mama before she replied with an unbending, "I don't want to be blatant here, but you've given me no choice. My objectivity, as you call it, has to do with common sense. My son is white and your daughter is black. They don't belong together because there's already been enough turmoil and confusion in my family and your daughter is to blame. So she is not welcome in my home or in my family and I will not have a nappy-headed—"

"Stop it, Abigail!" Johnathan bellowed in fury. "You've gone too far!"

"Now hold on just a minute," Daddy started angrily, right after him.

Mama calmly reached for the bowl of gravy that was sitting conveniently in front of her. "You know, Abigail, you've got one more time to insult my daughter and this bowl of gravy goes all over that expensive suit you're wearing," she warned angrily.

Oh, no. Mama did not have a good history with gravy.

"Mama," I warned softly.

Abigail scoffed, returning that same expression at Mama. "My dear, you do not scare me," she drawled with a mean smile. "Face it; your daughter will never be good enough for my son and she–"

Mama stood up abruptly and so did everyone else. I don't know how Daddy came all the way over to the other end of the table, but he did, in time to take the gravy bowl away from her.

"Josephine, no! Not like this," Daddy said, holding Mama's arm.

Abigail remained seated in her chair and grinned at Mama with satisfaction. Reneé and I hasted over to Mama to try to calm her down.

Johnathan and youngest offspring said simultaneously, "Okay, we all need to relax, here."

"You see, Johnathan, I told you; this is how they are. That is why I have a problem with this. This is what happens when the races get together — anarchy. Blacks and whites should never mix with each other and this is why," Abigail went on, pointing at Mama. "Look at her, Johnathan. This woman has no class at all. She's ready to fight me just because of words. Words that mean no harm and aren't personal."

Now, she was talking about my Mama and despite the anxiety and stress I was feeling, I got hot. I started to defend Mama but she was already ahead of me.

Mama wrestled free from us calmly. "Not personal, you say?" She leaned over the table with her knuckles and glowered at Abigail. "Okay. Since you suggested that words don't hurt. Let's see how these words grab you."

Reneé and I both sucked in a breath, realizing where Mama was going. We were right.

Mama's words were slow and deliberate as she announced, "You're ...going...to be a grandma!" Abigail's eyes widened in horror immediately. Mama nodded her head insistently with a broad smile. "Mmm, hmm, that's right, Abigail. You're going to have a beautiful *black* grandchild. Don't you just love it?"

## Tony

*Huh?*

I stood stock still, in stupor, gazing at Josephine.

Mom sprang from her chair and screamed, "That's a lie! That girl is not pregnant!"

Josephine straightened up and said with an amusing chuckle. "Every truth in it... Grandma."

I glanced from Josephine to Lacie. Lacie returned my look with wary eyes and started toward the living room. I gulped, suddenly overwhelmed with emotion and followed Lacie in bewilderment.

"What? Is this true?" I heard my Dad say as their conversation faded in the background.

"Lacie?" I asked, coming up to her hastily and turning her around gently so she could face me. "Honey, am I going to be a father?" I asked, studying her intently and cupping my hands around her face.

Scared brown eyes responded only by darting toward the commotion that ensued in the dining room as my mom cried out, "She did this deliberately! She tricked him!"

"What in John Brown's name would she do that for?" Josephine hollered.

"Because she wants his money!" Mom hollered in return.

"No, honey...look at me," I said to Lacie quickly. "Shut them out because all that matters right now ..." I pointed softly with my index finger to her chest and then to mine "is you and me," I declared with a small gulp. "Are you really...?"

"You know what, Abigail? You really need Jesus!" I heard Josephine shout at Mom. "You are pathetically paranoid. Lacie doesn't want or need Tony's money!"

With a last glance in the dining room at Josephine and Mom continuing their arguing, Lacie heaved a big sigh and nodded. "Yes," she replied meekly.

"Oh, my God!" I whispered hugging her tightly after the beautiful words came out of her mouth. "Oh, honey!" I released the embrace and held her at arms length to get a look at her. "Wh...when did you find out? Ha, how far along are you?" I stumbled out anxiously.

"Yes, she does and that's why she made herself get pregnant! She did it to force him into marriage!" Mom accused.

Lacie's eyes were disbelieving, staring at me just as I'd done at her a second ago. "You're really...okay with this?"

"I don't think she'll have to force him," I heard Mason state.

"Yes!" I answered swiftly. "Oh, babe of course I am," I said, giving her another hug with a kiss on the cheek. "Why wouldn't I be?" I whispered in her ear.

"Ha! That's the only reason he'd marry her!" I heard Mom shout back.

"Abigail, you need to calm down," Dad said.

"I just thought..." I felt her sigh, deeply. "I...I...just didn't know how you were going to react with everything going on and then there's your mom..." She let go and her eyes beseeched mine. "Tony, this wasn't planned. I'm just as surprised about this as you are."

"Calm down, Johnathan? Do you see how much damage this is going to do if our friends and family find out about this? Can you imagine the ridicule?" I heard Mom cry out.

"This woman has gone absolutely nuts!" Josephine said.

I smiled and touched Lacie's chin with one finger before I pulled her back into my arms. "Babe, listen, I—"

Without warning, Mom rushed over to us. She tried to push me out of the way in order to grab Lacie, but I held her off. What in the—

"You can't have this baby! Do you hear me? You just can't!" Mom screamed at Lacie, still reaching for her.

Angry and fed up, I yelled, "Mom, stop it! Have you lost your mind? She's pregnant!" It was a good thing I was holding her off because in the corner of my eye, I saw Mason and Reneé holding off Josephine as well.

Dad came over swiftly and pulled Mom away. It was the first time I'd ever witnessed him using any type of physical force on her.

By this time, Lacie had broken down and I was holding her in my arms. "Mom, what is wrong with you?" I belted out.

Mom suddenly crumbled. "Anthony, she's trying to trap you!"

"Mom, stop it! Just stop it!" I shouted.

Time seemed to stand still and there was an eerie silence as my eyes scanned the apartment in sad disbelief. Reneé was crying and Mason and Josephine had somber expressions while he continued to hold Josephine's arms. Dad was holding a now sobbing Mom and Lacie was trembling in my arms.

Dad broke the silence. "Abigail...it's time we left," Dad said sternly.

Mason nodded. "Yeah," he uttered wearily. "I agree. Reneé, will you get their coats, please? I've got your Mama."

"Dad, you and Mom go on. I'll meet you downstairs in the lobby," I instructed.

Dad nodded in compliance and looked at Mason and Josephine. "I'm very sorry about this," he expressed gravely.

"We all are," Mason replied with a sympathetic smile.

Dad nodded again and started to veer a dazed Mom toward the door, cleverly managing to keep her away so he could shake Mason and Josephine's hand.

I turned to Lacie and wiped the tears off her face after Dad and Mom walked out. "Hey, it's going to be okay," I soothed. "I'm going to drive my parents back to my apartment and I'll be back. I'm going to come back so we can talk, okay?" She nodded tearfully. I kissed her forehead. "I love you."

Reneé came into view carrying the coats.

"Reneé, I'll take them," I said, walking over to her, holding Lacie's hand. I took the coats and gave her a kiss on the cheek.

Still holding Lacie's hand, I walked toward Mason and Josephine. Mason gave me a grip and Josephine gave me a tight hug.

She whispered in my ear, "I'm so sorry, Tony."

"Don't worry about it," I whispered in return. "I know why you did it. Thank you." Releasing the embrace, I gave her a kiss on the cheek and then winked at her.

After, I gave Lacie a soft, quick kiss, said, "Remember, it'll be okay," and left the apartment.

Oh, there was no doubt it was going to be okay. I was going to propose to Lacie tonight and nothing was going to stop me.

Not even my mother.

# Chapter 68

## Lacie

"I swear that woman brought the flesh out of me!" Mama exclaimed once Tony left. "I'm so glad she's gone."

Tearfully, I stared at the closed door after Tony walked out. As predicted, dinner had been a disaster, but for some insane reason, I'd hoped that it would have been peaceful.

"Uh...I'm going to start clearing the table," Reneé offered quietly and walked to the dining room.

I wiped my tears away with a big sigh and walked past Mama and Daddy to start for the kitchen. I heard Mama say to Daddy, "Mason, you'd better not say one word about the way I acted tonight, because if you do, I–!" Mama warned sternly. "Lacie?" I heard her call, followed by her and Daddy's footsteps as they joined me into the kitchen. "Sweetie, are you okay?"

I leaned against the counter for support. "No, Mama. I'm not. Dinner was just horrible. Just horrible," I expressed. "I mean, can you believe his mother? Did you see how she reacted to the news?"

"All I saw was a black eye that she was going to get if she put her hands on you," Mama said tersely, sitting down at the table.

"Thank God, I grabbed you before you did," Daddy remarked, joining her.

For a moment, there was silence in the kitchen as we sat in deep thought. Mama stood up suddenly and came over to my side.

"Lacie, you're not upset with me, are you?" she asked and I shook my head. "I only told her because I knew it was the best way to hurt her because she'd hurt you so much. Anyway...Tony needed to know."

"I know." I nodded and started welling up again. "I just wish that things would have gone better."

"Lacie, you could have had an eight course meal catered by a famous chef and it wouldn't have done a bit of good," Daddy rationalized, coming up to us with a supporting hand on my back.

"But I didn't want this for Tony. I wanted everything to go well so this wouldn't be so difficult for him," I contended somberly. "I mean, why can't she accept my relationship with Tony? Why can't she accept me?"

"Lacie, it's not about you. It's her. She's the one with the problem," Mama declared. "If she's unwilling to accept your relationship with Tony, you, or that baby you're carrying, it's her loss."

Daddy smiled at me tenderly. "Lacie, aren't you forgetting something?" He didn't wait for my answer and said, "Johnathan likes you. He seems to like you very much, indeed. He's not like his wife. And what about Tony? You were so worried about how Tony was going to react and yet he was ecstatic. There was nothing but joy on his face when he left here. Shouldn't that give you a little comfort?" Daddy suggested.

I was unconvinced and looked at him with a forlorn expression. "But what good is that if he can't even share that joy with his mother?" I replied softly with a shrug. "Either way, everyone loses."

Miserably, I left my parents in the kitchen, walked past Reneé carrying a few dirty dishes and went straight upstairs. I had appreciated my parent's joint effort in their attempt to make me feel better, but nothing was going to change the ill-fated facts.

Tony was in love with me—a black woman who was carrying his child and his mother clearly detested that. No prophecy was needed to know that Tony was going to have to make a choice between us.

And that did not sit well with me.

# Chapter 69

# Tony

The ride to my apartment had been excruciating.

Mom had not ceased from talking about the dinner, and by the time we entered my apartment, I'd had enough.

"To believe that…that…that Josephine woman had the nerve to attempt–" Mom continued as she walked into the living room.

I slammed the door and she jerked around with shocked, wide eyes. Dad, having gone straight for the bar, looked up casually from pouring himself a brandy and imperturbably went back to it.

"What was that for?" Mom screeched.

"Because I have listened to you carp and whine about everyone else but yourself!" I expressed bitterly. "Do you realize how embarrassed I am with your behavior tonight? What possessed you to go after Lacie that way? What has gotten into you?"

Unruffled, she went on the defensive. "What has gotten into *you*, Anthony? How could you get that woman pregnant?" she blared obstinately in return, standing straight. "Haven't you ever heard of using condoms?"

"Yes…I have." I grimaced. "But that's hindsight. She's pregnant now and I have to take action. First, we have to get something straight," I avowed with a nod. I walked toward the bar. Without a word, Dad took another glass and poured a shot for me.

Mom straightened her back and marched over to us. She sat on the barstool, leaned in close to me and squinted. "Just what, pre tell, do we have to get straight, Anthony?"

Oh, she was ready, all right. But so was I and there was no backing down.

I picked up my glass and held it in my hand and fixed her with an unyielding glare. "I will no longer tolerate your verbal abuse toward Lacie." I shook my head in disapproval. "You have been unyielding and obnoxious in your continuous disregard toward her and me; to top it off; you were very disrespectful to her family. I'm telling you; this stops now."

She squinted even more and blared, "How can you stand there, Anthony, and defend them when I was almost attacked by that mother of hers?"

"You threw the first punch, Abigail," Dad interjected in reproach.

Her eyes darted to him. "And you. You are supposed to be my husband. You just sat there while I was being attacked and just...just... offered no help at all."

"Because I was embarrassed too!" Dad exclaimed with a thunderous slap on the table, which seemed to rattle Mom some. "I implored with you before we left to behave and give this dinner a chance. Why couldn't you just leave well enough alone?"

"I...didn't...want to," Mom retorted furiously. "Don't you dare mention chances here, Johnathan," she said, then turned to me. "Because I wasn't given one, was I, Anthony?" She threw up an arm angrily. "We came up here to New York to surprise you and instead we're surprised to find you with a black woman. Now we find out that you're going to have a bastard child her!" I clenched my teeth. "How can I pretend to support this ludicrous affair of yours when it's ripping this family apart? Is all of this worth it for a little piece of—"

"Yes, it is!" I interjected her vehemently. "How many times have I told you that I love her, Mom?" I didn't wait for her to answer and said, "I see now that I'm just going to have to show you this because...you are having a very hard time comprehending what I'm saying to you," I added quickly. I reached into my left jacket pocket for the box, took it out and held it in the air. "Here. See this? This is proof of my love for her and how serious I am about her." I slammed the box on the bar angrily. My peripheral vision showed Dad picking it up and and opening it.

"Oh!" Mom exclaimed, raising her arms. "There you have it, Johnathan," she said, giving him a momentary glance. "Proof that

that girl is a trouble maker. She's gotten pregnant on purpose so he'd feel obligated to marry her. He's falling right into her plans." She shook her head at me. "How gullible can you be, Anthony? Don't you see that she's using you?"

Was she serious? I cocked my head to the side to peer at her, ready to spring my trap to see how far she was willing to go.

"You really think she's using me?"

"Of course, she is," she said with a mock chuckle. "She's a gold-digger that wants to get her hands on the family fortune. I've seen it happen so many times, Anthony. Girls see rich available guys, they go out and sleep with them. Then miraculously, they get pregnant. C'mon! It's a game! She doesn't love you."

I sat there sickened by my mother's twisted notions of Lacie and offended that she'd think I'd be so naive. "Uh-huh. What do you think I should do?"

Her eyes lit up. "Make her get an abortion," she said without missing a beat.

I glanced at Dad quickly and saw that he had the same expression—the one that said that she had to be out of her mind.

"Really?"

"But of course." Her eyes widened and a large smile came on her face fast. "I know a good place where the procedure can be done…"

Thunderstruck, I stood and moved toward the few feet to the living room to distance myself from her. I stared at the fireplace while she continued her speech.

"…our friends will be appalled if this gets out. This has to be done promptly and quietly, so there won't be any evidence of this little faux pas of yours. The family won't be disgraced and you can go on with your experimentation. But marrying this girl, Anthony…is definitely out of the question," she asserted with confidence.

I turned around slowly as everything came to light. Dad just stared at Mom in mortification with his mouth wide open.

"Mom…you actually believe that I would go along with this? That I would want to get rid of my child?"

She tilted her head to the side and replied with a disturbingly persuasive tone. "Anthony, son…it's the only way to handle this. This is a terrible, terrible mistake—"

I narrowed my eyes. "You're calling my child a mistake?"

She took a breath. "Technically, it's just a fetus — tissue–"

"It's my child!" I roared with outrage, looking at her in disbelief. "My God, Mom! Do you hear what you're saying? Have you been listening to any blasted word that I've said?" I pointed to the door effectively. "I love that woman, I *am* going to marry her and her being pregnant makes it that much better."

She was slightly shaken, but held her ground. "Anthony, what kind of hold does this girl whom you claim to love so much, have over you? Is the sex really that good for you to ignore advice from your family? From your own mother? The people who've known you all of your life. Why can't you see that we are concerned about you?"

I scoffed. "This isn't about concern and you know it. It's about control, Mom. All of my life and throughout all of our lives, you've had some sense of control and say so over what we do and how we live."

"It's called preservation, Anthony. I don't apologize for it."

"No. You've not been very good at apologies lately, have you?" I uttered sarcastically. "The only thing you continue to see is Lacie's color. You haven't even tried to get to know her. No attempt at all. Nothing. Just don't care at all about how I feel or how very important she is to me." I shook my head sadly. "Well, you know what, Mom? I've made a decision and I'm sticking to it. There's nothing you can say to convince me otherwise."

"Anthony, I implore you. Do not…do this. Why are you trying to hurt us? This is going to bring so much shame to this family. She's not worth it," she pleaded. "You can do so much better with another girl."

"He doesn't want another girl, Abigail. Why are you being so irrational?" Dad asked strongly.

She turned to him swiftly. "I just cannot accept my son being with a black woman. He's worth more than that!"

378

I looked at her in incredulity. "When did you become so prejudiced?"

"When my white son brought shame to this family by bringing a black gold-digger home, that's when," she shot back.

I shot her a steel glare. "Mom, that ring *will* go on her finger tonight. I *will* marry Lacie and there's not a damn thing you can do about it."

"You are sorely mistaken," she countered, sucking in her breath and letting it out. "I'm letting you know now, Anthony, that if you continue to see this woman or even attempt to marry her, I will disown you. I will not attend your wedding and furthermore you will be cut off from the family fortune."

"You're not going to do that, Abigail. I won't allow it!" Dad bellowed going over to her.

"Yes, I am and you know you can't stop me Johnathan," she declared, her eyes never leaving mine. "Butt out!"

"You're threatening me — giving me an ultimatum. Is that it?" I asked with a penetrating stare. "What was all that jargon about you looking out for my best interests?"

She stuck out her chin with watering eyes, but her stance was unwavering. "I am."

Our eyes never left each other as we stood our ground. The saddest and most agonizing few seconds of my life was at hand. My mother was making me decide between her and Lacie. The sick part was that she actually thought she was doing this for my welfare, when it was nothing but her self-centeredness, fear and ignorance behind it.

Mother. It hurt to say the word and I couldn't believe that it had come to this.

I took my eyes off her and looked at Dad with a final nod. "Dad… make sure the door is locked when you two leave." With a fleeting look at my mother, who's eyes had widened in shock, I uttered, "Good-bye, Mom." I walked swiftly to the bar, grabbed the box and then headed to the front door.

"Anthony, if you go out that door, I will make good on my promise. You won't get one dime of my inheritance. Do you hear me?

Not one di–"

With a cool glance over my shoulder, I retorted, "As if I need it!" before I walked out and slammed the door.

She was my mother, but I was not to be bullied.

# Chapter 70

# Lacie

Tony looked awful.

His hair was tousled and his eyes were red as he leaned against the doorway with his hands shoved deep in his pockets.

"Hey, you," he whispered.

"Hey. I've been worrying about you ever since you left," I said. "How did everything go with your parents?" I stepped aside to let him in.

He sighed. "Not good," he said, strolling into the living room. "I've been driving around the city, just trying to calm down from everything." He stopped in the middle of the living room and turned to look at me. "How are you feeling?"

I shrugged as I joined him. "Just stressing out over what happened at dinner. You know I'm not Lacie if I'm not stressing," I stated with a little smile.

He looked around casually. "Everyone else okay?"

"Yeah, everybody's fine and in their rooms. We're trying to get back to normal." I took a deep breath. "You want to tell me what happened?"

He gave me a brief synopsis of what happened and after, opened his arms wide with an unhappy grin. "So...I've been disinherited and my mother has disowned me."

"I'm so sorry." I winced, seeing his pain. "Tony, I'm so very sorry. I didn't want this to happen."

He replied with a grim smile. "Me either."

"I feel like I've started trouble between you and your mother."

"You haven't." He came up to me and took my hands in his. "But listen, I don't want to dwell on that right now," he replied, gazing at me intently with those blue green eyes of his. "I want to know why you didn't tell me that you were pregnant when you first found out." I gulped. "Why did I have to find it out the way I did? I'd have liked to have been told in a different way. Not by your mother while she's arguing with my mother. I thought we were closer than that."

"We were. I mean we are," I corrected quickly. I grumbled with frustration. "Ugh! Look, Tony, I didn't know how to tell you or when to tell you," I hunched up my shoulders. "I had to come to terms with the idea myself and I was worried about how you were going to handle the news. Despite what Mama, Daddy, Reneé, Carrie and Dawn said, I–"

"Wait a minute, here," he interrupted softly. "You mean, they all knew and I didn't? And *I'm* the father?"

I glared at him incredulously, releasing one of my hands from his grip to put it on my hip. "Tony, it's not like we've really talked about children—or marriage." He raised an eyebrow and I stumbled to rephrase my words quickly. "Not...not that I wa...want...to marry you or anything because I can raise this child myself. I'm perfectly capable of–"

"So...you don't want to marry me?"

I felt my face getting flushed and I struggled to find the words. "I...I...that's not what I'm saying–"

"So...you do want to marry me?" he pressured.

Was it getting hot in here or was it me? And why was he smiling?

"I...I...I'm not saying tha–"

"What are you saying?"

"Will you give me a chance to answer?" I barked at him, annoyed.

"I've given you plenty of time to answer but you keep fumbling over your words," he teased. "Here, let me make it easier for you," he stated calmly. He got on one knee while he continued holding my left hand.

"Tony, what are you doing?"

"Shh! Will you be quiet and let me do this right?"

"Do what right?" I frowned as he reached into his coat pocket. "Tony, I was trying to explain–"

"Woman, please. Quiet!" he commanded, taking a square shaped, royal blue, suede box out. I sucked in a breath when he opened it to reveal the largest diamond I'd ever seen in my life. "Lacie, will you do me the honor of marrying me?"

My answer got stuck on my tongue as I gawked at the huge stone.

"Lacie?"

I managed to get some words out while still fixating on the rock in front of me. "T...T...Tony...if this is some twisted way of you trying to get back at your mother or if you're just asking me because I'm pregnant—I'm not the one. I don't want you to ask me if that's what you're doing."

"What?" he asked, giving me an incredulous look. "Is that what you think?"

I stuck out my chin. "Well, you sure didn't ask me before. With you finding out that I'm pregnant and after that disaster of a dinner, do you blame me for thinking that way?"

He looked at me in bafflement. "Lacie, do you know what time it is? It's almost eleven o'clock. How am I going to get a ring at this hour?" he asked. "I bought it way before I knew you were pregnant and way before this dinner even happened."

Feeling a little foolish, I gulped and hunched my shoulders. "When...exactly...did you get it?"

"Are you kidding me? You're actually going to interrogate me while I'm on my knee? I'm asking you the most important question in my life!"

"Yes, because I want to know."

I wanted to laugh at the look on his face as he gritted his teeth and replied. "I bought it last weekend in Connecticut."

I sucked in a surprised breath and started tearing immediately. "You did?" I asked tenderly. "When you went to that shop?"

"Yes, honey," he replied with emotion.

I gazed down at him with my tears dropping onto his coat and put my hand under his chin. "Tony...are you sure about this? Babe, I don't want to be a burden or for you to regret—"

He cut me off swiftly and looked up at me with watery eyes. "Lacie, I've never been sure of anything in my life and you will *never* be a burden to me, babe. You are…heaven sent. I cannot imagine my life without you. My God, how I love you and I'm so happy that we are going to have a baby."

"You are?"

He replied with a nod. "Yes! Now will you marry me…damn it?" he asked, chuckling.

I could hardly see through the rainfall of tears as every emotion came over me. I replied tearfully, "Yes! Yes! Yes! I'll marry you!" I started giggling hysterically as he slipped the ring onto my finger. "Oh, my God, Tony. This is so beautiful," I remarked, putting a hand to my chest.

He stood up and cupped my face with his hands and kissed me passionately. "I love you, Lacie," he said, coming up for air. "I… love ….you! And I can't wait for you to be my wife," he said.

"Baby, I can't wait either," I agreed, kissing him again.

There we were just laughing and hugging and kissing each other in the living room- in complete bliss.

Then we heard, "What in John Brown's name is all of that ruckus down there?" Mama shouted. She and Reneé were leaning over the upstairs balcony looking down at us.

We heard Daddy come out of his room to inquire also.

We smiled at each other and shouted in unison, "We're getting married!"

Mama's eyes widened and then she and Reneé screamed and hurried down the stairs. Daddy said, "Hot damn!" and clapped his hands together as he came over instantly to grip Tony and slap him on the back.

Mama and Reneé took my hand and marveled at my ring when they came into the living room. I looked at Tony as he and Daddy started talking and he winked at me. All I could do was smile.

Tony had chosen me — despite his mother's wishes.

At the time, it might have seemed somewhat selfish to be so happy, knowing that Tony had basically forsaken his mother for me.

But hey…I was worth it.

# Chapter 71

# Dawn

I didn't know how I was going to tell Lacie now.

When Tony saw me in Joe's apartment, all I wanted to do was crawl under a rock. Joe, on the other hand, was bitter and defensive. He felt that Tony was a hypocrite for pointing fingers at us because of that whole thing with him and Lacie.

Honestly, I had to agree with Tony. We were wrong—dead wrong, but Joe couldn't see that. I'd tried to tell him just as much, but he wasn't too happy about it. As a result and because we were both upset with each other and at being caught red-handed, we got into a little tiff. The mood had been broken and I asked him to take me to my mother's. Really, all I wanted was to get away from him.

Going to Mom's was a big mistake. All she said was, "Umm, hmm. What's done in the dark God always brings into light." My mother's favorite sayings — and in my case, very true.

With all of these events taking place, I'd mustered enough courage to visit Lacie on Sunday afternoon and tell her. First, I had to find out how dinner went so I would know how to tell her.

*"Whaaaat?" I exclaimed, after she'd pulled me in the apartment with a strong tug. Then she flashed the fattest diamond I'd ever seen in my face. "Oh, my God! Oh, my God!" I screamed and then we started jumping and squealing and hugging like schoolgirls.*

*"I know, girl. I know!" Lacie gushed, brushing happy tears from her eyes. "Isn't this the biggest rock you've ever seen?"*

*"Girl, it's a boulder!" I declared, taking her hand and bringing it closer to my face. "Wh...when did Tony propose?"*

*"Girl, last night. He got down on his knee and with the most tender expression asked me to marry him. C'mon, c'mon, sit down. I've got to*

*tell you this, girl," she managed to say amidst uncontrollable laughter as she ushered me to the living room sofa. "He knows about the baby." she said, plopping down next to me.*

"Whaaat?"

*She nodded and giggled. "Yeah, girl, that's right."*

"How did you tell him? How did he react?"

*"Well, how he found out is a long story," she said, laughing. "Actually, it's quite funny. But oh, Dawn, when he proposed! Girl, you should have seen us. We were all emotional and crying and laughing and all that."*

*A thought came to mind.* "Now wait a minute, Lacie. Are you sure that he only asked you because you're pregnant?" *That was really stupid, Dawn.*

*"Girl, no," Lacie replied excitedly. "I mean, that's what I thought at first, too. But it turns out that he'd gotten the ring when we were in Connecticut!"*

"Isn't that something," *I remarked with amusement for a second. Then I urged,* "Look, tell me what happened at dinner with his parents."

*"Oh, it was bad," replied Lacie easily. "Child, Mama was about to pour gravy on Tony's mother if Daddy hadn't stopped her."*

"Whaat?"

*"Mmm, hmmm. Sure was," Lacie said. "Girl, it was a scene!" Lacie laughed. "Woo! Miss Abigail showed her tail and Mama was getting ready to get into it, too. You should have seen it, girl. There was Daddy and Reneé, with her big belly, holding Mama off and Tony's dad, Johnathan, holding off Abigail.*

"Where were you and Tony?"

*"Here in the living room. Tony was trying to find out why I hadn't told him I was pregnant after Mama had blurted it in front of his parents. Then, girl, guess what?"*

"What?"

*"His Mama rushed up to me, girl. She came up to me and tried to shake me and told me that I had to get rid of the baby!"*

*I gasped.* "No, she didn't!

*"Yes, Dawn, yes," she exclaimed, taking a breath. "But Tony held her off and then Johnathan pulled her out of there and they all left. Girl, it was a trip!"*

*"Whoa, girl, you really went through!"*

*"Huh, me and everyone else," Lacie said.*

*"You really are taking this well," I remarked.*

*"Remember, this is the day* after *everything has happened," Lacie chuckled. "Dawn, I was so worried about everything, you know? I mean, I was really not happy with myself and about being pregnant. You know about my concerns about Abigail. But now, it's a new day. Things have come full circle and I'm deliriously happy because I'm marrying the man I've been in love with ever since September."*

*"It's about time," I said, then I looked around the apartment. "Lacie, where is everyone?"*

*"Tony took Daddy to lunch and Mama and Reneé went to an afternoon program at church. Rose went with them, too."*

*I'd just started thinking that this would be the perfect time to talk to her since we were alone, when I heard my mother's name. I gulped. "Oh."*

*Lacie continued. "I guess Tony and Daddy wanted to get that father and son to be son-in-law talk down. You know how that is," she chuckled, with a sigh. Then she looked at me and smiled. "You know, Dawn, despite last night, I really think things are going to work out. I mean, I just feel so happy. You know?"*

*She really wasn't making it easy for me to tell her.*

*I took a deep breath and started with, "Uh...Lacie...I...I...came by because I wanted to tell you so–"*

*She interrupted me by coming closer and putting her hand in mine. "Yeah, and I'm glad you came by. We haven't had much time to talk to each other and I wanted to ask...if you'd be my maid of honor?"*

*Why did she have to ask me that?* Because you're supposed to be her best friend, remember?

*I swallowed hard and said, "Huh?"*

*She slapped my hand playfully and mimicked me, "Huh? Is that all you have to say?" she asked, leaning back and eyeing me with a raised eyebrow. "Dawn, don't act so surprised, girl. You know how much I love you and you know that we always said that we'd be each other's maid of honor whenever one of us got married. Don't you remember?"*

Yeah…I remembered.

*"Are you gonna do it or what?" she asked.*

*She was staring at me very closely so I put on a fake smile and answered,* "Sure, Lacie, girl, you know I've got your back."

Dawn, don't ever say that again.

*"Great! Whew, girl!" Lacie said. "For a second there, I thought you were going to say, 'no'."*

*I sure was thinking it.*

After that conversation, the opportunity to tell Lacie was gone.

Lacie was in such high spirits and I couldn't spoil her joy just like that. I don't think anyone could have. I was a backstabber, but I wasn't insensitive.

My guilt-ridden complex grew even more when everyone came back to the apartment — at the same time. Lacie and Miss Josephine started fixing dinner while the rest of us were in the living room. Everyone talked and laughed animatedly about the engagement whenever Lacie and Miss Josephine would come out of the kitchen for a few moments. But I couldn't get into it. It didn't help either when I'd make eye contact with Mom or Tony and when each managed to pull me to the side.

*"I see you didn't tell her," Mom complained. "What happened? I thought you said today was the day?"*

*"Mom, I tried," I snapped in return. "I was just about to tell her when you all decided to show up. How could I, with all of this excitement and you all around?"*

*"That's no excuse, Dawn," she said and walked away.*

*I just rolled my eyes.*

*"When are you planning to tell her?" Tony whispered a moment later, standing by the bathroom door as I came out.*

*I jumped in surprise. "Dag, Tony, you scared me."*

*"Sorry," he said quickly, glancing around the apartment. "When are you going to talk to her?"*

*"Well…Tony," I exasperated, narrowing my eyes at him. "I really couldn't do it today because you decided to pop the question and plant that boulder of a ring on her finger, now could I?" I huffed sarcastically.*

*He gave me a blank look. "You're trying to break bad on me, when you asked me to cover for you and hide this from Lacie?"*

*He had a point.*

*I sighed. "You're right, Tony. I apologize," I said. "I didn't mean to snap on you."*

*He waved it off with a wry expression and said, "It's okay. I know this must be eating you up inside." I nodded. "Yeah, me too." He took a deep breath. "Listen, just give me a heads up before. I'd like to be there for her when she finds out, okay?"*

*I appreciated that and was just about to say something when Lacie came around the corner and asked with a little smile, "Find out what?"*

*Tony and I gave each other nervous glances. Then, thinking quickly, I put my arm around her shoulders and said, "Oh, nothing, girl. Don't worry about it. I'll tell you later."*

*As I steered her away, I put one hand on my forehead. This lying was getting too easy.*

*I was such a Judas.*

Mom and I stayed for about thirty minutes after dinner and left for home. Ten minutes later, I was leaving to go see Joe.

"You still ain't learned your lesson, yet?" Mom asked, glowering at me as I strolled past her to the front door.

"Being in love makes people do stupid things," I explained with a shrug and opened the door.

"You got that right," she expressed, following me to the door.

"Bear with me, Mom," I said. I gave her a quick kiss on the cheek before I opened the door and said, "I love you."

I didn't look back when I got in the cab. I just had one goal in mind and that was to see Joe. Seeing him would be my alcohol, drug and therapy all in one.

Joe looked relieved when he opened his door. "Hey," Joe said softly. "I'm sorry, gorgeous. I'm so sorry." My eyes started watering at that moment and he studied me. "Did you tell Lacie?"

I sniffled. "I couldn't, Joe."

He sighed and opened his arms. "Come here."

The tears fell and I went into his arms, feeling the emotional pit of quicksand that I was in.

"How am I going to tell her, Joe?" I muttered with my face buried in his shoulder.

"I wish I had the answer for you, gorgeous. I really do," he soothed, embracing me tighter.

I did too.

*Chapter 72*

# Lacie

I was on cloud nine.

Even the congestion of the hustle and bustle of the morning rush on the trains as I went to work couldn't break my spirit.

That's how happy I was and it felt so good.

I strolled through my department cheerfully, greeting the few that had arrived with a bright smile and a 'good morning'. In response, there were some questioning glances and raised eyebrows as I strolled toward my office gaily.

A few minutes later, I was in my office, looking through some files in my file cabinet, barely realizing that I was humming, *You and I* by Stevie Wonder when I heard the door open and close. Tony handed me a bouquet of roses, kissed my neck and with his melodic voice, started singing the words in my ears.

"Mmm, good morning and thank you," I greeted, turning around. I took a whiff from the bouquet. "You know, when we get married, I hope you don't lose your romantic side."

He raised his brow and caressed my back. "Why do you say that?"

"Because you're really starting to spoil me and I don't want it to stop. These are beautiful!" I said, taking another whiff.

He chuckled. "You don't have to worry about me losing my romantic side—ever."

"I'd better not," I said. "Hey," I responded, giggling to his playful slap on my butt. "No kinky stuff until after we're married."

"Mmm, speaking of kinky," he replied, kissing me hungrily.

"Okay, down,,boy. Down," I laughed, pushing him away after a moment and looking at him pensively. "Listen, I just thought about something. How are we going to let everyone here know about us?"

He shrugged. "I don't know. Make an announcement, maybe…" he trailed off. We both shook our heads. "No, I agree with you."

Then we said, "Carrie."

"Perfect," Tony said with a small chuckle. "That's all settled," he said, leaning in to me with a devilish smile. "Now about that kinky stuff…"

"Tony?" I giggled.

"What, woman? Come on, now. The door's closed," he said, giving me a daring look. "What up? Not up for the challenge?" he teased.

"Oh, you're going to go there?" I raised my eyebrow. "Come here," I purred and pulled him by the tie and devoured his tongue.

Deep into the kiss, we didn't bother to stop when the door opened.

"Oh, c'mon! Get a room!"

Slightly embarrassed, we stopped and laughed at the sound of Carrie's voice.

"Carrie?" I scolded lightly. "Why didn't you knock?"

"Girl, please. I'm not worried about you two. Been there, done that and more than what you two have ever even thought of," she dismissed with a wave of her hand.

"Uh…good morning, Carrie." Tony cleared his throat, keeping his arm around my waist as he turned in Carrie's direction. Then he looked at me and we just started laughing again.

"Okay, okay," Carrie said, holding up a hand. "What's the joke? Let me in on it."

With a last little chuckle, Tony planted a kiss on my cheek and said, "I'll let you handle this one." He went over to the door to leave then stopped at the door abruptly. "Carrie, is Joe in his office?"

Carrie shook her head. "No, not yet. But he should be here any minute. You know how punctual he is."

He nodded. "Okay, I'll get with him, then." He winked at me and then looked at Carrie. "Carrie, how do you like the roses? They're gorgeous, aren't they?" he asked and walked out.

Carrie turned to me then looked at the roses and her eyes got wide. "Lacie…are you and Tony…?"

I giggled as I looked down and understood the reason for Carrie's expression. Tony had cleverly put the roses in my left hand where my engagement ring was. I responded with a wide smile and nodded.

"Married? You're getting married?!!!" Carrie exclaimed loudly.

Just as Tony and I'd thought, that did it. It was barely nine o'clock when Carrie had found out. By nine-fifteen, everyone in the whole building had heard the news.

Nothing but good came with the remainder of the day. So many people came to me and Tony, congratulating and wishing us the best. Word of my large diamond had traveled faster than the news of my engagement as throngs of women came in and out of my office. Eyes popped open in awe and I was besieged with questions about the wedding plans and so on. It was amazing how I was able to get through my meetings and get any work done as people continuously trickled in.

Among them was Trevor.

"So…Whitey popped the question, huh?" he drawled, leaning against the doorway of my office.

I glanced at my desk clock. It was fifteen minutes till five o'clock and he had to come in and try to spoil it.

I looked up at him and with a raised eyebrow replied, "No, *Tony* popped the question."

"Yeah, that's what I said," he said, ambling in casually. "What'd he do, knock you up?" he asked dryly.

Was he psychic?

"Is that any of your business?"

He shrugged, coming closer to the desk. "No…but it would explain all of the decaffeinated coffee you've been drinking and you looking so horrible for the past few mornings," he remarked.

I smiled with wonder. "Trevor," I said, opening my arms wide and then putting them on the desk. "Why…are you constantly all in my business? Why are you paying so much attention to what's going on in my life?"

He just grinned. "You still didn't answer my question."

"I don't have to," I spewed back, standing up to gather the documents on my desk.

"Ah...," he said with a satisfactory nod. "So you are pregnant." He tsked, tsked. "A mulatto in the family. Tony's Mama won't like that I'm sure."

Ouch! His statement was a painful reminder of the weekend. But I smiled anyway.

"Trevor, you know what?" I held up my hand so he could get a good look at my diamond ring and said, "Plaa-cow! That's what I've got to say to you and Tony's mother. This is symbolic of the love Tony and I share. I *am* going to marry Tony and we are going to be very happy. "

He grinned even wider. "Are you trying to convince me or you?" He chuckled and held up a hand to stop me from answering. "Don't answer that," he mocked. He turned around to leave. "By the way, nice big cubic-zirconia."

"No, diamond, man. Diamond, all right?" Tony retorted suddenly, coming in the door.

Trevor snickered and with a last fleeting look at me said, "Yeah, right. Whatever, man."

I went to get my coat. "Tony, don't pay any attention to him."

"I'm not," he said, walking over to help me with my coat.

"Good. I'm glad," I asserted, giving him a quick kiss on the cheek. "Listen, I noticed that you and Joe seem to be talking again. Did you get everything settled between you two?"

He nodded. "Yeah, we're cool. I told you, it wasn't anything for you to be worried about."

"I know, but I just didn't like seeing the tension between you two. You've been friends for a long time."

"We're still friends," he assured with a little pat on my behind. "Now, come, on. You ready?"

"Hey," I scolded lightly, pointing my finger at him. "I said the kinky stuff is not until we get married."

"Ummm, promises, promises," he countered with a chuckle.

Once Tony and I came to my apartment door, angry voices rang out. I looked at him and just sighed, tiredly.

Why was it that every time I left my own apartment, people were always arguing when I came back? I'd been having such a good day, too.

"Danny, you can't do this! I won't let you!" Reneé was yelling and crying hysterically when we came in.

"You don't think I won't? Just try me and see what happens!" he threatened loudly.

"Hey, hey, what is going on here?" I said, once Tony and I entered the living room hastily and stood between them. "Danny, what are you doing here?"

Reneé answered for him. "He's threatening to sue me for full custody. That's what!" she yelled tearfully. "He's trying to take my baby away from me!"

"What?" I exclaimed, swinging my head around to look at him in shock. "What?

Danny shook his head at Reneé. "You're not telling her the full story, Reneé," he protested. He looked at me. "I only said that because she said she wouldn't let me see the baby unless she wanted to."

"Reneé," I said, swinging my head sharply to look at her.

"That's right, I said, it!" she confirmed, eyes piercing into his. "You don't deserve to be a father to this baby! Not after the pain you've caused me," she said, putting a protective hand over her belly.

"That's my baby, too, Reneé!" Danny argued.

Oh, my goodness!

Tony and I looked at each other and nodded.

Tony took action. "Okay…Danny, it's time to go, man. C'mon, I'll take you home. You two aren't going to get anything solved tonight— not like this." He slapped him on the back lightly and started leading him toward the door. "C'mon, man. It's cool."

Danny hesitated for a second, keeping a furious eye on Reneé.

"Go on, Danny. I'll talk to her. It's going to be all right," I urged, nodding toward the door.

"Don't bet on it!" Reneé shouted at his back as he retreated.

"Reneé...if you don't be quiet," I threatened softly.

Danny turned back around and looked at her with a frown before he walked out the door. Tony blew me a kiss before closing the door.

Reneé broke down and covered her face with her hands once the door shut. I just looked at her sadly as I rubbed her back.

Finally, I asked. "I guess I don't have to tell you that you were wrong, do I?" She shook head. "Okay...good. 'Cause I'd really thought you'd lost it for a minute." I sighed. "Oh, come here. Come here. It's going to be all right," I soothed, hugging her. When she'd almost composed herself, I leaned back and asked, "Hey, let's order Chinese and have some good old fashioned girl talk. You down for that?"

She nodded tearfully. "Yeah. Mama and Mason went out to the movies anyway, so they'll be out for a bit," she told me.

"Movies?" I asked, stunned. "Together?"

"Yep...together," she sniffled.

Well, I'll be.

ℰℭ

It was déjà vu as Reneé and I sat in the living room pigging out on Chinese.

"Reneé, remember the first time we broke bread like this? You weren't even pregnant then. You'd imposed yourself on me and wouldn't leave my house," I chuckled.

"Oh, don't even," she replied. "You know you enjoyed having me for company."

"Yeah," I nodded meditatively. "That's true. But you're still a pain, though," I teased, pointing my finger at her.

"Whatever," she said, rolling her eyes.

"Now...time for the elephant in the room," I started with a deep breath.

"I already know what you're going to say, Lacie."

"Oh, really?" I raised my eyebrow. "Okay, enlighten me, then."

She breathed in. "You were going to say, that I shouldn't have threatened Danny," she started.

"Okay...go on," I urged, taking a shrimp from my shrimp and broccoli meal.

"And that he is the father and he has as much rights as I do," she finished.

"Ummm... not bad," I murmured. "You're learning, you're learning." I peered at her and smiled. "You're still in love with him, aren't you?"

"Yeah...doggone it!" she scolded herself, looking at me. "I wish I didn't."

"I know, honey. I know," I soothed. "But...as you know from my own experience...we can't always help who we fall in love with. Sometimes that can be good or bad — depending on the situation." I shook my head. "But dangling that child in Danny's face though, honey, was not the mature way to handle your differences. If he wants to go, fine. Let him go. But let him be a father to his child. Don't deny him that. There are so many black men who aren't in their children's lives. And Danny wants to be. That's something that's unfortunately very rare so take advantage of it. It shouldn't be rejected."

She was holding her head down and picking her food with her fork. "Yeah...you're right."

"Hey," I said with a comforting smile. "Why don't you go upstairs and talk things out with him? Straighten everything out while it's still fresh," I suggested.

She made a face. "Do I have to?"

I shrugged. "Hey, you don't *have* to do anything. But should you?" I nodded. "I believe you already know the answer to that question."

She squinted at me. "You're tricky, you know that?"

I blew on my fist and rubbed it on my blouse. "Yes, I know this."

I laughed when Reneé rolled her eyes and struggled to get up from the sofa to go upstairs. She would do the right thing, I knew.

I stood and gathered the empty Chinese cartons off the living room table and headed to the kitchen. When I came back for the rest of the trash, the doorbell rang. Thinking it was Mama and Daddy and that Mama had probably forgotten her key, I hasted to the door, ready to tease them about their little excursion. I was completely thrown by the person in front of me when I opened it.

Abigail Douglas.

Damn!

# Chapter 73

# Tony

I chuckled softly as I listened to Danny talk non-stop about Reneé when I was driving him home.

He was still in love with her. When I'd called him out on it, he balked and denied it—a clear sign that he still had feelings for her. Like most guys who'd been caught cheating with another girl, while really still in love with their girlfriend, he'd gotten himself in a jam. Now tenacious pride hindered him from getting out of the jam he'd wished he'd never gotten into.

I could identify with him slightly. I'd gotten into a jam also and had to wait on others before I could get out of it. I thought of the conversation I had with Joe when he walked into my office this morning.

*"What up, man?" he muttered, after knocking on my open door.*

*I looked up and was surprised that he'd come to me first. He'd always been the stubborn one.*

*"Hey, man. What's up?" I asked, standing up.*

*He walked in slowly and stood in the middle of the office. Both of us eyed one another, holding our own. After a good minute of tight silence, he held out his arms wide and put them down in defeat.*

*"All right, look, Tony. I'm sorry," he said with a sigh. "You were right, I was wrong. You had every right to chew me out on Friday," he muttered.*

*"Naw, Joe, I'm sorry too," I said. "Maybe I shouldn't have come over your house unannounced, breakin' bad on you like that. Perhaps I was being a hypocrite," I offered.*

*He waved his hand. "C'mon, man, you're talkin' crazy. You know you can come over anytime and…" Another sigh. "You're not a hypocrite. I was just mad at you and at myself, really. That's why I called you out.*

*You know we squashed that whole thing with Lacie a while ago. So don't sweat it."*

I nodded with a relieved smile and walked over to offer my hand. "So…are we cool or what?"

He smiled in return. "Of course, man. You crazy?" he chuckled as we gripped and embraced each other. After, he said, "Man, I'm glad we got that straight."

"Me, too," I said. "But we still have…"

"I know… Lacie," he finished. "This is a tough situation, Tony. I mean, Dawn came over my house bawling last night because she couldn't bring herself to tell her."

"Well…" I winced, making a face. "As she so eloquently put it, I didn't make it very easy for her."

"Why? What's up?"

"I asked Lacie to marry me, Joe" I said, not being able to contain the huge grin on my face.

"What?" he laughed, giving me another grip. "Are you for real?"

"Yeah, man." I chuckled. "And guess what? I'm gonna be a dad, man."

"What? Lacie's pregnant?" Joe asked a little too quickly.

I paused and asked perceptively, "You already knew, didn't you?"

He hunched his shoulders with a guilty grin. "Yeah… I did. Dawn told me when Lacie called her and told her."

"I should have known," I said, shaking my head with a smile.

"So how do you feel about this, man? You're engaged and getting ready to be a father. I mean that's huge, man. You ready for that?"

"Joe, honestly, I believe I was ready the moment I met Lacie."

"Really?"

"Yeah, man." I shrugged. "I can't explain it. I love her that much and ain't no other woman ever bit me like she has."

"I feel you. I feel you." He nodded. "So how do your folks feel about it?"

I shook the pain off. "My dad's cool about it, but my mom's tripping out." I shook my head. "You should have seen her, man. My parents ate dinner over Lacie's house and my mom straight flipped." I sighed.

"Yo, man, I'm sorry about that," Joe said.

"Joe, I'm marrying the woman I plan to spend the rest of my life with and there ain't a damn thing to be sorry about."

He said in wonder. "I can't believe it. My partner's getting married. Umm, Ummm, Umm. Hangin' up your player's hat. Such a shame," he teased.

"Man, what're you talkin' about? Yours is falling off your head as we speak," I shot back.

He laughed and nodded. "You're right. Dawn's got me. She really has."

"I hear you, man. Lacie's got me too and I'm never letting her go. Believe that." I blew hard. "That's why Dawn has to hurry up and tell Lacie, man. Because I hate this. Me lying to her and all that."

"You're not lying to her," Joe offered.

"But I'm not telling her either," I objected. "That's just as bad. When I had my suspicions about you and Dawn, she asked me straight up what was wrong and I didn't tell her. The brew we'd just had piqued her curiosity even more. I didn't tell her then, either." I shook my head. "No, man. I can't keep this up."

"You're right. But to let you know, Dawn's planning on coming here tomorrow to invite Lacie to lunch. She's gonna tell her then."

"Good. So are we all gonna go out together or what? I've got to be there with Lacie when this goes down."

"Yeah, man, that's cool. I think that's a good idea," he agreed, thoughtfully. "But look, man. We can't let Trevor know where we're going because he already knows about me and Dawn. He almost let it out at lunch that time and I'm sure he'd take the opportunity to do it again." He took a deep breath. "If Lacie finds out from him, it's not going to be pretty. She's a black woman and being one, I wouldn't be surprised if she got to cuttin'," he joked.

"Thank, Joe. That really makes me feel better," I uttered sarcastically. Then, "What makes you so sure that Trevor might do it again?"

With a mischievous look, he said, "All I'm going to say is that I'm on to something."

"What? You're just gonna leave me hangin'?"

*"Got too, man—too many ears around here. I'll holla about it with you tomorrow. All right?" he asked, starting to walk out the door.*

*"All right, cool," I said, frowning at his retreating figure thoughtfully. Then I thought of something, "Hey, Joe?"*

*"What up?" he asked easily, stopping to turn around.*

*"I forgot to ask you if you'd be my best man."*

*"Tony, you didn't even have to ask," he answered with a smile.*

*Joe turned and walked out. Right after he did, Trevor stopped in front of the door, looked directly at me, and then walked by with a huge smirk on his face.*

*He'd probably heard every word of our conversation.*

I drove my car into the underground parking lot of my apartment building and pulled into my parking spot and sat pensively. What was Joe not telling me? Did he have something on Trevor? It was a couple of minutes before I shrugged it off and got out my car.

I didn't know what was going on. What I did know, was that I didn't want Lacie to get hurt and if Trevor said anything to her before Dawn, Joe or myself, then I was gonna clock him.

And I meant it.

# Chapter 74

# Lacie

It took an extreme amount of will power for me not to slam the door in her face. Her only saving grace was that she was Tony's mother.

"Is there something I can do for you, Mrs. Douglas?" I asked with mock politeness.

Standing erect with a demure expression, she was dressed from head to toe in expensive business garb.

"May I come in?" she asked with a slight nod. "I'd like to talk to you."

I put one hand on my hip and gave her a good once over pensively. "I think we've had our share of 'talking' don't you, Mrs. Douglas?" I replied.

"We've talked, but I don't think we've accomplished anything," she said. "Matter of fact, I know we haven't. So please, may I come in?"

Did she actually say the word 'please' to me? I cocked my head to the side and studied her before I moved out of the way for her to enter. I couldn't help but feel as if I'd just let Dracula into my domain and had giving him direct access to my neck. I put a hand to my neck self-consciously and followed her into the living room.

"Okay...what is it that you want to talk about?" I asked, folding my arms. I watched her eyes gaze over the paper bags, plastic cups and plates on the table. I swore inwardly, mad that she'd just picked this particular moment to come when I hadn't even finished cleaning.

Finishing her thorough sweep of my living room, she turned around slowly with a grave expression. "Anthony is very angry with me," she said.

*You think, Abigail?*

With a confounded expression, she sat down. I halfway didn't appreciate that because I hadn't told her to.

"He's never been this upset with me before," she continued.

*There's a first time for everything, Abigail.*

I was just about to sit down when she got up abruptly and walked over to the large window.

*Okay...I'll stand up too, Abigail.*

"Together, Johnathan and I have raised five children. We've traveled all over the world together, exploring new places. It was quite difficult at times because we moved around so much and the children never really had a foundation—something to call home. Still, we've always remained close." She glanced over her shoulder fleetingly at me, then turned back to the window. "I shouldn't say this, but out of all my children, Anthony is my favorite. Yes, he is the baby in the family, but..." she put a finger to her lips. "there was something so very special about him when he was born. He started walking and talking at six months, reading at three and could sing...." She put her hand to her chest. "....like an angel."

I listened patiently as she reminisced over Tony and all of his accomplishments from grade school to high school. She continued on while I waited for her to explain why she'd come. She didn't.

With respect, I waited for her to pause and then queried, "Uh... Mrs. Douglas, you still haven't told me what you wanted to talk about. Why are you here?"

Her face was stoic when she turned around. "I'm here because I need your help."

"My help?" I asked her dubiously, pointing a finger to my chest.

"Yes." She nodded. "I need you to help me keep my family together."

"I don't follow."

"I want you to break up with my son," she stated seriously.

"What?"

C'mon, Lacie, you should have sensed that when she came. She didn't come for reconciliation.

She nodded her head with a blank expression. "Yes. I need you to break up with Anthony. My family is being torn apart. My husband and I aren't speaking to each other, Jessica is upset with me and now my Anthony will not even pick up the phone when I call." She narrowed her eyes at me. "All…because of you."

I took a deep breath. "Mrs. Douglas…the problem is not me. It's you." She shook her head, stubbornly. "Yes, you," I insisted. "You have some gall to blame me for your shortcoming in this matter. You're the one that's holding on to this unbending prejudice that's hindering you from seeing how much in love Tony and I are. If you would just open your eyes and accept what my relationship with Tony is—undying love."

With eyes watering, she said, "No. That's not what it is."

"It's not?" I raised my eyebrow along with my hand that had the fat rock on it. "Then why did Tony ask me to marry him?"

Her lips tightened. "Because you are…pregnant. That's the only reason. You tricked him."

I wasn't perturbed. "Really?" I scoffed. "I wasn't the only one in his bedroom, you know. He did have a part in it."

She responded with a thin grin. "His part is going to be over."

I narrowed my eyes at her. "Excuse me?"

Within an instant, she pulled a check out of her purse and held it up with one hand so I could see. I just stared at her, not immediately comprehending what she was doing.

"This…is a blank check," she stated. "Write whatever amount you want on it. Cash it, abort this baby, take the rest and walk away."

*No she didn't.* I rolled my eyes upward in irate disbelief. Here we go with this simple soap opera bull-

"I'll pay whatever—" she continued.

"You actually think that I'd take your money and get rid of this baby?" I cut her off. "Lady, your screws are loose," I said, pointing a finger to my head. "You really are." I looked at her incredulously. "You must really feel threatened by me for you to go to such extreme and absurd lengths. This also means that you *do* know how much your son loves me. That's what scares you. Tony is happy with me. He loves me and chose to be with me, in spite of what you told me that weekend.

**405**

He made you look like a complete idiot and you can't stand that."

She strolled over to me slowly like a lioness, steady, stalking and ready to pounce on her prey. "No, what I can't stand, is you. I want you out of my son's life—period. As I was saying, before you rudely interrupted me. I'll pay whatever you want. Just get out of Anthony's life!"

I sneered at her defiantly. "Lady, I'm not going anywhere. I'm going to marry your son and I *will* have this child. Bet on it."

It was her turn for a raised eyebrow. "Are you challenging me?"

"I didn't stutter," I retorted.

She folded her arms and leaned her head to the side. It was a shame but she looked just like her son then.

"Do you want Anthony to be disinherited?"

I shook my head adamantly. "I didn't make that decision, you did."

"Do you want to see the constant hurt and pain on Anthony's face because he no longer has the kind of relationship with his mother or his family that he loved so much?"

I knew where she was going but was determined not to let her get to me. "Like I said. I didn't make that decision. You did."

"Do you want Anthony to be jeered and back lashed by his peers because he's with you? Do you want him to be frustrated because he can't deal with the discrimination he will face by being with you?"

Her words were starting to sting. "He's been dealing with it thus far."

"What about your child? Do you want him to have an identity crisis for the rest of his life? To be tormented and ridiculed at school and not accepted from either race because he's not considered white or black?"

Cringing, I just frowned at her with no comeback and she gave me a satisfied grin.

"Hit a nerve?" she asked. "I thought it would."

Fed up with her insults and her taunts, I came up to her closely, but stopped just a few feet away from her and asserted with seething animosity, "*Abigail*, I have respected you above and beyond what you deserve. Just because you are Tony's mother, I have dealt with your bitterness, your cruelty and your racist remarks. But now I'm pissed and I don't give a damn anymore. Get out of my house before I throw you out! Get out!" I stressed my point even further by moving aside and pointing toward the door. I didn't care if I was kicking my fiancé's mother out. I just wanted her butt gone.

With a smirk, Abigail walked past me to the coffee table and placed the blank check on it. Then she strolled slowly toward the front door.

I didn't even turn around as she said, "I told you before that I'm a realist. All that I have said just a minute ago can become a tragic reality...for you, my son, and this unborn baby. If you truly love Anthony, then you will abort this baby and this relationship. Let him have his *real* life back."

I was so glad that the lump in my throat waited until after she slammed the door to form into tears and trickle down my face.

Amazing—two strikes in one day.

I wondered when the third was coming.

*Chapter 75*

# Tony

"I've got bad news," Joe said after he'd knocked on my door early Tuesday morning.

I frowned. "What's up, Joe?"

When he closed the door, I knew it was serious.

He walked up to my desk and with a deep breath said, "Our contractor is MIA, man."

"Say what!" I exclaimed, immediately standing up at the news.

"Yep," he said with a forlorn nod. "Gone. Vanished. Not a trace left."

Perceptively, I uttered, "And all that money is…"

"Gone with him," he confirmed grimly.

"Oh, hell!" I exclaimed, running an angry hand through my hair.

"That's what I said too, man."

Mind racing, I asked, "Richard and William know?"

"Not yet. I just found out and came to you."

I scoffed and looked at him shrewdly. "You already had an idea this was going to go down, didn't you? This was what you were going to tell me yesterday."

He hunched up his shoulders. "I had my suspicions Dude was dirty…"

"Why didn't you tell me, man?" I interrupted.

"I didn't have the facts, Tony. We were going to need to have our guns ready if we were going to dispute this contractor. You should know that from the trick Trevor pulled on us at the meeting and with how ecstatic Richard and William were. We couldn't go in there half–"

"Yeah, yeah, yeah, I know. You're right." I murmured grudgingly. "What tipped you on it?"

"This whole bid's been irking me ever since it went down and needless to say, I didn't appreciate the way Trevor flipped on me and Dawn at lunch that time. Matter of fact, it pissed me off and so… the results," he said, flopping a report on my desk.

I picked up the report and flipped through it while he waited. My eyes bulged at what I read.

"This is bad, Joe. How in the hell did this get overlooked?" I looked up at him quickly, then back at the report. "I mean, this contractor's got an armload of grievances and lawsuits pending against him." I shook my head. "Heads are going to roll because of this, man."

"Yep and Lacie may be one of them…" he added.

"…because she signed off on the bid first," I finished. "Damn!" I threw the report down on my desk.

"Look, man," Joe said hastily. "We might be able to resolve this. We find the man. We find the money."

"Easier said than done," I said. "It's hard to find someone if they don't want to be found — especially if they're carrying millions of dollars."

"Still, it can also make them an easy target," he suggested. "Spending habits always make for an easy mark." I just stared at him blankly, understanding the hidden meaning. He shrugged with a mischievous smirk. "Hey, what can I say? The streets are still in me."

I took a deep breath and glanced at my watch. "Look, before we go to any extremes, we need to have a private meeting with Richard and William — fast." I shook my head when he was about to speak. "I know Lacie's not here yet, but we can't waste time." I started toward the door with him on my heels. "It's millions of dollars missing and we've got to find it."

I just hoped we could—for everyone's sake.

# Chapter 76

# Lacie

There were strange pains in my side and my head was throbbing when I woke up.

Last night I'd forgotten to set the alarm and now I was already an hour behind schedule for work. But for the first time in a long while, I wasn't concerned.

Abigail's words and her sordid attempt at bribery never left my mind since last night. They were still there when I entered the office building.

Mama and Daddy had walked in the door about fifteen minutes after she'd left.

*Mama immediately asked, "Was that Abigail I saw getting in a limousine outside?" while Daddy helped her with her coat.*

*Smoothly, I picked up the blank check and put it into my pocket. "Yeah, that was her," I muttered.*

*My parents stopped, looked at me, and then at each other.*

*Mama frowned. "What'd that witch come here for?"*

*"A peace offering."*

*"Peace offering?" Mama repeated, walking over to me.*

*I took a deep breath. "Yep."*

*"Mmm, hmm," Mama uttered. "Very timely that she happened to come when your dad and I weren't here. What was that that you put in your pocket?"*

*"Nothing, Mama," I lied. "Just trash." I just stared at the door fixated after Daddy had walked away from it and joined us in the living room.*

*"You okay, baby girl?" Daddy asked, putting a comforting arm on mine.*

*I mustered up a bright smile. "Yeah, I'm fine." They didn't look convinced. "I'm fine, really," I insisted.*

*"Mmm, hmm," Mama uttered.*

*I wanted to get their attention off of me and nodded upstairs. "I'm not sure about Reneé, though."*

*Daddy frowned. "Why? What happened?"*

*I explained. "...so, she's been upstairs for the past half hour or so, probably talking to Danny. Hopefully, they've worked something out," I said, finishing the story.*

*Mama squeezed her eyes tightly. "What? He did whaat?" she exclaimed.*

*I spoke quickly. "No, no, Mama, calm down. Danny only said that because Reneé threatened him with not seeing his child. He was just mad. Let them try to work it out themselves. I'm sure it'll be okay," I told her.*

*Mama let out an exasperated breath. "All right, all right," she said. "but if Reneé comes down here upset, then I'm gonna work it out." She raised her arms in the air. "You know what? I'm just going to go in the kitchen and start working on dinner. Maybe that'll calm me down." She stalked off toward the kitchen, mumbling, "The nerve of him to come over here and get a pregnant girl all riled up, knowing that she's had complications already."*

*Daddy and I watched her go to the kitchen and then he touched my arm. "Lacie, what did Abigail say to you?" he asked perceptively.*

*I wanted desperately to tell him, but I knew that if I did, I'd start crying. "Daddy," I replied, managing to give him a small assuring smile. "Don't worry about it. Just go in there and see if you can calm Mama down. Reneé and I just got through eating Chinese, so I probably won't eat dinner but Reneé might want to eat later." I started toward the stairs then turned and said as I reached the bottom of them, "I heard about your little date today." I winked at him. "Not bad, Daddy. Not bad."*

I thought of my dad and my mother on a date as the elevator stopped on one of the floors and a few people stepped in. Things were looking up for them.

I leaned against the elevator wall and thought of Abigail wanting me to get rid of my baby and wanting me out of Tony's life. What was her problem? What did I do to that woman that she would consider me so cheap as to offer to buy me off? All I wanted was to love her son. I couldn't help it if I was in love with him. Now, I had the added stress of deciding whether I was going to tell Tony. I mean, how could I explain to him that his own mother had offered me money and also asked me to abort his child?

"Crap!" I exclaimed out loud.

A few of the other elevator passengers looked my way. A second later, the elevator stopped on my floor and I pushed through the crowded elevator irritably. The front receptionist who normally speaks to me when I arrive every morning just stared at me as I walked by. I must have really looked pissed.

With a few 'hello's' to some of the office workers, I hasted toward my office. I just wanted to get in my office, take an aspirin and be alone for five minutes to gather my thoughts.

It was wishful thinking.

A minute or so later, Carrie burst through my door excitedly. "Girl! Did you hear the news?" she asked.

I looked at her dubiously. "Carrie, I just got here. How can I hear anything that fast? Didn't you get my message that I'd be in late?" I said crossly.

She stopped in mid stride with a blank stare and pointed her index finger at me. "Is this one of those pregnancy days when your hormones are all out of whack so you snap at everyone that comes your way?"

I let out an exasperated sigh and leaned back in my chair. "Carrie.... girl, will you please give a sista a minute! Just a minute, that's all I'm asking," I stressed.

Ignoring my request, she hasted to my desk and urged, "Lacie, you ain't got a minute. Right now, Anthony, Tony and Trevor are in a big conference with Richard and William. No one else was allowed in. Something serious is going down, so you'd better go find out what it is!"

I sat up straight at the news. "What?" I exclaimed.

Carrie nodded. "Just get in there now, Lacie, because it is not looking good!"

Now, what?

CREO

"I'm telling you, Richard, I researched this guy fully and he was referred to me by a close associate!" Trevor was saying when I entered the conference room. "I gave you all of the stats on this guy and... Lacie," he said, seeing me enter. "tell them, will you? You reviewed the information too, right?"

"Uh...what information?" I said unsurely, glancing fleetingly at the stone expressions around the large oval conference table. "Can someone fill me in on what's going on?"

None of the men replied as I went to sit next to Tony. Finally, Richard spoke up and looked at me with a soft expression.

"Lacie, I'm afraid we have a very bad situation, here. The contractor that you and Trevor were so anxious to accept the bid from...is missing. The millions of dollars that we advanced him are gone also," he explained.

I blinked in disbelief. "What?"

Richard just nodded. "We're not the only company he's done this to. He's got a very bad history of it."

"B...but...the report..." I sputtered.

"The report was on the money, but the list of fraudulent activities and suits against him outweigh it," Tony added. "There was not enough research done on this because *someone*," he said, nodding toward Trevor, "was too anxious."

Trevor's face tightened with rage. "I don't understand this."

"What's there to understand, Trevor? He took the money and ran. It's simple," Joe snapped.

Richard took a deep breath. "What's not simple is the predicament we're in, people. As a high profile company, this can be very embarrassing for us. If word gets out about this, it could very well jeopardize future business endeavors. We will have a lot to explain and potential clients will not want to risk their money with us if we're this irresponsible."

·"The gravity of this issue is undeniable. We might lose the other

**413**

investors more money and more man hours will have to be dedicated to fixing the mayhem of this project," William added, staring directly at Trevor.

I leaned back in the chair, depleted from the news. "I am so... so...very sorry," I uttered.

Richard gave me a small nod, inhaled and glanced around the table fleetingly. "We need to get pass this and do some damage control." He turned to Trevor. "William and I will handle things on our end. Trevor, consult with other lawyers on the authorities and the legalities. Tony, Joe and Lacie, round up the rest of the team and plan an alternate course of action for another contractor. We also need a plan of action for press, investors and potential clients. This is a setback, but as a company, we must continue to move forward. Let's get our heads together tomorrow and regroup. Trevor, Lacie — you're excused. William and I need to talk to Tony and Joe privately."

"This is some bull–" Trevor was saying as he stormed out of the conference room in anger.

Confounded, disturbed by the events, and the sea of faces a blur, I followed Trevor out and walked down the hallway slowly to my office in a daze. What had just happened? Had I just become the accomplice in the possible demise of a very important and lucrative investment? Was my job now in jeopardy?

I didn't even have time to sit down in my chair when a door slammed behind me. I turned swiftly, startled by the sound.

"You just had to sit there and act like you didn't know anything, didn't you? Why didn't you speak up when I asked you to?" Trevor accused with a roar.

He had picked the wrong time and one thing I couldn't stand was someone slamming my door in my office — let alone behind my back. My head was still throbbing and the pains in my sides were flaring up again.

Annoyance slowly building and aware of the other workers outside my door, I remained standing behind my desk. I supported my arms with my fingers as I leaned over my desk and managed, "Trevor, you need to leave—*right now.* Because you are the last person that I want to see or deal with."

As expected, he paid no heed to my calm demand. "Let me ask you something," he asked, nearing my desk with one full stride. "Was this a plot so you, Joe and Tony could diminish my credibility? Are you trying to make me look bad? Was this Tony's idea?"

I fought back the expletives that wanted to escape from my eager lips and flared, "You are such an obsessive, finger-pointing, egotist. You know that? Everything is not about you, Trevor! My job is on the line and you want to accuse me of being involved in a plot to discredit you? After I put my butt on the line and signed that bid when we should have waited?"

"You didn't say anything," he insisted.

"So what, Trevor?" I argued. "I didn't know what was going on!!" I held up a finger. "You know what? This is not about me and you know it. This is about you always trying to showboat and one up someone because of your own insecurities when your behind should have been playing for the team all along. We've all had to put up with your indignant and self-righteous attitude — including Tony. But all the while you've been the one who's been unfair, ungrateful and unrelenting!"

"I'm damn well proud of it, too!" he declared obstinately. "I've always had to take a back-seat to Whitey when I did all the work and he got all the credit. This project was my idea in the first place and I had every right to take initiative and do what I thought was right and in the best interest of the project."

"But it backfired, didn't it?" I disputed. "Instead of being humbled up, you're assed-down. Now we're both up the creek because you wanted to shine all by yourself." I shook my head. "You know what else, Trevor? This Whitey name-calling is getting tired. That's another issue you have. You are extremely prejudiced and you let that very own prejudice of yours get in the way of progress. That's why you're in the predicament you're in now." I grinned thinly, remembering what Tony said a while back. "You let the wrong color get in your way. Instead of concentrating on the green you concentrated on black and white."

**415**

"That's right, because The Man will chew you up and spit you out every time!" he stressed. "That's all that matters in this world, is black and white. How many times do I have to tell you that, woman!"

I looked at him in awe and just raised my arms up in frustration and then back down in defeat. "You don't have to tell me a damn thing, Trevor. I just want you out of my office," I declared, sitting down to ease the pain I was feeling.

He still didn't want to recognize his own culpability and insisted on using the race card and I'd had it. Had it with him, Abigail, and their black and white notions.

He didn't comply and leaned over the desk with a mischievous smirk. "You don't believe me, do you? You're still holding on to the belief that your fiancé is this great stand up guy."

"I don't believe. I know," I retorted. "Get out, Trevor."

He quirked a brow. "Really?" he asked, putting a hand to his chin. "Is he honest with you?"

What was he suggesting? I shook it off, not wanting to fall for whatever he was using to trap me.

"Trevor, just get out. I don't have to validate my relationship with Tony to you," I asserted with a frown and winced.

He grinned. "I didn't ask you to. I just asked if he was honest with you. It's a simple question."

Why was I falling for it?

"Tony's *very* honest with me," I declared, raising my chin. "Now get out, Trevor."

"You're absolutely sure?" he asked, not moving. "He's never hidden anything from you?"

I stood up, angry with his persistence. "Yes, I'm sure and he's never hid anything from me. Now get out!"

He knew he was gaining ground. "Why didn't he let you know about the meeting?"

That was a good point. I pointed at the door. "Get out, Trevor!"

"Why didn't he defend you?"

I was just about to answer when the door opened fast and Tony barked, "Didn't you hear her tell you to get out? What is with you, man? Haven't you caused enough trouble?" He started gunning for Trevor but Joe got in the middle, holding him back.

Trevor wasn't perturbed. "Ah, Tweedle Dee and Tweedle Dum, ebony and ivory," he accused. "The conspirators coming to rescue the damsel in distress!"

"What are you talking about, man? Ain't nobody conspiring against you!" Tony argued while Joe continued to hold him back.

I rushed to the door and closed it, conscious that the angry exchange had been witnessed by a few of the other office workers. Then I got in between them. "Tony, calm, down," I tried to soothe.

"That's right. Go ahead sista, and be a traitor by pacifying the man that is trying to damage my career!" Trevor accused.

"Look, Trevor," Joe said, easing Trevor back gently. "You need to calm down and relax."

Trevor was adamant, pointing his finger at Tony. "What for, man? This dude is trying to make me look like a fool. He's trying to ruin me, man!"

Carrie burst through the door looking concerned and alarmed. "What is going on in here?" she asked.

I put one hand to my forehead. Thank goodness she had the sense to close the door behind her.

"Point your finger at me again, man and I'm gonna break it," Tony threatened with a snarl.

"Tony, please calm down," I pleaded, holding him back.

"Ain't nothing between us but air and opportunity. C'mon, man. Leap, if you're feeling froggish. I've been waiting to punch that perfect chin ever since I met you–" Trevor taunted.

That's all Tony needed and he started for Trevor again.

"No, Tony!" I shrieked as Carrie helped me hold Tony back.

"Look, ain't nobody going to punch anyone out. All right?" Joe stated, holding Trevor back with one hand and looking at Tony. He looked back at Trevor and shook his head. "You're mad at the wrong person, Trevor. *I* found out about the contractor. Tony had nothing to do with it."

Trevor wasn't convinced. "Man, c'mon, don't stick up for him. He's been against–"

"He's hasn't been against you, Trevor. You've been your own enemy, man. Can't you see that? C'mon man, enough is enough," Joe said. "Own up, man. Admit your mistake and let's work this out." Joe took his hand off Trevor's chest.

It took a second for Trevor to realize that Joe was telling him the truth before he looked at him in shock. "You dimed on me, man? Sold me out?"

Joe took a deep breath. "I didn't sell you out, Trevor. Something wasn't right and—"

"What?" Trevor interrupted Joe sharply with a face full of wrath. "You couldn't come to me and let me know what was up? You had to go to Whitey first and make me look like a fool?"

Joe frowned. "Enough with the Whitey comments, man. Tony's my friend. Respect, man. Resp—"

Trevor slit his eyes at Joe with an irate glare. "Man, you ain't nothing but an Uncle Tom, man."

"Oooh," Carrie and I both exclaimed softly, cringing.

That was the ultimate insult a brotha could give another brotha.

"Man, I've had enough of this—" Tony started again, trying to get around me and Carrie. It was hard, but somehow Carrie and I managed to block his way and use the weight of both of our bodies to press him against the wall.

Joe took a fleeting look at Tony and said calmly, "It's all right, Tony. I got this." He stepped right up to Trevor and pointed his finger in his face. "You know, I've been dealing with your funk ever since you came back into my life. Dishing out insults to my friends and all that. But despite everyone's reservations, I decided to back you. I put in a good word for you with William and Richard, put up some of my own money and even considered going in with you on that jazz club. Now you're gonna get all personal? When everyone worked their butts off for this deal to go through you're gonna have the nerve to buck and disrespect me and my fri—"

"Man, don't even talk about respect," Trevor interrupted him again with a bitter snort. He paused before his mouth turned up into a calculating sneer. "You wanna tell Lacie about you and Dawn?"

I heard Carrie gasp and suddenly felt Tony's hand on my arm. I glanced at both of them, observing their nervous glances at the exchange between Joe and Trevor.

What about Dawn and Joe?

Joe's threat was soft and deadly. "Watch it, man."

After a quick glance at me, Trevor smirked at Joe and continued with his antagonizing homily. "What, man? You're the one that brought up the word respect. Tell her about how you and Dawn have been sleeping around behind her ba—"

Pow! Trevor was down on the floor before anyone could blink.

"No!" I yelled.

Joe had socked Trevor with a straight shot across his nose. I was sure Carrie muttered, "It's about time."

Just as my mind was reeling from Joe slugging Trevor and from what Trevor had accused Dawn and Joe of, Dawn burst through the door.

"What the!" she spurted with wide eyes, seeing Trevor on the floor.

At the first sight of Dawn, Trevor staggered to get up. Tony immediately swiveled around us to get by Joe's side. Both men stood in a defensive stance, ready for whatever Trevor might attempt. I blinked in dismay. This was unreal.

With a slight weave, Trevor shook his head and wiped the blood from his nose with his sleeve. "D...don't worry. I...I'm not gonna put up a fight," Trevor assured with a nod and with another sweep of his nose. Carrie kindly offered him a tissue from her pocket but he refused it. "It's cool. I guess I deserved it." He let out a cold laugh. "Oh, Joe... always the street fighter and never the gentleman. That's all right, man. You got me—this time," he said with a gleam in his eye. He brushed past all of us but stopped at the threshold of my office and looked back at me. "Oh, and Lacie...remember you said something to me about Tony never lying to you?" He nodded toward Tony. "Dawn and Joe aren't the only ones that have been keeping it from you. Think he's such a stand up guy, now?"

I heard several soft curses behind my back. I turned around very slowly and witnessed three guilt-ridden faces.

Dawn, Joe and...Tony.

# Chapter 77

# Tony

Woo!

Joe had warned me about a black woman's fury, but he could have never prepared me for the look I saw on Lacie's face.

She stood there, frozen, staring at us. No one spoke because I'm sure we were all — at least Dawn, Joe and I, anyway—afraid to.

Carrie blew out a soft whistle. "Uh...I...I...I'm gonna leave you all alone to talk," she uttered before she walked out and closed the door behind her.

I ran a hand through my hair wearily and started toward Lacie. "Ah...listen, Lacie...we–"

Wounded eyes flashed and stopped me as she stepped back and held up a hand. "Is...this...true?" Her voice was barely above a whisper as she stared at all of us again for an answer.

"Uh...Lacie, maybe we should go somewhere else and–" Joe began.

She sliced him with her voice. "I *said*...is this true?" she demanded, her voice breaking.

This time she looked at Dawn, who by now was shedding rapid tears. At the sight of Dawn's reaction, Lacie sneered through clenched teeth, "Incredible! In...credible!" She looked at the ceiling and put her hands on her hips.

Dawn moved toward her but Lacie swiftly turned her back and went to the coat hanger. "Lacie...I'm–" she began.

"*Don't*...Dawn!" Lacie turned around and shot her down with fuming, watering eyes. "Right now, you are *really* not my favorite person." She turned back around and started to put on her coat. A crushed Dawn backed away and I moved forward to get near her. As if she sensed me coming, she warned harshly, "Neither are you, Tony."

Joe sighed.

"Where are you going?" I asked, fretfully. She was too agitated to go anywhere by herself.

"Away from you, away from this friggin' place and especially away from Dawn!" she exclaimed. It was only a second before she gathered her things, swung the door open and stormed out.

I hasted to my office for my coat and left Joe and Dawn in her office. She'd already gotten on the elevator and it was going down when I reached the front receptionist. By the time I'd reached the downstairs lobby, the guard told me she'd gotten in a cab and left.

Next place for me—the garage.

⚜

"Lacie, c'mon, open the door! Let's talk about this!" I yelled at the door after banging on it.

It was a good thing no one else was home and that she and Robert were the only tenants.

"Lacie, c'mon, honey. We need to talk!" I pleaded with another bang.

The elevator came up then and opened with her in it. I let out a relieved sigh. Her expression turned from weariness to disappointment when she looked at me.

"What did you do, break the speed of sound trying to get here?" she quipped, walking over to me tiredly.

"I wanted to make sure you were okay," I replied.

I noticed that she winced when she unlocked the door and opened it. "Does Richard know you're here?" she asked.

"I called him on my cell on the way over here. He'd already heard about what happened." I followed her inside and closed the door, noticing how slowly she was walking toward the sofa.

"Umm, as well as everyone else, I'm sure," she muttered. She winced again as she threw her belongings onto the sofa. "Care for anything to drink?"

"No thank you," I replied, watching her closely and following her toward the kitchen. "Lacie, are you okay? You don't look so well."

She was leaning against the counter with a Diet Pepsi in her hand when I entered. She took a huge swallow and answered, "I'll be fine, Tony."

"Are you sure? You look tired and you keep wincing as if you're in pain."

She put a hand to her forehead, closed her eyes for a second and expelled a frustrated breath. "Tony, I have a headache and I've got some pains in my sides—"

"What kind of pain?" I asked, moving toward her.

Lacie backed away. "Tony, just go, okay? I'll take some Tylenol and lay down. I'll be fine. I just want you to leave."

"Lacie, I'm not leaving you like this."

"Tony, can't you see that I want to be alone?" She let out a loud grumble and held out a hand. "I'm about to lose my job because I lost focus and my sense of judgment by following the advice of an egotistical worm, almost jeopardized a multi million dollar deal and I just found out that my best friend has been lying to me and sleeping with my ex- fiancé!" she exasperated. Then she pointed a finger at her heart. "But what hurts the most is that my soon-to-be husband, my lover, the one that I want to spend the rest of my life with, has known about this the whole time and never bothered to tell me—not once! Do you know how embarrassing that was to hear… from Trevor, of all people?" She put her hand to her head again. "So Tony, I want you to go, because I've had enough drama for today!"

"I wanted to tell you, Lacie," I said easily.

"So, why…didn't…you?" she demanding, bearing her sad eyes into mine.

I sighed. "Dawn asked me not to."

With an incredulous look and a slow nod, she uttered, "Dawn asked you not to."

I shrugged. "Yeah."

She made a face. "Since when in the hell do you listen to Dawn and forsake my feelings for hers?" She slammed the soda can on the counter.

"It's not like that, Lacie. Dawn wanted to tell you herself and to be honest, I really didn't think it was my place to tell. I hated keeping it from you, but I knew that it was the best thing."

"Oh, so now everyone is an expert on what's best for me, right?" She looked at me wearily and winced. "How long have you known, Tony?"

"Lacie, c'mon...that was your third wince," I said, trying again to move closer to her. She backed away again. "C'mon, let me take you to the doctor. You don't look good."

She ignored what I said and put more of her weight against the counter. "Just answer my question."

I was worried about her but she wouldn't let me get close to her. I let out a defeated sigh and held out my hands. "I'd just had suspicions, really..."

"You should have told me, Tony."

"I said, they were suspicions, Lacie! Not facts," I defended.

"I don't believe you've been keeping this from me," she said accusingly.

I didn't like her statement. "Wait a minute. I'm not the bad guy, here. I've been trying to shield you from getting hurt!" I grumbled softly. "Look, I'm very sorry about this, but you've got to understand how difficult it would have been for me to tell you with all of the chaos that was going on in your life and in mine. Nobody wanted to hurt you, Lacie. Especially Dawn," I maintained. "Did you really expect it to be easy for her...or for anyone of us?"

She put her fingers to her temple and grimaced. "Do you think it was easy for me to find out that she's been with Joe?" she spat out.

I folded my arms and peered at her, feeling a twinge of jealousy from her statement. "Tell me something. Are you mad over the fact that she's seeing him or the fact that he's seeing her?"

"What?"

"I don't have to explain. You know what I mean."

"I don't see that there's a difference," she replied.

"Oh, there's a difference, all right. I'm just waiting to see what your answer is going to be."

"What are you implying?"

"Do you still have feelings for Joe?" I asked her directly.

She looked at me stupefied, mouth wide open. "You're really asking me that question?" She pointed at herself.

I knew it was my male ego asking. Even so, I just shrugged and waited for her response.

"I don't believe this." She raised her eyes up toward the ceiling and let out a breath. "After all of the crap I've taken from Trevor and your mother. After all of the sneers and jeers and looks I've had to deal with because I'm with you. You're going to question my love for you?"

"I don't doubt that you love me, Lacie."

"Then you shouldn't have asked me that question, Tony! I'm carrying your child, for crying out loud!" she yelled. "Just get out, Tony. I want you to…ow!" She suddenly doubled over, holding her stomach.

I dashed over to her and grabbed her so she could support herself on me. "Lacie, what's wrong?" Lacie only answered with a small painful scream. "All right, that's it. I'm taking you to the hospital."

"No," she managed weakly.

"You don't have a choice," I said, leading her to a chair to sit down. "Sit here while I get your purse and coat."

Within five minutes, I had her downstairs and in my car, heading to the hospital.

# Chapter 78

# Robert

Dad was gone.

Although Ma and I'd braced ourselves for it, it still hit us hard. Death can be such a painful thing.

I'd never wept so much in my life and neither had I seen my mother weep so hard. I was upset that my dad was gone and grieved for my mother who was now alone.

Eventually, after an exhausting cry at home, and with Ma's help, we were both able to stop the tears from rolling and somehow find some comfort. The comfort was in knowing that my dad was no longer in pain. Knowing this, gave us a sense of closure because we didn't have to witness his suffering anymore. It had been a very tough battle and Dad had been a trooper, right to the end.

Ma had already made peace with that, I had to, too, and I did.

Everything was going to be all right.

Now, it was time to call Lacie.

# Chapter 79

# Lacie

*"What?"*

I must not have heard the doctor correctly.

He cleared his throat before he repeated, "I'm afraid you've suffered a miscarriage. You've lost your baby." My body went numb and I just stared at him. He cleared his throat again. "Mrs. Adams don't get disheartened. You're still young and you can try again…"

I didn't want to hear that. I'd just lost my child. What the hell did he know? Silent tears started to fall and I held my hands against my face as the doctor continued to speak. This couldn't be. Not now. Not after everything that has just happened. No. This had to be some horrible nightmare.

I realized it wasn't when he continued with, "There are a few things that we have to do before we discharge you, so it might be a while. Your husband's outside making a call. Before I bring in the nurse, would you like me to tell him to come in so you can break the news—"

"He's not…my husband," I sniffled quickly, wiping my face with my hand with one fast sweep.

"I'm sorry. I just thought—," the doctor replied uneasily.

"It's fine," I said tersely. "If you don't mind, I'd like a few minutes before you tell him to come in here."

With a nod, he said, "Certainly."

It took only a half a second after the doctor left for me to softly wail out, "Oh my, God!" I rocked back and forth on the hospital bed, shaking and weeping as I held my hands over my face.

It was just last week that I was thwarted with the news of my pregnancy and had made such a big stink about it, too. Instead of appreciating it as a blessing, I'd doomed it a curse. The superficial stuff—my career, my reputation, what my peers thought, what Tony thought and lastly, what his mother thought—had mattered. Well, I didn't have to worry about it any longer, did I? I wasn't pregnant anymore. Just that quickly, my baby was gone, and that was deeply painful.

Then, of course, were all of the events that had recently occurred. All of it had been paradoxical and now I'd miscarried. Was all of this a sign? Were Tony and I supposed to be together?

"Lacie?" Tony called out softly, interrupting my thoughts as he came into the room with intense concern. With a sniffle, I wiped my face quickly as he walked up to me and took my hand. "I uh... I managed to get an answer from your house. Your parents and Reneé are on the way." He swallowed nervously. "How are you? Ha...How's the baby?" I could only muster a small shake of my head. Words were out of the question. "My God," he uttered, choking up automatically and embracing me. "My God, I'm so sorry, Lacie. I'm so sorry," he continued to say while we cried in each other's arms.

"Excuse me," a nurse said, popping her head in the door a moment later. "But we're going to need you to leave us with Ms. Adams, while we—"

"Yeah," Tony snapped, glancing over his shoulder. "Give us a minute, will you?"

The nurse pursed her lips and said, "Yes, sir."

Tony turned his attention to me and took my hands in his when she closed the door. "Listen, I'll be back. I'll just be down the hall in the wait—"

I'd already made up my mind and cut him off. "Tony, that's okay. Go on home. I'll be fine."

He looked shocked. "Lacie, I'm not leaving you here."

"Tony, you said that Mama and Daddy are on their way. I'll be fine. Go home."

He paused to stare at me, but I turned my head to avoid his eyes. "Lacie—"

"Tony, please go. I want to be alone," I pleaded. "So much has happened already. Don't push it. I just want some space."

He inhaled. "Lacie, the baby was mine, too."

"But *I* lost the baby," I declared.

"You didn't lo–"

Geeze!

"Tony, just go, all right! I told you, I want some space," I voiced, turning my head to look at him.

He took his hands off mine abruptly as if they'd burnt him. "Okay," he murmured. He straightened up with a tight and wounded expression. "I'll give you a call later on to–"

"Don't call me. I'll call you if I need you," I said sharply, turning my head from him. I didn't like being rude to him deliberately, but I had to.

His tone was just above a whisper. "Lacie....how much space are we talking about?"

I couldn't bear to look at him. "I don't know."

"*When* will you know?" he asked.

I didn't answer. Shoot, I didn't even have the answer myself. I just wanted him gone.

There was a long ominous, pause before he scoffed and said, "Wait a minute. Lacie...wh...wh...what's going on? Lacie, look at me," he ordered. I turned around reluctantly to see his piercing eyes. "Are you trying to break up with me?"

"Tony..." I struggled tearfully. "We have been through a hell of a lot in the past few months. More than what a couple should have to go through with a relationship so fresh," I sniffled. "With everything that happened this weekend and today..." I trailed off and put my head down a second before I gazed into his eyes. "Tony, we've just had so much pain...so much heartache."

"So you're giving up on us that quickly?" he asked. "When we've just experienced something traumatic? We should be supporting each other instead of giving up!"

"It's more than that, Tony. It's your–" I almost blurted and stopped.

"It's my what?" I held back because I didn't want to go down that road. "Lacie–"

"Tony, we've had problem after problem after problem and they just keep coming. It seems like we just can't win and I don't think we will,"

I contended in tears.

He frowned. "Lacie, what have I been doing since we've been together? Fighting for our relationship. Defending our relationship to my friends, my family — my mother!" he declared, strongly. "I've been disinherited and my mother and I aren't even speaking because we're together! Because I love you. Because I believe in us!" he argued. "Shouldn't that show you how much I'm devoted to you and how far I'm willing to go to be with you?"

"Yes!" I cried suddenly, thick with emotion. "But it hurts because I see the sorrow in your eyes every time I look at you, knowing that you've forsaken your family for me. I saw how upset you were at the shop in your hometown when I was discriminated against. I saw the surprise, hurt and disappointment in your face at your mom and brother's rejection of me. I saw the anger in your eyes at dinner. I saw it all and it hurts, Tony. It really does! But out of everything — losing our baby hurts the most," I uttered. "I think it would be best for us to end this relationship now since we're no longer tied to each other."

"No longer ti–" he broke off. The look on his face was beyond words as he choked up some. He stopped himself and then cleared his throat. "Is that what you want?"

I didn't like that he was leaving the defining moment up to me. Nonetheless, I strained out, "Yes," and turned my head dismissively.

I heard him utter a curse before he said roughly, "Fine. You want some space. You got it!"

I cringed as the door slammed shut.

"Oh my, God!" I burst out again, suddenly realizing that I'd literally just pushed the love of my life out. I'd let a good man go.

I hadn't wanted to do it, but everything from the drama at work, the disastrous dinner, the incident at the wedding, the shop, and my miscarriage, had all taken its toll on me. In addition, were the irrational comments and the offer from Abigail. I wasn't going to take her bribe, but I didn't want Tony to lose his family. I didn't want him rejected and mistreated.

Trying to get myself together, I took a tissue from the stand next to me to wipe my nose and noticed my cell phone vibrating. I'd forgotten to turn it off. I knew I shouldn't be thinking about answering it in the hospital, but picked it up anyway. Dawn's cell number came up on the caller I. D. There was no way that I was talking to her. I waited for the vibrating to end and was just about to turn it off when it vibrated again. Robert's cell number came up. I answered it because I hadn't heard from him in a while.

"Hello?" I whispered, wiping my nose and trying to be as quiet as possible.

"Dad's dead," Robert's voice choked tearfully on the other end.

Hearing him sob uncontrollably tore me to pieces and automatically my pity party and my worries were put on the back burner. They didn't matter.

Forget about me. I had to be there for my friend.

# Chapter 80

# Dawn

Lacie's reaction had been worse than I'd thought it would be.

Not so much that she'd broke bad, but it was the incredulous look of betrayal that she'd given me in her office.

That had been the first time I'd ever seen her that hurt and I was cross with myself because I'd been the culprit. It wasn't Joe's doing and I didn't blame him. I felt the onus even more when her eyes lingered on mine when Trevor spilled the beans. They just slowly rested on mine in utter shock. I'd thought I'd felt guilt before, but none such as this.

When Joe and I left her office, all eyes were on me. The other office workers had clearly heard everything and had glared at me with reproach when I walked through the department.

Joe had tried his best at consoling me, but it was useless. I'd hurt Lacie and the only thing I wanted to focus on was how to repair the damage. I'd called Lacie's cell and house number over and over again, but she never picked up. I didn't blame her for it, either.

She'd expected more from me and I'd let her down.

Her best friend.

# Chapter 81

# Joe

The secret was out.

The bad part was the way it came out and that the two women I cared for were upset.

I'd been the executor of the wrongdoing. The one that had pursued Dawn — selfishly.

I'd given myself plenty of excuses throughout our clandestine affair and it was all for naught. I'd possibly broken up a lifelong friendship and didn't know if there was any mending it.

While I drove us to my apartment, I watched helplessly as Dawn shed tears while she continuously rang Lacie's cell phone and then shed even more at every sound of the voice mail. Dawn sniffled beside me in the car.

*Well, you got what you wanted, Joe.*
*Now look at the mess you made.*
*So much for your impulse, huh?*

# Chapter 82

## Tony

I was steaming when I left Lacie in the room at the hospital.

I ran into her family on the way out and told them where she was before I left. Sensing something wrong, Mason tried to stop and talk to me but I politely excused myself. They were going to have enough to deal with, with Lacie and all.

I did need to talk to someone, though. In the state that I was in, I knew I shouldn't be alone. So I called Joe without giving him the news. Hearing the anxiety in my voice, he invited me over.

"Man, you look rough," Joe remarked, opening the door so I could come in.

"I feel it," I grumbled, stepping into the living room.

"I see," Joe said, joining me. "How's Lacie?"

"Lacie's in the hospital. She lost the baby."

His eyes widened in shock. "Aw, man, I'm sorry, Tony," Joe expressed sorrowfully. "What...how did this happen?"

"Joe, before I get into that with you, I've got to have something to drink," I replied grimly. "I'd prefer something strong, but that wouldn't be a good idea, considering I've got to drive back home."

"Yeah, yeah, sure man," Joe said and I followed him into the kitchen. He looked in the refrigerator and asked, "A Pepsi okay for you?"

"Yeah, that's cool. Thank you," I said, taking a swig once he handed me the bottle. After, I asked, "Is Dawn here?"

"Yeah. She's asleep in my bedroom. Dawn's really taken this thing with Lacie hard, man. She's been in tears ever since we left the office. She just now went to sleep," he replied. "Man, this whole thing stinks," he sighed. "And now you're telling me that Lacie lost the baby?" I nodded and he sighed again. "I'm so sorry, man. Really, I am. How's Lacie taking it and what are you doing here when you should be with her?"

I swallowed some more soda before proclaiming, "Joe, Lacie kicked me out of the hospital and broke up with me." Joe's mouth dropped. I told him what happened. "...and I feel so bad, man, because we'd just been arguing over everything that happened at work and then she got sick. Now the baby's gone," I finished.

"Man, this wasn't your fault," Joe offered.

"Deep down I know that, but it doesn't help, man. I'm torn up, too. That baby might have been my son, man! I loved that kid, already!" I swallowed a tear.

"I know, man. I know," Joe murmured and put a hand on my shoulder. "Man!" Joe uttered, holding his head down. He looked up a second later and asked, "Tony, do you really think she wanted to break up with you?"

"I don't know. My heart tells me no, because I know that she's upset, which might be why she flipped out on me the way she did."

"Tony, Lacie probably needs time to heal," Joe offered reasonably. "Listen, a miscarriage is a very difficult thing for any woman to go through."

"Yeah, I know and you're right." I nodded and sighed. After a pause I added thoughtfully, "But I will tell you this; I don't believe Lacie was telling me everything."

"Why?"

"I just feel that she was holding something back and wanted to tell me but felt like she couldn't."

"What do you think it is?"

"I don't know. That's what I've got to find out."

Joe shook his head. "Man, things have got to get better — and fast. We've got two beautiful black women on our arms that are upset, hurt, angry and going through drama. That ain't good. I know. I have a mother and a sister."

I uttered wearily, "So you keep telling me."

# Chapter 83

# Lacie

"Lacie, are you crazy? You just had a miscarriage!" Mama had exploded when I told her my plans as soon as we all got home. "You shouldn't be taking a flight anywhere!"

"Mama, I'm fine. They got me all fixed up in the hospital. The doctor even told me that I could even go back to work tomorrow if I wanted," I claimed, sitting down on the sofa easily.

"To work, but not on an airplane!" Mama objected.

Daddy looked at me. "Lacie, your mother has a point," he stated. Mama looked at him in surprise. "You've just had a terrible tragedy. Maybe you shouldn't go."

"I agree, Lacie," Reneé concurred. "At least wait a day or two before you fly out there. This has been a very emotional day for you."

"And what about Tony?" Daddy pointed out. "Shouldn't you be trying to work things out with him before you go gallivanting down there? It was his baby too, Lacie."

"My *terrible tragedy* is nothing compared to Robert's and I told you that I'm not ready to talk to Tony just yet. My life and my emotions do not count right now, so they can wait. I'm going," I stated firmly. All three huffed. "Listen, my mind is made up. Daddy, could you call the airports and find out the earliest flight schedule for me?" I asked, standing up to head to the stairs. "I'm going up to my room to pack. Mama and Reneé, you two can join me while you attempt to change my mind." Then I added, "If Tony calls, I don't want to speak to him and definitely don't tell him that I'm leaving."

It was late evening by the time my bags were packed and my trip was booked for the next day in the early afternoon. Despite Mama and Reneé's best efforts, they couldn't convince me not to go. They even offered to come with me, but I immediately rejected their offer because there were issues to be settled at home.

Reneé still had school and as a result of a peaceful conversation with Danny, was working on a compromise with him. While I was gone, Mama could focus on Reneé and give her guidance and emotional support and take advantage of some peacemaking time with Daddy. Not to mention, I was ready for a break.

I planned on going in to work and ask for some time off. I had some stored up vacation time and once I told Richard about Robert's dad, I was sure he'd understand. I needed to be away from everyone and all of my problems.

Being with Robert and helping him through this difficult time would deter me from my own and allow me to focus all of my energy on his.

❦

The sky was still dark and the moon hadn't gone down when I went to the office the next morning. Richard was fully dedicated to the success of his company. I knew he usually arrived in his office right before the cleanup crew left. This was the perfect time to talk to him.

"Come in," Richard answered to my knock. "I'm glad you came to see me," he remarked when I walked in and sat down.

"You are?"

"Yes." He replied, studying me. "I meant to call for you later on today, but you beat me to it."

*Oh, oh.*

He continued. "I'm concerned about you and what happened with this whole deal. I want to hear your side of the story."

I sighed. "Trevor came to me early one morning and presented the bid to me. I…I admit, that I wasn't really feeling well so I wasn't looking for any work talk right then. But he kept pressuring me about this contractor and wouldn't leave." I shrugged, meekly. "So…after looking over the bid carefully, I signed it."

"Mmm, hmm," Richard muttered, still studying me. "I understand that you all were supposed to agree on it before anyone signed it. Is that correct?"

I was starting to get nervous and gulped. "Yes, that's correct. But Trevor had the last say, so. At least that's what he's been saying in all the meetings since we've started this project," I replied.

Richard let out a sigh. "This is not like you, Lacie. You've never let something slip like this before." I started to interrupt and he held up a hand. "I'm not really blaming you. I know Trevor's been manipulating and pushing his weight around here. Carrie's been keeping me pretty updated," he informed me casually. "But mistakes like this are critical and are not needed in the business that we're in. They must not be repeated. We were on a limited timetable, but we very well could have waited. It wouldn't have cost us so much time and money." He peered at me. "Can you give me an idea of what's going on or what it is that might be affecting your work? I know that Trevor has not been the best person to work with. I also know that you and Tony are engaged. Con—"

"We're not anymore, Richard. We've broken up," I interrupted him.

"Oh. I'm sorry to hear that," he said, astonished.

Last night came into mind and I shook it off. I didn't want to tell him about last night so he could pity me. "But to answer your first question, there are some things...quite a few things that might have had some roundabout...but not direct affect on my work."

He nodded. "Are you feeling burnt out?"

Honestly, I was. "Yes. This project has been challenging," I admitted.

"There are many more challenges you will have to face if you stay with this company, Lacie." Did he say *if*? "You'll have to learn to manage them along with your personal affairs. The hours will increase as well. If you're having trouble managing your problems now, how are you going to handle them later?"

I swallowed hard. "Richard, I've never complained about the work or the hours that I put in — especially with this deal," I defended.

"I know you haven't and I appreciate everything you've done. But are you able to fully maintain the responsibilities that will undoubtedly arise if you stay with this company?"

There was that '*if*' word again.

I was speechless and looked down at my hands solemnly.

"Listen, Lacie, I don't want you to think that I'm here to hang you or anything. I know you're a hard worker. You've done such a great deal for this company, but the bottom line is that we cannot afford to have mistakes like this made. Not when there are millions of dollars on the line."

I held in a breath and nodded, ready for the worse. "I understand."

Obviously contemplative, he stared at me for a good second before he said, "I think it would be a good idea if you took a few days off to figure out a few things. Kind of get a perspective if you will," he suggested.

I swallowed the lump in my throat and said shakily, "Why do I get the sense that this will lead to you firing me."

He shook his head with a friendly smile. "That's not the case. I just want you to take a few days off and think about your career here. When you come back we can talk things over some more."

I smiled thinly. "Are you expecting me to come back?"

"That's what I hope, yes."

I scoffed, lightly. "It's ironic that you're telling me now to take a few days off when I was going to ask you for the same thing."

"Oh, really?"

"Yeah, a very good friend of the family's dad has recently passed and I wanted to be there for him so—"

"Ah…I see," he said. "I'm very sorry about your friend's dad, Lacie. Considering the circumstances here, this might be what you needed—a break."

I stood up, held in my emotions and reached for his hand. "Understood, Richard. Thank you."

He shook it firmly. "No. Thank *you*, Lacie. For everything."

Although I'd gone in to ask Richard for some time off, hearing him *advising* me to do it was upsetting. I felt like I'd just gotten broken down and despite his handshake, I was feeling worse than when I did before I walked in.

Riled and flabbergasted with the idiosyncrasies in the chain of events, I took the elevator down to the department in a haze of tears, fully intending to get to my office, retrieve a few things and jet. I was so glad I'd come in early.

I hadn't come early enough.

Trevor was standing by one of the copy machines when I walked toward him. The sight of him alone was infuriating.

*Keep walking, Lacie.*

He automatically showed his teeth with his slimy grin when he noticed me coming near. His expression changed to a frown when he saw my tears.

"Lacie, what's wrong?" he asked immediately, following me to my office.

"Trevor, if you know what's good for you, you'll leave me alone. I'm serious, now," I warned, entering my office and going to my desk to look for a few items.

Of course, he didn't listen.

"Lacie, for real, I'm concerned. What's wrong?" he asked.

"Trevor, there's nothing you can do about it anyway, so just leave me alone, okay?" I went to the closet to get a box and went to the file cabinet.

"Did Richard fire you?" he asked, straightforwardly.

I turned and looked at him. "No," I replied. "As he put it, he's just giving me a couple of days off so that I can reflect on my career with the company. But I feel that it's been assigned a death sentence." I turned back around.

From behind, I felt his presence and his eyes on me, but I continued on with my mission.

He cleared his throat and started with, "Lacie, listen, I'm sorry—"

He picked the wrong time to attempt to apologize.

I turned on him in justifiable wrath. "You're sorry?" I scoffed. "*Now* you say you're sorry. You've clearly enjoyed spewing your insults and taunts and making trouble for me, Tony and everyone in this department and now you want to apologize!" I exploded. "You know what, Trevor? I don't want to hear it! Not one syllable, not a word, nada, nothing!"

"Lacie...I want to help," he contended.

"You want to help me? Okay. Get out of my office! That's how you can help me, Trevor," I snapped, while I continued to retrieve the files from the cabinet and flung them into the box. "I gotta tell you, I've just about reached my limits. I might not have a job when I get back, my sister's going through baby daddy drama, my best friend and ex-fiancé have been secretly doing each other, my good friend, Robert's, dad just died, Tony and I have broken up, and his mother offered me a bribe to end my relationship with her son and abort my baby that I've just miscarried!" I yelled and slammed the last file cabinet drawer and looked at him angrily. "Oh, yeah, I have really reached my limits! In a way, I guess I should thank Richard for giving me a few days off because I truly believe that I am on my way to having a nervous breakdown!"

With that last statement, I threw the last folder in the box, picked it up and didn't look back as I walked past Carrie's surprised expression.

I didn't even stop to talk to her.

I just wanted to leave and couldn't wait to get out of New York City.

# Chapter 84

## Tony

I'd been up all night worrying about her.

Despite how early it was, I wanted to hear Lacie's voice as soon as I woke up to make sure she was doing okay. I didn't care if she didn't want to speak to me. When the voicemail on her cell phone kept coming on, I decided to try her house phone. I was shocked when Mason answered it and told me that she'd already left and was heading to the office.

*"Tony, she's uh…"* Mason had started but finished with, *"listen just talk to Lacie and see if you two can work it out."*

Without a second thought, I hurried off the phone and didn't worry about what Mason had tried to tell me and quickly got ready.

"Damn!" I muttered when I came to Lacie's closed office door.

I looked around and saw Carrie coming over with a cup of coffee in her hand and turned to her. "Carrie, Lacie hasn't come in yet, has she?"

She slowed down and sat her coffee on her desk. "Yes, but she left just a few minutes ago."

I frowned. "Huh? Why?" She didn't say anything and just stared at me warily. "What, Carrie? What's going on?"

She let out a small sigh. "Lacie is on a leave of absence."

"What?"

She nodded wearily. "Yep. She came in early this morning and had a meeting with Richard. According to my sources, it was a mutual decision for her to take time off."

"Oh, hell!" I grumbled.

"Tony, she walked right past me and didn't say anything when she left. She was very upset and it looked," she said with a casual nod toward Trevor's office, "as if she'd just had an argument with Trevor, too."

"I'm gonna–" I started, heading over to his office.

"Tony, don't," Carrie advised, blocking my way. "There's been enough trouble. Anyway, Richard has been looking for you. He wants to have a private meeting with you, Joe and Trevor and asked me to come see if you'd arrived. Joe and Trevor are already up there as we speak."

I was boiling with aggravation while I took the elevator up to Richard's floor, wondering what was going on.

"They're all waiting for you," his secretary stated once the elevator door opened.

"Thank you for coming on such short notice, Tony," Richard said once I entered. "Have a seat." He cleared his throat and paused before speaking. "I brought you three gentlemen here for one thing, to settle matters once and for all," he said, looking at us sternly. "I am aware of the incident that happened downstairs in Lacie's office and I want to convey to you, that whatever it is that's going on, ends now."

All of us shifted uncomfortably.

He leaned forward and looked at Trevor hard. "Trevor, I thank you for your initiative and your idea for this project. You've been aggressive and hard working, but at the same time you've been a pain in the rear. From the beginning of this project you've brought your personal beliefs and feelings and attitude into a professional atmosphere and this firm is suffering because of it. You need to thank William for going to bat for you, considering that I strongly advised him to eliminate you from his counsel. This project is continuing just because of William. So, from now on, every word that you say and every movement you make will be scrutinized until this deal is done. If you try to cause anymore confusion or make one wrong move, Trevor, you're out," he threatened.

He leaned back and linked his fingers together. "Now that I've gotten that out of the way, let's get to the good news." He took a deep breath. "William and I have pulled our resources together to work with law enforcement in this ordeal. It looks like we are coming up on a lead."

I heard Trevor breathe a sigh of relief.

"But the battle is not over," Richard cautioned. "So," he gave a nod to Joe, "Joe, you've offered help in finding this man and I'm taking your offer. Trevor and Tony, the show must go on and we still have a lot of work to do. Settle your differences and let's make this deal happen. We're all in this together and there is a lot of money to make." He stood up. "Okay, that's it for now. I wanted this resolved to make sure that we all recognize what the primary focus is…to get this project done. Thank you for coming." Then he added, "Tony, Joe. I want to speak with you individually for a second. Tony, first." He waited for Joe and Trevor to leave before saying anything.

His face was somber as he spoke. "I'm sure by now that you've heard that Lacie is on a little leave of absence."

"Yes. I know."

He looked gullible. "I'm afraid, Lacie, took my suggestion the wrong way," he said. "I think I might have been a bit too hard on her. I don't want her to leave this company."

"She's been going through a lot, Richard," I disclosed, trying not to choke up. "Yesterday was not a good day for her or for me."

"I'm aware of that–" he began.

"No, Richard," I said. "Lacie had a miscarriage last night."

He blinked in shock. "I…I'm sorry, Tony. I didn't know. She didn't tell me." After an uncomfortable pause, he remarked, "I guess it's better that she left, then. She'd just informed me that a good friend of hers father has died and she was going to ask for some time off for the funeral."

I expelled a sad breath, instantly knowing that it had to be Robert's dad that passed. "Did she say when she was leaving?"

"No, but my impression was that it was immediate," he replied. "Tony, even though we have a lot of to clean up here at work, I'll certainly understand if you left to be with her."

"Thanks for the offer, Richard, but I don't think she wants me to be there with her."

"Just the same, the offer still stands."

Trevor was waiting for me in my office when I came back downstairs.

Remembering Richard's instructions, I suppressed my annoyance and lightly grumbled, "What's up, man? What do you want?"

I walked over to my desk and turned on my laptop and sat down.

I heard him take a deep breath before he said, "I came to make peace, man."

I looked up at him sharply and quirked a brow. Had I heard him right?

"You want... to make peace," I stated with slow skepticism.

He held out his arms with a shrug. "Hey, it's like Richard said. We're all in this together. If the objective is to make money, then we might as well get along, right?"

"Man, we've been trying to tell you that from jump street!" I claimed.

"Yeah, yeah, I know," he answered hastily, holding up a hand. "But look, for real, we've got a huge problem, here—"

"You mean, *you've* got a huge problem—"

He nodded with a little grimace. "That too, but the bottom line is that if this deal doesn't go through, all of us will be done. Richard's already given us fair warning about the griping so..." he suggested, trailing off with another shrug.

I studied him, still not believing his game. "Trevor, what's up with the sudden change of heart?"

He hunched up his shoulders. "It's something I just realized, that's all and..." The look on my face must have said it all and then he took a deep breath. "All right, all right. I'll fess up. Richard chewed me out before you all came," he confirmed humbly. Then just as quickly, "But the situation remains the same. It's not going to help if we're not working together."

I chuckled softly, marveling that he was still trying to save face even when his behind was on the line. He surprised me further when he came closer to my desk and extended his hand.

"So…are we all right?" he asked.

I questioned his sincerity and hesitated, but because I was never one to hold a grudge, I stood and gave him a grip. "Yeah, man…we're all right," I chuckled.

"Bet," he replied with a look of relief. "But look, Tony. Another reason why I came in here is because of what happened yesterday."

"Trevor…we just squashed it. Leave it alone," I warned.

"Naw, man, look. Some real ill stuff went down yesterday and I'm not happy about any of it."

"Uh, huh," I murmured. "Because Joe punched you in the nose, right?"

"No. That's not it. I mean, no, I didn't like being punched in front of everyone, but…" he took a breath. "Lacie got hurt man and I didn't want that."

"Other people got hurt, man–" I started.

"Yeah, yeah, I know that," he stopped, frustrated. "I know that," he said softer. "I know about the baby, too, and I'm sorry." My expression spoke for itself. "Lacie blurted it out to me earlier but I don't think she realized it." He shook his head. "But something else is up Tony and she ain't telling you."

"What?"

He took another breath. "Your mom's been pressuring Lacie, Tony. Hard."

"About what?" He seemed reluctant to tell me. "What, man?"

He really looked sorry when he said it. "Your mom is bribing Lacie, Tony."

"What?" I growled.

"Yeah, man. I saw Lacie early this morning, just fresh from her talk with Richard. And she was up-set! You know seeing me only made her more upset." He shook his head. "Lacie let everything out all at once, man. She mentioned all of the trouble at home and with your mom and along with her miscarriage. Then she let it slip that your mom offered her money to get an abortion and to stay away from you!" I sat down hard on my chair. My ears and my eyes started to burn while I struggled to maintain my composure from what Trevor had said.

"Hey, man…you all right?" he asked, staring at me with a frown.

"No. I'm not," I strained and then cleared my throat. "Why are you telling me this, Trevor?"

He sighed. "Look, man. I know that I gave you and Lacie a lot of grief with you two being together. And although I don't really enjoy the fact that she ain't got a brotha on her arm, the fact is that you two love each other. Despite all of my attempts at trying to break you two up and busting her chops about her being with you, she never wavered man. Not once. She loves you. Believe me, I know. I've tried my charms on her and even attempted to get a kiss from her, but she–"

"Wait a minute…did you just say that you tried to kiss her, man?"

"Yeah, I did. But it didn't work, Tony. She shot me down — cold." He shrugged. "She is crazy for you. Man, I wish I had a woman that crazy for me!" he exclaimed, with a glance at the ceiling. "She's a good woman, Tony."

"She is that," I agreed with a contemplative nod.

"Lacie shouldn't be going through that kind of drama with your mom, man. I figure she didn't tell you because she is your mom. So that's why I told you," he said. "With her just having a miscarriage and all, she really needs you. You need to find her and see what's up."

"You got that right," I said decisively and started piling my briefcase. I was taking Richard up on his offer. "I'll tell Richard and Joe what's up and arrange to have conference calls with you all while I'm gone. I want to be notified on any–"

"Look, man, I'll tip them on what's going on. Joe and I and the rest of the team will work on getting things done with this deal. Don't worry, we'll handle it," he assured. I gave him a skeptical glare. "Man, if I'm lying then Joe can punch me again. I swear! Just handle your business!"

Well, what do you know. Ol' Trevor pulled through.

I shouldn't have even been driving in my condition, I was so mad.

I made it to my parent's place in record time, playing everything over in my head from when Lacie first met Mom to Trevor's allegation of Mom bribing Lacie. I swerved into my parent's driveway, ran up the steps and hammered the door with my fist.

Dad saw my fury when he opened the door and immediately held out a peaceful hand. "Anthony, what's wrong? What are you doing here?" he asked at once, letting me in and closing the door behind him.

I stepped into the hallway and said loudly. "Is Mom here?"

He frowned. "Yes, she's here. She's in the kitchen. Why?"

On a mission to the kitchen, I didn't bother to answer his, 'what's wrong, Anthony?' I just wanted to find out if what Trevor had said was true. Although, I didn't doubt it. Trevor's track record for dishing out bad— but this time, in my case, helpful—news was on the money of late.

"Mom! Mom!" I yelled, walking through the house.

"What's going on?" I heard Jessica say, running down the stairs.

Mom met me in the doorway of the kitchen apparently getting ready to come out in answer to my call. "Anthony, what is it?" she asked in alarm.

I stepped by her and went over to the other side of the kitchen where the back door was. I took a deep breath as Jessica and Dad joined us. Everyone's eyes were on me.

"Mom," I began, struggling to remain calm since I didn't have the facts as of yet. "Did you happen to go back to the city recently?"

Her eyes were cleverly secretive as she moved over to the stove and looked at me. "Yes, I did. I went to visit the Sanders. Why?" she opened the oven and put a roast beef in it.

"Did you go anywhere else?" I prodded.

Mom shot back up and stuck her chin out, immediately understanding. Dad and Jessica were oblivious.

Dad said, "I already feel the negative energy that's coming from you, Anthony, so let's just have it okay?"

Another breath and, "Mom?" I questioned. "Care to tell them what you did?"

Her eyes flared. "Not particularly," she replied.

Jessica caught her look and groaned, "Mom, what did you do?"

Dad said, "Abigail?"

Mom didn't utter a word as we stood there expectantly. I scoffed. Sure as my name was Tony, she'd done it. Trevor was two for two.

"You did it, didn't you?" I asked with calm certainty.

"What did she do?" Jessica asked.

"She–" I'd started

"I gave Lacie a blank check and told her to get an abortion!" Mom exclaimed suddenly, cutting me off.

"You what?" My father bellowed.

"Mom!" Jessica cried out.

Mom glowered and nodded at me while I stared at her in disappointment. "She told you didn't she?" she asked. "That little–"

"Lacie didn't tell me anything!" I shouted and Mom smirked. "Not a damn thing! Do you know why? Because she knew that it would hurt me!" Expelling a frustrated breath, I beseeched, "Mom, how could you do this?"

"Abigail, we are going to have a serious conversation about this," Dad expressed angrily.

"We're not going to talk about anything, Johnathan!" Mom declared, looking at all of us defiantly. "What I did, I did for us—our family. I saw us breaking apart and I took action!"

"Oh, Abigail," Dad uttered with frustration.

"Oh, shut up, Johnathan! I did what I had to do!" Mom burst out.

"Mom, Lacie's not the one breaking us apart. You are," Jessica uttered, shaking her head. "You refuse to accept her."

"I will never accept her!" Mom spat out bitterly with an angry shake of her head. "The sooner everyone realizes it—the better."

There was no convincing her, I acknowledged. No compromise, on her part.

"You know what, Mom, I do realize it. But I won't let you disrespect Lacie or me anymore. This stunt that you've pulled was the last one!"

I exploded, my limit gone. "If you don't accept her— you don't accept me!" I stomped out angrily past Dad and Jessica.

"Tony, Tony, c'mon, don't go. Let's talk this out!" Jessica implored as they all followed me as I headed toward the front door.

"Anthony! Anthony!" Dad shouted as I opened the front door with a jerk and hasted down the front stairs.

"Let him go!" Mom yelled. "See if that girl will stay with him when he has no money. He'll find out sure enough. So let him go. Let him go back to his black whore and that bastard child of his!"

"Abigail, shut up!" I heard my Dad shout.

The last statement by my mother halted me in my tracks and I jerked around quickly in rage.

"She's not pregnant anymore, Mom! She had a miscarriage!" I shouted and Mom backed away slightly.

"Oh my, God!" Jessica cried out, bringing a hand up to her mouth.

Dad flinched in sorrow. "Anthony, I'm sorry, son."

"Are you happy now?" I scowled at Mom. "Isn't that what you wanted, Mom?"

I wasn't prepared for what came out of her mouth next. "I'm sorry, she lost the baby, but I'd be dishonest if I said that that I'm not relieved."

What?!!!

"Damn it, Abigail!!" Dad exploded.

Jessica flew down the stairs like lightening and held me off with her hands on my chest when I started for the stairs. Dad got in front of Mom.

"No, Tony....just let it go," she pleaded, tearfully.

I grimaced and looked up at the woman who'd given birth to me, for the last time. "I know you had some fault in this and you'd better be happy that you are my mother!" I bellowed.

"Tony, just go! Go get in the car. Dad and I will take care of her," Jessica implored, her voice cracking with emotion.

I suddenly heard the sorrow in my sister's voice and looked down at the tears falling from her eyes and almost broke up with her. I realized then, that this would probably be the last time that I'd set foot in the place that I called home—the place my family celebrated Christmas. But it was out of my hands now.

I cupped my sister's face in my hand and planted a kiss on her forehead. "Goodbye, Jessica. Take care of them for me. Love you."

I didn't look back at my parents as I got in my car and sped off.

I didn't even look back at the house. It was dead to me now.

And at that moment so was my mother.

# Chapter 85

# Lacie

"My Lord, do I hate flying," the elderly lady sitting next to me stated in a shaky voice. "I especially hate landing."

I smiled at her warmly and patted her hand for comfort. "It's okay. You can hold my hand when we're about to land if you'd like," I offered.

"Bless your heart. That's mighty kind of you," she said, grabbing my hand in a vice grip.

I smiled and chuckled softly. We weren't due to land for a least another twenty minutes, but I didn't mind her holding my hand. Actually, she'd been a great side-seat passenger, talking animatedly as soon as she'd taken the seat next to me. She'd had my attention for a good minute, but as she went on, my thoughts slowly drifted toward all of my troubles that I'd left behind in New York.

I looked out the window thoughtfully while the elderly lady started talking again.

*"Lacie, I know what happened at work. Carrie told me when I called your office,"* Mama started as soon as I came home and entered the kitchen. *"Why didn't you tell me what was going on?"*

*"I didn't have time, Mama, and did you forget that I went to the hospital?"*

*"Yes, baby, but —"* she began.

*I stopped her by holding a hand up.* *"Mama, it's been an extremely rough couple of days and you know what I've been through in the past twenty-four hours. I'm emotional as it is. I don't want to talk about work, Tony, or Dawn and Joe."*

*"Lacie, Dawn's been calling all day and she's worried about you. You must know that she's got to be sorry. You should tell her what's happened..."* Mama pleaded.

*"Drop it, Mama."*

*Mama sighed and looked thoughtful. After a pause she said, "You know, something told me that Dawn was getting some. She was just too happy and had a certain glow about her. You know when a woman's getting some—"*

*"Mama!" I cut her off sharply, surprising her. "Please…no more."*

*"Well, did you at least talk to Tony and tell him that you were leaving? He was so sad, Lacie."*

*"Mama, I'm trying to hold on here, and you're not making it any better," I said, voice quivering slightly. "Robert is all I want to be concerned about right now. Okay?"*

*She was silent for a second and then put a soft hand on my arm. "Okay, baby." She took a breath. "I'll get your daddy to call for a cab and then we'll all go to the airport with you."*

*"No, that's okay. I'll go by myself."*

*"Lacie?" Mama asked surprised.*

*Emotion running through, I couldn't speak and just held up a hand and exited the kitchen.*

೨ාଓ

My tears fell once Robert's figure came into view in the walkway of the airport terminal. We ran to each other and embraced tightly.

"I'm so glad you came," he murmured into my ear, rubbing my back.

"I'm glad too," I replied. "I just wish it was for a different reason."

We stood in the terminal for a long time and held each other. Finally, he let go and said, "C'mon, let's get your bags."

೨ාଓ

"So…how have you been dealing?" I asked Robert carefully as soon as he pulled out of the airport parking lot.

He glanced at me quickly, shrugged and let out a deep sigh. "I'm not going to lie. It's been hard. Ma and I let a lot of our emotions go when we came home from the hospital but once we realized that my father was in no more pain. it just seemed like a heavy weight had been lifted. Ma seems to be handling it okay and after our good cry, she just heaved a big sigh and said, "Well, he's finally at peace. He's gone to be with the Lord, now.'"

"What about you?" I asked, gazing at his face steadily.

He shrugged. "The doctors had pretty much prepared us for the worse, so..." he trailed off, clearing his throat. "He's not suffering anymore, Lacie. My father's at rest and he's in a much better place."

I took his hand. "What do you need me to do?"

He looked at me with a grateful smile. "You're doing it. You're here and that means a lot," he said, giving my hand a squeeze. "Dad had just about everything arranged — right down to the obituary. All we needed to do was call the undertaker and he took care of the rest. He went to school with him so..." He smiled reflectively. "Yep, Dad always handled his business."

"When's the funeral?"

"It's Saturday at one o'clock. It's a pretty big church and Daddy was a popular minister in the community. There's going to be a lot of people there."

"All right, I'll make sure to get there in plenty of time."

"You won't have a choice. You'll be leaving from my house."

I looked at him in surprise and he nodded. "No, Robert. I'm getting a hotel. I can't impose like that. You've got family–"

"Yes and just about all of them live in town and attend the same church where he preached. There's plenty of room at our house, Lacie and I won't take 'no' for an answer. Not to mention, Ma's expecting you to stay," he squeezed my hand again. "You're staying."

"Okay," I chuckled.

"So...now that you've heard all about me, let's talk about the sad face and the tears in the airport." Robert said casually, glancing at me when he stopped at a red light. "Are you okay?"

I attempted a smile and replied. "I'm fine and Robert, I came here for you. Not me. The drama in my life is on hold for the moment."

He eyed me. "Even though I'm glad that you're here, I'm instantly

**453**

reminded of how stubborn you can be. I should be mad with you for coming so soon." In answer to my curious expression, he said softly, "I know about the miscarriage, Lacie, and I'm sorry." My eyes welled up and he squeezed my hand. "I also know about Dawn and Joe." I blew hard and he looked at me. "Josephine called me an hour ago and told me. She told me to watch over you while you're down here and to try to talk some sense into you."

I dragged out a deep, irritated breath. "That's not going to happen because we're not going to talk about me. Didn't you hear me say that just a second ago?" I jibed.

He shrugged. "Yeah, I heard you. But was I listening? No." I sucked my teeth and he ignored it. "Listen, Dawn called me this morning," he said tactfully.

"And?"

"And she's tore up, Lacie. She feels really bad about everything."

"She's not the only one," I quipped.

He nodded. "Okay. Continue to be stubborn — for now. But Dawn's arriving early Saturday morning for the funeral. I'm letting you know now that as a friend of both of you, this matter is going to be taken care of when she gets here." I rolled my eyes upward. "I saw that."

&#8450;&#8450;

Robert's mother, Ann, had to be the sweetest mother on earth.

She showed hardly any signs of a grieving widow. When she welcomed me in her arms, I felt her good spirit and amazing strength. It was also nice that she had already had dinner waiting for us when we arrived.

Their large dining room table was set with a wide variety of dishes, compliments of many family, friends and neighbors paying their respects. With the food, came countless visitors. After calling home to let my family know that I'd arrived safely, I joined Robert and his mother as visitors came in and out, paying their respects, laughing, and remembering his dad. By eleven o'clock, after the last visitor had left, Robert, his mother and I, went straight to bed, exhausted.

∞℃℞

The next day came too soon and Robert dragged me out of bed early to go on errands with him. We left the house around nine after another family member came to stay with his mother and wait for company.

While Robert and I traveled around town taking care of business, I realized that it was the first time in a while that I'd felt a sense of relief and contentment. I was glad that I'd come to see him and he was as well. We'd really missed each other.

It was nice listening to him while he reminisced about his childhood, his mom and dad. All of my cares and concerns were on him and my baggage of troubles and worries seemed to dissipate.

Of course, he'd tried to prod and pick my brain again, but I was adamant. No talk about me. Only he and his mother.

That was my plan. It was not someone else's.

I recognized the sleek black Mercedes in the driveway once Robert pulled up to his house and let out a nervous sigh.

Tony.

# Chapter 86

# Tony

The trip had been long and I was tired.

Seeing her and wanting to get things straight between us had been worth the drive.

Robert got out of the car and came up to me and gave me a grip. "Hey, Robert. I'm sorry about your loss, man," I said immediately.

"Thanks. I appreciate that," he replied. "I'm sorry about..." he trailed off.

"Yeah," I said swiftly, swallowing a painful lump. "Thank you." I sighed. "So, is there anything you need? Anything, I can do...?" I asked.

"Like I told Lacie...you're doing it," he replied. "You're here and that's enough." With a nod and a glance at Lacie still sitting in his car, he said, "But look, get this thing situated with her. She's been putting up a good front, but she's been a mess ever since she arrived." He gave me a pat on the arm and walked to the entrance of the house.

I could see the uneasiness and apprehension in her eyes as she started to get out of the car. I rushed over and held the door open for her.

"From your expression, I guess you're surprised to see me," I said pleasantly.

"Surprised, is one word, yes," she said. She slammed the door and leaned against it, crossing her arms.

"Lacie, we need to talk." I began.

She shook her head. "No, we don't."

I put my hand over her head onto the hood of the car. "Why did you run away?"

She lifted her chin. "I didn't run away. Robert called me after…"
She paused, and exhaled. "Robert called and told me about his dad.
He needed me and…that's why I'm here."

"So you decided to just leave without letting me know anything?
You could have at least answered your phone," I said. "I was worried
about you."

"Didn't I tell you that I wanted some space?" she asked with an
annoyed glare. "I'm a grown woman, not a child, Tony."

"Then don't act like one and run away from your problems," I
retorted, shooting her with the same look.

"I said that I was here for Robert," she snapped.

"Yeah, right," I returned.

"Okay…so how are we doing out here?" Robert asked, coming
from behind me suddenly. "Is everything all right with you two
lovebirds?"

"We're fine," she replied through clenched teeth.

"No, we're not," I said and Lacie gave me a hard look.

"O…kay," Robert said, glancing at both of us as we stared at each
other. "Uh…why don't you two come inside and eat with the rest of
us? Tony, I want you to meet my mother," Robert said easily, slapping
my back lightly, heading back toward the house. We didn't budge. "I
said, 'c'mon,'" he commanded in a more forceful tone.

I motioned for her to get in front of me with my hand and stepped
back. With a quick nod she proceeded to the house and I followed.

I blew out a deep breath.

Lacie wasn't going to make this easy.

# Chapter 87

# Lacie

I was so mad at Tony.

Mad because he looked so damn good and mad that everything that I had been trying to ignore was coming back in full force.

Within respect and because the house was full of visitors, I tried not to let my anger show when we entered the house. Family and friends came in and out, brought more food, ate and laughed. The atmosphere was endearing and it was good to see the throngs of people visit who seemed to have really loved Robert's father.

I noticed that Tony got a few curious glances. Being the only white guy, he stuck out like a sore thumb. Still, he mingled and talked with everyone. Ann took to him instantly and had him sit right beside her on the couch and just started talking away with him.

I stared at them in awe. Tony never ceased to amaze me. Wherever he went, no matter what the circumstances, he always seemed to blend in. It was remarkable.

"Now…are you ready to stop being so stubborn and talk to him?" Robert came up behind me and whispered.

"No," I whispered back.

"Lacie, did Carrie, Josephine and I scheme to get you two together for nothing? C'mon, girl. Isn't that big. expensive, rock on your finger and the fact that that man drove all the way down here evidence of his undying love for you?" he whispered anxiously. "You know he had to be pushing the speed limit for him to get down here so fast."

"I didn't ask him to come," I replied. "Anyway, I told you I was here—"

"Yeah, yeah, I know," Robert interrupted me quickly. "And I appreciate you being here, but you've had this pitiful and sad expression on your face ever since you arrived here yesterday. And to be honest, that's not helping. You look terrible. This may be a funeral but I don't want people acting and looking like it is and that's what you're doing. This is a home going celebration and my father is at rest. That's something to be happy about," he stressed.

"Okay...I'll talk to him after–"

"No, you'll talk to him right now!" he demanded, grabbing my hand and taking me over to Tony.

"Robert," I protested softly.

He ignored my protests and guided me in full force where Tony was sitting with Ann and a few family members.

"Tony, you and Lacie need to talk," Robert said aloud. "Take her upstairs in my bedroom and don't come down until you've got her lipstick all over your mouth. Now take her hand and go!"

I was embarrassed and looked at Ann and everyone uncomfortably while they laughed.

With an amused smirk, Tony said, "yes, sir."

SOCR

"Thank God for Robert," Tony remarked softly. He closed the door behind us as we entered Robert's bedroom. "If it wasn't for him, I don't know when we'd get the chance to talk."

I turned around and faced him. "Okay, so we're here. Now what?"

He only responded by coming over and giving me a breathtaking kiss. My knees weakened immediately and he supported me with his arms. "That's... what," he said. He smiled and put a hand under my chin. "I've traveled a long way to do that."

Heated, I moved away from him to gather my cool. "That wasn't fair," I murmured, narrowing my eyes at him.

He held out his arms. "All's fair in love and war. Isn't that what they say?"

"That's not what I say."

"Uh, huh," he nodded, raising a brow. "Lacie, that kiss was the only positive response that I've gotten from you since I've been here. Do I have to do that again to get you to come to your senses?"

"No, that's not necessary," I said immediately, turning my back on him.

"Then what is?" He paused. "What is it going to take for you to realize how much I love you?"

"I know you love me, Tony," I replied, turning around to face him.

"Then how could you break up with me? How could you shut me out?" he asked earnestly. "Don't you realize that losing our baby was agonizing for me, too? I wanted us to mourn together, but you just shut me out. That hurt."

"I know it hurt, Tony," I uttered softly, trying to keep myself together. "But from the beginning until now, hurt has appeared to be the unyielding quandary in our relationship."

"Is that all you can say about our relationship? What about our love?"

I raised my hands up in frustration. "Tony, will you stop bringing up love?!"

He shifted his foot and argued, "No. I'm going to keep bringing it up because I believe in it. Otherwise, I wouldn't be standing here fighting for it — for you — for us!"

"But *I'm* tired of fighting, Tony!" I stressed, putting my hands up to my head. "My God, Tony! Look at what we've been through. I mean, have you ever heard of any couple going through so much in such a short amount of time?"

"No, I haven't," he admitted. "But I'm still here, aren't I? My love for you hasn't changed. I still want you to be my wife and want to have kids with you. Shouldn't that account for something? Shouldn't that show you that despite all of the negative garbage, I'm never going to stop loving you?" he avowed tenderly.

I groaned and turned around. "Oh, God, Tony, I don't know..."

There was a good pause before he uttered softly, "Listen, Lacie, I understand the arguments that you have tried to convince me of. But there's another reason, isn't there? My mother got to you." Shocked, I turned around quickly to the question. "That's the real reason why you are trying so desperately to make me give up on you. Am I correct?" he asked, coming over to me.

How did he know?

I gulped nervously and my eyes started to water when he reached me. He took both of my hands in his and kissed them. Then he put a hand under my chin so that I could look into his eyes. At once, my tears started to fall at his gentle and affectionate gaze and I dropped my head.

He pulled it back up gently with two fingers and said compassionately, "My God, Lacie, why didn't you tell me? Why didn't you tell me what she did to you?"

"Because she's your mother, Tony," I strangled out frantically and tearfully. "She gave birth to you. How was I going to contend with that?"

"You didn't think I'd believe you," He surmised, wiping tears off of my face.

"Honestly, I didn't know," I sniffled. "All I knew was how close you are with her and your family. I didn't want to get in the way. After I had the miscarriage, I was so emotional with everything going on and I started having these irrational thoughts about what your mom said to me. She said that she didn't want to lose you. She said that I was the cause of all of the trouble between you two and that if I really loved you—"

"No...no," he interrupted. "Lacie, listen to me," he stressed. He closed his eyes tight and then opened them with such passion and conviction. "I...love...you. Do you hear me? I love you!" He kissed me and looked at me again. "If my mom can't accept that or..." He broke, shaking his head. "That's her problem. That goes for anyone else in my family for that matter. But this is *my* life. Mine! Ours! You got it?! Who cares if people don't like that we're together. What matters—"

Gee, he sounded so convincing.

Then I cut him off and shook my head sadly. "This is not just *people* we're talking about here, Tony. This is your family and I can't go through life knowing that you chose me over them when you've known them all of your life."

His eyes implored into mine and I melted. "And I can't go through life without you." He held up a finger. "Lacie, we're talking about only one member of my family. Just one and that's my mother. I refuse to let her ruin my chance at happiness."

I looked at him through a haze of happy tears and managed to utter, "You would do that for me?"

"No. I'm doing this for *us*." He traced my cheek softly with his finger and said tenderly. "I want you to be my wife, Lacie."

Still apprehensive, I swallowed through a midst of tears and stressed, "Are you sure, Tony?"

"Do you love me?" he asked.

I sniffled, wiping the tears from my face. "Of course, I do."

"That's all I need to be sure." He smiled and touched my cheek. "Lacie Adams, will you marry me?"

I nodded. "Yes," I cried out softly.

Elation spread over his face and he just picked me up and twirled me around in the room. "Oh, thank God! Thank God! I'm so glad you said 'yes'," he uttered with emotion. He put me down and just started kissing me all over my face and I giggled tearfully. Then he looked at me seriously. "Listen, I want us to get married as soon as we can."

"What?" I asked, stunned.

He nodded insistently. "Yes, honey. We can have the biggest wedding or a small simple one now and later a big one. I don't care. I just want us married."

"What are we going to do about your mom? What about your family?" I asked.

"No." His tone was adamant, but gentle. "All… I care about is seeing you walk down the aisle."

I stared at him in astonishment. He was for real. But man, was his suggestion tempting. All at once, my mind started racing about what kind of wedding we'd have. Where it would be? How could I get a wedding done so quickly?

"Lacie?" Tony asked, bringing me out of my mulling state. "How about it?"

His eyes were bright and filled with excitement as he slowly smiled. Then I smiled and we both said, "Lets do it!"

We hugged and laughed ecstatically.

There was a quick knock on the door and Robert peeped in.

"Is everything straight between you two? I won't have to lock you in here?" Robert asked.

"No," Tony said, beaming. "Everything is great!"

"Good," Robert expressed, rolling his eyes upward. Then with a fleeting look at me, he said easily, "Now... for round two."

I was about to ask Robert what he meant when he opened the door wider. Dawn and Joe came into view, right beside him.

Tony drew in a nervous breath.

I groaned and drew in one also, as my elation drained from me all at once.

What was she doing here so soon?

# Chapter 88

# Dawn

It was the fear of the unknown.

We didn't know what each other was thinking as we stared at each other, fixated.

Against my reservations, I boarded a plane with Joe and we came. I'd already told Robert that I would only make it down for the funeral, but he'd insisted on me coming today. I didn't know why, but I agreed to. Now I knew.

*"Look, you two are friends—best friends at that. You gonna let some man come in between your friendship?" he asked on the phone, after I'd filled him in on everything from beginning to end.*

*"It's not me, Robert...it's Lacie. She hasn't answered any of my calls and I've called her several times. I've been worried even more about her ever since Joe told me she miscarried. She's not going to want to see me, Robert. I want to be there for her but I don't think she's going to forgive me for this," I replied sadly on the other end.*

*"Listen, just let me handle, Lacie. Just nab Joe and bring your butts down here. Pronto!" he demanded.*

Now looking at Lacie, she seemed to be just as shocked to see me.

Robert that scheming, son of a —

"Okay, now. We're all gonna play musical rooms. Tony, you come out here and Dawn, you go in there," Robert instructed coolly.

All of us stayed still.

"Tony! Dawn! *Move it*!" he demanded with a snap.

With haste, Tony and I did as told. When I entered, Lacie crossed her arms and moved further into the room to stand by the window.

"Now, ladies, there'll be no punching, no biting, no scratching, no hair pulling or anything of that," Robert bantered. "Let's make this swift and clean so that the only drama left in this house will be for my mother or myself. Move out of the way, fellas," he instructed, closing the door on Tony and Joe's worried expressions.

After, I turned around to see Lacie's penetrating eyes on mine.

And I was frightened by the look in them.

# Chapter 89

# Joe

"You think this is a good idea — leaving them in there alone?" Tony asked me, looking worried as Robert passed us to go down the stairs.

With equal concern, I said, "I don't know, man. It's hard to say with women. If this had been between us, we'd have fought over it and it'd been squashed by now."

"Good point." He nodded, starting for the door. "Maybe we should— "

"Come on, men. Don't stand by the door. Give 'em their space," Robert called from the bottom of the stairs suddenly.

"Guess that takes care of that," I murmured with a sigh. "Come on, man, let's go. I'm sure it'll be all right."

# Chapter 90

# Dawn

I took a deep breath and started the confrontation.

"Are you okay?" I asked softly.

She nodded, understanding my question. "Yeah, I'm fine. It's been difficult, but I'm making it through."

"That's good to hear."

She didn't reply and there was a long, silent and uncomfortable pause as we looked at each other.

I took a deep breath. "I guess this is long overdue."

"Yeah, you can say that," she muttered, arms still crossed.

I inhaled. "Look, let's just get this whole thing out in the open. I've been worried about you and miserable ever since. This silent treatment has been driving me crazy."

She appeared to be steadying her voice as it shook with thick emotion. "I wasn't giving you the silent treatment, Dawn. I just wasn't ready to talk to you." I wiped my face. She sighed. "But now that you're here and since Robert has given us no choice…do you want to tell me how this all started between you and Joe?" she asked, simply.

Although we hadn't spoken since that fateful day and I knew she was still obviously upset, I couldn't help but marvel at her initial attempt of harmony — despite Robert's help. I took her invitation willingly and told her as we both sat on the bed.

"…and we just kept seeing each other. One thing led to another and…here we are," I finished telling her.

"Wow," she murmured. "This was going on right in front of me, the whole time and I never saw it. Wow!" She stood up from the bed and went to the window. Then she turned to me with a perceptive glare. "You're in love with him, aren't you, Dawn?" she asked. I nodded my head and she sighed with frustration. "Why did you keep this from me? I kept asking you what was wrong and was wondering what was up with you. But you never told me. Why...didn't you just tell me, Dawn?"

I hunched my shoulders meekly. "I...didn't know how."

"Dawn," she sniffled. "We've been through a lot and have always been good with communication. I have never given you the idea that you couldn't come to me—for anything. I mean, you never gave me a chance, here!"

"This was different, Lacie," I expressed, shaking my head. "You used to be involved with Joe. You were engaged to the man."

"But that didn't stop you from seeing him, did it? From keeping it from me!" she cried tearing. She swallowed. "Listen, I'm not trying to be a hypocrite here, because I'm not an angel, myself. After all, Joe was very hurt when I broke up with him and told him that I was in love with Tony. But I do want to make something clear, here. I'm not upset about you being with Joe. Honestly, I'm not. Yeah, I still love Joe—but as a friend. I love Tony and I'm very happy with him. Nothing and no one can change my feelings for him. Joe and I are over. *And*...I would have told you that if you'd have just trusted me and been straight with me from the beginning!" she exclaimed.

"I didn't want to hurt you, Lacie. Can't you understand that?" I claimed, choking up in tears while I frantically grasped to explain. "I...I...I mean at first, I thought that I was seeing your man and your leftovers because you two had just broken off your engagement. At one time I actually thought that he was still in love with you and was only using me. I even broke up with him because of it, but he wanted to continue to see me and honestly, I did too. We started out as friends, first and then we became more than that. Yet, I still considered myself his second choice because he'd been yours, first. Then he told me he loved me and that's when I knew I really had his heart," I said softly, still tearing. "But still, I didn't feel right. I didn't feel I could tell you because I felt bad about what I'd done and you were going through so much already. I felt like such a backstab—"

"All you had to do...was open up your mouth and tell me, Dawn," she interrupted simply with a crushed expression. "That's it. Instead, you hid it from me and that's what's so sad about this whole thing. You didn't *want* to trust me and deep down you didn't *want* to tell me!" She shook her head as she shed tears. "That's not what best friends do, Dawn. I wouldn't have done that to you, because I love you too much. You were more than a friend to me. You were my sister!" Disappointed, she turned her head to the window.

I wiped the tears from my eyes before I said with a shaky voice. "So..." I shrugged meekly. "What do we do now? I mean, do you even want to be my best friend anymore?" I paused and inhaled. "Can you forgive me?"

# Chapter 91

# Lacie

*"Can you forgive me?" Dawn asked.*

I stood looking out the window for a while after she posed the question to me. I'd never thought either of us would have to ask that of each other and that we'd ever be in this predicament. And knowing her, I was sure she thought the same.

Then, within a flash, it hit me how silly this whole situation was and all I wanted to do was laugh. I started chuckling softly before I finally turned around and looked at her with a smile. Dawn quirked a brow and looked at me as if I was crazy.

"Oh, my goodness, Dawn," I said, still chuckling. "Can you believe this, girl?" Dawn said nothing and just continued to look at me warily. "Girl, we are here for Robert's father's funeral and we're up here in this room dealing with this foolishness." My eyes started watering. "Oh, my goodness life is too short for this. And life should be so much more than holding on to something so superficial," I whispered.

Dawn gulped nervously and tears started to fall down her face. "Are you saying that you for–"

I shook my head and tasted and swallowed the tears falling from eyes. "Dawn, I don't even deserve to be asked. Robert losing his father and me losing my baby has made me realize that tomorrow is not promised and that this storm that we're going through right now is way too trivial in comparison. Yeah, I'm a little hurt about the way I found out about you and Joe, but is it really that big of a deal that I can't get over it? No, it's not. My friendship with you means so much more than that. I just lost my child and I don't want to lose you, too." Dawn broke down in relieved tears and I started to choke up as well. "Dawn, you deserve to have a good man in your life and if Joe is who you want then I don't want to stand in the way. I love you and I want you to be happy. I've moved on with Tony and I'm happy. But I wouldn't be if I lost you as a friend." I stretched out my arms and she came over at once and embraced me. "Dawn, I'd be absolutely miserable without you."

"Me too," she cried in return.

"I just want you to trust me and be honest with me. I mean, we didn't have to go through any of this!" I let go and took a tissue from my pocket and handed her one and blew hard. "I'm so ticked at myself because with all of the time that has past, you should have been enjoying your time with Joe instead of worrying about my crabby tail."

It was her turn to blow her nose before she replied, "You wouldn't be Lacie if you weren't crabby and stubborn." She laughed and reached for another hug.

After a moment I let go and sniffled out, "Dawn, are you really happy with him?"

She smiled with a nod. "Yes, I'm very happy."

"Good," I uttered. "You'd better be after all of this drama," I declared with a little chuckle.

Dawn heaved a big sigh. "Lacie, I'm so sorry."

"No, I'm sorry," I said, shaking my head. "I love you, Dawn, and I'm so sorry that you felt that you couldn't talk to me."

"No, I'm sorry — because I should have known you better than that. You were right. I should have trusted you."

"No, I'm sorry–" I repeated.

"Oh, for Heaven's sake, you're both sorry!" Robert voiced, coming into the room suddenly. "You two are the most pitiful creatures. It's a shame that the two of you had to come all the way down here for my father's funeral, for me to get you two talking again."

I raised my eyebrow at him. "We know you did it deliberately, too."

"Hey, I'm not denying it," he said, putting a hand on one hip. "Now have you ironed out your differences? Are you two still best friends?"

Dawn and I smiled at each other then looked at him and replied in unison, "Forever."

ℰℐℭℛ

If one could call a funeral beautiful, then that's what Robert's father's was. Simply beautiful. The large church was filled to capacity with people and the minister's eulogy was moving. There wasn't a dry eye in the church except for Robert and Ann who sat remarkably composed, enjoying the minister's sermon.

As we ventured back to Ann's home, a sense of closure fell on everyone. Ann and Robert had laid her husband to rest and they were at peace. Tony and I were happily re-engaged and anxious to start planning our wedding. Dawn and Joe no longer had to worry about keeping their relationship a secret anymore and could enjoy being in love.

As for Dawn and I, well, I was happy for her and she was happy for me.

More importantly, we were still the best of friends.

# Chapter 92

## Tony and Lacie's Wedding—Two Months Later

### Tony

My God, was she breathtaking!

My eyes watered as I stood transfixed on Lacie's beautiful frame while she and Mason came down the aisle, stepping to the wedding march in her church.

Eyes still on her, my mind went back quickly to a couple of minutes ago.

*"Man, are you nervous?" Joe asked me in one of the side rooms.*

*"Not at all," I replied, beaming confidently, glancing at him. He hadn't stopped pacing since we arrived at the church. I chuckled. "You all right, man? You seem more nervous than I am."*

*Joe looked uncomfortable as he tugged at his necktie. "I don't know, man. You're getting married to Lacie. Now I'm beginning to wonder if Dawn's gonna want the same thing."*

*"What's so bad about that? You love her, right?"*

*"Yeah, I do, but," he looked around the room. "Being in this church and everything's starting to give me the creeps."*

*My dad came in with my brothers just as I was about to speak.*

*"You ready, son?" Dad asked, clapping me on the back.*

*"More than ever," I replied.*

*"Good. The pastor's ready and so is the bride. We'd better get moving," he stated.*

*"Right, right," I said, getting ready to go out the door and then stopped. "Dad, did Mom...?"*

*Dad paused and Mark and Matthew hung their heads. "No, son...I'm afraid she's not coming," Dad answered sadly.*

*I swallowed and took a breath and said, "All right, let's get the show on the road."*

I blinked back the tears as Lacie and Mason came up to my side with him between us.

"Who gives away this bride?" Rev. Jacobs asked.

"I do," Mason stated and placed Lacie's hand in mine.

I looked into Lacie's tearful eyes and winked at her and she managed a little giggle.

Yeah, everything was going to be just fine.

## Robert

Hallelujah!

After all that drama they were finally doing it.

Smiling, I watched my girl, Lacie, walk down the aisle, somewhat proud that I had helped them get together.

They were made for each other.

I was going to miss them when I moved but ever since Dad took sick, I had an idea that I'd move back to Georgia.

Still, change is good. Now that things were looking good for Lacie and Tony, I had a feeling it would be for me too.

I looked up at the ceiling, imagining my father in Heaven, then.. I was going to miss him, but I felt he was all right.

There was no question in my mind.

## Joe

Man! My homey was actually getting married.

I was happy for him. He was marrying a good woman.

I glanced at him as I stood next to him. Look at him, cheesing and tearing up at the same time. Man, was he whipped!

I suddenly felt eyes on me and turned to see Dawn staring at me. She licked her lips and stealthily, put her finger in her mouth. I got excited instantly.

Man, I was whipped even more!

## Dawn

I stifled a giggle and watched Joe's eyes bulge. He thrust his hands into his pockets. I winked at him and he winked back.

Then I looked at Lacie. She looked so beautiful. I immediately watered up and had to dab my handkerchief on the corner of my eye. Just in that instance, I started to feel a little twinge of jealousy and I looked at Joe again.

Maybe I was next in line.

*Naw, Dawn…you ain't never been one to settle down.*

I don't know, though. One never could tell.

## Lacie

This was coming true.

Even as members of the congregation and wedding guests stood and marveled at me walking down the aisle with Daddy, I still couldn't believe it.

Then I looked at Tony and the tears just started to flow. I was marrying a gift from God.

I held my gaze on him, recalling the hustling we had to do to have the wedding on such short notice. Wedding gown, wedding rings, wedding cake, groom's tuxedos, bridesmaid's gowns, reception hall, catering, transportation, honeymoon—it was amazing that we'd accomplished anything. But we were here and he looked damn handsome!

I was the happiest I'd ever been in my life. I was marrying the man I was made for, Dawn and Joe were in love, Mama and Daddy seemed to be rekindling their relationship, Reneé was due to pop any day now and although I was sorry to see him move, Robert seemed to have taken a new appreciation for the state of Georgia.

The outcome at work was better as well. Ryan had welcomed me with open arms when I came back, the missing contractor had been found and was now being held in jail without bond, the project was back on track, and Trevor had miraculously seemed to have had a change of heart about Tony and me.

I glanced at Tony's side where Johnathan, Matthew and Mark stood. Then I eyed Jessica and Jennifer on my side. They'd made every effort to be a part of this occasion. My only wish was that Tony's mother could be here. Everyone else in Tony's family had answered our invitations with a positive reply except Abigail.

Just for Tony's sake, I made a last ditch effort call to Abigail to plead with her to attend our wedding.

*"Douglas residence,"* she answered on the second ring.

*"Uh… hello, Mrs. Douglas. How are you?" I replied respectfully. Dead silence on the phone. Still, she didn't hang up. I cleared my throat. "Uh, I won't keep you long. I know that you and Tony have your differences, but he is your son. He hasn't said so, but I know that he'd want you to come to our wed–"*

*Her words were remote and acidic. "I have no son named Tony, anymore. He's dead." Without another word, she hung up.*

It was difficult to hear a mother say that about her own son. But I couldn't help her and what she needed was prayer. I'd just have to love her son enough for both of us, that's all.

Her ignorance or anyone else's ignorance, for that matter, wasn't going to hinder Tony and me. It wasn't going to hinder us from being happy and growing a family, either. That was my promise to myself and to Tony.

And I was going to hold onto it.

Until the day I die.

Lizzette Grayson Carter

*The Color Line* was a fantastic debut for first time novelist, Lizzette Grayson Carter. It preceded her expectations even further, by going into its second print in mass paperback production. Now, as a full-time author, with the release of her sequel, *Across The Color Line*, Carter has launched an audio book, book publishing and print on demand company. She continues to travel near and far for book events, lectures, speaking engagements, conferences and book club meetings. She is a resident of Mathews County, Virginia and lives with her husband, Michael and daughter, Brienna. She continues to devote her time to her Lord and Savior Jesus Christ, her church and many other Christian engagements.

For booking information, contact:

Michael T. Cater
C L Press
P. O. Box 1, Hallieford, VA 23068
804-725-2660 | 804-725-8227 cell
www.lizzettegraysoncarter.com
lgcauthor@yahoo.com

*C L Press*

proudly presents its premiere author,

Lizzette Grayson Carter

and the release of her sequel,

*Across The Color Line*

We hope you have enjoyed the novel.

This novel is an exceptional example of the quality of work produced by C L Press. As a newly formed audio book and book publisher, we also offer services for print-on-demand.

For the services listed above, please contact:

C L Press
Michael T. Carter
P. O. Box 1
Hallieford, VA 23068
804-725-2660

C L Press would like to acknowledge all of our business partners who helped make this project a success:

The Writer's Assistant
N'Digo Designs
J's Music Studio
Balloon Boutique & Party
Supply, Inc.
Chaney Robinson & Company

*The Daily Press*
B. W. Wilson
River City Graphics
Coleman One
Bayport Credit Union